SENTINALS ORIGINS

SENTINALS ORIGINS

PREQUEL PART ONE

SENTINAL SERIES

HELEN GARRAWAY

Published by Jerven Publishing

Cover designed by Jeff Brown Graphics

Maps by Fictive designs

eBook ISBN: 978-1-915854-10-0

Paperback ISBN: 978-1-915854-11-7

Hardcover ISBN: 978-1-915854-12-4

A CIP catalogue record for this book is available from the British Library.

Sign up to my mailing list to join my magical world and for further information about forthcoming books and latest news at: www. helengarraway.com

First Edition

*For those who dream of magical places,
and lost arifels who spread their wings and soar high*

ALSO BY HELEN GARRAWAY

<u>Sentinal Series</u>

o.5 Sentinals Stirring (Novella)

1. Sentinals Awaken

2. Sentinals Rising

3. Sentinals Justice

3.5. Sentinals Recovery (Novella)

4. Sentinals Across Time

5. Sentinals Banished

6. Sentinals Destiny

7. Sentinals Origins | Part One

8. Sentinals Origins | Part Two (Date TBC)

<u>SoulMist series</u>

SoulBreather

DragonBound

OblivionGate

<u>Standalone</u>

Harmony

<u>Anthology</u>

Secret Alliance (Part of Reign of Dragons Anthology) May 2025

REMARGAREN
PRE-FLOOD
ELOTHIA
TEROLIA
VESPIRI
BIRTOLI
VESPERS
DEEPWATER
GREENWATCH
MARCHWOOD
STONEFORD
AGLINTI
MOLINTI
PLINI
SENTI
ATOLEA
KIKER
RAMILA
EASTWATER
SOLARI
GESAR
KIRSHA
MINER
MISTRA

CONTENTS

1. Guerlaire — 1
2. Leyandrii — 11
3. Birler — 16
4. Guerlaire — 26
5. Birler — 35
6. Birler — 41
7. Birler — 49
8. Leyandrii — 63
9. Guerlaire — 69
10. Birler — 84
11. Birler — 91
12. Birler — 98
13. Guerlaire — 106
14. Birler — 111
15. Birler — 119
16. Guerlaire — 135
17. Clary — 140
18. Guerlaire — 145
19. Leyandrii — 154
20. Guerlaire — 158
21. Leyandrii — 168
22. Birler — 173
23. Birler — 184
24. Guerlaire — 193
25. Warren — 201
26. Guerlaire — 209
27. Tagerill — 211
28. Birler — 222
29. Birler — 233
30. Birler — 247
31. Leyandrii — 255
32. Guerlaire — 261

33. Guerlaire   268

34. Birler   273

35. Tagerill   285

36. Guerlaire   294

37. Birler   302

38. Birler   309

39. Birler   322

40. Birler   336

41. Melis   348

42. Birler   360

43. Serill   374

44. Birler   384

45. Birler   403

46. Guerlaire   416

47. Guerlaire   428

48. Birler   435

49. Tiv'erna   448

50. Birler   461

51. Birler   471

52. Birler   476

53. Kayer   486

54. Birler   492

55. Leyandrii   501

56. Birlerion   511

57. Leyandrii   515

Glossary   521

Acknowledgments   525

About the Author   527

Sentinals Awaken   531

SoulMist Series   535

Reader's Notes   537

1

GUERLAIRE

ELOTHIA, SEPU 1120

Effervescent magic flowed around Guerlaire in the moist Elothian air. Swirls of blue energy were attracted to him for some reason he couldn't explain, but no doubt, his beloved, the goddess Leyandrii, could. She had warned him that close association with her would affect him, but as usual, he hadn't listened. He really ought to pay more attention.

His skin tingled. The magic within him was eager to join the wild magic flirting with him. He smiled at the thought and then scowled as he slapped his neck. At the sting of yet another bloodsucking bug, Guerlaire cursed under his breath as he ducked under the low-hanging branch, attempting to take off his head. Could he use his magic to repel the bugs? Even if it seemed a little trivial, it would be worth it. The trailing vines tangled in his hair, and he pushed them away as the sailors continued rowing downstream.

They had taken the wrong tributary when the main river had split into multiple channels, costing them valuable time. Worse, he was nearly bursting with magical energy which was a constant itch under his skin, and he needed to return to Leyandrii to alleviate it. With the unexpected delays, he had cut it too fine, and now he was paying the price. Unable to keep still, he paced between the rowers, the only stretch of deck unencumbered by coiled ropes, barrels, or sacks of dwindling supplies.

From out of nowhere, a sudden squall rumbled overhead and drenched them in icy sheets of rain. The next moment, the air steamed with a muggy closeness, attracting those buzzing blood suckers that ate him alive, another symptom of the unexplained wild magic unbalancing their world. In the depths of Elothia, he shouldn't be fending off blood-sucking bugs. He should be wrapped up against freezing snowstorms.

Exhaling, he strode back along the deck of the sturdy two-masted ship he had hired for his explorations. He had been fortunate to get his old friend, the captain of the *Serpent Lady,* and his crew for this trip. Two teams of rowers replaced the huge white sails when they were inland. The crew were experienced and manoeuvred the ship with ease; the thick vegetation lining either side of the river blurred as they raced past.

The holds were full of his research, maps, and crates of specimens. They took up so much room that they had to pull in to camp on the river bank every night as there wasn't enough space below deck to sleep.

His fellow ranger and oldest friend, Chryll, raised a black eyebrow as he approached. Chryll was a giant of a man, broad-chested, deep-voiced, and highly intelligent—too clever for this jaunt of his into the depths of unexplored Elothia. Guerlaire suddenly wondered why Chryll had accompanied him. He must be bored out of his mind.

"Need a sparring session?" Chryll inquired, a small smirk on his lips.

"We'd capsize if we tried," Guerlaire replied, ignoring

the concerned expressions of the nearest rowers. They had seen some large predators moving through the waters earlier, and no one wanted to tempt them any closer.

"Then let's pull in and camp for the night. If you don't work off some of your energy, you'll explode into flames."

"I'm not that bad," Guerlaire growled.

"I beg to differ. Leyandrii will string me up if you don't return in one piece."

Snorting, Guerlaire inspected the banks. Rushes and bushes screened the view, and trees draped in trailing vines arched above them, blocking the dimming light as the day drew to a close. Chryll was right. They needed to set up camp before darkness descended.

"There." Guerlaire pointed to a gap in the vegetation further down the riverbank. "Pull in there, men. We'll camp in that clearing."

The boat's captain shouted a command, and the rowers leaned more heavily on one side and pulled their boat to shore.

Guerlaire jumped onto dry land and searched the clearing. It seemed unoccupied by any beast that might eat them. The sloping bank did suggest that it may be a watering spot, so they would have to keep a good watch. They were the interlopers here, not the local wildlife.

The sailors shipped their oars and turned into landsmen as they set up camp. They were skilled and efficient and ignored his odd requests, storing his finds and samples with the care they deserved.

Staring back out across the river, Guerlaire still couldn't see how the gods had created this world and yet knew nothing about it. Leyandrii, the daughter of the All-Mother and the woman, nay goddess, he hoped would one day be his, had stared at him in bemusement when he'd asked how she could not know the lands she'd brought into existence.

He imagined her exquisite face, her emerald-green eyes sparkling as she smiled at him and said, "Just because we created it, it doesn't mean we know every inch."

Guerlaire was determined to know every possible thing he could about the world he lived in, especially as everything that existed had come from within Leyandrii and her family.

The sound of a sword being unsheathed brought him out of his introspection. Chryll had been serious. He turned and drew his own sword. He hoped Chryll was ready because the power simmering beneath his skin needed an outlet, and once they started, he wouldn't be able to stop.

Chryll didn't give him a chance to speak but launched into an attack that had Guerlaire on the defensive. Powerful blows rained down on him, and he concentrated on deflecting the force aside, parrying thrusts and working into a position where he could attack.

He was lost in the flow of his body, his warming muscles, and the sheer exhilaration of not having to hold back when Chryll barked in his deep voice, "Stand down!"

Guerlaire immediately broke off. His chest heaved with exertion, and sweat dripped down his face. His muscles burned, and his shirt stuck to his skin, but the simmering spark of energy had eased, burnt off in the brutal sparring session.

With sudden concern, he inspected Chryll. "Are you alright? I didn't hurt you, did I?"

Chryll laughed as he turned away. "In your dreams. You didn't come close."

Guerlaire knew that wasn't true. In the brief glimpse he'd had of Chryll, he'd seen blood spatters across his slashed shirt. He grabbed Chryll's arm. "You *are* hurt!"

Chryll brushed him off. "I'm fine."

"You should have spoken sooner."

Chryll laughed again and bent down to pick up his sword

belt. He hissed his breath out, and Guerlaire was immediately by his side. "Where are you injured?" He helped Chryll sit and tugged his shirt open. Self-recrimination rushed through him as he saw the red marks down Chryll's side and the multitude of minor nicks and cuts on his skin. Nothing serious, but taken altogether, Chryll must have been in pain, even if he said he wasn't.

"I'm so sorry," Guerlaire murmured as he grabbed a canteen, soaked a cloth, and dabbed Chryll's torso.

"What for? It was a good workout. I should move faster."

"I didn't even realise I had hit you."

Chryll gripped his shoulder. "Stop it, Guerlaire. You did nothing wrong. I attacked you." He shifted awkwardly and sighed. "It was a good workout. Hopefully you won't need another for a few days."

"Chryll …"

"I mean it." Chryll glared at him. "Go get me something to eat. I'm starving."

Guerlaire rose, his exhaustion taking the edge off his simmering intensity. His constant need to burn off energy was eased by Chryll's sacrifice. He needed to find another way to control this power that bubbled under his skin.

Offering the sailor stirring the soup a brief smile of thanks, Guerlaire took the bowls and bread back to where Chryll leaned against a tree trunk with his eyes closed. "Here," he said softly, offering the soup and a spoon.

Chryll opened his eyes, and as he took the bowl, he said, "You need to show me that reverse manoeuvre. Where did you pick that up from?"

Guerlaire frowned as he stirred the steaming liquid, trying to remember the moves he had made. It must have been related to Apeiron, the discipline of the air, where mind and body melded into one. "I'm not sure. I think it was a variation of the Apeiron move in *Acknowledgement.*"

Chryll drank his soup. A crease formed between his brows as he thought. "Maybe." He dunked his bread in the soup to soften it. After weeks of travelling, they were left with hard biscuits and rock-like rolls. Chryll lifted the roll out of the liquid and stared at it for a moment before dunking it back into the soup. "I can't wait to taste fresh bread again," he muttered.

"Once we reach the main channel, we'll only be a few days away from the coast. It won't take long to return to Vespiri after that."

Nodding, Chryll ate his bread. "I imagine Leyandrii will be waiting for you."

Guerlaire grimaced. "She warned me about staying away for too long. Getting lost wasn't in the plan."

"At least you have enough research to keep you in Vespers for the rest of the year."

"True."

They were interrupted by a small, fluffy, tri-coloured creature with scaly wings and tail, who appeared in front of Guerlaire. She chittered loudly, scolding him.

Guerlaire laughed and held out his hand so the little arifel could land. Tufts of brown, black, and white fur stuck up in all directions, and once she flipped her wings back, she groomed herself. "Mia! How did you find us?"

Mia rubbed her cheek against his hand, and images of Leyandrii filled his head: worried green eyes, hands on hips, head tilted in question.

"I know we're late. Tell her we're fine and on our way home. A couple of days at most."

Mia tilted her head in a mimicry of Leyandrii, and Chryll snorted.

Guerlaire scowled at him. "We'll be home soon, I promise."

Mia chittered and disappeared.

Chryll grinned. "So, when are you going to propose to her?" Guerlaire choked on the mouthful of soup he had just swallowed, and Chryll patiently waited for him to stop coughing. "Well?"

"I'm a nobody. She's a goddess."

"You are the most senior captain in the Lady's Rangers. You command her palace guards, and she sends an arifel to check up on you. It's obvious she loves you."

"I have no family line, no lineage to offer."

"So? Has she asked you for one?"

"No, but her family will."

"I think Leyandrii can make up her own mind. After all, she *is* the goddess they left behind to run this place. If she is capable of that, then managing you should be simple."

"Thanks, I think."

"You're welcome." Chryll waved an airy hand. "I live but to serve."

Guerlaire grunted, though he wasn't deceived. Chryll was trying to distract him from the lines of pain creasing his face. They had run out of medicinal supplies days ago; that was why they had headed for home, and now he had caused his friend pain, and there was nothing he could do about it.

He rummaged in one of the bags a sailor had brought over and, using his knife, tore one of his spare shirts into strips. "Let's bind your ribs to give you some support," he suggested. Ignoring Chryll's protests, he forced him to remove his shirt and proceeded to strap him up. The red marks on Chryll's skin were turning a deep purple. "Once we are home, I'll teach you how to defend against a reversal," he promised, guilt blunting the edge of his restlessness even more.

.   .   .

Late the following day, a low growl rumbled overhead, and Guerlaire glared at the thickening clouds. "Doesn't it ever stop raining?" he grumbled as he wiped the water out of his eyes. He braced himself against the railing and watched the river rush by.

"The water levels are rising much faster than normal," the captain said as he hurried past. "We must stay in the main channel or risk hitting something."

Guerlaire peered down the river. "Isn't that where the fastest currents will be?"

"Yes, but we can't afford to have the bottom ripped out by submerged rocks near the fringes."

Guerlaire nodded in agreement and hung on as the ship was buffeted by surges of water swirling around them, driving them downstream.

"Portside, up oars!" the captain screamed as the ship veered drunkenly to the left.

The sailors whipped the oars up, all bar one, which snagged on debris. The ship continued to turn until the oar snapped and then it jerked upright. The starboard oars dipped in the water, and the sailors pulled strongly, trying the straighten the bow.

Rain slapped on the deck and stung bare skin; the rigging rattled and clattered as the masts swayed precariously. The river had seemed wide and deep enough, but this torrent of water was driving them too fast for them to be really in control.

Guerlaire's sword heated at his waist. When he unsheathed it, the blade glowed a brilliant blue, and he spun, searching for the threat.

An oily voice inveigled its way into his mind. *"You are far from home,"* it said, threat heavy in its tone, *"and unprotected."*

Guerlaire raised his glowing sword and searched the deepening gloom. "Who are you?"

"One who would demonstrate how feeble you really are."

"Show yourself."

"That is not necessary for you to meet thy doom."

A flash of lightning hit the deck, splintering the wooden planks beneath his feet, and Guerlaire leapt, twisting as he deflected a second strike back into the air. Another flash of lightning crackled as it hit the taller of the two masts, and golden sparks cascaded to the deck as loose rigging whipped across the deck, nearly beheading the sailor clinging to the capstan.

"Guerlaire!" Chryll's shout was lost in the ferocious wind that swept between them as his friend was forced back along the deck. He leaned so far forward that he was almost horizontal, but he couldn't reach Guerlaire.

The roar of rushing water, thunder, and wind deafened him and pushed Chryll further away.

Sweeping his blade above his head, Guerlaire called on the magic within him and imagined a barrier, one that would protect the ship from further attacks. This wasn't just bad weather, but someone intentionally targeting them. How and why, he didn't know.

The glow from his sword expanded, and he poured all his efforts into extending the barrier over the ship. The waters calmed as rain splattered on his shield instead of them, a sharp sting against his mind.

He gasped for breath, concentrating on holding his barrier over them as he inspected the ship. "Anyone hurt?" he yelled as a flash of lightning struck his shield, and he flinched as a spike of pain stabbed his temples.

"What is that, and how long can you hold it?" Chryll asked as he grasped Guerlaire's shoulders. He stared above them, his eyes wide in amazement.

"It's a shield, and I'll hold it as long as I need to," Guerlaire replied as another flash skittered over his barrier, sending a spike of energy through his body, and he shuddered.

Chryll hissed in pain and released him. He shook his fingers. "You cannot absorb that much power for long."

"Let's hope they exhaust themselves soon," Guerlaire mumbled as his vision blurred.

The deck bucked and Guerlaire stumbled into Chryll. The larger man grabbed him tightly, dragging in his breath as another charge ripped through Guerlaire.

"He's running out of steam," Guerlaire said, and he collapsed into Chryll's arms as the excess magical energy within him writhed in its effort to escape. His skin tingled, and his head throbbed.

"Who is? Who's attacking us?" Chryll's embrace tightened as the ship righted, and the sailors began rowing again. "You may be the Lady's Captain and her beloved, but you still can't hold that much energy, Guerlaire."

"I can hold enough of it to drain him," Guerlaire replied as the storm eased and the image of his friend's concerned expression faded into darkness.

2

LEYANDRII

VESPERS, VESPIRI

Leyandrii observed the chamber that was filled with rows of tiered seating rising up the walls. The burnished dark wood gleamed, polished to a shine, and the aroma of beeswax hung in the air. Timber supplied from the great forests of Vespiri, no doubt. Above the seating, four golden onoffs floated in the air, emitting a dim glow that only increased the depth of the shadows, almost depleted. They needed recharging.

The tiers were slowly filling with members of the Administration, the men who managed her world on a day-to-day basis and managed to irritate her more often than not. Why did they have to be so difficult?

Her instructions had been simple: keep the peace and ensure that the people were free to live their lives. How difficult was that? Why was it that as soon as these men put on their green robes, all their common sense dribbled out the bottom of their boots?

Leyandrii slowed her breathing and calmed her nerves. Her bottom was already protesting about the hard cushion she sat on, but that had been deliberate. She didn't want to get comfortable. She needed to pay close attention to the proceedings today.

Someone was scheming, and the balance of power was shifting. She had her suspicions, but today would be her proof. Once she was certain, the next problem would be what to do. She had tried to distance herself from the Administration and allow the ministers to rule as they saw fit, but she wouldn't let them exploit her people.

Hers was the voice of reason. She was saddened that she had to interfere, that these ministers were so easily corrupted.

She let her senses drift through the room. Most of the ministers' thoughts were light and innocent, nothing sinister. They were wondering how long the session would last before they could get back to more important matters.

Her lips twitched as the ministers began low conversations as soon as they saw her seated in the place of honour. Many uncertain glances flicked in her direction, and Leyandrii noted who huddled with who—important information she was collecting for free.

There was one man whose thoughts were closed. He emitted nothing and was surrounded by silence. Leyandrii inspected him. He was a large man, powerfully built. He had a thin, drawn face with a sour expression permanently etched in place. Gilbert Clary, the uncle of the current Lord of East Mayer.

No doubt, the fact that his nephew had inherited the estate instead of him had soured his disposition. Clary was like a brooding cloud in the midst of all ministers, and the golden onoffs only made him seem darker as they revealed the arrogant sneer firmly fixed on his lips.

The noise level rose as more ministers arrived. There were more than she remembered. She wasn't sure if that was a good thing or not. The meeting room wouldn't hold many more, and it would be cramped and uncomfortable.

The only person who approached her was Oren Asher, the commander of her rangers. Straight-backed and lean, his hair greying at the sides, Asher strode down the centre aisle and up the steps to where she was seated. He wore his uniform instead of robes; its deep grey suited his bronzed complexion.

"Lady Leyandrii! It's so good to see you!"

Leyandrii smiled and offered her hand.

Asher bent over it, and his lips were warm on her skin. He peeked up at her from under his black lashes. "Any news on when my captains will return?"

Leyandrii chuckled. "Soon. They got lost."

Asher rose with a laugh. "I see my rangers need some map-reading lessons."

"I'd agree, but I fear the maps would not be of much assistance these days," Leyandrii replied, staring out across the chamber. "Too many people are trying to flex their muscles."

"Do you know who?"

"I have my suspicions."

"As do I. It has been subtle, but there is one faction gaining the more influential seats. And they are quick to bring in their friends."

Leyandrii pursed her lips. "I had so hoped that they would work *with* our world and not against it."

"Power has a way of changing people," Asher said as he gazed out over the chamber and then back at Leyandrii. "The more they have, the more they want."

"It seems we are the centre of attention."

"Wherever you are, you will always be worthy of all our attention," Asher said with a grin.

Leyandrii laughed, and as the room quietened, she rose. Her gaze swept the room, and she was disappointed to see only men. There were still no women in the

Administration. She wondered why. Something else to investigate.

"Gentlemen. I see the Administration grows. I welcome the new ministers to your position of authority and responsibility. You may influence the direction of discussion, but you have an obligation to my people. A duty to ensure that the world they live in gives them the freedom of choice. To live their lives how they desire, in safety and with opportunity. Your job is to create and maintain that environment. I look forward to hearing your proposals."

She swept her hand through the air, and the golden globes suspended above the chamber glowed brighter, illuminating each of the ministers seated in the tiers.

"Please introduce yourselves so that I may know you."

Leyandrii sat and waited as the ministers organised themselves. She tensed as a faint voice teased the back of her mind, and she threw her awareness out into the city, frantically searching as she acknowledged the new ministers.

She had heard the voice before, demanding her attention, but it was so faint that she had never been able to pinpoint it. Today, however, it was near the site where her temple was being built, and she wished she could just leave this shambles of an assembly and find him. It was a male, young, very determined, and drawn to her temple, as she had planned.

She had to find him before it was too late. Deep in her bones, she knew the child would not last much longer on his own.

But for now, she would know her foes. The men planning her downfall would soon find out she was more than a match for them. They might only see a young woman. More fool them.

A surge of power disrupted her sense of the world's magic and she cast her mind out, searching. That it came from Elothia was concerning. She wasn't surprised when she felt Guerlaire's intense concentration, nor the impressive amount of energy he was expending to shield himself and the sailors. They were safe for now, but targeting her beloved was an attack on her.

She traced the magical surge, with the pulse weakening as the wielder drained their power. Northern Elothia! Before she could pinpoint exactly where, the surge cut off. No doubt, the wielder was unconscious possibly even dead if they hadn't thought to retain enough energy to keep their heart pumping.

Leyandrii gritted her teeth, smiled serenely, and observed the proceedings. She rigidly suppressed her desire to grab Guerlaire close and not let him out of her sight. Just as she didn't like to be suffocated, neither did he, and she would never make the mistake of assuming he couldn't look after himself.

3

BIRLER

VESPERS, VESPIRI

Chill winds whipped through the empty back streets of Vespers, eddying around the scrawny child crouched in the gutter. His only response was an involuntary shudder, but he didn't stop watching. A runnel of filthy water flowed under his bare feet unnoticed—his feet were wet and dirty already—nor did he notice the way the wind tugged at his ragged clothing or the goosebumps that ran down his arms; he was used to being cold.

He only had eyes for the procession wending its way down the muddy street. The bright colours of the Guardian's flags, a splash of depth and richness rarely seen in the poorer streets of Vespers. His gaze was riveted to the swathes of green, red, and gold material, and he felt a sense of yearning at his fingertips. He needed to touch those colours, just once.

He curled his grubby fingers in denial.

It was safer not to be seen. Why risk all just for a moment of pleasure, as fleeting as it would be?

Ducking back unseen, away from the noise and the gaudy pomp, he hesitated as the regulated stamping of the guards' feet snared his attention. His gaze flicked around the few people lining the streets. They were better dressed than he, but they still blended into the drab building, as if they, too, were embarrassed to be seen.

The guards passed by in their dark grey and black uniforms, a muted counterpoint to the colourful Guardians, so fair and beautiful, or so it was said. Never having seen them, he wondered if any of it were true and which one had just passed by him. He watched the tail end of the procession turn the corner and disappear into the streets of Vespers.

It wasn't often that he came into this part of Vespers—the clean streets were no place for a filthy wharf rat—but still, he lingered, drawn. The golden stone of a huge building rose high above him, the marker that the city was ahead and the Harbourtown behind them, clinging to the slopes that led to the port. The building must have been important because it had many glass windows and towers with rich-toned bells that chimed as the day passed. Birler had no idea what it was for.

On the other side of the muddy road, amongst the trees and bushes, the groundworks of a new building drew his eye. Piles of white stone gleamed a seductive invitation, and after another sharp glance around him, he drifted across the street and into the camouflage of the trees. The sweet scent of roses tickled his nose and relaxed his tense shoulders. Scowling, he observed the beginnings of a new temple that was being built in the gardens; their time would be better spent building houses for the people.

Leaning against a tree, its rough bark catching the calluses on his skin, he peered at the groundwork. He couldn't help it; he needed to touch that white stone, so clean and bright. The ring of metal on stone echoed through the gardens, the sound of chisels at work as the masons smoothed the edges. It was foolish to stay. There was only one family in the whole of Vespiri who could afford such work.

Finally, listening to his sense of caution, he retreated across the road and scurried back to where he belonged, in the back slums of the city of Vespers. He hesitated on the corner across from the Squalley, the local alehouse frequented by most of the dockers.

The door slammed, loud in the damp air, and a dark-haired man staggered out. He was wide across the shoulders, though skin and bone like most residents of the back alleys. The boy stepped back into the shadows and watched the drunken man lurch down the road. He fingered his sling but stayed his hand. As the man negotiated the corner, he waited, and then he moved on towards the harbour and the sea.

Breathing in the clean salt air, he exhaled the lingering taint of the slums. It usually took him two days' worth of searching for driftwood to earn a copper vail, and he had already wasted the morning. He searched for likely pieces of wood on the beach, piling the most usable above the tide line. Once he had achieved an armful, he headed back up to the harbour, his bare feet sinking into the cold sand.

He skirted the cavernous barns and trudged into the smelly alleys, his eyes alert for someone bigger or tougher than him. They would take his chance for food without a second thought. His tummy grumbled at the idea; he hadn't eaten for two days.

The back door of the Squalley was ajar. He squirmed through the gap and hovered on the threshold of the kitchens, waiting for the man who was the thin line between life and death in this city. The cook saw him and nodded, and he dumped his armful of driftwood into the wood basket by the ovens. He backed out to the door, hovering hopefully, watching the plump man with some desperation.

The cook grumbled under his breath and searched out a copper. "Birler, your da was in earlier. You be careful. He knows you're coming here."

Birler nodded, his gaze flicking around him. The cook was a good man. He couldn't look after every waif and stray in this city, though, on occasion, he tried. Birler whipped in and grabbed the dark brown roll and the tiny copper coin the cook had placed on the table and was gone before the cook could say anything further.

The cook tutted as he turned back to his work.

Birler scurried through the alleys, his heart light and his treasure tucked in his pocket. You didn't display anything you wanted to keep; it was an invitation to those who believed they were stronger. He made his way back down to the sea and trudged towards the far end of the beach, towards his shelter. A tree trunk with a tangle of branches had been flung high up above the tide line, and he was small enough to squirm under it into the relative warmth out of the wind and rain. It was far enough away from the harbour that few bothered to make the hike this far.

Considering his treasure, he inspected his hands. He was filthy; maybe he should wash. His mother would not have been pleased. A hazy image of a soft face smiling at him formed in his mind. He vaguely remembered the sensation of someone holding him because they wanted to, not because they wanted something from him.

He shook the memory away as the wind howled around his makeshift home, and he tore the bread in half and then in half again; it would last him four days if he were careful. He nibbled at the bread, with the yeasty flavour stirring more memories of better days as he stared at the driftwood around him. He had pushed the sand up to fill the gaps, and it held quite well; the damp air stuck the sand together like mud.

Wrapping the bread in the cleanest rag he had, more to

keep the sand out than to keep it fresh, he tucked it into his makeshift wall and hunkered down. He ought to go and search for more wood, more stones, more something, but he was exhausted. His stomach eased for once, and he relaxed. His eyelids drooped, and he slept.

Birler dreamt he was drowning. It was so real he could feel the cold and frothy water creeping up his thighs. He shivered, reaching for the delicate hand that was held out to him; someone wanted to help the likes of him. Reaching to accept the help, he hesitated when he saw his rough, grimy hand, daring to take such a precious offer, and he woke, choking on the saltwater that swirled around his home and tugged at his body as it receded.

Horror rushed through him, and he lurched upright as the furious wind tore at his little shelter, with the wood creaking as it shifted. He stuffed his bread in his pockets and patted himself down. Sling, stones, copper. Another wave tore through his shelter and dragged both him and the sand back towards the sea. His heart rate spiked when he realised sand blocked his entrance. He furiously began digging, only to realise it was a waste of time as the next huge breaker lifted him off his knees and filled his hole with sand again.

Grasping the wood to keep himself in place, he pushed against the solid branches he had relied on to protect him, now an impenetrable cage restraining him. Why he was so determined to live, he wasn't sure. Maybe he was just stubborn; maybe he wanted to prove to his pa that he didn't need him after all. Whatever it was, he was not dying here. He worked his way up the branch, snapping dead wood off where he could, hanging on when grasping waves tugged his body and sand scoured his skin as it swirled around him.

The branch gave under his hand, and he scrabbled to pull it apart, frantic in his panic as the storm crashed around him. He squeezed out of the branches, scraping off skin as he struggled, shedding the shelter like a juvenile crab seeking a new home. He staggered up the beach above the grasping sea, the driving winds buffeting his slight frame. The rain drummed against his skin, cold and hard enough to bruise.

He stood there defiantly, draggled and drawn, as he watched the waves slowly tug his home apart. The water persistently drew the sand away, digging the wood out by its foundations and dragging it back into the sea from whence it had come.

A particularly vicious gust of rain-laden wind drove him to find some shelter. He huddled in between the dunes, sheltering against the strength of the winds and protecting his eyes against the flying sand. The broiling clouds clashed above him as if it were all his fault. Waves crashed on the beach, and the wind roared around him. Swirling gusts of sand abraded his skin, making it sting as he huddled there all night, slowly buried by the shifting dune.

When the winds finally eased, Birler crawled out from the sands. Shaking the grit out of his clothes, he stared around him. Even in the dark of the night, he could see the dunes had shifted. A fine drizzle persisted, a reminder of the storm that had moved on to some other poor soul. He was bone cold and wet, but he had survived. Again.

Birler turned his face up to the rain and opened his mouth. The fresh water washed the sand off his face and cleansed his mouth of grit and salt. Spitting out sand, he patted his clothes, checking he still had his meagre belongings. Relief eased his tight muscles when he found he still had his sling and some of his stones. The bread, though, was a pulpy mess of sand and salt, so he left it for the birds. His tiny copper coin was at the bottom of his pouch, among the stones, and he thanked the Lady for leaving him something.

A glance around revealed deserted dunes. He stripped and shook out his clothes, using them to wipe the gritty sand off his body, though it stubbornly stuck against his damp skin. He eventually gave up and just stood in the rain, letting it clean him as best it could. He debated bathing in the sea, but the thought of the stinging salt drying on his scraped skin made him stay where he was.

Shivering in the cold air, he dressed in his tattered shirt and trousers. The wet cloth clung to his sore skin, reminding him how exposed he was. Strapping his pouch around his waist and under his shirt, he considered his options. The sea was a frothy darkness behind him, and the deep roar of the surf on the beach was still a sign that it hadn't calmed down yet. It was safer to go inland, but to where? He preferred the deserted beaches to the filthy streets.

An image of leafy trees intruded on his thoughts, and his feet moved of their own volition.

<hr>

Serill threw his pack on his bunk and looked around the barracks. He had made it, finally. This would be his home for the foreseeable future, a bare wooden hut with ten beds. The uniform of a cadet in the Ranger's Academy hung on a peg, and his fingers drifted to the dark green cloth. It had cost more than his family could spare, though they had clubbed together and offered him what they had; he was their future. He swore he wouldn't let them down.

Loud footsteps preceded more cadets arriving, and he turned, his face expressionless as he faced those who would be his new family. They would become as close as brothers or sisters, or so his mother said, to be relied upon, and in turn, they would depend on him to protect them and the people of Remargaren. As he watched the cadets enter, he hoped she was right.

A red-headed youth took the bed on his right, his

sparkling blue eyes bright in his round face as he raked Serill with a hard inspection. Serill wondered what he saw apart from a thin face thatched with light blond hair and grey eyes. The youth stuck his hand out. "Tagerill Descelles of Greens," he said firmly, a sly dimple creasing his cheek.

"Serill of Marchwood," Serill replied, no ancient family name to offer.

Tagerill nodded and looked around him. "So, this is home, is it?" He watched the other cadets and then suddenly strode across the room. "Ty, when did you sign up?" he asked as he grabbed a blond-haired lad by his broad shoulders.

The boy laughed. "When m'father said I had to. He'd had enough of us scrapping. He shouldn't have had so many sons, should he?"

Tagerill dragged Ty over to where Serill stood watching them. "This is Serill. Serill, Tyrler," he said before heading off into the crowd of cadets again, leaving the two to size each other up. Serill stiffened under Tyrler's intense inspection.

"Where are you from?" Tyrler asked, jutting his chin out.

"Borders of Marchwood," Serill replied. "You?"

"Tyrler Clary of Mayer," he said, dismissing Serill and heading back to his chosen bed.

Serill watched him go. So that was how it would be? Maybe it had been naïve to think that the cadets would be above lording it over each other. After all, they were supposed to be equals. He should have known better. He watched Tagerill bouncing around the room; he either knew everyone already or, if he hadn't, he did now. He was effusive, talking to everyone, badgering all for their names and status. Not that he seemed to care one way or the other; he just wanted to know, but then he didn't have to be concerned. Tagerill was from an old, respected family, just as Tyrler was.

Serill sighed and, overcoming his inherent shyness, went to introduce himself. Tagerill pounced on him as soon as he came within reach. Serill couldn't help but smile at his enthusiasm and allowed himself to be pitched into a whirl of introductions, all of which he soon forgot.

It didn't take long for them to lose all their preconceptions as they were swept into the rigorous training regime that recruits were put through. There wasn't the time or the energy for anyone to lord it over anyone else. Weary cadets fell into bed each night, and they were cruelly roused at dawn each morning.

Tagerill tucked Serill under his wing for some reason, and Serill soon became the owner of far more information about the Descelles family than he had ever wanted to know. He was more frugal with his own history, there not being so much to tell, but Tagerill wheedled it out of him in the end.

"You're lucky," Tagerill said morosely one evening after he had collapsed on his bed at the end of a particularly gruelling day. The rising wind whipped around the barracks and rattled the shutters.

"How so?" Serill asked with interest, wondering how his circumstances could be better than Tagerill's.

"You don't have to live up to ridiculously high expectations. You don't have a brother and a sister who have already excelled through the academy and become rangers. Being the youngest sucks. There's nothing I can improve on; they've already done it."

"You should think yourself lucky, then; they can't expect anything more. My family have invested everything in me. They expect me to succeed and, once I graduate, to repay them many times over." Serill stared at Tagerill, a brooding expression on his face. "I'm not so sure the military will pay them what they expect."

"Families, eh? Who'd have 'em?" Tagerill made to sit up and groaned. "My back, my legs. I swear my muscles will have muscles by the time they've finished with us."

Serill laughed. "Only four more weeks to go, and then the real work starts."

"Don't remind me. I'm not looking forward to that either, though having a sword in my hand will be a relief. I never thought I would complain about not sparring."

4

———

GUERLAIRE

AT SEA

After hastily sluicing himself down with the remainder of the rain water in the barrel, Guerlaire watched the Vespirian coastline with hungry eyes. For five more days he had suffered while the crew repaired the rigging and then finally rowed the ship into the open sea. Even after raising the sails, it had taken another four days to sail down the coastline, and at last, the Port of Vespers was in sight.

His skin hummed, with every brush of cloth sending flashes of sensory torture along his nerves. He had never been so on edge or skittish in his life. He was overloaded with magical energy, and the flaw in his plan was that he didn't know how to release it. Worse, he had no idea who had attacked them or why. Who had such power that they could target one vessel in the middle of Elothia with such accuracy?

His brooding was interrupted as Chryll leaned on the railing beside him, his bulk a reassuring presence, though he had shifted a little further away, which would have been insulting if Guerlaire didn't know the reason why.

"I said you should have sparred again." Chryll frowned at Guerlaire. "You are crackling with energy; it's quite painful to be near you."

"I can't help it. You're not fully fit, and I'd end up killing anyone else."

"I'm fit enough to spar with you. You shouldn't have absorbed so much magic; you should have let it dissipate."

Guerlaire rubbed his face. "Not knowing who was attacking us, I didn't want them to be able to draw it back in and reuse it against us."

"Who has the ability to wield magic so?"

"I don't know."

"Can't Leyandrii"—Chryll waved his hand in the air—"teach you how to control it better? You suffer needlessly."

"She has, but it's my fault. We should have returned earlier. I've stayed away too long."

"Are you sure you want to be tied so close? You shouldn't be dependent on Leyandrii to control your power."

Guerlaire sighed and stared at the approaching port. It wasn't Leyandrii's fault. She had warned him his association with her would affect him in both body and spirit, and he had laughed her words off. He should have known she wouldn't have said it if it weren't important.

If he wanted a goddess for a wife, there were things he would have to live with. And live with them, he would, for Leyandrii. Her power enhanced his, and he was changing as a result, but he didn't care. His eyes were changing from blue to an emerald green, just like hers. It was the one change he loved. It strengthened their connection and was a visible sign of his love for her, a love so deep it physically hurt on occasion.

She had also warned him that he wouldn't be able to hold all the magical energy collecting within him and she would have to siphon it off periodically or his magic would spill over and he would begin to affect others without realising it. He could even implode under all the pressure. If he hadn't expended so much energy creating the shield, it could have been a real possibility.

Usually, he had no worries about magic overload because Leyandrii came up with the most imaginative ways to siphon off his energy, and he enjoyed every moment of it. But he had miscalculated this trip, and Chryll was paying the price.

Chryll shifted as the air crackled, and a pained expression crossed his face. "Half a chime, Guerlaire. The limited space means you have to control your moves even more. Enough to take the edge off; otherwise, you won't even be able to enter the palace."

Knowing Chryll was right, Guerlaire joined him on the deck. "Half a chime only. And if it gets too painful, you call a halt. Promise me." Sailors watched them, and a low murmur rose as they traded bets on how many hits Guerlaire would make.

Chryll scowled.

Shaking his fist at them, he said, "Give me some credit. I will make at least one hit." And the sailors began betting on how long it would take him to get his first strike. Chryll laughed, his deep voice a comforting rumble, and he squared up to Guerlaire.

The confined space made them much more even, and when Chryll made his strike, the sailors groaned. Guerlaire laughed and redoubled his efforts. Before he knew it, the captain was calling his sailors to break out the oars as they approached the harbour entrance, and he called the session to a halt. The buzz under his skin had calmed, and he blessed his friend for insisting they spar.

Chryll peered across the harbour. "Looks like someone was expecting you," he said as he gestured at the coach and horses waiting on the quay.

Guerlaire clapped him on the shoulder. "Expecting *us*," he replied as he sheathed his sword and collected his possessions. The boxes of samples, journals, and specimens would be transported up to the Chapterhouse later. He would spend months sorting and cataloguing it all.

He waited impatiently as the boat docked and planks of wood were run out so he could disembark. Chryll followed, inhaling the salty air tinged with the perfume of roses. "Nice to be home," he murmured as he climbed into the carriage beside Guerlaire.

Guerlaire strode through the palace corridors, nodding at the guards on duty. They were the men and women he had chosen to protect the most important person in his life and in the whole of Remargaren. That Leyandrii had laughed at his over-protectiveness made no difference to him. He knew he couldn't protect her himself; he would suffocate her with his fears. That was why he went on his travels—so she would always welcome him back. But if he had to go, then he wanted some reassurance that she would be safe.

The Lady's Guards were the result. He was their commander, and he chose them, and Leyandrii let him with a smile of understanding. They were even more important now than they had ever been. He had tried to persuade Leyandrii to call forth her own Guardians, but she always refused, saying she didn't need them. He knew she was wrong.

The governing body in the Administration was causing an upswell of discontent, questioning Leyandrii's rule. Ever since the elder Guardians had departed many decades ago—how and to where, no-one knew—and left Remargaren in her hands, there had been questions. They thought she was too young, even though no one knew how old she really was. She was a Guardian; of course she was older than she looked. *She was a goddess,* he thought viciously as he stomped down the corridor. How dare they question her validity, her right to rule the world that her family had created. *Created.* If it hadn't been for her family, none of them would even be here.

He took a deep breath, trying to control his anger, though he knew it was hopeless. She'd known what he was feeling ever since he had stepped off the boat onto dry land down at the harbour. The journey up to the city hadn't helped alleviate his growing restlessness as much as he had hoped.

He nodded at the guard on duty and waited for her to open the door. Passing within, he came to a halt as soon he saw Leyandrii. She was ethereal and delicate, yet the sight of her slammed against his senses. He took a deep breath and tried to steady his frantic heart. He had stayed away too long, and he was overwhelmed and distraught in the same breath. Leyandrii hurried to his side, her green eyes enormous.

Wrapping her arms around him, she soothed his frazzled nerves and pulled him towards her. "You fool," she said, kissing him. She cupped his face, and he stared into her emerald eyes and was lost. She covered his face in kisses, and he melted into her embrace. A shuddering sigh of relief escaped as he hid his face in her neck and breathed in the scent of her skin.

Leyandrii held him tightly until the shudders died away and he was able to draw breath.

"What did I tell you?" she scolded.

"I know. We got lost. I hadn't intended to be so late," Guerlaire said as she released him.

"And was the trip worthwhile?"

"All trips are worthwhile," he murmured. "Otherwise, why go?"

"Ah, does that mean you will be lost to the archives for the foreseeable future?"

"You need me here. We need to discover where the wild magic is coming from. The weather in Elothia was unpredictable and out of season. The river's path was unexpected at times. That's why we got lost; the maps were almost useless."

"That's not all that happened. I felt a surge of magic. Your shielding was impressive."

"We were attacked; by whom, I don't know, but they were strong."

"It came from the north of Elothia, though I couldn't pinpoint the location exactly. I'll speak to Asher and request he investigate." Leyandrii scowled at Guerlaire. "I'll teach you how to retaliate should such an attack occur again. I never thought our magic would be used for such terrible purposes. Whoever it is, they are dabbling in things that should not be touched."

"Then it's time to stop them before they do irrevocable damage."

Leyandrii slowly nodded, her gaze distant. "I had so hoped the people of Remargaren would see reason and embrace magic as a way of life. But there are some who will not listen to me. The Land is weary, and their thoughtless actions pain him. It is almost time for him to sleep the long sleep, but not just yet."

Guerlaire narrowed his eyes. "And what happens when he sleeps?"

"A new Guardian will be chosen." Leyandrii cast him a brilliant smile that lit up her face. "But there is no point worrying about that. We have other matters to discuss. There is one calling for me in Vespers; his voice is getting stronger, and you must find him. But before that," —her eyes sparkled with mischief, and he was lost in their seductive depths—"we have time for something else."

Guerlaire managed a chuckle, his mind already rushing ahead of him. "I timed something right, then."

"You always time it right, my love. Come, let me show you how well," She grasped his hand and led him to her private rooms. "You can tell me everything about your trip later. I have something to show you first," she said with a secretive smile as she closed the door behind him.

Tugging at the leather straps, Leyandrii unbuckled his jacket and pushed it over his shoulders and down his arms. Guerlaire let it fall to the floor. She unbuttoned his white shirt, spreading it wide so she could kiss his broad chest, and he sighed into her hair and reached for the back of her gown. "I should really bathe first."

"You mean you didn't stop to bathe before you came to see me?"

"You know I didn't."

Leyandrii smiled against his skin, and the sensation caused a flash of desire to spread through his body. "You still have to undress to bathe, and anyway, I like how you smell. It means you're home."

A shudder trembled through him as she slid her hands down his flat stomach and then unbuckled the belt at his waist. She unbuttoned his trousers as he toed off his boots and allowed her to push him on the bed so she could tug them off.

Groaning, he reached for her. He still hadn't released her from her gown, but with a soft chuckle, Leyandrii shimmied, and the silk slid down her body to gather at her feet. She stepped out of it and paused as Guerlaire raked her with a scorching gaze. Heat flared within him; he was about to combust. Blue sparks of energy crackled around him, and she slid her cool body against his, quenching the fire and absorbing his excess power.

He sighed in relief as the pressure behind his eyes eased, and the crackling presence he knew he emitted on occasion subsided. Sliding his hands down her body, he pressed his lips against hers. She moulded herself against him as he lost himself in the kiss. They were such a perfect fit, and she encompassed him in her love, a swirl of heady emotions and sensations, teasing and playful, soothing and sensual.

All thoughts of bathing left his brain as he struggled to catch his breath, and he tensed beneath her, straining to follow her touch, his skin sensitised by her every caress. Every kiss stimulated his senses, and she let out a long, low chuckle of delight as she brought him to the edge. Then he roared his release as she worshipped him as much as he worshipped her.

Guerlaire shivered as a cool waft of air caressed his sweat-slick skin. He inhaled Leyandrii's scent, soothed by the sweet aroma of roses, and he knew he was where he belonged. He kissed her neck and nibbled her ear as she settled in his arms.

"I missed you," he whispered.

"I know. I have missed you too," Leyandrii replied. "Though, much as I wished you stayed home, I know you are a restless creature and would not be happy here all the time."

"I will be home for the rest of the year now. I have plenty of records and maps to update and many samples to log."

"That's good, then."

Guerlaire smiled. "I saw your temple is coming along."

"It is. Father Menaret is preparing a lovely service of dedication. The temple is very excited."

"I'm sure it is," Guerlaire murmured, ignoring the baffling fact that a building could be happy. He stretched, with satisfaction running through every muscle, and Leyandrii laughed.

"We must bathe. Marguerite will join us soon for dinner."

Guerlaire groaned. "I don't want to move."

Leyandrii sat up, her golden hair caressing his skin. She clasped his hand, threaded her fingers in his, and kissed his knuckles. "We often have to do things we don't want to, but let's enjoy the things we do like." She peeped at him from under her lashes as she rose and tugged his hand. "Let's bathe."

5

BIRLER

VESPERS, VESPIRI

irler watched the plump father circle the temple building site. He knew he was the Lady's priest because of the brown robes he wore, robes made of nice thick material that Birler coveted just for the warmth they would provide. The swirling material dwarfed the small man, but he strode confidently around the site regardless.

The father visited every day, casting an eye over the progress, stopping to speak with the man in charge at the end of every inspection. The tall overseer was always enthusiastic, waving his arms as he explained their progress.

Each night, Birler had taken to walking through the building, finding comfort in the glowing stones as they gradually rose around him. He patted them to say well done, as if they needed his approval; he knew they didn't, but he gave it anyway. He had taken to sleeping in the tall oak tree which stood in the gardens, having found a hollowed-out nest in the fork near the top. He scampered up the tree out of sight when a woman unexpectedly flitted through the building and almost caught him.

From his eyrie, he watched the woman float through the

half-built structure, caressing the walls much as he had. He couldn't see who she was; the moonlight bleached all colour from her hair and robes, making her a gauzy shadow that barely made an impression. She hesitated at his favourite place, the central altar. A base had been set above three shallow steps, and he wondered what would be placed on top of it.

She mounted the steps and spun, her skirts flaring around her, and Birler witnessed her sheer joy as flowers bloomed by a burbling stream at her feet. She slowed and stared up through the open ceiling and looked straight at him. He froze as his gaze met her startling green eyes, and warmth suffused him, chasing away the chill night for the first time in years. She bent her head in acknowledgement of his vigilance on her behalf before she turned away, and the temple was reclaimed by the night. He stared at the marble statue of a young woman on the central altar, her skirts swirling and with a plethora of flowers covering her bare feet. The scent of fragrant roses drifted on the night air, embracing him and lulling him to sleep.

The next morning, Birler was back on the beach, gathering his driftwood. He alternated the beach for the temple gardens, with the gardens giving up as many branches and kindling as the beach in his nightly searches. He didn't wonder why or how; he just accepted what he found and continued to guard the temple as it grew within and around him.

That evening, Birler trod his nightly rounds, communing with the temple. He knelt at the Lady's feet, and her flowers swayed before him, giving off that lovely scent of roses. He liked to think it was just for him. The sound of trickling water was soothing in the night air, and he lingered until the brilliant moon passed behind the rising walls and the temple was cast in shadow. He finally left and settled in the tree for the night.

The moon was particularly bright that night; it kept Birler awake, shining in his eyes, no matter how he lay. He gave up and watched the glowing sphere slowly progress across the night sky, leaving a trail of sparkling stars in its wake. As Birler observed the twinkling stars appear and flicker as the moon passed, he wondered what they really were.

His musing was interrupted by the sound of running feet, and Birler peered out of his nest and watched the father run under the oak tree towards the temple, his breath loud and gasping in the soft night air. The temple gardens were still, and a sense of caution hung in the air.

Birler readied his sling; his fingers filled with stones before he had even considered there was need. He climbed the tree and positioned himself over the entrance to the gardens.

There were four thugs, large and threatening. They gripped thick sticks for clubs; the father didn't stand a chance. Birler didn't hesitate, and the air hummed as he released his sling; the first stone dropped his target as the second was released. The men scattered in panic from the unexpected attack, and his third stone ricocheted off the knuckles of one of the men, who dropped his club, howling in pain. Stuffing his broken hand under his armpit, the man scuttled out of the temple grounds.

"Show yerself, yer scum. Hiding like a coward. Where are yer?" One of the men had found his voice as he searched the gardens. Birler watched him. He was getting close to the father. His sling whirred, and his stone caught the brute on the back of the head. The man spun, cursing, rubbing his head. "I'll getcha, yer bastard. Yer'll pay for that."

"He's up the tree." The other man had spotted him.

Birler ran along the branch and climbed higher as the father slipped away and out the other side of the gardens.

Birler waited. He only had a handful of stones left. The smaller of the men began to climb the tree, and Birler took aim and let go. The stone hit the man between the eyes, and he crumpled, crashing out of the tree to land at the feet of the last man standing. Birler grinned as the man cursed and then retreated at the sound of fast-approaching horses.

Birler slid down the tree and hid in the temple. He hushed the walls as they shimmered in greeting, shrinking back as he heard a decisive voice cut the night air. "You're sure it was the boy?"

"Yes, Guerlaire. He was up the tree. If it hadn't been for him, I'd have been in serious trouble." The father's soft voice filtered through the walls.

"Well, it doesn't look like he's up there now. Father, if you see him, let me know. Leyandrii is worried."

The father sighed. "I've tried; he just disappears."

"I'll leave you a guard; we should have left one before." The man's voice was receding as he walked away from the temple, and Birler breathed out a sigh of relief.

The father's voice carried on the still air. "I *have* a guard, Guerlaire, and he hasn't failed yet." Birler didn't hear the other man's reply. He crept out of the temple and retreated through the gardens. His safe place was compromised; he would have to find somewhere else to sleep, though he didn't know where. He was reluctant to leave the temple when she wasn't finished, but it was no longer safe to stay.

The temple was Birler's downfall; he couldn't stay away. He wanted to see her finished. The Lady's voice called him, and he couldn't resist. He slunk into the nearly finished temple early one morning before the ceremony of comple-tion was due to be performed. He stood before the altar in awe; the statue of the Lady mesmerised him. Water trickled at her feet, and the scent of the flowers overwhelmed him, fixing his feet to the floor. But it was her green eyes that held him in place. Her voice embraced him as the temple celebrated his return, its stones shimmering in happiness. It was intoxicating, a sense of belonging that infused his body; he belonged here.

"Gently," the father's voice intruded, breaking the spell. He held Guerlaire's arm, preventing him from stepping forward.

The child spun, startled, though his hand didn't stray to his belt as Guerlaire had half-expected. His lips twitched in sympathy as he saw the boy's face; it was open and awestruck. His dark blue eyes were distant, still seeing something he didn't. He had been well and truly ensnared, though he didn't know it. The echo of the temple's exaltation shivered over Guerlaire's skin. No wonder the boy was stunned.

And he *was* only a child, maybe early to mid teens. It was difficult to tell because he was ill-nourished, gaunt-faced, and bone-thin. His clothes were dirty rags that couldn't possibly keep him warm. His sling was tucked into his waistband, visible through the holes in the material. Guerlaire wondered how he had survived for so long. He also wondered how he was going to fulfil his Lady's demand. He didn't think she realised how desperate or ill-prepared the child was.

Guerlaire deliberately leaned on the temple's excitement, and, extending an open hand, knelt before the altar. "The Lady bids you welcome," he said, tempering his voice.

The boy stared at him, his eyes focussing on the here and now and alertly flicking around the temple, looking for an escape.

"She offers you shelter, food, work," Guerlaire said. "She needs your help."

"I can't. She's not finished yet." The boy's eyes strayed back to the altar.

"After, when she's finished. You won't need to sustain her any longer. She will sustain others." Guerlaire wasn't sure where the words were coming from, but they seemed to make sense to the boy.

The boy tilted his head, bird-like, and considered Guerlaire's words. He nodded sadly. "She won't need me anymore."

Guerlaire felt the temple's denial at the same time the boy did.

Resting a grubby hand on the altar, the boy smiled.

Guerlaire froze in shock as the stone shimmered in response.

"You know I'll always be here for you," the boy whispered, almost too quietly for Guerlaire to hear. The temple steadied, and he stood back. "She'll be finished later."

"Yes," Guerlaire agreed.

"I've got nowhere else to go," the boy said, staring at Guerlaire. Whatever the boy saw, Guerlaire didn't think it was him.

"You won't need to go anywhere else," Guerlaire promised, slowly standing. "My name is Guerlaire."

The boy nodded as if he'd known all along. "Birler," he replied.

6

BIRLER

RANGERS ACADEMY, DECU 1120

Birler hesitated on the threshold of the barracks. He didn't belong here; he knew it. He yearned to return to the temple, to the peace and quiet. He clutched an unfamiliar bundle of clothing, more cloth than he remembered seeing in his whole life, all for him.

The man at the temple had turned out to be a captain in the Lady's Rangers, Captain Guerlaire, and he had taken Birler to a nearby tavern, where he'd been given a bowl of watery soup and a slice of bread. Half the bread was now in his pocket, though the soup had settled the gnawing hunger he had suffered most of his life. He'd also been given a bath. His skin was scrubbed clean, and it didn't feel like it belonged to him; it tingled and smelt different.

He'd been told to take bed four, so he counted the neat cots and moved towards the fourth one. Small trinkets stood on the box next to the beds on either side, alongside a book, a real bound book with gilt lettering. Birler stared at it as he perched on the edge of the bed, not sure what to do next.

After a moment, he peered into the unadorned box, stuffed his new clothes into the empty space, and then sat on the bed, listening for anyone approaching. The sound of voices echoed down the corridors, and he stiffened as they grew louder. Captain Guerlaire had told him the academy was a place of learning, a place where he could build his strength and learn to fight. He said the Lady had asked him to stay and study.

Birler stood as the voices turned into boys, a jumble of healthy, strong boys, all bigger and older than him. They paused in surprise at the sight of him. A blond-haired cadet with heavy brows that hung over his eyes stepped forward. "What sort of runt are you then?" he asked, looking Birler up and down and not liking what he saw.

Birler glared back at him. He wasn't *that* much shorter than him.

"We have a reputation to uphold, and we don't need the likes of you dragging our scores down."

More cadets arrived. "Let us get to our beds, then. You know we've only got a quarter-chime to change." A slender lad squirmed through the ring of boys and took the bed to Birler's right. His words galvanised the others to move, and they pulled out their clothes.

"Serill," the slender boy said, holding out his hand.

Birler shook it. "Birler," he replied.

A much larger, red-headed boy took the bed on the other side of Serill. He cast Birler a searching glance but didn't speak.

Serill nodded. "You need your training kit, black cutoffs, white shirt, running shoes. Change quick. We have to be on the field in five minutes."

Birler did as he was told and followed the boys out of the barracks. Once on the field, they were sent running around the perimeter. The slow pace was galling, and Serill laughed as Birler reached him. "We have to do ten laps. Pace yourself; this is about stamina, not speed."

Birler slowed his pace and wondered why anyone would want to run for so long. He was used to darting escapes, not long-winded chases. If someone chased him through the city, he would be dead, not running.

After two laps, Birler thought he might die. His breath was coming out in deep gasps. He thought his lungs might explode, and his chest hurt with each breath he inhaled.

The training master loomed up beside him. "Stop running before you do yourself an injury," he said, inspecting the boy. "You're new. What's your name?"

"Birler, sir," Birler gasped out as he bent over, hands on knees.

"You're not ready for this. You haven't the strength. Weren't you told to report to me?"

"No, sir."

The master frowned. "Very well. The rest of this week you do one lap. Then you come to me. You will build the laps as I tell you. Now, stretch out." He took Birler through a series of stretches to soothe the muscles that would be protesting on the morrow.

Next, he moved Birler to the first stage of the air disciplines to build his control and, once he had the routine down, left him to continue as more boys came up to join them, gasping out plumes of steam in the chill morning air. They were soon doing their stretches and eyeing Birler as he smoothly performed the routine they had been struggling to remember for the last week.

The master came down the line and raised an eyebrow as he saw Birler, but he continued back up the line, correcting as he went.

He came back, calling the boys to order. "Apeiron, the first discipline, controlling the chaos around you. You are grasping the air and acknowledging that it is chaos. Until you acknowledge, you cannot move on. You are not listening. You are not paying attention. All except him." The master pointed at Birler. "This is his first day, and he has already understood. I suggest you ask him how. Because, unless you do, you will be languishing here whilst those who do understand proceed to the next level. So, again, acknowledge the chaos. Begin."

The master kept them working for another chime, and the boys grumbled at the slowness of it all. Birler enjoyed the way his body seemed to mesh together in alignment.

They were released for lunch. Even Birler was ready, though he was so used to being hungry that he hadn't really acknowledged that it was lunchtime. He followed the boys into the mess hall, shying back from the rush of people and the racket of plates and crashing crockery. The boys behind him shoved him aside unceremoniously and rushed to get into the queue ahead of him. Birler tagged on the end, watching everyone and everything with enormous eyes. The boys had piles of food on their plates, enough food to last him a month.

He stood speechless as he reached the hatches at the top of the room. "Chicken or stew?" the man behind the counter barked. Birler stared at him in bewilderment. The man slopped some lumps of meat on a plate and shoved it at him as Serill appeared at his shoulder.

"Take the plate," Serill murmured. "He'll have potatoes and greens as well," he said, grabbing two rolls and some cutlery. He steered Birler to his table and plonked him in the seat next to him. The red-haired lad from the barracks sat opposite him, watching him with interest. No one else sat at their table.

"Eat," Serill said, digging into the food piled on his plate. "You need the food. You'll burn it off this afternoon, and you don't have enough fat on you to sustain the pace of this place. Eat."

Birler looked at the mound of food on his plate and dug his fork into the potatoes. There was no way he could eat it all. He broke the bread in half and then half again and nibbled it, his eyes darting around the room.

"You're gonna need to eat more than that," the boy opposite him said with a grin, "and faster. We only have half a chime, and then we're in class."

Birler swallowed his bread and gulped his water. It was clear and clean. He took another mouthful, savouring the freshness.

He stabbed a piece of chicken and concentrated on the texture; it was chewy but tasted smooth and warm. He ate some more. He had only eaten maybe a quarter of his plate when a single bell clanged. His stomach thought he had eaten a whole chicken; it was heavy and uncomfortable.

"That's us," the red-haired boy said. "I'm Tagerill. I know you're Birler. C'mon, we put the plates in the stacks at the end." His eyes widened as Birler slipped a piece of bread in his pocket. "You don't need to worry. There's more food later. The way they work us, you'll need three meals a day just to survive. You won't go hungry."

Birler flushed, but he didn't replace the bread.

Afternoon class had Birler leaning forward with wide-eyed interest, watching avidly as the master explained the coding used for maps. He absorbed the information like it was the air he breathed, and he had the symbols memorised before the master had finished explaining them. He looked at the piece of paper on the desk before him; they expected him to *mark* the paper?

Birler hesitated, watching the boys around him bend over the paper, quills in hand, frowning at the symbols on the boards and then the paper before them. Shrugging, he picked up the quill, annotated his map, and then sat staring at the words. He wondered where the map was of. It would be very useful, he was sure. He frowned at what he assumed were the names of places, tracing the first letter. It meant nothing to him.

"Right, who can tell me what this symbol is for and where it is on the map?" the master said as he rose. His stick tapped the board.

"It's a temple, and it is in square C8," Tagerill's lazy voice said from behind Birler.

C8? Birler scanned the map. There were numbers across the top and what must be letters down the side. He had marked the temple. He followed the lines back to the edges and traced the letter C and the number 8.

He paid close attention to the other letters and numbers that were offered, taking care to memorise each one.

"You, in the middle, this one." The master pointed at Birler and then the symbol on the board.

Birler traced the lines. "A bridge, D4."

"Very good." The master moved on whilst Birler sat in amazement. He had read letters on a map and got it right!

The day proceeded, and Birler held his first sword. He had no idea what to do with it, so he faded into the background and watched. Tagerill was a natural. Birler could see that the sword was just an extension of his arm, and he devoutly hoped he would never have to fight him.

The end of the day was a shower and a change of clothes and then back into the mess hall for another enormous meal—This one, fortunately, not so rushed. Birler found himself at the same table with Serill and Tagerill.

He listened to their good-natured bickering and nibbled his food. He was eating beef for the first time, and he chewed slowly, identifying the flavour.

"So, where are you from?" Tagerill asked, turning to Birler, the worst of his hunger satisfied.

"Down by the harbour," Birler replied.

"Vespers, you mean? Didn't think there was much housing down that way."

Birler shrugged.

"What made you join the academy? You're not quite what a recruit usually looks like, are you?"

"What does a recruit look like?" Birler asked after swallowing his mouthful.

Tagerill gestured to the room. "Can't you tell?"

Birler shrugged again. "The Lady said," he replied, taking another mouthful.

"You mean you think the Lady told you to join up? Didn't know she was recruiting." Tagerill laughed at his own joke.

Birler gave him a glimmer of a smile and concentrated on his food. Greens—now, they were interesting and a bit slimy. He poked them. They looked like the seaweed he found on the beach.

Serill gave him a sharp glance. "They're good for you, or so my mother says. Gives you strength."

Birler looked at them dubiously.

"Haven't you had greens before?" Serill asked very quietly.

Birler shook his head.

"Try them. If you don't like them get something different next time."

Birler took a mouthful and chewed—a bitter taste but fresh. He tried some more. They weren't slimy after all, and he was surprised when they were all gone.

"Dessert," Tagerill said, rubbing his hands, his eyes brightening. "Which do you prefer? Pie or cake?"

Birler didn't know what the difference was, though cake sounded more familiar. "Cake," he said slowly.

Tagerill nodded. "Good choice. Chocolate or berry?"

"Berry?"

"Sure?" Tagerill leapt from his seat and came back with two plates, one with a brown sponge swimming in a dark brown sauce and one covered in a frothy white substance and a pile of colourful berries.

Birler stared at it in awe.

"Go on then. Eat." Tagerill grinned at Birler's expression and dug in.

Birler flashed Serill a quick look from under his lashes. Serill grinned. "Eat."

Birler took a mouthful and thought the Lady had blessed him, as she surely had. The sweetness melted in his mouth, and as the berries popped, they flooded his mouth with tart flavours. His senses were on overload.

Later that night, he stumbled out of his bed and threw up in the flower bed outside the barracks. He collapsed to his knees and shuddered as the heavy weight in his stomach forced its way out, leaving him spent and weak.

Shivering in the night air, he wiped his mouth and then covered his mess with dirt. A quick visit to the well had him drawing some water to rinse his mouth and face. He drank the cold water, hoping it would soothe his sore stomach, before crawling back into bed and hunkering down under the blankets—nice warm blankets that made him feel over-heated. He tossed them off until he shivered again and then pulled them back up again.

Finally, he slept as the grey dawn lightened the sky.

7

BIRLER

RANGERS ACADEMY

The days progressed to weeks, and Birler found his way. He absorbed everything that was offered, except for the food. He reduced his food intake instinctively, no matter what the others said; his stomach knew what it could take. Gradually, he ate more as his body demanded more fuel.

Tyrler and Tagerill laughed at his efforts with the blade, united in their superiority of sword handling. It finally came to a head during a sparring session as Birler stood opposite Tagerill and waggled his sword feebly.

"What's he doing here?" Tyrler jeered. "He's not big enough to hold a sword. Tagerill, I could beat him one handed."

Birler clamped down on his spurt of anger. "You could try," he said, his voice low.

Tagerill grinned, his eyes bright. "A challenge." He tucked his left arm behind his back and dropped into his opening stance. "Come on, then."

Birler firmed his stance and tried to copy Tagerill. He knew it wasn't going to work; his body didn't feel right. He flowed into the first discipline instead and aligned himself to the air. Birler swung his sword, and Tagerill parried, his eyes widening in surprise. Tagerill retaliated far too fast for Birler, whose sword went spinning. Birler shook out his hand as the vibration from the strike shivered through his arm.

A cadet handed him back his sword, and he flinched as Tagerill's sword caught him across the ribs, and he landed on the floor, breathless. He winced as he stood and rubbed his side. He managed to block a strike, but once again, the flat of Tagerill's sword slammed into his ribs, and he collapsed, wheezing as spiking pain spread through his chest.

"Had enough?" Tagerill grinned, bowing as the cadets applauded him.

Struggling back to his feet, Birler struck back, driving the unprepared Tagerill across the ring. Once Tagerill got his feet under him, he soon gathered himself and struck back. Birler barely deflected the first strike, and the second pounded his ribs again, and then he was back in the dust, gasping for breath.

"Stay down," Tagerill said fiercely, a little breathless.

Birler glared back at him and slowly stood, holding his aching side with one hand. He raised his blade.

"Stand down." The sparring master stood between them. He glared at Tagerill. "Mr Descelles, it seems you have forgotten the rules. Maybe a week on basics will remind you. Mr Birler, it seems you have no idea what you are doing, so you will join him—after you have been to the healerie to make sure Mr Descelles here didn't break your ribs. You'd better not have," the master warned Tagerill, with ice in his voice. "Accompany him and escort him back to the barracks. Your practice is finished." The master turned back to the other boys, called them round, and, ignoring Tagerill and Birler, began a demonstration.

Tagerill sighed and offered Birler his hand. "C'mon, I didn't break your ribs, did I?"

"Not sure," Birler huffed with a grin. "It hurts to breathe," he admitted as he stumbled out of the ring. Tagerill steadied him.

"I didn't mean to. You've got a wicked swing there. Once you learn control, you'll be a worthwhile opponent. I'm sorry. I get a bit carried away sometimes."

"Doesn't matter. Got to learn somehow," Birler said, his voice still breathy, and Tagerill frowned in concern.

"I'll help you. We'll have plenty of time next week. We'll do the drills together, and you learn quick; you'll be fine. You're even getting some fat on those bones," Tagerill joked, though Birler knew that compared to the other lads, he was still distressingly thin, and what he had was all strappy muscle.

Tagerill steered him into the healerie, swallowing as he saw the senior healer on duty, Healer Demeren. "Birler here took a couple of raps to the ribs. He says it hurts to breathe," Tagerill said, releasing Birler into the care of the healer.

Healer Demeren glared at Tagerill before leading Birler deeper into the healerie. Tagerill trailed after them. The healer helped a wincing Birler remove his shirt, and Tagerill scowled at the sight of the deep bruising already purpling across Birler's chest, along ribs that could be clearly seen and counted.

The healer prodded gently, and Birler flinched. Sweat dewed his face as he swallowed, concentrating on controlling the nausea that swept through him. A faint hissing filled his ears and he gritted his teeth.

Watching him closely, the healer grunted. "You're lucky, just badly bruised. You'll be stiff for a couple of days, and then you can return to sparring. I'll tell Pallinten. Use this." He placed a pot in Birler's hand and took a handful of ointment out of another. As he slathered it over the bruised area, Birler tensed. "Morning, noon, and night. If *you* can't, then you do it." The healer glared at Tagerill until he agreed. "If it's no better in two days, come back. If you have any trouble breathing, any trouble at all, you come back straight away, understood?"

Birler nodded.

The healer handed Birler a glass. "Drink it." He waited, tapping his lip, before taking the empty glass. After peering at Birler again, he helped him back into his shirt. Once he dismissed them, he turned away to make some notes on a pad.

Tagerill led Birler back to the barracks and helped him lie on his bed. He stood over him, frowning in concern. "You gonna be alright?" he asked.

"Yeah, jus' tired," Birler murmured, closing his eyes.

Tagerill wasn't so sure as he inspected Birler's ashen face. Sitting on Serill's bed, he watched Birler doze, his brow creased in thought. Birler didn't make any sense. He was painfully thin, didn't seem to know much about food, and hardly ate anything, yet he had held his own.

Unease burrowed its way into Tagerill's thoughts. He knew he hadn't held his punches. The deep bruising on Birler's ribs was proof of that. As he watched Birler, guilt prickled his conscience. Wherever Birler had come from, and his dark hair and eyes suggested the desert borders, he wasn't a pushover.

As the evening drew in, Tagerill woke Birler. "It's time for dinner."

"You go. I'm not hungry."

Tagerill left and went to track the healer down. "Birler

says he isn't hungry, but there's nothing of him; he hardly eats anything."

"Starvation does that to you; your stomach shrinks. He probably can't eat it, not because he doesn't want to but because he physically can't. Leave him tonight. If he won't eat tomorrow, let me know." The healer looked at Tagerill. "You're in the same barracks, aren't you?"

Tagerill nodded.

"I was considering supplementing his food. I think I should do it anyway. If I'd known, I could have started him weeks ago," the man muttered to himself. He made up a draught in a mug, whisking it with a spoon. He peered at Tagerill. "I know what you boys are like. No teasing him. It's no fun starving to death. Count yourself lucky you've never been in his situation."

Tagerill nodded, his eyes wide. "Lady's honour, not a word."

"Very well. Take this. Make sure he drinks it tonight. If he refuses, threaten him with a night in the healerie. That should kick him into line. He won't want to come back here." The healer sighed. "I'll send another over in the morning."

Tagerill returned to the barracks, carefully carrying the covered mug. His face pinched as he watched Birler wake. "Here, drink this," he said. "The healer sent it over." He helped Birler sit up and stood over him as he drank it. After taking the mug, he helped Birler back into bed. "Just sleep in your clothes; worry about it tomorrow. Sleep. You'll feel better in the morning," Tagerill promised, tucking the blankets around him.

Birler stared at him. "Why are you being so nice?"

Tagerill grinned. "I need an opponent worthy of my sword. You're not much use sick, are you?"

Birler thought about it for a moment and then gave up and closed his eyes. His breathing smoothed, and Tagerill went to lie on his own bed. He folded his arms behind his head and stared at the ceiling, thinking furiously, putting two and two together and making at least eight.

Serill scowled down at him when the cadets returned that evening. "Where have you been?"

"Looking out for Birler. Healer Demeren put him on bed rest for the rest of the day."

"And that meant you not eating dinner?" Serill said in disbelief.

Tagerill shrugged. "One meal won't hurt. I'll have a big breakfast to make up for it."

Serill looked at Birler. "Is he alright?"

"No, not really, and it's my fault."

"He could have stayed down," Serill said loyally.

"Would you have?" Tagerill asked with a snort.

"No, but I have some skill. He doesn't even know how to hold a sword. He was foolish."

Tagerill laughed. "Some might say, but I think he was probably the wisest of all of us."

"But you're on basics for a whole week." Serill said, obviously aghast at the idea.

"Do me good, and it'll give me a chance to help him lay in a good foundation."

Serill laid a hand against Tagerill's forehead. "Where is the Tagerill we know and love? What have you done with him?"

Tagerill laughed ruefully. "Learning a painful lesson, but then, those are supposed to be the most valuable, aren't they?"

Birler was thankful the next morning that the healer's assistant arrived before anyone was awake, especially as he stood over Birler until he drank the proffered mug.

Sitting up had been uncomfortable, and Birler felt stiff and sore, but his ribs didn't grab so painfully. He swung his legs out of bed and made for the shower. He felt grubby, having slept in his clothes, and he shook his head at the irony of it all. How quickly you got used to the comforts when they were offered. He had slept in one set of clothes most of his life, yet here he was, feeling grubby after one night.

He still hadn't got over the novelty of the shower. The sensation of soapy water on his skin was one of the most satisfying feelings he had ever experienced. He liked being clean, and he thought that would be the thing he missed most when he had to return to the real world. His hands stilled under the shower at the possibility that this wasn't real, just a brief reward for something the Lady believed he had done. If that were so, it was a cruel reward, and Birler knew he would struggle to survive on his own after experiencing such a different way of life.

He dried himself off and returned to the barracks, intending to use the salve before dressing. He paused on the threshold, his towel wrapped around him and his clothes in his hand. Tyrler Clary blocked the way.

"You think you're clever getting Tagerill in trouble?" he snarled in Birler's face. "You'll pay for it. Scum like you shouldn't be here." Birler took a step back in response to the sheer spite that filled Tyrler's voice. "Watch your back," Tyrler said, the threat clear in his voice. "You will pay for it."

He turned away as Tagerill hurried in behind Birler from the showers.

"C'mon, get a move on. I'm starving." Tagerill hurried to his bed and dressed. He was beside Birler before he had even finished buttoning his trousers. He grabbed the salve. "Turn round," he said as he scooped the gloopy salve out and gently smeared it over the violent purple bruises on Birler's side. "Give it a chance to soak in before you put your shirt on," he added as he returned to his bed and pulled his boots on. He was back in a trice and kneeling to help Birler with his socks and boots, ignoring his protests. He had realised Birler would not be able to bend down and pull them on, as he had struggled with his trousers.

Serill watched them while waiting patiently at the end of the bed. "You two ready?" he asked.

Tagerill stood and grinned. "Just about." He led the way out, his stomach audibly growling. True to his word, he took a double helping of everything. His plate was overflowing.

Birler averted his eyes from so much food; just the sight of it made him feel ill. "There's food, and then there's too much food," he said with revulsion.

Tagerill laughed as he dug in. "I don't know how you did it."

"Did what?" Birler asked with a frown.

Tagerill dropped his voice. "Survived on nothing," he murmured.

Serill leaned forward. "What do you mean?" He leaned back soon enough as Tagerill frowned at him.

"Nobody can survive on nothing," Birler said.

"You know what I mean."

Birler shrugged and sipped his kafinee. Tagerill had brought him a mug, and he was hooked. He had never tasted the like, and kafinee was his favourite drink now. He eased back in his seat and cupped his mug.

Tagerill watched him with a slight smile. "What?"

"This doesn't seem real. It's a different world," Birler admitted.

"It's a good world. The Lady protects, and this is just a small corner." Serill watched him with interest.

Birler cringed, knowing this was the most he had said so far. "What if it doesn't last? What happens then?"

Serill frowned. "What do you mean?"

"Nothing good lasts. Someone always wants more," Birler said as he assessed the room.

"The Lady wouldn't allow it," Tagerill scoffed.

Birler brought his gaze back to him. "She allows people to starve. What makes you think she can protect against everything that's out there?"

Tagerill stilled as Serill laughed. "No one would dare oppose the Lady. The Guardians created this world, and they hold it in their hands; no one could threaten them."

Birler stayed silent and sipped his kafinee. Tagerill stared at him, his thoughts obviously elsewhere.

Serill glanced at him. "You can't seriously be listening to this, Tagerill."

Tagerill forced a smile. "Of course not," he said, relaxing back into his seat.

For the next week, Tagerill and Birler diligently spent every morning going through the basics until Birler could hold the sword correctly and eventually disarm Tagerill. Every afternoon, Birler explained his understanding of the disciplines until Tagerill understood the first two stages and reached "Awareness". His swordplay improved significantly, and the little Birler had improved was wiped out by Tagerill's new understanding of himself and his surroundings.

Birler grinned wryly. "I wish I could improve with the sword as easily as you do with the disciplines."

"Years of practice. M'father had a sword in my hand as soon as I could walk. Nothing can replace practice. It just takes time."

"So, I'll never catch up," Birler said, moving into the third movement.

Tagerill stopped his exercise and watched him. "That's new. What are you doing now?"

"Understanding," Birler murmured as he flowed through the movement and spun to a close.

"What is your weapon of choice?" Tagerill asked, watching the strength inherent in the moves with new eyes.

"Sling," Birler replied, starting the movement again.

"Sling?" Tagerill repeated in astonishment. "How is that a weapon? How do you defend against a sword with a sling?"

"You don't," Birler said, his body moving in alignment, his eyes closed. "The idea is not to let them close enough to threaten you with a sword. If you do, you're dead."

Tagerill's eyes bulged. "Show me."

Birler stopped and opened his eyes. "What?"

"Show me what you can do with a sling."

Birler dragged a hand through his hair. "I don't have any stones."

"But you have a sling?" Tagerill asked, his eyes bright.

"I can make one easily enough. But I need some smooth, round stones about the size of an arrowhead."

"I'll find the stones, and you make the sling. We'll try it out on the archery range tomorrow."

"Won't we get into trouble?"

"The master told us to practice the basics." Tagerill laughed. "What's more basic than a sling?"

The next day, Tagerill handed Birler a handful of pebbles and waited expectantly. Birler grinned. "What do you want me to hit?"

Tagerill looked down the range. There were three targets, each one about fifty feet further away than the last. "Hit each of those targets."

Birler assessed the distance. The first two were easy. The

third … he wasn't sure if he had the strength to reach that far. He shrugged and raised his face to the breeze. It was light, nothing to worry about, and he loaded the stones between his fingers. He whirled and rapidly fired the three stones down the range.

Tagerill gaped. "That was so fast you didn't even pause to reload."

Birler laughed and rotated his shoulders. He ought to practise more. "Let's check that I hit them first," he said, leading the way down the range. Tagerill excitedly dug the stone out of the centre of the first straw target. They moved on to the second target, and Tagerill repeated the action. He was silent as he dug the third stone out of the bullseye of the last target.

He gave Birler the stones. "I wouldn't have believed it if I hadn't seen it."

"As I said, the idea is not to let your enemy get close enough to do you any damage."

"Makes sense for the situation you were in."

"Situation?"

Tagerill grimaced. "You're from the harbour. No family, starving, fearful. It doesn't take much to realise you were living on the streets."

Birler shivered. "I couldn't have been. I'm here now, aren't I? If I was on the streets, I couldn't afford to be here."

"Oh, you could if the Lady decreed it. And you said the Lady commanded you."

Birler stared down the range. "Are you going to tell them?"

"Are you crazy? Why would I do that? Your secret is safe with me. You're my friend."

Birler looked at him with surprise. "Why?"

"Why what?" Tagerill asked as they walked back up the field.

"I didn't think you thought much of me."

Tagerill grunted. "Let's say the Lady opened my eyes. You deserve to be here, Birler. Don't let anyone tell you otherwise."

The weapons master was waiting for them when they returned.

Birler let Tagerill do the talking. The weapons master showed an interest in the sling, and Birler demonstrated his skill a second time. The master accompanied them down the range and dug out the stones himself. He stood holding the stones, his gaze distant.

Abruptly, he walked back up the range and Birler and Tagerill trailed behind. He led them into the storage room, which smelt of timber and oil. "Choose a bow," he said, standing back.

Birler hesitated, staring at the racks of bows lining the walls.

"Go on. You can use a sling; you can *make* a sling. Choose a bow," the master said, watching intently.

Tagerill grinned encouragingly, and Birler walked down the rack. He pulled a couple out and replaced them. His hand hesitated on a shorter bow. He lifted it out and smoothed his hand down the dark wood. He sighted the bow and pulled the string back. It was powerful. It felt right.

"This one," he said, looking at the master.

"Why?" the master asked.

Birler shrugged. "The others are too long. If I ever grow, I might be able to use them, but for now, I need the power this bow has. And it feels right."

"Let's see you use it, then," the master said.

He led the way out to the range and handed Birler a quiver of arrows. He demonstrated how to use the bow and then had Birler take a turn. He adjusted Birler's stance and then said, "Start with the middle target. If that is too comfortable, move to the further one."

Birler grinned as Tagerill's jaw dropped as he stared at the master. Tagerill hadn't managed to hit the nearest target yet. Snapping his mouth shut, Tagerill kept quiet as he watched.

Birler flexed the bow a couple of times and then turned sideways to the target. Looking up at the sky for a moment, he breathed out the tension in his shoulders, and then he sighted the bow down the range. His hand unerringly found the arrow and slotted it in place. He sighted the bow again and released. He reached for the next arrow. The master almost spoke, but he held his tongue as Birler smoothly nocked and released, relishing the rightness of the motion. Birler repeated a third and a fourth time and then shifted slightly and repeated until he had no arrows left. He lowered the bow and looked down the range with a small smile of satisfaction on his face.

The master let his breath out. "Let's go see, shall we?" he said and he walked off down the range. Birler followed, and Tagerill tagged behind.

The first target had four arrows in it: one a bit off-centre, the other three tightly grouped together. The master moved on without comment.

He exhaled as he reached the second target. All the arrows were grouped in the centre; some had even split the shaft of the previous arrows in situ. "Well," he breathed as a smile of delight spread over his face, "I would suggest that you don't need to excel with the sword. Focus on the bow. I expect you will be just as accurate with daggers. You'll improve with the sword, but this will always be your weapon of choice." He looked at Tagerill and grinned at his stunned expression. "We'll leave these in. It will be good for your classmates to see what they are aspiring to."

He turned back to Birler. "Keep the bow. Practice whenever you need to. When not in use, unstring it." He demonstrated how to unstring and restring the bow and watched Birler's nimble fingers repeat the action. Then he nodded and strode off with the smile still on his face.

LEYANDRII
LADY'S PALACE, VESPERS

Leyandrii rubbed Mia's fluffy ear and scowled at the message the little arifel had brought. Serene images of a sunlit pool and carousing arifels diving into their burrows in the side of a cliff filled her mind, and her scowl eased.

"It looks very pretty," Leyandrii murmured as she dropped the parchment onto her desk and leaned back in her chair.

Golden sunlight lit her study, burnishing old wood and picking out the yellow thread in the patterned rugs. A full-length portrait of her mother and siblings adorned the wall opposite her, and she smiled as she named each one of her brothers and sisters.

Her eldest brother, Desalin, tall and elegant. Her next two oldest brothers, Averdeus and Kaenera, as different as day and night and very noble in their courtly clothes. Herself and then her sisters: Asilirie, blonde, petite, and very reserved, seated on a bench, holding their baby brother, Reynald, who was as cute as a cherub; Leyarne, dark blonde, blue-eyed, intense, and intelligent; and their youngest sister, Marguerite, the only brunette, dancing around them.

Even after all these centuries, she missed them. She wondered where her mother had taken them next, who had been left where as she had scattered her children across the universe. Sometimes, she thought Asilirie should have remained here on Remargaren with her instead of Marguerite. Asilirie would not cope well with being thrust into a position of responsibility, but Leyandrii supposed her mother knew what she was doing.

The little arifel walked onto her lap, curled up with a rumbly purr, and went to sleep.

Leyandrii exhaled and let her mind drift as she stroked the little creature. Mia's fur was soft beneath her fingers. They were so cute and cuddly, very affectionate, and often mischievous, yet they rarely mixed with humans, preferring to breed in remote locations like the one Mia had shared with her.

Instead of her worries about the Administration, she'd rather think about Guerlaire's latest report on Birler. The boy was a delight. Now that he was eating properly and flexing his mind with new information, his echo, resonating in the back of her mind, was calmer but more intense, an indication of the intelligence waiting to erupt.

He simmered with magic, nascent at present, waiting for the right time to surface. But he would be a power to be reckoned with when he came into his own. She was just relieved that she had found him in time to help him flourish. Now she just had to deal with the idiots who would try to block those opportunities.

Her thoughts drifted back to the Administration. Now they wanted to be called dominants instead of ministers. Why waste so much time and effort on a title when there were more important things to be resolved?

Did they think they could dominate her?

Leyandrii swirled her wrist and stared at the golden flare of light hovering above her hand. She twirled her fingers, and the light danced above her fingertips. Mia lifted her head and chuffed. The light transformed into a shower of sparkles, and Mia snapped at them.

With a single thought, Leyandrii created an onoff and pulled the parchment towards her. Under the golden light, she dipped a quill in the ink, scratched a note on the bottom, and tossed it aside. Reba, her assistant, would deal with it.

Before Leyandrii could move on to the next missive, the door opened and her younger sister danced in. Marguerite could never keep still; she was a constant blur of movement and delight. Today, she was burdened by two mugs, and as a result, her movements were much curtailed.

"You've been working for chimes, Leyandrii. It's time for a break," Marguerite said as she kicked the door shut behind her. "I brought you some cremlia."

Leyandrii smiled as she rose. "That sounds lovely." She met Marguerite by the sofa and sank into the cushions before accepting a mug. "You are very thoughtful." Cremlia was a creamy concoction made from vanilla beans, cinnamon, and milk. A sweet and decadent luxury.

Marguerite raised her eyebrows as she sat next to her. "Now, that's not something you hear often," she remarked.

Leyandrii inhaled the spicy aroma and sipped. She moaned her appreciation, and Marguerite giggled.

"Usually, you are shouting at me to make haste or stop gallivanting about."

"I do not shout," Leyandrii replied, cupping her mug in her hands as she cast an eye over her sister. Marguerite seemed very bright and bubbly. Her auburn curls bounced around her shoulders as she fidgeted on the sofa.

"You have received some good news?" she asked.

Marguerite flushed and toyed with the silk ribbons on her gown before replying. She took a deeper breath. "Taurill's unit has returned to Vespers."

Ah. Her sister's beau. Taurill was one of the rangers posted to Elothia. Asher had diverted them to search for signs of Guerlaire's attackers. It was frustrating that they still had not found any evidence of magical use or its wielders. Somehow, they had managed to disappear. "I am glad to hear it. How long has he been away in Elothia?"

"Three months."

"And …?"

"He wants to take me out to dinner."

Leyandrii smiled at her sister. "You don't need my permission to go."

Marguerite pleated the material of her skirt. "I know. I just wondered if you and Guerlaire wanted to come with us?"

Surprise made Leyandrii hesitate. "Wouldn't you prefer him all to yourself? You've not seen him for three months."

"I don't want to appear too needy. I'm afraid I'll overwhelm him."

Chuckling, Leyandrii leaned forward to grasp her sister's arm and give it a shake. "Don't be silly. I'll bet he is as desperate to see you as you are him."

Marguerite kept her face down. "I don't want to assume," she whispered and then looked up, her blue eyes gleaming. "And anyway, we're all the family that's left. We never go out together."

"True," Leyandrii said. "We don't, do we? Why not? Where were you thinking of going?"

"A new tavern just opened in the city centre. They offer small plates of dishes from different regions. I thought it would be interesting to try. We could go tomorrow night?"

"Sounds lovely. I will confirm with Guerlaire that he is

available. Let me know the time and place, and we'll meet you there."

Marguerite relaxed and sipped her cremlia. "Where do you think Mother and the others are now?"

Leyandrii shrugged. "Who knows? There are many places they could have gone." She gave her sister a wicked grin. "They could even be off creating more new worlds."

Marguerite rolled her eyes. "Do you think they intend on making a world for each of us?"

"Can you imagine Asilirie ruling over a world?"

"Well, maybe not her, but Kaenera would have leapt at the chance, as would Averdeus and Leyarne. I was surprised Kaenera didn't challenge you for Remargaren."

"I think that Desalin's bonding with the Land scared him off. He wasn't ready to make a similar sacrifice."

Rubbing her finger around the rim of her mug, Marguerite frowned. "Why did Desalin need to bond with Remargaren? I don't understand the need."

Leyandrii stared off into the distance as she collected her thoughts. "I think our mother left too much magic scattered around this world and wanted a sentience in the land to absorb some of it. There are certain people that attract it." She flashed Marguerite a smile. "Guerlaire being one of them. He crackles with power, and if I don't siphon it off, it will become uncontrolled magic. It is our job to find those people and help them learn to control it."

"What about those who don't want our help?"

"Then we have to drain them of their magic before they kill someone—or someone uses them as a weapon."

Marguerite's eyes darkened. "Why would anyone do that? Do you think that is a real possibility?"

"I believe so. There are more power surges than there used to be. There is wild magic in the air. The Administration has a new voice, and now they are calling for more power. They want to remove my oversight. They don't believe they need it any longer."

"Ah. Are our people all grown up now?"

"They are hardly out of their infancy, but that is the joy of people. They never believe they have reached their limit. It is our job to guide them so they don't overextend, but still take every opportunity offered to them. It always amazes me with what they come up with next."

"And what has Guerlaire invented now?" Marguerite asked.

"He won't tell me, only that it will blow my mind."

"That confident, is he?"

"Always," Leyandrii said with a laugh, and she drained her mug. She rose and leaned over to her sister to give her a hug. "Thank you for the cremlia."

"My pleasure. I'll see you tomorrow evening. Don't be late."

"We won't be."

9

GUERLAIRE

CHAPTERHOUSE, VESPERS

Guerlaire finished inking in the final section of his plan and stepped back. After tugging out the cloth from his belt, he cleaned his fingers and smiled. It was finished. Now he just had to figure out how to build it.

The lantern flickered as the candle gave up and expired. The aroma of burning wax drifted in the darkness as he fumbled his way over to the door. He had been so focussed he hadn't realised the candle was low.

Stubbing his fingers on the metal latch, Guerlaire hissed his breath out and dragged the door open. A dim light intruded into his workroom and as he peered down the corridor, his breath plumed in the chill air. Lanterns lit the passage. He had worked into the night again.

Leyandrii would not be amused. He was surprised he hadn't been bombarded by arifels to chivvy him home. She was being reticent, and that worried him even more. This had maybe not been the time to get sucked into a new project.

If he weren't paying attention, Leyandrii wouldn't tell

him what was going on; she would try to handle the Administration and the unknown magical threat on her own.

After a quick glance around his office, he belted on his sword, grabbed his jacket, and locked the door behind him. His project could wait. He hurried down the passage to the stairs and climbed out of the lower levels of the Chapterhouse.

The sky was dark, lit only by a spray of stars and a sliver of a new moon. The air was freezing and full of the scent of roses. Ice glittered on the ground, a warning to take care. Across the road, white stone gleamed through the trees, Leyandrii's temple rising into the sky. He felt her regard rest on him for a moment, like a warm embrace, and then she was gone. He frowned. What was she still doing awake at this time?

His footsteps echoed on the cobbles as he hurried through the dark city streets. Shivering, he tucked his hands in his pockets; he should have picked up his gloves. With his head down, he hunched his shoulders against the cold and wished he could just transport himself home.

The slight scrape of metal was his only warning of trouble as he spun, drawing his sword to meet the attack. The blade hummed in his grip, a subtle glow defining the edges, and power rippled through his veins.

Four shadows detached themselves from a nearby building, and Guerlaire inhaled, calming his thrumming heart. A spark of worry in his mind told him that Leyandrii had caught his brief spike of fear. They were so attuned that it was difficult to hide strong emotions from each other.

"You don't want to be doing this, boys," Guerlaire said as he spread his arms and backed away. He risked a glance over his shoulder to make sure there was no one behind him and stiffened as another two shadows came into view.

The leader scoffed. "You shouldn't go upsetting people willing to pay for you to be dead."

"And who would that be?" Guerlaire asked as he rotated, inspecting what little he could see of his opponents. They were all dressed in black, blending into the shadows.

"Wouldn't you like to know?"

"Actually, yes, I would. Who wants me dead?"

Instead of answering, the men launched their attack, and Guerlaire responded. His sword glowed with energy, and blue sparks showered around him as his weapon struck metal and he spun, parried, and held firm.

He held his own for the first few minutes, but there were too many of them, and his arm vibrated with each jarring shock. He switched hands as his arm went numb. Then, shaking his hand out, he grabbed a dagger and flicked it at one of the men rushing him.

He was fighting off three of them and struggling when a flash of light briefly blinded them all and an arifel dived at the face of one of the other men, all teeth and claws. The man jinked back, shrieking, and the arifel blinked out of view.

Guerlaire took the opportunity to slide his blade into his opponent's ribs and spun to face the next man. A burning slash across his side made him falter, and he inhaled pain. A blow to the back of his head had him sinking to his knees, and his sword was wrenched out of his hand as he fell.

"Your loss will hurt her more than you!" a man snarled as he thrust his blade towards Guerlaire. Sluggishly, Guerlaire rolled, and the blade flashed by, missing by a hair's breadth. His power shimmered, and a blue glow expanded to surround him, and then he was suddenly in the midst of men and women in familiar uniforms.

The rangers soon held the ground, and he released his shield. Chryll was beside him, stuffing a wad of cloth against his ribs and hugging him tightly. "You injured anywhere else?" he asked, his voice tight.

"Hit m'head," Guerlaire gasped, his relief making his eyes water, and he sagged in Chryll's arms.

Chryll carefully felt his head and hissed his breath out when he found more blood. "Leyandrii's waiting for you. I said I'd take you straight back. It was the only way I could convince her to stay in the palace." He lifted Guerlaire in his arms, ignoring his protests, and laid him on the cushions in the carriage.

"Did you leave anyone alive?" Guerlaire asked as he struggled to sit up. "We need answers. I want to know who ordered the attack."

"We've got it. Anter will interrogate them."

Hissing his breath out, Guerlaire slumped in the corner and closed his eyes. He patted his side and lurched upright, his head pounding. "I lost my sword."

"Again?" Chryll asked as he sat beside him. "Leyandrii is going to be annoyed with you."

"Everyone likes my sword," Guerlaire mumbled. His side burned, and the warmth of fresh blood running down his skin made him tighten his grip on the cloth, but it sapped his strength. His eyelids drooped, and he sagged against Chryll. "Don't say it," Guerlaire muttered.

Chryll snorted. "Only if you accept a personal guard. You are not invincible, Guerlaire, no matter how much you want to be."

Guerlaire exhaled. "I know."

"The man finally agrees," Chryll said with mock surprise.

Grunting, Guerlaire twisted his lips. "They were right about one thing."

"Who was?"

"My attackers. They said my death would hurt Leyandrii

more than me. I never meant to become a weapon to be used against her."

"You're not if you let us protect you." Chryll moved to clamp his hand over Guerlaire's, and Guerlaire hissed his breath out as the pain spiked.

"You're losing too much blood." Chryll released Guerlaire and leaned out the carriage window. "Get us to the palace as fast as you can!" he yelled. He was back before Guerlaire could draw breath. "You're too pale," Chryll muttered under his breath. "You sure you've not got any other injuries?" He tugged at Guerlaire's clothes, refolding the cloth and pressing it hard against the wound.

Hissing filled Guerlaire's ears, and he swallowed as saliva filled his mouth. "I don't feel too good," he said into the velvet material used to upholster Leyandrii's carriage. How had he ended up face-planting the seat?

Hands tugged at him, rolling him over, as lanterns flashed above him, the glare from their flames blinding.

He squinted as a rustle of silk and a soft voice took command. A soothing warmth filled his mind, an embrace that could only be Leyandrii. The absence of pain was a shocking relief; he hadn't realised how much it had consumed him. Someone tugged at his side, and he tightened his grip.

"Sleep," Leyandrii said, and as her soft lips touched his, he drifted into a cocoon of love and reassurance. They were the last words he heard.

Leyandrii sat beside Guerlaire and clasped his hand. His skin was heated as his body still fought off the effects of the poison that must have coated the blade. It wasn't until she had cleaned out the wound that she realised blood loss and concussion weren't the only issues. Someone had wanted Guerlaire dead, no matter the method. She had purged his blood and healed his skin, but his body was still trying to recover from the shock.

She inspected his face, noting the lines of strain that hadn't been there when she'd first met him. His hair was thick and black, with no sign of grey, and it was just long enough to tie back. He hadn't got around to cutting it short since his last expedition. She threaded her fingers through the strands in a soft caress.

He had been a cocky, young ranger when she'd first met him, full of confidence and not afraid to stand his ground. But it wasn't just that; there was a presence about him that just drew her to him, and she hadn't wanted to resist when he had met her gaze. The air had crackled as his vivid blue eyes had consumed her.

Guerlaire was her match. He was *hers*, and the thought of losing him had her tightening her grip on his hair. When her bedchamber door opened, she raised her gaze from her inspection of Guerlaire's face.

Marguerite flashed a glance around the room, noting the guards, and then hurried over.

"How is he?"

"Holding his own," Leyandrii replied and rotated her neck, easing the stiffness. She needed to move.

"You need to eat. Your breakfast is in the little parlour. Go and eat it while it's hot or the cook will be after you."

Leyandrii smiled and stroked Guerlaire's hand. "He hasn't moved."

"Then he won't miss you. I'll sit with him while you eat. We don't need you fainting through lack of food."

Leaning over to kiss Guerlaire, Leyandrii caressed his cheek and then sighed. Marguerite was right. She had expended a lot of energy healing him. Now she had to give him time.

"I'm sorry about dinner. We'll have to reschedule."

"Pfft! Taurill is guarding your door. He is more concerned about Guerlaire. We can have dinner another time."

"I'll try not to be too long, but I want to speak to the rangers. This was an attack against me, and I want to know who ordered it."

"Anter was hovering in the corridor. I asked him to escort you to the parlour. You can ask him."

Leyandrii flashed her sister a smile. "Thank you."

Marguerite pushed her towards the door and sat in her seat. She reached for Guerlaire's hand, and Leyandrii suppressed the brief flash of jealousy at the sight, that anyone else could replace her. She hurried out the door before she said anything. Jealousy was unbecoming, and Marguerite was no threat; she was doing her a favour.

Just as she told Guerlaire he couldn't do everything himself, neither could she.

Anter was waiting for her, as Marguerite had said. Another large man, broad-shouldered, with shaggy blond hair and light blue eyes. A competent ranger and one of Guerlaire's peers.

"How is he?" Anter asked, with lines of concern creasing his skin and a frown between his eyebrows.

Leyandrii twisted her lips. "Sleeping. It's the only way to keep him still."

Anter's chuckle was a rumble deep in his chest. "Good. We don't need him dashing off, thinking he can get his revenge."

"What have you found out?" she asked.

"Nothing."

"How can there be nothing?"

"The men don't know who hired them. It was all arranged anonymously. They didn't even know who they were attacking; they just had a place and a description of their target."

"And they didn't care who they were assassinating?"

"The amount of coin offered removed any concern."

Leyandrii growled. How could money negate conscience? "What is wrong with these people?" They entered the parlour, and she sat with a thump in a chair. She waved Anter to another chair. "Please join me."

"Thank you, my Lady."

Leyandrii fiddled with the cutlery. "Do you think there is any point in me speaking to them?"

"Unless you can read minds, I doubt you'll get a different response."

Squirming in her seat, Leyandrii grimaced at her plate. Anter stared at her. The silence drew out until Anter said, "Can you read minds, my Lady?"

"I don't like to," she admitted. "It's like overhearing a conversation you're not supposed to; you never hear anything good about yourself. And men without conscience probably have the worst thoughts."

"They may be aware of something they don't realise. If you could, we may find something we could follow up on."

Leyandrii gave a sharp nod as she flicked out her napkin. "Very well. Where are you holding them?"

"At the cell blocks in the Justice building."

"Not the barracks?"

"No, the Justice building was closer."

Leyandrii wrinkled her brow. The thought of the ministers having access to the prisoners first rankled her. If the dominants were behind the attack, which was her suspicion, then they would try to remove any links to them.

"We'll visit them next and see what they are hiding."

Leyandrii observed a rather battered man chained to the wall. His clothing was worn and mud-splattered, his face gaunt and lined. His anguish and despair filled her senses, and she pushed them away. This man had tried to kill Guerlaire; she would not feel sympathy for his plight.

She pushed past his weak mental defences, noting that others had been in his mind before, and her concern mounted. Who had found a way to persuade others to act on their behalf?

Images of altercations, terrified victims, blood, and gore filled the man's mind. His enjoyment of hurting others explained why he had been chosen for this task. The man's mind was a sewer, and Leyandrii veered away from some of his more horrific actions, though his recent memories were vague and uncertain. He wasn't sure what had happened or how he had ended up in a cell. He didn't remember attacking Guerlaire, which was ridiculous.

Leyandrii latched on to a wisp of a persuasion. A shadowy man, his features hidden. The passing of coins and the promise of more. And then the memory faded, and she couldn't find it again.

"He's been tampered with."

"What do you mean?" Anter asked, peering over her shoulder at the cowering man.

"Someone has altered his memories since he's been here. Check who has had access to him."

"That's not possible. No one has been allowed entry."

"Someone has because he has no memory of attacking Guerlaire."

"I never did," the man spluttered. "Only fools go after the Lady's Captain."

"True," Leyandrii replied, "but all the same, the blood

on your hands says otherwise."

"I swear I never did."

"This is a waste of time. Are there any others?"

Anter led her to another cell, but the occupant was just the same, almost an exact replica of the first prisoner: no recent memories and adamant that he hadn't attacked anyone.

"Who are the guards?" Leyandrii asked as they left the cell. A tug on her awareness and a rush of exhaustion quickly smothered made her shake her head. If Guerlaire thought he could hide his emotions from her, he was mistaken.

"Severen and Ellaer."

"Let's have a quick word with them on the way out. I need to return to Guerlaire; he is waking." She gathered her skirts and hurried up the stairs.

After a quick skim of the rangers' memories, she found the same tampering: a suggestion to forget. Whoever had discovered the skill hadn't yet perfected the art of hiding their tampering, though that would come with time. But now she would recognise the hand if she came across it again.

Her jaw tight, she decided there and then that she would teach Guerlaire how to mentally shield, and teaching his peers would keep him out of trouble while he recuperated. Her rangers would not be vulnerable to these unscrupulous people.

A few days later, Guerlaire swung his legs out of bed and paused for a moment as the room wavered around him. He was back in his bedchamber. Leyandrii must have sedated him while he was moved because he didn't remember it. Gritting his teeth, he levered himself upright and winced at the ache in his side. It shouldn't take this long to get over a wound like the one he had received. It was that damned poison that was complicating things.

He tottered over to his desk and grasped the edge, leaning on it heavily until he reached his chair. He collapsed into it, cursing under his breath. This was ridiculous; his limbs were trembling from the effort. The distance back to the bed seemed insurmountable.

A tray with a jug and glasses lay on the desk, and his hand shook as he poured out the water. He took a gulp, leaned back in his chair, and closed his eyes, concentrating on calming his breathing. He opened them when he heard the door, and Leyandrii entered.

She hesitated in the doorway and rolled her beautiful eyes. Shaking her head, she closed the door behind her and crossed to the desk. "It's only been three days. You really can't rest for longer than that?"

"No," Guerlaire replied, sipping his water.

"Well, we need to talk, so I suppose it's good you're awake."

Guerlaire leaned forward. "What's happened?"

"Apart from my captain being attacked and not being able to find out who did it?" Leyandrii asked as she sat in the chair opposite him. She smiled, and Guerlaire caught his breath. That such an exquisitely wonderful woman loved him shocked him sometimes. His brain stirred into motion as her words hit him.

"We got nothing from the prisoners?"

"No, someone tampered with their memories."

"Who? How?"

"We don't know. They also tampered with the guards' memories as well."

"I'll search all of Vespers if I have to," Guerlaire vowed. "I will find out who they were and who sent them."

Leyandrii smiled. "I have no doubt of that, but in the meantime, I need to teach you how to shield. You need to teach my guards and the rangers."

"Me?

"Yes, you won't be cleared for duty for at least a week, so in the meantime, you can teach everyone how to shield. The alternative is that I keep you asleep for the next few days."

"Don't you dare."

"I will if you overdo it."

"Don't worry. I'm not going far. I just couldn't lay in that bed for another chime."

Leyandrii nodded. "You have a natural shield, but it won't hurt to strengthen it, and then you will know when someone is trying to probe your mind. Most of the time, if you are unaware, you'll never know."

Guerlaire frowned as the ramifications occurred to him. He rubbed his temple. "This has never been a problem before. What's changed?"

"Someone has discovered *Mentiserium*, a way to control people's minds and actions. I have no idea how they learned it. I expect someone did it accidentally, and it's grown from there. It's not something that's discussed because we don't want to scare people."

"And a mental shield is the only defence?"

"In effect, yes. Now that we know *Mentiserium* is being attempted, you need to maintain a shield at all times for you to repel it."

"What do I do?"

Leyandrii smiled. "I love you."

Guerlaire raised an eyebrow, surprised by her declaration. "I love you, too." A sudden push against his mind made him stiffen, and he pushed back.

"That was a mental prod. I made it obvious so you would

feel it, but others can be more subtle, so you won't always be aware."

Guerlaire stood, walked over to the bed, and lay down. Leyandrii rose and followed him. "I thought you said you weren't tired?"

Guerlaire stiffened and sat up, looking around. He patted the bed, trying to figure out how he got there. He frowned. "I-I don't remember laying down."

"Because it wasn't your choice. I told you to go to bed."

"No, you didn't. You said you loved me."

"That was a distraction while I planted the suggestion."

A spike of fear flashed through him, tightening his chest. Guerlaire fought to keep his expression neutral, but the ease with which Leyandrii had planted the suggestion and the fact that he hadn't even felt it terrified him.

"See," Leyandrii said, a wry smile on her lips. "You fear me now."

"I could never fear you." The words were out before Guerlaire even thought them.

"But you fear what I could do."

"I'm terrified of what someone without your scruples could do with this."

Leyandrii leaned over him and kissed him on the lips. Heat flared through his body, and he pulled her closer as he kissed her back. "Teach me how to defend myself," he murmured against her lips.

"We should probably return to the chairs."

"No." Guerlaire pulled her down on top of him. "This is distracting. Teach me while I'm distracted."

Leyandrii laughed. "You'd better not use this technique while you're training your colleagues."

"I promise I won't. This is only for you. I'll make them spar. They will be distracted trying to defend themselves."

"I thought I said this was supposed to be a sedentary training."

Guerlaire rolled her over so she was beneath him. "This *is* sedentary. At least we're lying down."

"You are incorrigible."

"That's why you love me."

"True." Leyandrii squirmed beneath him, and he shifted so he was lying beside her. If she wriggled too much, he wouldn't be able to concentrate at all.

"Close your eyes and visualise your shield."

Guerlaire did as he was told and imagined a stone wall with a thick oak door, locked with heavy metal clasps. He braced, expecting Leyandrii's attack. The door creaked as she pushed against it. She pushed again, and the planking splintered.

"You have a weak link in your defences," Leyandrii murmured against his throat.

Guerlaire shivered as her warm breath caressed his skin, but he removed the door and infused the stone with his love for Leyandrii. She huffed her breath out in surprise as she couldn't budge it.

"Much better."

"But I don't want to keep you out of my head," Guerlaire said as he kissed her nose.

"Then you can choose to let me in, but no one else."

"How do I do that?"

"You give me permission, a key that will allow me through."

"That won't weaken my defences, will it?"

"No. No one else will have the key."

"Good. How do I keep it in place without having to continuously think about it?"

"Practice, to begin with. Your shield will fail if you don't concentrate, but the longer you hold it in place, the quicker it will become normal. After a few days, you won't even have to think about it."

Guerlaire's barrier rang as Leyandrii thrust again. "Ouch," she said. "I just stubbed my mental fingers."

Guerlaire chuckled and raised her hand to kiss her fingers better.

Leyandrii reached up to kiss his chin. "Next time, you can try and break through my shields. You'll need to know how for the training sessions. I've also thought of a way for you to control your power when it gets to be too much. We can work on that as well, just in case you get lost again!"

"I was not the only one who got lost, you know." Guerlaire kissed her on the nose. "Though a way to relieve the pressure would be good. How do you suggest I do that?"

"I think you can use your sword to siphon off the excess. The sword will store the magic until I can release it." She frowned. "I should have thought of that before, but for now, time for a rest."

"But I lost my sword. They took it."

"I retrieved it for you."

"You did? How?" Fear spiked in his chest. "You didn't go searching for it on your own, did you?"

"I did, but not how you are thinking. I was quite safe. As I've said many times before, they underestimate me. But now you should rest."

"A rest, you say?" Guerlaire replied, kissing down the smooth column of her neck as his fingers hunted for the laces at the back of her gown. "I have a better idea."

10

BIRLER

RANGERS ACADEMY

Birler wasn't sure when he first realised he had a friend, and not just one, but two. Both Tagerill and Serill had begun to include him in everything they did: waiting for him in the morning, escorting him to breakfast, and sitting next to him in class. He didn't think they noticed what they were doing; it was as natural as breathing.

But it wasn't natural to Birler. He wasn't used to people paying attention to him, watching him, or asking him what he thought or how he felt. It was as if he were being dragged out of the shadows and into the sunlight, and he wasn't sure how he felt about that.

There was safety in the shadows. Once noticed, others wanted what you had, and the academy was no different. The problem with the academy was that there were few places to hide, and you couldn't hide for long as you were expected to go places at certain times, which meant you were sure to be found.

And once found, you were the target.

Birler exhaled as he followed Tagerill into the classroom. He gripped his book, trying to disguise the fact that he was shaking. This was the worst lesson of the day. No matter how hard he listened, he couldn't read what was in the book. Half the time, he wasn't sure he was on the right page.

Once pointed out, he memorised the text, tagging the subject to a keyword he would recognise. He would be able to regurgitate it thereafter, but if asked to rephrase or rewrite, he would be caught out.

Today, he was relieved to find he was sharing a book with Tagerill. Tagerill was flicking through the pages, pausing at the images of various people.

"What's it about?" Birler asked.

"Politics. History of the Administration."

"What administration?" Birler asked, peering at an image of an elderly man. "Who is that?"

Tagerill laughed. "Don't you know anything?"

Birler flushed as he reared back, and Tagerill was quick to apologise. "Sorry. I forget you haven't …" He didn't get the chance to finish as the class was called to order.

Birler sank back in his chair and learned more about the "Administration" than he wanted to, and he agreed whole-heartedly with Tagerill as they escaped the classroom that politics was boring. But he needed to learn so no one could accuse him of being ignorant.

Fortunately, Tagerill had commandeered the book, so Birler hadn't had to find anything. Birler wasn't fooled, though. Tagerill had glanced at him keenly enough from under his lashes as the lesson had progressed, and he'd pointed out specific sentences and waited expectantly for Birler to say something.

Later, after they had eaten, Birler returned from the well house, and his heart sank as he saw his friends waiting for him. Tagerill had obviously spoken to Serill because they were both hovering by his bed as he entered their barracks.

"What?" Birler asked as he approached them.

Serill looked at him and then he held his book out. "I wanted you to read us some of this book."

"Why?"

"Because you keep looking at it as if it's the most amazing thing you've ever seen, and I think you need to read it."

Birler flushed and shifted awkwardly. "It's your book."

"I don't mind sharing." Serill smiled and opened the book. "Here, see? It's about the Lady."

Birler was drawn closer by his words, and Tagerill glanced at Serill in admiration. Birler hesitated as his finger traced the first letter on the page.

"That's an 'ell'," Serill said.

Birler froze.

"You can't read, can you?" Serill asked as he sat on Birler's bed, drawing Birler with him. Tagerill sat the on the other side.

Trapped, Birler shook his head.

"Don't worry; we'll teach you," Serill offered, a hesitant hand resting on Birler's arm as if aware how fragile the connection was and was afraid of scaring him away.

Tagerill huffed. "He means *he'll* teach you; he's the patient one," he said with a grin.

"How have you managed to get through class? You've fooled everyone, including the masters," Serill asked.

Birler shrugged. "I remembered the shapes."

Tagerill and Serill exchanged amazed glances. "So, you know the shapes, but you don't know what they mean?"

Birler shrugged again, at a loss to explain what he had been doing.

"It's alright," Serill said. "We'll start tonight. No one else will know. It will be our secret. We'll practice every night once everyone is asleep."

Guerlaire split his time between cataloguing his finds in the Chapterhouse and teaching his friends how to strengthen their mental shields.

When he explained what *Mentiserium* was, Chryll had been horrified, though Anter had been unsurprised, seeing as he had been with Leyandrii when she questioned the prisoners. The fact that Leyandrii had gone into the cells and dredged the minds of those scum while he had been incapacitated tied Guerlaire's guts up in knots.

More concerning was that some of the other rangers had been interested in how it worked. *Mentiserium* was a skill no one should have. Corrupting someone's mind, the callous invasion of a person's privacy, was unacceptable.

As the weeks passed, Guerlaire walked the halls of the Chapterhouse, watching, listening, and learning to ignore his personal guard. Today, an older ranger called Darll followed him as he walked down darkened corridors lit by sparse lanterns and wended his way back and forth, up spiralled staircases and down steep slopes. Wooden doors lined the corridors, concealing small chambers and study booths. There were as many floors below the ground as there were above.

In the depths of the Chapterhouse, you could forget that winter was turning into spring and the sun was chasing away the clouds and warming the air.

The scholars were usually a good indication as to what was being discussed in the Administration. Ministers' aides often came to the Chapterhouse to research topics and garner opinions.

Guerlaire sat at the back of the debating chamber, and a chill settled in his chest as he listened to a young scholar expounding on the need for more freedom for the people of

Vespers. Living under the oppressive oversight of a goddess meant the people of Vespers didn't have the same freedoms as other territories.

Some of Guerlaire's fears eased as a young female scholar stood and rebutted the other scholar's points. The scholars debated back and forth, eventually deciding that Leyandrii enabled the people of Vespers to reach their full potential. It was more the fact that the topic had even been tabled that worried Guerlaire.

He exhaled, knowing Leyandrii would say they had the right to debate whichever topic they wanted. The Chapterhouse was for learning, and she wouldn't interfere.

Guerlaire waited for the chamber to empty before he rose and descended the stairs. He collected Darll outside in the corridor and was relieved that he didn't have to say anything. Deep in thought, he didn't see the scholar scurrying down the corridor, and papers flew everywhere as they collided.

"My work!" the scholar exclaimed as he scrabbled on the floor, with pages floating down on top of him.

As Guerlaire helped him gather the parchment, Darll hovered behind him. There wasn't room for all of them to crawl about on the floor.

"Don't look at it! It's not finished!" the scholar said, his voice rising as he grabbed the parchment off of Guerlaire.

"My apologies. I didn't see you." For such a dedicated scholar, the man risked tearing his papers in his panic. This particular corridor was dimly lit, as a couple of the lanterns had gone out.

"How could you not see me? I'm tall enough! There are glows everywhere." The scholar glanced around and then glared at Guerlaire as if to dare him to contradict him. His grey eyes hardened as he took in Guerlaire's ranger's uniform and Darll standing behind him. "What are rangers doing here?"

"Rangers can be scholars as well."

"Rubbish. All you do is stir up trouble and cause fights."

"That is a rather narrow view for a scholar. I thought scholars were open-minded."

The man snorted. "I don't have time to waste on nonsensical discussions. I have more important work to do."

"And what are you studying?"

"You think I'm going to tell you? You'll steal my work. That's happening more and more often, you know."

"What is the point of that? I thought all scholars were adamant about their sources and proud to claim their work as their own?"

"That's how you can tell who the true scholars are. Too many lazy entrants lately. We need to tighten up the entry requirements."

"Surely the scholar-deane discourages such behaviour?"

"Not that you'd notice." The man scowled, glanced around, and then pushed past Guerlaire.

After watching the scholar hurry away, Guerlaire continued down the corridor. The smooth walls gave way to narrower, rougher tunnels, honeycombed with storage rooms. Most of his shelving and brackets were built in situ, as the corridors were too narrow to carry fully assembled bookcases.

Guerlaire paused as he peered into one of the chambers and smiled at the sight of the shelving and a selection of drawers for his samples. "Excellent. We can start populating the samples we have of the flora of Elothia." He had spent the last month or so ensuring all his specimens had been dried and pressed. Now he needed to draw a record so he could compare the different samples more closely.

Months of work when he needed to be beside Leyandrii, supporting her against the growing dissent within the Administration. His time would be better spent understanding the motivations of the current Administration, their staff, and their recent decisions before he went off on his next exploration.

All decisions had a ripple effect, and Guerlaire needed to know what they were so he could advise Leyandrii. She was already swamped with requests for aid from the outer regions. They never seemed to stop. Maybe it was time he investigated some of those as well, or at least the rangers did. He would have a word with Oren Asher and the scholar-deane. Make a few suggestions.

He groaned, torn between staying in Old Vespers, or leaving for Terolia. He would spend some time in Vespers ensuring Leyandrii was safe, and then, before the heat of the summer months hit, seeing as he had promised the Chapterhouse that he would visit Terolia next, he would explore the Kharma Ridge. While he was there, he could search for any signs of dissent within the nomadic Families; Leyandrii needed to know if there was trouble brewing, though they had their own Family Law, and it was unlikely they would break with tradition. Honour and duty were sacrosanct to the Families. But, even so, he needed to make sure there was no threat hidden in the deserts of Terolia.

11

BIRLER

RANGERS ACADEMY

The cold grip of winter thawed into spring. Birler wasn't sure which month it was, but it was definitely getting warmer, and he was beginning to find his place in the academy.

He drifted around the deserted barracks, trying to decide what to do. The room was empty, the silence suddenly oppressive. For one used to being alone all the time, he was surprised he no longer liked it. He enjoyed being part of a tight-knit group and having friends. They had begun to rely on each other, learning each other's strengths and weaknesses, and supporting each other as needed. Well, most did. Tyrler still gave him the evil eye, blaming him for Tagerill's downfall, even though it was clear to everyone else that Tagerill hadn't cared about being placed on basic training all those months ago.

Those who had family visiting were in the city, enjoying a day of freedom. They were halfway through the academic year, and the reward was a day pass. Tagerill had been hauled away by his elder sister, Marian. She was tall and elegant, with lustrous black hair that curled around her shoulders, framing an intelligent face with a creamy complexion that made her brown eyes smoulder. She had graduated the year before, and most of the cadets were swooning over her.

Marian ignored all the cadets except her brother, waiting impatiently as he finished polishing his boots. "You should have done that already, Tage," she said, her voice low and rich. "Why are you never organised?"

Tagerill grimaced at Birler and tied his boots. "See you later," he murmured as he followed Marian out of the room. Her voice echoed in the corridor as she continued to nag him.

Serill laughed and offered Birler his book. "You can borrow this if you like; it's really good."

Birler smiled and raised his hands. "No, I'd hate to damage it. Thanks, but I'll be outside most of the day."

Serill shrugged. "I'll leave it here for you if you change your mind."

And here he was now at a loose end. Sighing, he left the barracks. Maybe he would run; that was usually good for letting the mind drift. He wished he could have gone into town and visited the Lady's temple. He could feel it on the edge of his awareness, burbling happily as people visited. Trying to ignore it, he set off around the track.

Serill sat on the edge of his chair and gritted his teeth. He had forgotten how cloying his family were. It wasn't as if they really meant it, but they just didn't know when to stop. They had saved all their money to make the trip and were making a big deal of having a meal in the inn they had booked.

"You shouldn't have spent the money," he said, glancing around the room to make sure they weren't overheard. "You need it for the plantings."

His father grimaced. "Your mother was worried; she wouldn't have it any other way. I told her you'd be fine."

"You never know," his mother said, smiling at him. She was comfortably plump, with curly blond hair, and her blue eyes shimmered with happiness. "We know you're capable; we just miss you."

"We won't be able to come again until after the saplings are transplanted." His father was a small man, his skin creased and weathered by the outdoor life he lived. He worked in the Marchwood nursery, tending the new growth, the future forests.

"Pa, honest, next time, the pass will be for longer. I'll come home."

His pa nodded. "That might be best," he agreed, relieved.

His mother beamed at the other occupants; they were seated in a small parlour used for entertaining guests. "We don't mind coming here; this is a bit of a break. Staying in a nice place, having people serve us for a change."

Large framed paintings of unknown landscapes hung on the wall, hiding the bare walls behind them. There were three other tables with groups like his own. The cadets looked just as stressed as he felt.

The meal wore on, and Serill wondered when he might reasonably escape. He tried to answer their questions, his voice soft as he described the barracks and his friends.

"A Descelles? You need to be careful there," his father said, impressed. "They own the lands to the north of the East Road. Good timber up there."

His father measured everything in terms of the timber. If you didn't have core stock, then he wasn't interested.

"It's good you have friends; they sound nice." Serill's mother patted his arm. "Your friend Birler sounds nice, too.

You should bring him with you next time if he has nowhere to go."

Serill flushed. He hadn't meant to tell his family about Birler's situation, not that he knew if it was true, even if Tagerill believed it so. Still, Birler's lack of family had come out in conversation, and Serill's mother had gone all maternal over him, worried that he was on his own.

"I'll ask him," Serill finally promised, if only to stop his mother from going on.

***

Tagerill hugged his brother Penner and grinned up at him. Penner was tall and stockily built. His dark brown hair was swept off his face, cut in neat layers, and he reminded Tagerill of an official out of the Justice buildings. Versill and Tagerill were fiery redheads like their father. Penner and Marian followed their mother in looks.

"You didn't say you were coming," Tagerill said as he sat opposite his sister, Marian, at the table in the dining room of their family townhouse in Vespers.

Penner laughed, his brown eyes crinkling at the edges. "I don't tell you everything, you young scamp. So, how's it going?"

"Fine, they finally finished torturing us, and we've begun to learn some new stuff at last."

"You mean you might be able to last more than five minutes in the ring now?" his brother teased.

"I can last longer than you can," Tagerill cried. Penner was the only Descelles sibling who hadn't joined the academy, being his father's heir, but that didn't mean he couldn't hold his own in the sparring ring.

"Not at the table, Tage. Penner, don't start him off for goodness' sake," said Tagerill's mother, Melis, rolling her eyes as she joined them. Tagerill sprang to his feet to engulf her in a hug, and she flung her hand up to protect her hair as she laughed up at him. She patted his face, her brown eyes sparkling as he released her. Her deep green skirts swished as she sat in the chair that Penner stood to hold for her.

"Your father said not to wait. He'll be here as soon as he can."

"Where is he?" Tagerill asked, sitting back down and reaching for his brother's hand as Melis said grace. Blessing complete, he helped himself to the bowl of potatoes.

"Leave some for us," Marian scolded, swapping the beans for the meat platter Penner offered her.

"He went up to the Administrator building, some commotion or other," Penner said. "How far have you got to, then?"

Tagerill watched him. "Why didn't you go with Pa?"

Penner sighed. "Because I wasn't invited. Now, eat and tell us what you've been up to."

Tagerill took a quick mouthful and then described his barracks. "You know all this. It's no different to Versill or Marian."

"Of course it's different," Melis laughed. "It's your turn. It won't be the same as the others because it's you."

"And what do you mean by that?" he asked, taking umbrage.

"That we're surprised we haven't heard of any warnings yet," Marian interjected.

"That's not fair," Tagerill began, stopping when the door opened and a tall, broad-shouldered man entered. He was an older version of Penner, though with red hair tamed by streaks of grey. Tagerill rose and went to hug him.

His father chuckled, holding him away from him. "Academy life seems to suit you," he said as they approached the table. Tagerill slid back into his seat, watching his father sit. He looked tired, and his face creased into lines as he smiled at Marian while she served him. "So what were you arguing about when I entered? I must admit home is quite tame without all of you around."

Tagerill grinned sheepishly. "I was about to say there is no reason to expect me to get any warnings."

His father chuckled. "Don't try too hard, Tagerill. There is plenty of time left."

Tagerill made a face, but he applied himself to his food. His father looked at Marian. "How about you, Marian? Have you heard where you'll be sent yet?"

Marian shook her head. "The lists should be released next week."

Her father pursed his lips. "It sounds like there's trouble up north, so be prepared if you get sent up there."

"The rumour is we'll be on the Terolian borders, but you know how accurate they usually are."

"The administrators are pushing for the expansion into the northern reaches. They think there is something up there we need. Lady knows what."

"Is it true, then? The Lady will open it up?" Penner leaned back in his chair. "She's been under a lot of pressure recently. It's a lot of responsibility for one so young."

His father tutted, and Marian bristled. "She's old enough. People seem to have forgotten who she actually is."

"I'd have thought people would trust a goddess to protect them." Penner frowned at his father.

"If people were sensible, then I would agree with you, but they are not, and it's causing some panic in the upper echelons, shall we say," Warren said. "Fortunately, saner heads prevailed today, but I doubt this was the end of it."

Tagerill looked at his father and Penner. "Are you saying the Administration won't support the Lady?" he asked in shock.

"Hush, Tagerill. Those words should not be repeated. Ever." His father frowned. "We stand by the Lady no matter what. Be careful what you say. These are difficult times; Lady Leyandrii will need our support."

"Of course." Tagerill flushed as he stared at his plate—as if he would do anything else. The Descelles were staunch supporters of the Guardians. He hadn't been aware that some were not. Birler's comment all those months ago rang in his ears. Maybe he hadn't been far wrong, even then.

12

BIRLER

RANGERS ACADEMY

Birler was sitting on his bed in the barracks, polishing his boots, when the first of the cadets returned, Serill among them. Serill threw himself on his bed and scowled at the ceiling. Birler grinned at him. "What's up?"

"Families," Serill huffed. "Be glad you haven't got one." Then he realised what he'd said and sat up. "Birler, I'm sorry. I didn't mean that."

Birler shrugged and stared at his boots. "Doesn't matter," he said, keeping his voice neutral.

"I'm a thoughtless idiot. I am sorry." Serill moved to sit next to him.

Birler dredged up a smile. "It's alright."

"No, it's not. They just rile me so. They are so *nice* it sets your teeth on edge. I can't say anything because they mean well, but they can just be so … so suffocating." Serill stood and paced restlessly.

Birler watched him fidget. He reminded him of Tagerill when he had energy to burn, which was most of the time. The room filled with returning lads, and the noise level rose, which seemed to put Serill on edge even more.

"Go for a run. I'll come with you if you like," Birler offered, setting his boots down. He folded his cloth and stuffed it in the box.

Serill flinched as a strident laugh cut through the air. Tyrler was regaling his friends with a story. "No, I think I'll go and spar for a bit. I feel on edge. I need to hit something before I hit that oaf over there."

"It's too late. We could get up early and go," Birler said, hoping to persuade his friend out of breaking the one rule the academy was strict about. "Tagerill should be back soon."

"I can't wait. I *need* to go now."

"I'll go with you if you want," Birler offered, wanting to help.

"No, I'm the one with the energy to burn. We don't both need to get in trouble."

Birler watched him leave and rose to go and wash his hands. Maybe he ought to follow discreetly and make sure Serill was alright. The sparring rings were closed for a reason.

After a quick check around the well house, he followed Serill down to the sparring grounds. He crept around the outside, making sure no one else was around, and then positioned himself so he could see Serill and the approach from the barracks. The moon was hidden behind thinning clouds, casting a subdued light over the buildings, darkening the already deep shadows.

Serill was right. He had needed to burn off the energy. Sparks flew off his friend as he spun and twisted around the target; the target took the brunt of his frustration. After a chime of punishing exercise, he finally came to a halt, his chest heaving. Serill pushed his hair out of his sweaty face before replacing the batons he had been using. Birler rechecked the surroundings, pausing as his eyes caught a flicker from the other side of the arena, but there was nothing to see, so he faded away, back to the barracks, as Serill walked towards him.

Birler was lying on his bed, staring at the ceiling, when Serill returned. "Feeling better?" he inquired.

Serill grinned. "Much," he said as he headed off to take a shower.

Tagerill didn't return until the last possible minute, eking out the time with his family. He blew in just before midnight, laughing at the other boys' complaints, and he groaned when they were roused the next morning at dawn.

The next day, they were back into their routine, running around the perimeter. Birler was now running ten laps with the others, his gauntness a mere memory. The healer's supplements were no longer required. He was still slender, but he had filled out, and his strength was now commensurate with the other boys. His deep blue eyes sparkled with health, and he was no longer a pushover in the sparring ring.

Tagerill drew up beside Birler. "So, what did you get up to yesterday?" he asked as they completed their fifth lap.

"Had a nice, peaceful day with no snide comments or remarks."

Tagerill laughed. "You can come home with me next time. We've got plenty of room."

Birler smiled, warmed by the offer. "If you are sure your parents won't mind." He didn't know who to ask to get permission, or even if permission would be granted.

"Nah, my pa was complaining about how quiet it was. The more the merrier."

Birler nodded, and they ran in companionable silence. They were stretching out and moving on to the morning session of Apeiron when a message arrived calling Serill to the commander's office. He shrugged at Tagerill and Birler and left.

Tagerill and Birler rushed back to the barracks after the morning session to change, hoping Serill would be there waiting for them to go to lunch. He hadn't returned from the commander's office, and Birler had an awful feeling he knew why, though he didn't say anything to Tagerill. Tyrler had been suspiciously smug all morning.

His heart sank as they arrived. At the other end of the room, a silent ring of boys surrounded Serill, who was stuffing his clothes into a sack, his anger sparking off him.

Tagerill pushed his way through the boys. "Serill, what's happened?"

Serill stilled for a moment before he straightened. Tagerill flinched back from the scorching glare he received. "Someone," Serill hissed, "told Commander Asher that I was in the sparring grounds last night."

"And were you?" Tagerill asked, aghast.

"Of course I was. How else was I going to get over a home pass?"

"But who knew?"

Serill moved his gaze to Birler.

"I never told anyone," Birler said, immediately knowing where this was going.

"Where did you go last night? After I left?"

Birler hesitated. He didn't want to admit to following Serill; that would just compound the problem. "I was here. I had a shower," Birler lied.

Serill saw the lie. "How could you?" he spat, his face fraught at the betrayal.

"I didn't, Serill. I swear on the Lady. I would never betray you to anyone," Birler said hurriedly, but it was too late.

"I should have known better than to befriend someone from the gutter. You don't know what the word 'honour' means. I doubt you can say it, let alone spell it!"

Birler flinched away from his heated words. The boys stirred, muttering between them.

"Serill, you don't mean that." Tagerill grabbed his arm, but Serill turned on him angrily.

"Don't protect him. I've been expelled because of him."

Tagerill dropped his arm in shock. "Expelled?"

"Expelled." Serill's anger was shocking in its intensity; everyone cleared a path as he stomped out of the barracks.

"I swear, Tagerill, I never told anyone," Birler whispered. He couldn't stop shaking. His stomach roiled, its acid burning his throat. Tagerill nodded. Sweeping his gaze around the barracks, he caught Tyrler's smirk.

Tagerill was across the room in a flash. "It was you, wasn't it?" Relief briefly made Birler feel weak, and he collapsed onto his bed. But seconds later, Tagerill had Tyrler pinned up against the wall.

"Tagerill, don't. He'll get you expelled, too." Birler jumped up and hung off Tagerill's arm. Tagerill took a breath and let Birler tug him back.

Tyrler laughed. "Don't spend too much time with the gutter rat; he'll drag you down into the slums with him."

Tagerill tensed, but Birler dragged him back over to their beds. "What do we do?" Birler asked, his voice hushed.

"We can't do anything," Tagerill rasped, his eyes fixed on Tyrler.

"There must be something. We can't let Serill leave."

"He's not leaving. He's been expelled. He doesn't have a choice."

"It's not fair."

Tagerill laughed, but his face was hard and cold. "Who said anything about fair? You should know that better than anyone."

Birler flinched.

Tagerill took a breath. "I didn't mean it like that." But it was obvious that Serill's words had opened a wound that would be slow in healing, especially as the boys across the room were sharpening their knives to keep it raw.

———

Later that afternoon, Birler tapped on Commander Asher's office door. He opened the door as a deep voice commanded him to enter. Closing the door behind him, he hesitated. The office was large and airy. A brightly coloured rug covered the floor, out of place in the severely furnished room. Tall windows lined the far wall and looked out over the training complex. The commander could see the whole academy at a glance.

Commander Asher was sitting behind his desk, a large man with a ruddy face and dark brown hair peppered with grey. He stared at Birler in surprise. "How did you get in here?"

Birler swallowed nervously and cleared his throat. "Through that door," he said, jerking his head behind him. "Sir," he added as an afterthought. His gaze was caught by the glowing ball suspended over the commander's desk, casting a yellow glow over the stack of papers in front of him.

The commander's lips twitched. "That was not quite what I meant. However, now that you are here, what do you want?"

Birler dragged his eyes from the glowing ball and squirmed under the commander's clear gaze, wondering why he ever thought he could help. "It's about Cadet Serill, sir."

The commander raised his eyebrows. "You want to report him, too?" he asked.

"No, sir. It's more that you shouldn't be expelling him, sir."

"Why not? He broke the rules."

"For a good reason, sir, not because he wanted to."

"Oh? If a rule is broken, then it's broken. The person breaking the rule knows the consequences. It doesn't matter why."

Birler struggled to put his thoughts into words, still hovering by the door. "He came back from the day pass upset. He's under a lot of pressure from his family, sir. They don't mean to do it, but they are dependent on him to do well. He is their investment." Birler stared at the commander earnestly, hoping he understood.

"And?"

"You're teaching us to be soldiers. To harness our power and control it, to use it for the good of the Lady, to protect her people for her."

"So?"

Birler frowned. "But sometimes, there is an … an excess. An excess of energy. It's dangerous if you don't control it. But sir, there is nowhere to go and deal with it after class. The only place Serill could go to was the sparring ring. He had to work through the energy for his own good. There needs to be somewhere we can go when needed." Birler faltered at the shocked expression on the commander's face. "I didn't let him go on his own. I followed him to make sure he was alright. He didn't go alone, though he thought he did. I could see it, the energy sparking off him, sir. He did what was necessary. He shouldn't be punished for it."

The commander stared at him.

Birler tried once more. "The Lady needs him, sir. He shouldn't be expelled."

"What does the Lady need him for?" Asher asked, leaning forward and resting his hands on his desk.

Birler considered him. "She will expect him to die for her, sir."

"Is that what you expect to do for her?"

"She already knows I will," Birler said.

"I see." Asher considered him. "If I do not expel Cadet Serill, what punishment should he get? He did, after all, blatantly break an academy rule."

Birler, in turn, considered the question carefully, and Asher almost smiled. "The Lady requires assistance. Maybe he should be assigned to her for a week, for her to instruct as needed."

"And would that be a punishment?"

"He'll be terrified," Birler said frankly. "Sir."

At that, Asher did laugh; he couldn't help it. He straightened and steepled his hands on his desk as he thought. "I will consider the matter."

Birler nodded. "Thank you, sir. Umm, may I ask another question, sir?"

"Was that what you were doing?" Asher asked. He waved his hand. "Continue."

"Cadet Descelles invited me to go home with him next pass day. I didn't know who to ask permission from, sir."

Asher smiled. "I would have thought that would be obvious. I'll speak to Lady Leyandrii on your behalf when I next see her."

Birler bobbed his head. "Thank you, sir."

"You'd better return to your barracks. Off you go." Asher rose, and Birler scuttled out the door.

13

GUERLAIRE

VESPERS, VESPIRI

Guerlaire inspected the surrounding buildings as he stalked down the street towards the tavern known as the Squalley by the locals, accompanied by Chryll and a couple of the palace guards. He wrinkled his nose at the state of disrepair and the general air of dilapidation in the area.

If the citizens lived in such a poor state, maybe that was why they were open to attacking others for money. He would find out who had sent those thugs to attack him if he had to go door to door to find the culprits.

He and Chryll both had copies of the rough portraits one of the scholars had drawn of the two men they held in custody and of those Guerlaire had killed. Someone would know who they were. Once he found where they drank, he would find out who they associated with.

Whoever it was would soon learn it was a mistake to target him or Leyandrii. He knew how to persist in an investigation. He grinned viciously. He would make their lives so difficult they wouldn't have time to worry about anyone else.

Arriving at the Squalley, they split up. The guards would

patrol the outside while Guerlaire and Chryll went inside. They had taken the precaution of dressing down, though it would be obvious they were strangers. Guerlaire hoped the offer of a few drinks and maybe a few coins would loosen tongues.

Two chimes later, Guerlaire scowled at the piss-poor ale and wondered how anyone could drink it. He thought he might vomit if he drank anymore. The air smelt of stale ale, and the fire in the grate smoked terribly. His feet kept sticking to the floor, and the chair creaked every time he moved.

Initially, not a single person would speak to them. They had turned their backs and ignored them. It wasn't until Guerlaire had thought to check for signs of tampering that he realised the majority of the men were under the influence of *Mentiserium.*

Sweeping away all the persuasions and reassuring the men that they were fine and not suffering from some strange illness had taken up most of the time. Now they were just beginning to get to the names.

"That were Jake," the man was saying, pointing at the sketch and confirming what the previous person had said. "He lives down Wall Street with his missus. Worked with us at the warehouse most days. Likes ter throw himself about, yer know. Thinks he's tough."

"And who is your foreman at the warehouse?"

"Mr Lafferty. He don't live round 'ere. Rarely see him 'cept at the warehouse."

"And which warehouse does he manage?"

"All of 'em."

"All?" Guerlaire sat back in shock.

"Yeah. That's why we don't 'ave no choice. Got ter work for him. There ain't anywhere else."

"I see. Do you have any idea how I can get hold of him?"

The man shrugged. "'e'll be at the office in warehouse one tomorrow."

"Thank you."

"Yer know, thinking on it," the man said, scratching his armpit as he scowled in thought. "Yer should go speak to Danner. Works in the 'ostelry up Market Street. 'e was the one who brought that furriner to speak to us."

"What foreigner?"

"Dunno 'is name. But Danner said we 'ad to listen to 'im. It would be worth our time." The man scowled again. "Do yer think it was 'im that made us work for nothing? That ain't right." He stood and looked around the tavern. Raising his voice he said, "Oy, tomorrow, we demand more pay or we walk out! I ain't working for coppers no more."

Other voices joined him in agreement and Guerlaire leaned back in his chair. His work was done here. He stood and stretched his back. Catching Chryll's eye, he jerked his head towards the door. He inhaled deep breaths as they left the tavern, though the rancid odours in the street didn't help much.

Guerlaire coughed. "Let's get out of here. We can compare notes back in my office."

"Gladly," Chryll replied, and once they were joined by the guards, they hurried away.

When they arrived back at the palace, Guerlaire and Chryll descended on the kitchen to beg for kafinee and something to eat. Seated at the kitchen table, Guerlaire moaned as he sipped the creamy drink.

"So much better than that ale. I don't know how they drank it."

"Probably what they're used to," Chryll muttered. "They don't know any different."

"True. Anyway, we have two more people to track down. We are making progress. I will find out who is targeting me."

Late the next morning, Clary hovered by the window of his town house and glared down at the street. Breathing deeply, he clenched his fists and tried to control his anger. If he could get hold of Guerlaire, he would have him ripped in little bits. The man was causing untold difficulties. He must act but without alerting Guerlaire any further.

For now, he would concentrate on Elothia. Once he had the array restored and working properly, he would replicate it in Vespiri. He just needed to get the right configuration that would provide the most power. His people were working on it.

The mines were producing plenty of crystals; at least his plans there were uninterrupted. He would prioritise the delivery of crystals for Vespers. He would show Guerlaire who had the power.

At a tap on the door, Clary turned away from the window and resumed his seat behind the desk. He ran his finger along the smooth, old wood. This desk had been his father's and his grandfather's before him. Years of family history had been decided at this desk, and now it was his.

He had been determined that this was one family heirloom that the upstart Mayer wouldn't get. This desk grounded him, validated him. He was all-powerful, and soon, everyone would know what he could do.

"Come in."

His steward entered with a silver salver in his hand, upon which lay a letter. "Just arrived, m'lord."

"Thank you." Clary ripped it open and skimmed the contents. Immediately, he was on his feet. "Who delivered this? Are they still downstairs?"

"No, m'lord. It was an errand boy, and he left straight away."

Clary ground his teeth. "Get me Danner. Immediately!"

"Of course, m'lord." The steward bowed his way out and shut the door.

Clary strode back to the window, unable to stay still. Guerlaire had swept through Harbourtown and undone all his persuasions. The workers had gone on strike. He had lost his workforce and his thugs in one fell swoop.

How was he supposed to get his wagons loaded? His goods moved?

The situation was untenable.

14

BIRLER

RANGERS ACADEMY

Over the next couple of days, Tagerill and Birler attended their classes by rote, their worry and concern obvious to those who knew what had happened. At last, Commander Asher called them to his office.

Birler squirmed under his relentless inspection and stiffened when Asher sighed.

"I wanted to inform you that your associate, Cadet Serill, has been duly reprimanded for breaking the academy rules. He is currently serving out his punishment." Asher's lips twitched, and Birler worried he'd made it worse for his friend. "He will return in two weeks, and that will be the end of it. In the meantime, I expect exemplary behaviour out of you two. If I have a single report of any misbehaviour, I will split you three up. Understood?"

Their response was immediate: "Yes, sir."

"I have also, under due consultation with the sparring master, set up an after-class sparring schedule, available on request, should the need arise. The request should be submitted through my office. The sparring ring will be made available within a half-chime of the request, with an overseer available to assist. Understood? There will be no further visits without permission."

Birler's eyes widened. "Understood, sir," he breathed as a smile spread over his face.

"Good. Return to your duties." Asher dismissed them.

Tagerill hauled Birler out of the office and around the corner. "What was that all about?" he demanded.

Birler looked around him, trying to look innocent. "What was what all about?"

Tagerill sighed. "For someone who had to live off his wits, you are a terrible liar."

"Who said I lied?"

Tagerill laughed outright. "You are practically squirming right now, but seriously, why did the commander just tell us about an out-of-class sparring service? What did you do?"

Birler squinted at him and then exhaled. "I told him that, sometimes, we need to let off excess energy, and there's nowhere to do it; that's why Serill was in the sparring ring that night."

"And when did you tell him that?"

"Just after Serill got expelled," Birler admitted.

"And just how did you get in front of Asher?"

"I knocked on his door," Birler said, unsure of the issue.

Tagerill gave a crack of laughter. "You just knocked on his door?"

"Yes."

Tagerill stilled. "You're serious, aren't you?"

Birler glared at him. "I knocked on his door, and he told me to enter, so I did."

Tagerill shook his head in disbelief. "You've got balls, that's for sure. Tell me everything. What did you say to Asher?"

Birler watched Tagerill as he recounted his meeting. He didn't think Tagerill's eyes could get any bigger.

Tagerill exhaled. "I'm glad you're on my side."

Birler looked at him in confusion. "I'm not on anyone's side. I am the Lady's."

"You're on the right side, then," Tagerill said, dragging Birler away from the office block. "C'mon, we've got to survive two weeks."

They made it to two weeks but no further.

Everything fell apart the day Serill returned to the academy. There was no time to talk, to reassure, but the three of them were reunited, and that was enough.

It fell apart in the after-lunch lesson when the master handed back the papers from the previous week's test.

"Birler, out front," the master said, his voice sharp.

Birler slowly rose and walked up to the front of the class. He turned and faced his classmates. Tagerill frowned in concern as Serill watched the room, adjusting to being back.

"We do not tolerate cheats and liars in the academy," the master said, his voice cutting.

The boys gasped, as did Birler. "I am no such thing," he blurted, shocked.

"Papers don't lie," the master said.

"I did not cheat," Birler said, squaring his shoulders at the accusation.

"This academy values honour and truth. You lack both."

Birler stood rigid.

Tagerill observed his pale face and the wrath writhing behind his dark gaze.

The master hesitated at the strength of the emotion in

the boy's eyes. But he stiffened his resolve. "Hands out," he rapped. "We punish liars and cheats in this academy."

"He's not a cheat."

Serill's angry voice was overridden by Tagerill's furious one. "He's not a liar."

The master stared at the two boys who were standing when they shouldn't be. "Sit down," he growled. "I'll deal with you later."

"Surely, if there are no liars in the academy, you should be interested in the truth?" Serill asked, his voice so sharp it could cut.

Tagerill shuddered as the master brought the stick down across Birler's hands with a strength born out of his anger, harder than he had first intended. Birler gasped and wavered before stiffening. Tyrler slouched in his seat and scoffed, though he stopped as he caught Tagerill's vicious glare. Tyrler swallowed and dropped his eyes.

Tagerill gripped his desk and willed Birler to stay still. He stared at Birler, worried by the taut lines that accentuated his suddenly gaunt face. Birler stared back at him, and their gazes locked with an almost audible click.

Tagerill's anger grew with each strike. He had never felt so coldly dangerous in all his life, but he felt it today. His knuckles whitened as his grip tightened, and he offered Birler his strength as the boy stood tall and stared at him, unblinking, while the master shredded his hands.

"Enough," Tagerill said, his voice cutting across the room as his chair scraped back violently against the floor, unable to bear it anymore. The master instinctively stopped at the command in his voice. "You have the right to punish but not to irrevocably damage," he snapped, holding himself rigid so he didn't explode into the violence that was building within him.

The master stared at Tagerill before looking back at his

work, and he visibly swallowed at the sight of the Birler's hands. He raised his eyes to look at the boy's face. Birler's face was stiff, with an expression of pain and desolation frozen in place, but he hadn't murmured a sound. "Return to your seat," the master rasped, breathing heavily.

Birler stood fixed to the spot, unhearing, uncaring. Tagerill knew he had passed beyond simple obedience. His eyes were locked on Tagerill's, and he couldn't let go. His gaze was the only thing keeping Birler together. He looked like he might fly apart at any moment.

"I said sit down." The master was recovering his composure and his temper.

Serill stood, no doubt seeing what the master hadn't. Moving quickly, he carefully wrapped an arm around his friend and, ignoring the master, led him out of the room. "Tage," he breathed as they passed, and Tagerill fell in behind them.

Serill led them to the training grounds as if aware of Tagerill's failing restraint.

"How can they?" Tagerill growled. "Truth? They wouldn't know truth if it hit them between the eyes." He grabbed a stick and battered the sparring target again and again until the stick broke, and then he reached for another.

"Tage, stop."

Tagerill glanced across at them at the sound of Serill's worried voice. Birler was shaking uncontrollably, his eyes wild, a storm brewing. Tagerill was on his knees beside them in moments. "Birler, it wasn't your fault. We should have argued more," he said bitterly, glaring at Serill.

"Yes, we should have," Serill agreed, trying to hold Birler still. Tagerill helped him.

"What is it?" Tagerill asked as the strength of his friend's shudders frightened him.

"I don't know, shock or something maybe?"

Tagerill wrapped strong arms around Birler and held him tightly. "You're safe now. I've got you," he murmured. His anger drained away as Birler shuddered in his arms. He tightened his grip as Birler slowly relaxed and rested his head on Tagerill's shoulder, his arms hanging limp at his sides.

"We should take him to the healerie before someone comes looking for us," Serill said, stirring out of the three-way embrace, reassured by Birler's stillness.

A deep voice split them apart. "If he needs the healerie, you should have taken him there first."

Tagerill reared up in front of his friends, Serill behind him, providing an effective barrier between him and the injured boy behind them.

"I won't hurt him," Captain Guerlaire said gently, raising his eyebrows at their swift reaction.

Tagerill's eyes flashed, and a crackle of energy surrounded him. "It's too late for that."

"Go find Sparring Master Pallinten. Tell him I sent you," Guerlaire said calmly. "You need to work off your pent-up anger before you injure yourself."

Tagerill hesitated.

"You've protected your friend. Now look to yourself," Guerlaire commanded.

Tagerill flinched at the slice of power in Guerlaire's voice, but still, he hesitated. He looked at Serill, who frowned at him and jerked his head.

Tagerill glanced at Birler and back at Guerlaire and then left.

Serill stiffened under Guerlaire's inspection, blocking his view of Birler. "What happened?" Guerlaire asked as he considered how to broach the next line of defence.

"The literacy master wouldn't believe us."

"About what?"

"That there is more honour in Birler's little finger than in this whole school," was the bitterly cold reply. "Birler is not a cheat." Serill's anger surfaced, icy cold and deadly.

Guerlaire stood his ground. "Why did the master believe he cheated?"

"I don't know."

"Why did the master say he had no honour?" Guerlaire asked.

"He called him a liar."

"Why?"

"He didn't say."

Guerlaire breathed out gently. "Now, why would Birler cheat?"

"He wouldn't." Serill's answer was immediate and instinctive. "And anyway, I'd only just started to teach him to read," he said with disarming honesty, and then he clapped his hand over his mouth and stared at Guerlaire in horror.

Birler stirred behind him and came to stand at his shoulder.

Guerlaire inspected him. He was pale, to be sure, his face taut as if he were concealing something, but he looked well enough. His eyes, though—they told a different story. A clash of wills, damage done, words heard meant to hurt, and not old enough to understand why or how to deal with them.

"What happened?" Guerlaire asked. This scalding emotion would damage—and damage beyond repair if not handled carefully.

Birler raised stiff hands. His fingers were curled around like claws, his palms red and oozing. They shook. A tremor passed through Birler's body, and Serill twitched and then stilled.

Guerlaire gritted his teeth, his jaw rigid, and he had to consciously relax his muscles. Leyandrii would be furious. "The healerie it is, then," he said with admirable mildness, his anger stirring. He would be joining Tagerill in the sparring ring if he weren't careful.

Guerlaire indicated for Serill to lead the way. He followed, herding them to the healerie, making sure they arrived, and making sure the healer knew that *he* knew they had arrived.

Fury raced through Guerlaire's veins as he strode through the halls. Did he have to do everything himself? Why couldn't they see what they were doing? Why destroy when they should nurture? It was inconceivable to him that anyone within these halls would not further the objective of teasing out those inherent abilities, those skills that would contribute to protecting Remargaren, turning out strong, competent, knowledgeable men and women who would stand forth and die for them. His hands ached from him clenching them so tightly. If they had undone all the hard-learnt lessons, his anger would know no bounds.

15

BIRLER

RANGERS ACADEMY

ealer Demeren tutted over Birler's hands and shooed Serill out of the treatment room. "Back again already?" he asked, peering at Birler over his glasses.

Birler grimaced, easing his aching shoulders. He wanted to fall on his bed. He could hardly keep his eyes open, as if holding himself together for the last chime had taken the last of his energy. Birler hissed as the healer dunked one hand and then the other in a clear, viscous liquid. The initial sting was deadened, and his shoulders relaxed down from around his ears.

"Who did this to you?" Healer Demeren asked as he potted about, retrieving the various tools he needed.

"Literacy master."

"I see." Demeren tutted. "I hear you are a bit of an archer," he said as he pulled one of Birler's hands out of the jar and patted it dry.

"Sometimes," Birler admitted, his voice low, watching the healer flex his fingers flat. He was surprised it didn't hurt. The welts were angry and raised.

"Where did you learn?"

Birler shrugged. "The Lady's gift."

The healer flicked him a glance. "Fortunate for you, then," he said, smoothing the salve over Birler's palm and then wrapping a bandage around his hand. He moved on to the other one, his touch gentle, his presence soothing. "Come back every day, and we'll replace the bandages. Try not to use them too much. I know that's asking a lot, but until the skin begins to heal over, we can't remove the bandages. Your friends can help you, can't you?" the healer asked, raising his voice.

Serill peered around the door.

"You'll have to be his hands for the next week. Do you think you can do that?"

"Of course," Serill replied with an injured expression on his face at the insinuation that he wouldn't help.

The healer's lips twitched. "Don't get them wet. No sparring, no archery. You can't do Apeiron for the next three days, and then you can run. I expect to see you this time tomorrow. Drink this." He held out a mug with a straw, and Birler slurped it obediently, his hands resting in his lap. Demeren looked at Serill. "What else did you have on today?"

Serill stared back at him blankly.

"What lesson should you be in?" the healer asked patiently.

"History," Birler said.

"Then go and sit in the library and read until dinner. Both of you. I will inform the master of your whereabouts." Demeren rose and cleared away his tools, turning his back in dismissal.

Birler stood and escaped with Serill. They spent a soothing chime in the quiet library. Serill chose a map, pointing out and naming the towns across Vespiri. Birler silently memorised names, landmarks, and locations.

Less than a chime later, Asher watched Guerlaire pace like a caged animal, back and forth. Guerlaire would wear a path in his much-prized Aliinia rug if he weren't careful, but Asher held his tongue and watched, hoping some of the ire would fade before the angry man in his office condescended to tell him what was wrong.

He had ever been thus, even as a student: passionate, intense, unstoppable. Guerlaire didn't treat anything lightly. If he was engaged, he invested his all, and Lady forbid those who got in his way. He was a coiled spring waiting to be released— the power within controlled but present. You would expect such an intense man to be larger than life, but Guerlaire was not. He was of middling height, muscular, but not overly big. He had a narrow waist on which hung his sword belt. Asher could feel the sword from where he sat. It was another sign of the man's inherent power, to be able to control such a sword.

Asher sighed, and Guerlaire flicked him a fiery glance before a small sheepish smile flittered over his mouth. He threw himself into the chair before Asher's desk, tapping the arm with his finger.

Asher watched him. "If you need to go and work some of this enviable energy off, please feel free," he said as he spread his hand out before him in a gesture of permission.

Guerlaire scowled at the older man seated across from him. "Are you offering?"

Asher smiled. "No, not today. There is much emotion in the air. I fear I could not withstand it."

Guerlaire grunted in disbelief, and Asher's smile

widened. He might be two decades Guerlaire's senior and starting to go grey, but his strength was undiminished, and his body remained strong and lean, and Guerlaire knew it.

"Young Tagerill, I hear, has found his inner fire," Asher said. "The sparring master is struggling to control it. What caused it to ignite?"

"One of your masters accused Birler of cheating and took his punishment too far."

Asher leaned forward. "What do you mean?"

"Birler won't be holding a sword, or anything else for that matter, for a week at least." Guerlaire scowled at him. "He's in the healerie as we speak. Both Tagerill and Serill were defending him."

"Which master?"

"Literacy, I believe."

"I see. I will speak to the master and find out why he believed Birler cheated."

"And curb his unnecessary violence towards the students."

"That goes without saying. We are here to teach, not to incapacitate our students."

"Birler continues to surprise us," Guerlaire said.

"Ah, not quite what you expected, I believe?"

Guerlaire sighed out his breath and relaxed in his chair. "I'm not sure what I expected. Leyandrii watches. Birler does seem to affect those around him, though he remains contained. I'm worried."

"As you should be," Asher agreed. "It is a difficult time for new powers to rise, especially when they are unseen."

"They will not surface through beatings, Oren. There is discipline, and then there is discipline. The boy has already been taught despair. He knows that lesson far too well; he doesn't need to be reminded of it."

Asher stilled. "I see," he said.

Guerlaire sighed out his breath. "Whilst he recovers, introduce him to the Chapterhouse. He won't be able to train for a while. Serill guards him. Send them both, or you may find Tagerill bursting back into flame sooner than you thought." He flicked Asher a cutting glance. "Serill is teaching the boy to read," he said.

"Really? He hid that well."

"Being illiterate doesn't mean you're ignorant," Guerlaire said, leaning forward. "It's a shame some of your masters haven't learnt that lesson yet."

"As always, Captain, your visits are enlightening."

Guerlaire gave a bark of laughter, and he levered himself out of the chair. "Let me know how he gets on. Leyandrii will be asking."

Asher watched him leave. "Leyandrii? Or do you mean Guerlaire?" he muttered, frowning in thought. He had been reluctant to take Birler on because of the very issues beginning to arise, but then, he was also a breath of fresh air, revitalising many jaded masters to face the challenge. And then, of course, there had been Leyandrii and Guerlaire, standing behind the boy like protective parents. You didn't refuse the Lady, nor the Lady's Captain, especially when this had been the one and only sponsorship Guerlaire had made in all the years Asher had known him.

Not that anyone knew, not even Birler, or so he hoped. The boy didn't need any more targets on his back.

The cadets were a very subdued group at dinner. Tagerill joined them, looking as exhausted as Birler felt. Birler smiled in sympathy as his friend collapsed in the chair opposite them.

"Where have you been?" Serill asked.

"Pallinten is evil," Tagerill groaned in reply. "He kept me sparring for chimes. He said I needed to learn to control myself. I've got three new routines, and he wouldn't let me go until I mastered them all."

Serill chuckled. "But it got you out of history, so you should be pleased."

Tagerill winced as he sat up. "Not when you're being battered and bruised by a monster," he complained. "Everything aches. On top of that, Pallinten said I had to catch up on anything I missed in my own time."

Birler grimaced, and Tagerill was quick to stand. "What do you want to eat? Looks like chicken or fish."

"Chicken, please."

Tagerill nodded and was soon back with a tray loaded with a plate of chicken, bread rolls, and a mug of sweetened kafinee. "Here," he said, his voice rough as he placed it before Birler. He went back to join the queue as Serill sat down beside Birler with his own tray.

While Serill cut up the larger bits, Birler drank his kafinee, relaxing at the taste of the sweet liquid. He stabbed the chicken pieces, awkwardly holding the fork with his fingertips. Serill broke up the bread roll, just as he had watched Birler do many times.

They were talking in low tones when Tyrler stopped by their table. "Tagerill, you got a moment?"

Tagerill looked up and stared at Tyrler. He seemed to debate internally for a moment and then rose.

Tyrler drew him outside the door. "Tagerill, what are you doing? Why do you keep sitting with those two losers? You're not doing yourself any favours, you know. People are noticing."

"Noticing what?" Tagerill asked.

"Who you are associating with. Tage, you're from a respected family. Don't ruin your chances."

"If I have a respected family name, surely it doesn't matter who I choose to associate with?"

"You know that our next step after the academy will be a result of how we impress the masters here. They decide where we go. You need to be more careful. Like should stay with like. Our families brought Vespiri to where it is today. We are the ones who will lead us in the future, not the likes of them."

"What's wrong with them exactly?" Tagerill asked, his voice growing cooler.

"Tagerill." The condescending note in Tyrler's voice made Tagerill stiffen. "You know better than that. They have no bloodlines; they are nothing. They shouldn't even be here. They take the place of someone more worthy."

"You mean like the people who make false claims?"

Tyrler flushed. "They shouldn't be here. They will soon realise this is not the place for them."

"Says who?"

"Says everyone. Look, Tage, you're my friend. I don't want to see you hurt, see your family disappointed."

"Why would I be hurt?" Tagerill's voice had an edge to it.

"If you take the wrong side, you'll lose," Tyrler warned.

"Since when have we had to take sides? Against who?"

"Against the likes of them," Tyrler said, jerking his head back at the room.

"Let me be clear. You think Birler and Serill are a threat to you?" Tagerill's voice rose in surprise.

"Of course not; they are nothing. It's you, Tage; they taint you. People will wonder if the Descelles have forgotten where they came from. Your reputation is at stake."

Tagerill snorted. "Don't be ridiculous."

"I'm not, Tagerill." Tyrler stared at him. "I'm warning you because you're my friend. People are watching."

Tagerill flicked a glance into the hall. Many eyes were

watching them, though Tagerill was sure that wasn't what Tyrler meant. "They're not watching well enough, then, if that is what you think."

Tyrler stepped back. "You've been warned, Tage. You should listen if you know what's good for you."

Tagerill nodded, restraining the urge to punch Tyrler Clary in the nose. "Duly noted." He strode back into the hall and returned to his seat, ignoring Birler's and Serill's concerned glances.

"Is everything alright, Tagerill?" Birler asked as Tagerill systematically destroyed a bread roll.

"I think I need to go visit Pallinten again," Tagerill said, scowling at the mess he had made. But he wouldn't say anything further. He was quiet for the rest of the evening, though he sat and polished Birler's boots for him before the bell was rung for lights out.

The next morning, they were back into their routine. Birler was sent back to the barracks, with a stinging reprimand in his ears for returning to training against the healer's instructions. A message was waiting for him, advising him of a changed schedule. His mornings would be spent in the Chapterhouse, where he would be learning to read and, once his hands were healed, to write.

He flushed at the shame of it: the fact that everyone now knew he couldn't read. Staring off into the distance, he sighed. At least he would be in the Chapterhouse. Maybe he could fit in a quick visit to the temple while he was at it. With some difficulty, he changed out of his training kit and into a shirt and trousers. He slipped his jacket on and, taking the paper with him, left for the admin office to request permission to go the Chapterhouse.

He watched a unit of second-years out on parade. They did look smart, even if every cadet hated the practice. It was so boring. Birler much preferred running to marching. He crossed the grounds, entered the office, and handed the adjutant the paper.

The adjutant made a note, wrote out a form, and handed it to Birler. "Keep that with you. Do not lose it; it's your permission slip. You need to see Scholar Diminter, and you are expected every morning for the next month. You may rejoin your class for the afternoon session." The man nodded a dismissal and returned to his paperwork.

Birler breathed a sigh of relief as he left the garrison. He hadn't realised how confined he had felt within the barracks. After living on the streets, where no one cared what he did, now he couldn't leave the academy without a permission slip. Breathing in his momentary freedom, he exhaled with a laugh. Light-hearted, he strolled down the road to the Chapterhouse. Pausing outside the building, he admired the golden architecture. The building looked warm and welcoming. The soft aroma of the Lady's roses drifted on the air, making him smile. He crossed the open entrance hall to the official on duty behind his desk.

He showed the man his permission slip. "I'm here to see Scholar Diminter."

The man took his slip and nodded before handing it back. "Second sub-level, third door on the left." He returned to his work.

Birler ventured further into the building, following the narrow stairs down two floors. He peered into the dim corridor, which had rough stone walls. The light from the lantern on the wall revealed a row of dark wooden doors.

He hesitantly tapped on the third door on the left, wincing at the sting in his palm.

A light voice bid him enter, and using his elbow, he raised

the latch and opened the door. He was surprised to see a slight young woman seated at the desk. There was a golden ball floating in the air above her, providing light for her to work by. She was dressed in the silver scholar robes, and she also seemed surprised, even though she was supposedly expecting him.

"Scholar Diminter?"

"Yes, you must be Cadet Birler?" The young woman tilted her head, inspecting him.

He flushed under her clear gaze. "Yes, ma'am."

"Well, you'd better come in and sit, then," she said, patting the empty chair next to her.

Birler pushed the door shut and sat, his eyes drawn back to that suspended ball in the air. How did it stay there? He couldn't see any strings, brackets, or anything. He waited, mesmerised by the light. He flushed as he realised the scholar was watching him. She smiled, and lines creased her face. She wasn't as young as he had thought. Then she tapped the ball, and the light went out, throwing the room into darkness. She tapped it again, and the light blared forth. "It's an onoff lamp," she said.

"A-a what?"

"You tap it to once to light up and again to go off. An onoff lamp."

"But how does it work? There is nothing holding it there."

The scholar laughed. "The Lady's magic, of course. But I'm not here to teach you about lamps. You are here to learn to read and write. Sit."

"Thank you," Birler said, flushing as he sat.

She pursed her lips. "What happened to your hands?"

He tried to hide his bandaged hands, but she checked the move, touching his arm. "Birler, I am not here to judge. I am here to teach. You are here to learn. So, tell me. What happened to your hands?"

Birler sighed out his breath and raised his eyes. "I was accused of cheating in a test." He raised his hands. "Punishment for being a liar and without honour," he said, dropping his eyes again.

"And are you without honour?"

"No!" The word exploded out of Birler as he raised his head in shock.

"Good," she said. "Then let's see what we can do about ensuring you don't get falsely accused again. I need to understand what you already know. See what you can read out of this." She pushed an open book in front of him. He smiled as he recognised it. He read the first line out loud, and she looked at him in surprise.

"I'm not really reading it," he admitted. "My friend has this book, and he read it to me."

"But you just read it to me."

"I remembered the words," he said.

"That is what reading is," Diminter said softly. "Recognising the letters and the order in which they are written makes a word, which has a specific meaning. The combination of a group of words makes a sentence, which starts with a capital letter and ends with a full stop. She pointed at an example of each. That is how we know that particular group of words are associated together. Those words provide information, descriptions, directions."

Birler nodded, his eyes alight with interest.

She continued. "Let's try a different book, then, one you don't know." She pulled another book over. "Read this paragraph."

Birler stared at the words. He recognised some but not others. He understood the gist of the paragraph but not how to read it. He said what he thought it meant.

Diminter smiled. "I see how you've been getting by. You can assimilate the information very quickly; it's the individual words you can't read. Very well. Let us go back to the beginning. She drew out a slate and a piece of chalk and worked through the alphabet.

Birler named them all without fault. "My friend has been teaching me the letters."

Diminter rubbed the slate clean and wrote a word. She showed it to him.

He spelt out the letters. "B-i-r-l-e-r."

"Do you know what that says?" she asked.

"Birler," he said. "My name." He pulled out his permission slip and stared at his name.

"Very good. Let's continue." Diminter kept them working until a small timepiece chimed on her desk. She sat up and closed the book. She smiled at him. "We've been working for three chimes. You've done well, very well. We will continue tomorrow, and next week, when your bandages are off, we'll start you writing."

Birler carefully folded his paper up and put it back in his pocket. "Thank you."

Diminter smiled. "You don't need to thank me. It's what I'm paid to do. But I'll take your thanks all the same. See you tomorrow, Birler. Same place, same time."

Birler nodded, took one last glance at the amazing light, and left her office. He made his way back up the stairs and out into the bright daylight. He wondered why the scholars preferred to be buried in the depths of the land. Maybe he would pluck up the courage to ask why by the end of the week.

The Chapterhouse bell chimed twelve, and he hurried up the road towards the academy. He hadn't realised learning to read took so much effort, and he was starving. Searching the hall for a friendly face, he came up empty. He realised how few of the boys he knew, and he suddenly wondered why.

Awkwardly balancing his tray on his arm, he selected a bowl of soup and a couple of bread rolls. It was all he could manage easily on his own. He sat at a table near the back and tried to fade into the wall.

He looked up in surprise as a stocky, blond-haired lad sat at the end of his table. He didn't seem much older than Birler was, maybe the same age as Tagerill and Serill. He didn't say anything, but he nodded at Birler and tucked into his meal. Birler relaxed slightly. It was as if the lad was a barrier against the accusing eyes in the rest of the hall.

Tagerill blew into the hall like a breath of fresh air. "You won't survive on that," he said as he looked at Birler's lunch. He looked around the hall with suddenly aware eyes. "Parsill," he said with a nod at the boy at the end of the table. The boy held his eyes and nodded back.

Tagerill went up to the serving hatch and loaded up a couple of plates. When he came back, he passed one to Birler, along with a kafinee. "You're slipping. I thought you couldn't get enough of the stuff," he said with a grin.

Birler smiled with pleasure. "I couldn't carry it all," he admitted, taking a deep gulp.

"Parsill, join us." Tagerill waved him closer. "Do you know Birler?"

Parsill slid his tray down the table. "We've not really met. Parsill Ferrantes, from Stoneford," he said.

Birler grinned. "Birler."

Tagerill leaned over and cut up his meat. "Thanks, Ma," Birler said with a resigned smile.

Parsill laughed. "Where did you go this morning?"

Birler made a face. "Well, seeing as I can't train for a few days, I'm assigned to the Chapterhouse."

"Lucky you," Tagerill said with feeling. "Sparring Master

Pallinten was his usual unfeeling self. My arms are still vibrating."

"You are the only one that can hold him off," Parsill said. "We'll have to gang up on him."

"We still wouldn't win," Tagerill said morosely. His face lightened as Serill joined them. "Where have you been?"

"Someone kindly told the lieutenant that my gear was out of order. He wouldn't let me go until I had put it all to rights."

Tagerill frowned. "Your stuff was fine this morning."

"Yeah, well, someone obviously thought it would be good to get me in trouble. I got a demerit and a week of shit duty."

Tagerill's frown deepened.

Parsill glanced at him and then down at his plate. "There is a growing consensus that entry to the cadets should be more restricted," he said.

"But we're already here, already accepted," Serill pointed out.

"They don't care. Personally, I think the cadets would be poorer for it, but money tends to speak loudest these days." He shrugged as Tagerill scowled at him. "It does."

"So, we should expect more of this, then?" Birler asked, raising his hands.

Parsill exhaled, his expression worried. "I hate to say yes, but I don't see it going any other way."

"Isn't there something we can do? Report them?" Serill asked, violently stabbing a piece of meat on his plate.

"Report who? What can you prove?" Parsill's gaze flicked around the room.

Warmth spread through Birler as he realised Parsill had taken a risk by sitting at the same table with him but had done it anyway. He hoped some of the more sensible would choose to join them.

They finished their lunch in a depressed silence before leaving for their afternoon classes. Birler watched intently as the words flowed past him. Tyrler smirked at him from across the room. It was obvious from Tyrler's behaviour that he was one of the ringleaders, but Parsill was right; without proof, they could do nothing. He had forgotten to go to the healer, so after class, he left the others to go and get his hands redressed. His hands still looked angry and sore. He could attest to the soreness. The salve eased the pain, and he relaxed with a sigh.

"You should have come back earlier," the healer scolded.

Birler grimaced. "I forgot."

Demeren shook his head and shooed him out. "Don't forget tomorrow."

Birler rejoined his classmates and watched them do their evening chores. "Can you believe we're over halfway through the first year?"

"I know. Another year, and we'll be graduating." Tagerill scowled down at his boots.

"I wonder where they'll send us."

"We've got to graduate first. Next year, our schedule doubles, on top of looking after our horses."

Birler stilled. "Horses?"

"Yeah, you can't go anywhere without a horse to ride. You know, takes too long to walk. Pass your boots over." Tagerill reached for Birler's boots and began polishing. He turned them in his hands. "You have small feet, don't you?" he said with a grin.

"They're big enough," Birler protested, though he had to grin, too, when Tagerill held one of his boots up beside it. Birler shrugged. "They are what they are. Can't see them changing much now."

Tagerill bent back over his work. Tyrler stopped beside them, watching Tagerill. "You call yourself a friend," he spat at Birler. "Yet you're prepared to let Tagerill lose everything. Haven't you noticed? No one speaks to Tagerill anymore. No one wants to know him, and that's your fault."

Tyrler stopped speaking as Tagerill rose and stood between them. "I suggest you keep your opinion to yourself, Ty," he said, his voice low. "Who I am friends with is my choice, and it has nothing to do with you."

Tagerill's back was to Birler, but Birler peered around him and saw Tyrler flinch. His face paled, and he stalked away. Tagerill sat back down.

"Tage, is that true? No one speaks to you anymore?" Birler hadn't noticed, but now that he thought about it, Tagerill didn't bounce around their fellow cadets like he once had.

"Of course not," Tagerill scoffed. "Who has the energy at the end of the day to do anything but collapse? Don't listen to anything Tyrler Clary says; he never says anything good."

Birler accepted Tagerill's reassurance and forgot about it as he gradually resumed full training and picked up where he had left off, returning each night as exhausted as his friends.

16

GUERLAIRE

LADY'S PALACE, VESPERS

Guerlaire debated long and hard about whether he should go to Terolia. Just because he'd made a commitment to the scholar-dean of the Chapterhouse, it didn't mean he had to honour it. Protecting Leyandrii came first.

But there had been no threats. The Administration was running smoothly, and Leyandrii was unconcerned. North Elothia remained silent and empty. The rangers dispatched to search had found no sign of whoever had targeted him and Chryll on the river, nor who had attacked him in the street.

It was as if they had completely disappeared and this made Guerlaire uneasy. His instincts told him this was just the beginning, a probing attack to see how they responded. The rangers' inability to find out anything did not bode well, which reinforced his need to get out and discover what was happening.

He had Clary's contacts, Danner and Lafferty, under observation. Instead of barging in and demanding answers as he had first intended, he had listened to Chryll's counsel and was being patient. Not something he was well known for but at least he was trying.

He looked up as a shadow darkened his doorway, and he smiled as Leyandrii entered his office.

"Still undecided?" she asked

Guerlaire grimaced

"You know, your restlessness was why Asher seconded you to the Chapterhouse as their resident explorer. He knew you would never stand still for long. And what you discover on your travels only aids him long term. Go, Guerlaire. Find out where they have holed up. See if you can discover who these Ascendants are. Find out what their real purpose is."

"Do you really think I'll find that in Terolia? Those dissidents are holed up in Elothia somewhere."

"Not just in Elothia, I fear."

Guerlaire lurched to his feet. "What have you seen?"

"I have 'seen' nothing. Clary's support of any group is enough for us to investigate," Leyandrii replied, hurrying around his desk to embrace him, "but it is logical to assume that those who would undermine me would need support from all regions, would they not?"

Guerlaire inhaled her scent and buried his face in her hair, allowing her to calm his fears. He stiffened as her reasoning percolated through his mind. "You think it is that widespread?"

"We would be stupid to think otherwise, wouldn't we?"

"I would suggest they are stupid to think you would ever harm any of your people."

"But they will force my hand and make me seem a monster."

"You *have* seen something."

Leyandrii patted his chest. "I've been around long enough to know that if we do not know who our assailants are, then we will not be able to plan our defence, let alone a resolution to any conflict. You need to find out what is really going on so I can stop it before it is too late."

"Why do you think Terolia is the source?"

"I don't. I think the source is closer to home, but there is something going on in Terolia, and I need you to investigate." Leyandrii gave him a feral grin that made his heart clench; such an expression truly did not sit right on her exquisite face. "Maybe if you stir things up a bit, someone here will get rattled."

"It's still hot in Terolia."

"It's always hot in Terolia," Leyandrii replied with a small smile.

"You know what I mean. We're still a month away before it begins to cool."

"By the time you get organised, persuade Chryll to accompany you, and then travel across Vespiri, I'm sure a month will have passed."

"Are you trying to get rid of me?"

"I think," Leyandrii said as she pushed him back into his chair and sat in his lap, "that you are making excuses."

"For what?"

Leyandrii kissed him, and Guerlaire relaxed as her soft lips caressed his. Then her tongue quested for entry, and his lips parted. She tasted like nectar: sweet, flowery, and very addictive. "Because you don't think I can protect myself," she murmured against his lips.

Guerlaire scrambled to find an appropriate response. Of course he wanted to protect her; she was his heart, his life, but that didn't mean he thought she was weak.

Leyandrii laughed as she pulled away. "My poor captain. Torn between honesty and desire." She placed a finger over his mouth as he tried to respond. "I know you think I am too pure and innocent, but sadly, I do know how to defend myself, and I am not without power." She frowned at him. "Do not make the mistake of thinking I would not use it."

Guerlaire's chest tightened. "I know you are quite capable and all-powerful; I just don't want you to have to be in a position where you have to act when there are so many of us who would protect you with our lives."

Leyandrii's frown deepened. "If by my action all those lives could be saved, then why would I not act?"

Guerlaire sighed. He knew this was an argument he would never win. Leyandrii would not sacrifice those supposed to be there for her protection, and that was what scared him the most. She would stand on the front line if needed, and his heart quailed at the thought.

"My heart," Leyandrii whispered, "the more we can find out about this shadowy threat, the more you can prepare our response so I won't need to act."

And there she had him. He exhaled and hugged her tightly. "As you command, my love." Relief percolated through him as Leyandrii laughed and hugged him back, nestling her head under his chin.

"As if you listen to any of my commands," she said.

"I respect every command you make," he replied in mock outrage.

Leyandrii huffed against his neck. "I will miss you," she whispered.

"As I will you." Guerlaire kissed the top of her head, blinking away the tears welling in his eyes.

Leyandrii had been right, of course. It took a month to organise his expedition, from drawing up the maps, stocking provisions, choosing the right men, and convincing Chryll to accompany him. Chryll had not been enamoured with the idea of travelling through the deserts of Terolia.

At last, they were on the road, and Guerlaire watched Leyandrii's palace recede. As buildings and trees hid it from view, he turned in his saddle and exhaled loudly.

Chryll chuckled. "I'm amazed you tore yourself away from her. I thought you were supposed to be holed up in the Chapterhouse with all your Elothian research?"

"I should be," Guerlaire muttered under his breath.

"Then why aren't you? You could be home in her arms every night."

"Don't," Guerlaire groaned and rubbed his eyes.

"Then tell me what is really going on and why you insist on going to Terolia right now."

Guerlaire glanced around him. The men and women forming the mounted column behind him were all trustworthy, but he still didn't like voicing his concerns aloud. "I'll tell you later."

Chryll cast him a sharp glance and then changed the subject. "Are you sure we've got enough provisions? Four mules do not seem enough."

"If we have more mules we'll need to carry more feed and water. We have enough."

Chryll sighed. "The joys of travel rations."

"At least you have a week of comfortable taverns to ease you in."

"And then the heat of a furnace all day, every day."

"Stop complaining." Guerlaire grinned at his friend as he urged his horse into a trot. "We haven't even reached the desert yet."

17

CLARY

VESPERS

Lord Clary sat in his office in his Vespers townhouse and scowled at the papers in his hand. Why was it that he always had to deal with incompetent underlings? He glanced up and pinned the fidgeting man standing before his desk with a piercing stare. The man was covered in road dust and grime, proof of the urgency of his recent journey across Vespiri. "This cannot be correct," he said, waving the report at the man.

"I am sorry, my lord, but the wagon was halted on the border and searched."

"By whose command?" Clary's voice cracked through the air, and the man flinched.

"Captain Guerlaire, sir. He said the wagon was overloaded and the weight needed to be redistributed."

"What was he doing on the border, stopping my wagon?"

"I don't know, sir. But when the wagon was offloaded, the sacks were discovered, and he confiscated them."

"How many sacks did he take?"

"All of them, sir." The man took a step back as Clary lurched to his feet, his fists clenched on the desk.

"What about the border guards I've been paying off? What did they do?"

"N-nothing, sir. Captain Guerlaire's troop wouldn't let them near the wagon."

"So, you are telling me that I've been wasting my money and that the last six months of mined crystals are now in Guerlaire's grimy hands?"

"Yes, sir."

"And you expect me to be happy with that?"

"No, sir."

"Then what are you going to do about it?"

"Get the sacks back, sir?"

"You'd better. And while you're at it, kill those idiots who overloaded the wagon. If not for them, we wouldn't be in this predicament."

"Yes, sir."

"Don't come back unless you have every single crystal that is missing, do you understand? Those crystals are critical to my plans!"

The man trembled and dipped his head in a quick bow. "Yes, sir." He spun and dashed from the room.

Clary exhaled and sat down. He picked up the report again. Guerlaire was headed into Terolia. Maybe this was his opportunity to deal with him once and for all.

He tapped his fingers on the desk, soothed by the low beat until a knock on the door interrupted him.

"Lord Selby, sir," his manservant said as he opened the door wider to allow his visitor to enter.

"Is it true?" Selby demanded as he strode into the room, his cloak swirling around him.

Clary leaned back in his chair and observed the other man. His thin face was flushed, his lips pursed tightly, but he was elegantly clothed and draped in glittering jewels. This was a man with wealth and one who knew how to flaunt it. It was a shame he didn't have the toned body to carry off his flamboyant choice of clothes.

"It depends on what you are referring to," Clary replied.

"The crystals, man. Have we lost them all?"

"Ah, yes, I believe so, for now."

Selby leaned on Clary's desk. "You don't seem very concerned. You know we need them for the main array. Everything is ready," Selby hissed, "except for the crystals. We can't wait another six months."

"We won't have to." Clary shrugged. "Guerlaire won't know what to do with that many crystals. We'll steal them back."

"This should never have happened." Selby sat and gripped the arms of his chair.

"True."

"How are we supposed to prepare if we don't have an array in place?"

"You'll have to send your men to the source; let them practise there." Clary smiled at the expression of distaste that crossed Selby's face. "I didn't say *you* had to go."

"I have no intention of visiting that hell hole ever again. It's a stinking pit of misery."

"Using slaves to mine is the only way we can get enough crystals fast enough."

"But I thought you said they followed you willingly."

"They did. But it costs a lot of money to clothe and feed that many people. Unless you want to pay for it, we will continue to operate the mines my way."

Selby scowled. "If you mistreat them now, they'll never follow you into battle."

Clary laughed. The man had no idea what he was talking about. "Don't worry about it, Selby. I have it all under control. I will retrieve your crystals, and you'll get to play." Clary leaned forward and picked up a stick with a round ball on the end. He tapped a small gong hanging from a wooden stand. At the sound of the resonant note, the door opened, and his manservant entered.

"Bring in the brandy and two glasses."

"Yes, m'lord."

Clary turned his attention back to his friend, who was now smiling more genially. The only reason Clary tolerated him, apart from his wealth, was the fact that Selby had discovered how to leverage the power of the crystals. He was training a small group of individuals who could help him identify and expand their abilities. One of them had managed to use the crystals to focus his energy to attack a ship in Elothia. Clary frowned. Until he had been repelled.

"How is Brindle doing? Has he recovered from the backlash?"

Selby scowled. "Far too slowly. We haven't figured out how to block a counterattack yet."

"I would have thought that would be a necessity," Clary murmured.

"Of course it is, but we have to be careful. We don't want to destroy the crystals unnecessarily. There are too few as it is."

Clary clamped down on the spurt of anger at the jibe. He needed Selby, even if he didn't like him. "Where are we with the resolutions? Are we ready to submit them to the Administration?"

The manservant returned with a tray, on which sat a decanter and glasses. In silence, he proceeded to pour the brandy. Selby smacked his lips and picked up a glass. He raised it in a toast. "Of course we are. To the next lord chancellor," he said and knocked the brandy back.

Clary raised his glass and took a sip. "Guerlaire is in Terolia. Get them submitted before he returns."

Selby paused. "In Terolia? Why?"

Clary held his gaze. "Choosing the place he wants to die. Be assured, he will not be returning from the deserts."

"Don't underestimate him," Selby said as he placed his glass back on the tray.

"Well," Clary replied, repressing his irritation, "if you think you can do better, have at him."

Pursing his lips for a moment, Selby grinned. "He would be excellent target practice." He nodded and stood. "Consider it done."

"Good. And when you've finished that, I'll have your array all primed and ready in Vespers."

Clary stared at the door for a long time after Selby left. Removing Guerlaire from the board would be a good start. The man was always interfering where he shouldn't, taking up valuable resources.

18

GUERLAIRE

TEROLIA

Guerlaire turned in his saddle and inspected his troop. He was pleasantly surprised by how well they were coping with the Terolian heat, all except Chryll, who drooped in his saddle. The big man was sweltering under the robes Guerlaire had forced him to wear.

"Don't you dare say it," Chryll snapped as he wiped the sweat off his face before it stung his eyes.

"I'm sorry. It shouldn't be so hot yet."

"It's not as if you control the weather, Guerlaire. Just get us to that river you keep telling me about."

"It's not long now," Guerlaire promised. They had made good time after the delays at the border. Stopping to reduce the load on that wagon had been the right thing to do. He had never expected to find such a large haul of crystals. No wonder the horses had been straining under all that additional weight.

He had left Lord Mayer trying to unravel who the wagon belonged to and sent the crystals on to Leyandrii to investigate. That they were being transported into Vespiri was concerning. What were they being used for? He had almost turned around and escorted them back himself, but that would have deterred him from his real mission: to find out more about these powerful men calling themselves Ascendants.

After leaving Ramila, they had spent the last few days heading east across the salt flats. Now having made good time, they were approaching the Kharma Pass. At least the flats were firm underfoot, not like the sifting sands further south.

On the other side of the Kharma Pass was one of the few rivers to be found in Terolia and an area of lush green growth and vegetation. The lands of Fuerte, where the Darian horses were bred.

If he could get Chryll there. Guerlaire handed Chryll his canteen. "Drink," he said.

"I can wait," Chryll replied, hunching his shoulders.

"Don't argue. Drink," Guerlaire ordered, shoving his canteen at Chryll. The large man was sweating too much. "I can refill it at the river. The pass is just ahead."

Chryll relented and took the canteen. He was raising it to his lips when the air suddenly became charged. He stiffened as a flash of light struck him, and he slowly fell out of the saddle.

"Chryll!" Guerlaire shouted as he leapt from his horse, and he ducked as a crack of sizzling energy struck the ground in front of him. He dived to the side, and his horse bolted as the other members of his troop drove their mounts forward to shield them.

"What is it?" Merill yelled as he held his horse in front of Guerlaire. He drew his sword and peered around.

"Ride for the pass!" Guerlaire ordered. "Find shelter."

"We're not leaving you exposed, Captain," Merill replied

as he swung his horse around, with the rest of the troop crowding close.

"No, spread out. Head for the pass. If we stay together, we're too big of a target." Guerlaire scrabbled over to Chryll. His friend was too still. He struggled to turn the man over, and suddenly, Merill was beside him, helping.

His heart racing, Guerlaire pressed his fingers against Chryll's neck. "He's not breathing!" He shouted. Then he ripped Chryll's robes open, ignoring the aroma of burnt skin, and pressed on his chest.

Merill bent over and breathed into Chryll's mouth as Guerlaire paused. Once Merill sat back up, Guerlaire started pumping Chryll's chest again.

"C'mon, Chryll, breathe for Lady's sake." Guerlaire muttered as he watched Merill. Calling on his magic, Guerlaire struggled to form a shield over them. It was threadbare at best, much weaker than the barrier he had formed in Elothia, but last time he had absorbed the wild magic swirling around him and used it. There was no wild magic available to bolster him now.

They continued in rotation for a few minutes until, at last, Chryll inhaled a gasping breath.

"Thank the Lady," Guerlaire said as he rested his head on Chryll's chest, tears stinging his eyes and relief turning his muscles to jelly.

"What was that, Captain?" Merill asked as they made Chryll more comfortable.

"I'm not sure. It's like an unnatural lightning strike, and someone seems to be able to control it."

Merill gasped. "You mean that was a deliberate attack?"

"Seems so."

"And they could attack again?" Merill peered up at the clear blue sky.

"I have a shield over us, but if you move too far away, they could attack you."

Chryll groaned, and Guerlaire hovered over him, offering the canteen. "How are you feeling?"

"Been better," Chryll replied, his voice low and breathy. Guerlaire raised his head and dribbled a little water into his mouth. There wasn't much left; most of it had spilt when Chryll had fallen.

"Well, stay still while we figure out what to do next."

"I'll just have a nap," Chryll said.

"You do that," Guerlaire agreed as he scanned the area. Their horses were long gone, as were the rest of his troop. He ran his hand through his hair.

"Can you call Leyandrii for help?" Chryll asked.

"I thought you were napping?"

"Too hot."

Guerlaire snorted, and Merill shook his head as he grinned.

"I could go and search for the horses," Merill suggested. "They won't have gone far."

Guerlaire didn't like it, but they didn't have much choice. "If the air gets sharp and smells extra clean, take cover."

Merill nodded, even though there was no cover in sight. After one last scan of the area, Merill darted off in the direction his horse had gone.

"So, is this the same people who attacked us on the river?" Chryll asked.

"I assume so," Guerlaire replied. "The strike is similar."

"Any way we can strike back?"

"You are not doing anything except resting. You nearly died."

"We can't stay here. There's no water, and we're exposed."

Chryll shifted and groaned as he held his chest. He took

a deeper breath. "How far away do you think they are? Here in Terolia or even further away? How do we combat that?"

"I have no idea." Guerlaire placed his hand on Chryll's arm. "Please, rest. Save your energy; you'll need it to get back on the horse."

"I'm surprised they haven't struck again."

At the tremor of fear in Chryll's voice, Guerlaire squeezed his arm. "They tried, but I have a shield up. We are safe for now."

"So, they know we're pinned down."

Guerlaire sighed. "You are not moving until Merill comes back."

"And if he doesn't?"

"He will."

Chryll fell silent and closed his eyes.

Guerlaire flinched as another strike skittered off his shield, and he hurried to reinforce it as it split. A shield was fine, but it was only defensive, and if they sent enough strikes it would collapse.

He needed to send a strike back. Leyandrii had explained the basics of how to deflect the strike back at his attacker, but they hadn't been able to practise it. He pondered for a moment, remembering how he had pushed back Leyandrii's mental strike. Could he do the same with his shield? Send the pulse of magical energy back to its wielder?

Sitting beside Chryll, he pushed his mind into his shield, feeling its smooth surface, the humming energy at its core. Shrinking the coverage to the area overhead, Guerlaire drew on his remaining energy and waited for the next strike. When it came, he tried to grab it, but it flashed away. His shield shuddered and energy crackled through his body. Hissing his breath out, he waited for the next attack.

When it struck, instead of grabbing at it, he drew it in, absorbing the magic and the sense of its wielder. He pushed his magic back along the path of the strike, following the disturbance in the air. He glimpsed a cave with red walls and four black-robed men grouped around a circle of tubular crystals. The crystals splintered under his pulse of magic. The men cried out as they flinched away from the shards, and the image blinked out.

Guerlaire exhaled and slowly released his shield.

"What did you do?" Chryll asked, his voice a faint whisper.

Guerlaire's lips tightened at the sight of Chryll's pale face. "How do you know I did anything?"

Chryll tried to chuckle, but his breath was more of a wheeze. "You crackled."

Guerlaire was saved from answering as Merill returned with two horses. "I couldn't find mine, but these still have your canteens," he said as he offered Guerlaire the water.

"We need to leave," Guerlaire said as he took a gulp of the tepid liquid. "We'll have to take turns to ride."

Merill nodded. "Are you able to keep the shield over us while we travel?"

"No need. I've dealt with it." Guerlaire rose. "Chryll, do you think you can ride?"

"Do I have a choice?" Chryll asked as he took Guerlaire's hand and sat up. He held his ribs. "I feel like I've got a pile of bricks sitting on my chest."

"Well, you can relax in a cool river soon enough."

"That no longer sounds as enticing as it once did," Chryll replied, accepting both Guerlaire and Merill's help to regain his feet. He swayed, wheezing out his breath. "Thanks." He stared at his horse as if it were an insurmountable mountain waiting to be climbed.

It took both of them to get Chryll in the saddle, and afterwards both Guerlaire and Merill leaned against the horse, gasping for breath at the effort.

Sweat streamed down Guerlaire's back, and he adjusted his robes, trying to waft a bit of air against his skin. "Let's get to the pass and a bit of shade. It can't be far."

They had only been travelling a chime when they were met by two of his troops with news that they had found a Solari horse trader who had a healer in his wagon train. Guerlaire exhaled in relief and followed his men into the shaded pass.

The Solari were wonderful hosts, offering good food and music to while the evening away, and even though Guerlaire tried to refuse, they topped up their supplies as well. Offering heartfelt thanks for all their help. Guerlaire passed on warnings about *Mentiserium* and how to combat it. The Solari laughed and reassured him that the Lady was close to their hearts and would protect them, but they would be on the alert. They said the warning was payment enough for their help.

Guerlaire shook his head but accepted the trade. Once the wagon train moved on, Guerlaire relocated his troop to a camp by the river. He joined Chryll, who was sitting in the shallows. The water was crystal clear, running through worn sandstone rock and merrily flowing onwards. Lush green reeds and plants lined the banks before giving way to clumps of spiky grass.

"Feeling cooler?" He sat beside Chryll and sighed as the cool water crept up his body, soaking his clothes.

"Not by much."

"Do you feel up to moving on tomorrow?" Chryll was still sluggish, though his breathing had improved. "We'll follow the river south until we reach Koav and then head for home."

Chryll glanced at him. "Don't change your plans because of me."

"I'm not. Two months is long enough to be away from Vespers, and I want to find out where those crystals were going. Now that we know what they are using them for, it is even more imperative that we find the source and stop them."

"Good point. We can't afford for those people to be able to attack us like that in Vespers. You're the only one that has any defence."

"I need to speak to Leyandrii about that. There must be more people who can create shields."

Chryll frowned in thought as he swished the water against his body. "Maybe it's like those Ascendants. It's only possible if we have crystals to enhance whatever inner power we have?"

"That is an interesting thought and one only Leyandrii can answer. Remember to ask her."

"How did they find us? Do you think they were deliberately targeting you?"

Guerlaire exhaled and scooped up a handful of water to rinse his face. "Seems to be too much of a coincidence, doesn't it?"

"That's what I thought."

"Glad to see your brain is still working."

Chryll splashed him.

"So, if they are targeting me, I must be causing them some problems."

"I'd think confiscating ten sacks of crystals might upset them, and before that, you were the only one to be concerned about the effects of *Mentiserium*."

"That was Leyandrii."

"Pssht, you or Leyandrii, there's no difference."

"I can assure you that there is a very big difference."

Chryll laughed. "You know what I mean. Your intentions are the same."

"We're aligned," Guerlaire said.

"That's what I said."

Guerlaire shook his head. There was a subtle difference, but he wasn't going to argue the point.

19

LEYANDRII

LADY'S PALACE, VESPERS

Leyandrii stared out the window as she waited for Minister Jarvaine to arrive. Her assistant, Reba, had primed her with all the Administration's recent decisions, and she had been growing more and more concerned as she reviewed them.

Few of these new laws had passed her desk for ratification. In fact, she hadn't even seen any drafts or discussion documents. She had piled the questionable decisions to one side and tapped her finger on the top paper as she watched the grey clouds accumulate on the horizon. It was as if someone had drawn a line across the sky. Below was pale yellow sunshine; above hung thick, brooding clouds promising heavy rain.

A tap on the door drew her attention back inside her office, and she smiled as Minister Jarvaine entered. She remembered the day he had been initiated: a young, intelligent man eager to help Vespiri grow. When had he become so jaded and worn? His hair was grey and receding, his blue eyes pale and watery. His shoulders slumped forward, making him look older than he was.

"Minister, please be seated. It was good of you to come."

"Of course, my Lady. It's my honour to represent the other members."

"How long has it been now? You've been leading the Administration for over ten years now, haven't you?"

"Indeed, my Lady. Thirty years in total."

"And are you still enjoying it? I remember how eager you were the day you started working for my government."

Jarvaine smiled fondly. "It was a very special day."

"And you are thinking of retiring now?"

Jarvaine jerked upright in his seat. "No! Why ever would you think that?"

"Well." Leyandrii frowned. "This proposal to elevate Dominant Clary to your position. I would have thought you would have advised me of your intentions to retire before suggesting a replacement."

"Clary is not replacing me."

"Oh?" Leyandrii held up the top paper on the pile before her. "But this draft legislation promotes Clary to leader of the Administration. There cannot be two people in that position."

Jarvaine frowned. "No, it doesn't."

"I can assure you it does." Leyandrii handed it over.

Jarvaine removed a small pair of eyeglasses from his pocket, balanced them on his nose, and peered at the paper. He muttered under his breath. "This isn't right. Who signed it off?" He flipped the paper over and spluttered when he saw his own signature. "I never signed this," he said, raising his head to glare at Leyandrii.

"That is your signature, though, isn't it?"

"Yes, it looks like it, but I did not sign this. Why would I agree to give someone else my job?"

"I thought it was strange," Leyandrii agreed. "So, you

are not prepared to step down in favour of Dominant Clary?"

"No, I am not. It is well known that my successor would be Montserie. He has been my deputy minister these last three years, and he is well able to step up should the need arise. Clary hasn't been in the Administration long enough to know how to get things done. He is a junior minister at most."

Leyandrii raised an eyebrow. "I would have said he's understood the procedures very well." She handed him another document. "He's given himself a raise."

Jarvaine's jaw dropped as he read the paper. "That is preposterous."

"I am glad you think so, because I am not prepared to approve it."

"What else has he submitted?" Jarvaine asked, his expression grim.

"He wants to create some new positions for his supporters." Leyandrii handed him the documents.

By the time Jarvaine had finished reading them, his eyes were glinting with anger. "I see. My apologies, my Lady, if it seems I am no longer fit for my job, but I assure you, none of these documents have been ratified by the Administration, and I would have presented them to you if they had gained support."

"I thought as much. I am happy for you to clean house." Leyandrii paused. "As long as you do it thoroughly. Revoke all of these unsubstantiated rulings, remind your peers of the procedures, and ensure the correct process is followed. All legislation from now on will need to be ratified by me prior to being implemented. I expect Clary and his followers' seats in the Administration to be revoked. He is not to be trusted with the lives of my people."

Jarvaine winced. "I cannot revoke his title. That is a lifelong accreditation. But I will see to it that he is not in a position to speak for the Administration, my Lady."

"Should it be a lifelong title? It isn't hereditary, is it?"

"All titles are lifelong. Usually, the final title you achieve before retiring is the title you retain. A reward for service to the Administration. But they aren't hereditary, my Lady."

"If it is a lifelong honour, then I expect you to tighten up the rules for entry into the Administration. Clary managed to usurp our procedures much too easily for my liking. The purpose of the Administration is to ensure Vespiri runs smoothly for the benefit of all, not for the benefit of the few."

"I assure you, my Lady, the purpose of our Administration aligns with your understanding."

Leyandrii nodded. "Good." She tapped her finger against her lip. This was an opportunity to strengthen her bonds with her representatives. "Maybe it is time to remind the dominants and administrators of their allegiance to Vespiri. What say you to a ceremony of re-dedication? It's time to appreciate all the work you do."

Jarvaine nodded. "That would be well received, I think. It would be good to remind everyone of what we have achieved over the last few years. Much of it goes unnoticed, but we are dedicated to improving life in Vespers and the outer regions."

"I am happy to host the event at the palace. Allocate one of your people to work with my assistant, Reba. She will make the arrangements and send invitations and such."

"Thank you, my Lady."

"I am glad we are in agreement. Let us reconvene in a few weeks to check progress and finalise the details," she said as she held out her hand and drew the meeting to a close.

GUERLAIRE
VESPERS, VESPIRI

J ulu had arrived by the time Guerlaire returned from his sortie into Terolia. He rode into Vespers and inspected the temple as he passed. The white stone gleamed through the trees and bushes, a beacon calling to all. He was glad to be back in the city. The heat of Terolia still warmed his bones, even after the long journey through Vespiri, but the knowledge that the Ascendants were so active burned through any satisfaction he had from being home.

Leyandrii would not be amused. The Ascendants had more influence than any of them had ever dreamed possible. He was glad he had taken the time to travel into the deserts. Feet on the ground was always the best way to discover the realities of a situation.

He inspected Chryll. His companion had suffered much. The heat had slowed his recovery from the Ascendant attack, and the long journey home had drained him. He would be on leave for at least the next month. Longer, if needed.

At least there had been no further attacks. Guerlaire must have damaged that cell enough to put them out of action, for which he had never been more thankful. He needed to work with Leyandrii to find the best way to fight against such power.

Fortunately, Chryll hadn't had to take the brunt of Guerlaire's excess energy, not that he had been in any shape to spar. Guerlaire's sword had siphoned off the swirling power, much as Leyandrii had suggested, and for the first time, he felt in more control after a long trip.

Sometimes, he wished there were speedier ways of travel, like an arifel, able to move from one place to another with a thought. Maybe he would ask Leyandrii if that was a possibility. It would be a great help and an advantage they could use in the future.

What he had seen in the deserts did not bode well. During their journey home, he had visited remote villages and spoken to patrols, yet he had felt the dissonance in the towns, a contradiction to the platitudes of the nomadic tribes.

The townspeople were being swayed by a different doctrine, and without any other rhetoric to rebut it, they were being persuaded against their better judgment. Nothing he'd said had countered their opinions, and he had resorted to skimming their minds and plucking out any persuasions he had found.

He couldn't shield their minds for them, but he did encourage them to call on the Lady for protection if needed.

Leyandrii was losing ground without even being aware she was in a battle, and he was sure this phenomenon was not restricted to Terolia. He needed to speak to Asher.

Approaching the Rangers Garrison, he rode around to the courtyard and slid out of the saddle. A plume of dust rose as he patted down his clothes. "I'll be leaving in about half a chime. Keep him ready," Guerlaire said as he handed over the reins.

"Yes, sir," the stable lad said as he led his horse away.

Guerlaire escorted Chryll to the healerie and explained what had happened, even though Chryll insisted he was fine and that he just needed a nice, hot bath. The man had been talking about it all the way down the East Road.

Guerlaire hid his grin as the healer took over and led Chryll into the treatment room. The much-longed for bath might be delayed, but Guerlaire was sure he'd get one in the end.

Leaving the healerie, he veered down the corridor which led to Commander Asher's office.

Actually, he wouldn't mind a hot bath, either, but first, he needed to speak to Asher, even though Leyandrii was impatiently waiting for him. He didn't *have* to report to Asher—he no longer reported to the Rangers, being the commander of the Lady's Guards—but it made sense to act as if he did until it was no longer necessary. A little courtesy cost him nothing, and it also gave him free access to the garrison and its resources, which was not to be taken lightly.

Asher's aide waved him in, and Guerlaire entered Asher's office, raising his eyebrows as the man himself rose from behind his desk and exclaimed, "At last!"

"I haven't been gone that long," Guerlaire said as he crossed the room.

Asher grimaced. "It is noticeable when you're not here. I don't know what it is, but you seem to repress the wilder notions of both the Administration and the rangers."

"I can assure you that is nothing to do with me."

"You underestimate your reputation."

Guerlaire shrugged and sat in the chair opposite Asher. "I am not invincible, as everyone keeps telling me."

"No, but you have a presence that is unmistakable, and people are more wary when you are around."

"Enough flattery! What do you want?"

"For you to stay in Vespers. We need you here, not traipsing around the world."

Guerlaire straightened. "I have an agreement with the Chapterhouse to bring back samples from Birtoli."

"Send someone else. Leyandrii needs you here."

"That is below the belt."

"Doesn't make it wrong."

"What's happened?"

"Dominant Clary is trying to get himself promoted to the leader of the Administration. He is proposing he becomes the chancellor of all Vespiri."

"How did he get that through?"

"We don't know. He caught us unawares. Fortunately, Leyandrii stopped it. There wasn't even a rumour of such a proposal."

Guerlaire scowled. "Do you think the Administration were tampered with?"

"Leyandrii says not. She said it's just old men wanting more power for themselves. They are trying to build their own power base."

"If this were in isolation, maybe I would agree, but combined with the rise of the Ascendant rhetoric and the cornering of the crystal market, I would say there is more going on." Guerlaire twisted his lips. "The Ascendants are rampant in the towns of Terolia. They are persuading everyone that they are the future, yet the only thing they are offering is slavery. No one sees past the words to their actions. They are too busy accepting their lies."

"What do you suggest?"

Guerlaire leaned forward, resting his arms on his knees. He looked at the floor for a moment and then raised his head to meet Asher's eyes. "I think we need to send more rangers out into the territories. Let them be seen, disrupt the Ascendants' rhetoric, prevent them from using *Mentiserium*.

Show that Leyandrii is watching over her people. The rangers have all been taught to shield. We can teach them how to identify and remove persuasions. The people of Remargaren need to make their own decisions, not those forced on them. If we don't act, we will be betraying everything Leyandrii stands for."

Asher nodded, his brow creasing as he considered. Guerlaire observed him, clamping his lips tightly as he noted the new lines on his skin and the thinning of his grey hair. Asher wasn't old, but he was showing signs of ageing.

"Are you well, old friend?"

Asher jerked up in surprise. "Of course. Perfectly well."

Guerlaire exhaled in relief. Now was not the time for the leadership of the Lady's Rangers to be in question. Leyandrii needed his support. "Good. I—" He was interrupted as a small black and white Arifel popped into view and chattered at him.

Asher chuckled. "Someone is getting impatient."

"Calm down. Tell her I'm on my way." Guerlaire extended his hand, offering the arifel a perch, but it fluttered its wings, scolded him again, and disappeared.

"I'd better go. I'll be in touch after I've spoken to Leyandrii."

"I'll expect you at eleventh chime tomorrow," Asher said.

Guerlaire nodded. "Very well." And before he could say another word, he disappeared.

Asher shook his head as he stared at the empty chair. Sometimes he wondered how anyone could oppose a goddess, but he supposed there was always someone who would try.

Guerlaire stumbled as he appeared in Leyandrii's study. He turned in a circle and frowned. "Why did you do that?"

"You were taking too long," Leyandrii said as she approached him. Reaching up on her tiptoes, she cupped his cheeks and kissed him on the lips. "Oren would have kept you all day."

"I wasn't even there half a chime."

"It was still too long. I haven't seen you in over a month."

Guerlaire kissed her back, sliding his palms around her waist. She was being kind; it was nearer two months. The deserts were large, the towns remote. Travelling took forever. "I'd be home sooner," he said against her lips, "if you could transport me around like you just did. We need a faster way of travelling."

"I can if I know where you are. That's why I sent the arifel. I could locate you through him."

Guerlaire deepened the kiss, preventing her from speaking. She tasted so fresh, and the aroma of roses filled the air. He felt road-worn and grubby beside her.

"I need a bath," he said.

"You always need a bath," Leyandrii replied. "I drew one for you." She tugged him out of the study and down the corridor to her personal chambers. The scent of roses increased, along with a humid mist, which thickened as they entered the bathing room.

Guerlaire inhaled, and the arid remnants of the deserts faded away, leaving his mind clear. He hurried out of his clothes, pausing only to lean his sword against the wall, and climbed into the bath.

Heat enveloped him, like a soft embrace, relaxing tired muscles and stiff joints. Gentle hands soaped his chest, and he realised he had closed his eyes as he sank into the water. He opened them again and smiled at the expression of concentration on Leyandrii's face.

The Goddess of all Remargaren was washing him. Him! A nobody from the city of Vespers. Strong fingers massaged his skin as if determined to remove every grain of sand that might still cling to him.

She ran her hands down his arms, and he lay there, luxuriating in her attention. She washed under his arms and between his fingers, and it tickled. She chuckled as he wriggled away and leaned over to kiss his chest, butterfly kisses that fluttered up to his throat, and he breathed in her floral scent as her hair tickled his nose.

Heat pooled in his groin as her hands worked their magic, and he shifted in the water as need replaced the desire to be clean.

"Ah, ah," Leyandrii murmured. "I haven't finished." She lifted his leg and ran soapy hands down his skin, between his toes, and back up his calf, up the inside of his thigh, avoiding the very place he needed her to touch. He groaned when her fingers caressed sensitised skin, before sliding back down his leg, and then she concentrated on his toes.

"Torturer," he said, gripping the side of the bath tub to stop himself from reaching for her.

She cast him a wicked smile. "This is what you get when you are away for too long. I have to reacquaint myself with every part of you."

"Every part?"

"Every single part."

"You missed a bit."

"I was saving the best for last."

"It's feeling left out."

"Well, we can't have that, can we?" Leyandrii lifted the abandoned part, and he hardened even more as the cooler air caressed his heated skin, and then she kissed the tip. "See," she murmured. "Leaving it to last encourages it to grow."

Guerlaire choked on a laugh as she peeked at him from under her long lashes. His hips bucked upwards, no matter how he tried to resist. His knuckles turned white at the strength of his grip on the tub as he watched the woman he loved bring him to the very edge. "You need to stop." He forced the words out.

Leyandrii smiled at him as she leaned up to kiss him, her hair trailing in the water. "Get out, then."

Guerlaire wasn't sure his legs would hold him, but he did manage to rise and step over the side of the bath and into the soft towel Leyandrii offered him. Drying off the worst, he dropped the towel and grabbed Leyandrii before she could lead the way out of the chamber.

Her kiss consumed his every thought as he offered her all that he was, and he groaned as her clever hands found his buttocks. He needed to remove her clothes, and fast, or he was going to disgrace himself in the bathing room.

Leyandrii must have helped because, suddenly, silky-smooth skin slid against his, and he was lost. Everywhere they touched, magic sparked. His power crackled under his skin, rising to the surface, where she continued to caress whichever part she could reach.

"You really mustn't stay away for so long."

"Never again."

"You promise?"

"I promise."

His reward blew his mind.

Lying in bed with Leyandrii snuggled into his side was the most perfect place to ever be. Guerlaire was floating in ecstasy, sated and relaxed, on the verge of sleep, but not wanting to let go of the moment.

Leyandrii's breath puffed against his skin in the gentlest of caresses, delicate and soft, and yet the sensation zinged through his veins, teasing the power simmering in his body, completing him. Magic swirled between them, twining with Leyandrii's love for him and entangling him deeper, entrenching his love for her where no one could touch it.

He was hers, and she was his, and no one would ever part them. He wove that vow deep inside himself, entwined in the strands of his being, knotted it tightly, and let it swirl back into Leyandrii. Her fingers tightened on his, and he knew she had accepted it.

They would be together forever, and he would protect her with his dying breath if need be. Not that he intended to die, but he *would* protect her. He would be the thorn that the Ascendants couldn't remove, and he would begin rooting them out here in Vespers.

Leyandrii muttered under her breath, and he relaxed, his breathing deepening as Leyandrii wrapped herself around him.

When Guerlaire woke, sunlight framed the edges of the curtains. He had slept later than he had intended, and he knew the reason why when he tried to stretch. Leyandrii lay half over him, one leg tangled between his, her arms tucked around him, keeping him prisoner. Her golden hair was splayed across his chest, the silky strands falling around his ribs like bindings.

He smiled. She couldn't have made her claim any more obvious—not that she needed to claim what was already hers.

He bent his head to kiss her shoulder, and she tightened her grip around him.

"Love, we need to get up."

"Not yet." Her voice was a warm caress in his mind as she slid her knee up between his legs, and he huffed out his breath. She was wicked.

He rolled her over, leaning on his forearms so he could cage her. He concentrated. *"Did I just hear your voice in my mind?"*

Leyandrii froze and opened her eyes. *"Oh!"* She smiled in delight. *"I can hear you, too."*

"What does this mean? Will it last?"

"Of course. Last night, we committed ourselves to each other. I think our magic knew what was in our hearts and took it as meaning much more. I think, my love, we are stuck with each other."

"Good. I wouldn't have it any other way." He kissed her, deep and heartfelt, and then he raised his head and grinned. Speaking out loud, he said, "But I do still need to go and speak with Asher. Make plans to deal with these Ascendants."

"Only if I can go with you."

Guerlaire smiled, recognising her need to be near him. He *had* stayed away too long. "Always, beloved."

Leyandrii stretched beneath him, her warm skin sliding against his, and then her bright emerald-green eyes snared him. "We have much to discuss."

"Asher mentioned some of it, and I have much to tell you."

Guerlaire shifted when she tapped his arm, releasing them to rise, wash, and dress.

21

LEYANDRII

ASHER'S OFFICE, VESPERS

Leyandrii and Guerlaire arrived in Oren Asher's office just on eleventh chime, their fingers entwined, their eyes bright, and with a swirl of magic sparkling around them as they appeared.

Asher stared at them. "Did you two get joined?"

"We've always been joined," Leyandrii replied with a grin. She sat while Guerlaire held the chair for her, and she entwined her fingers with his again as he sat beside her.

"You look …" Asher twirled his fingers as he searched for the word. "Exultant."

"We are," Guerlaire said with a grin.

"I don't want to spoil your happiness, but we have some serious topics to discuss."

"We know; that's why we're here," Leyandrii said. "I should have dealt with Clary before now, but I didn't want to be seen as too heavy-handed, and now he has the protection of the Administration."

"The Administration acts in your name, my Lady." Asher frowned at her. "You should approve all appointments. Can you not question the validity of his claim?"

Leyandrii wrinkled her nose as she thought. "I have. Jarvaine is revoking the proposal, but Clary's seat in the Administration is apparently lifelong. Another rule I have Jarvaine investigating."

Asher exhaled. "That's good."

"I thought it might be time to devolve power to the watches, as they do the work anyway. Keep the Administration accountable."

"Oh, yes!" Guerlaire grinned. "That would be perfect."

"That is actually a very good idea, my Lady. You should consider it," Asher said.

"I will, but for now, a reminder of who is in charge might not go amiss."

"We need a visible reminder of who you are," Guerlaire said. "And I know exactly what we need."

"And what is that?" Leyandrii asked.

"It will be a nice surprise. I've been working on it for a while, but I think maybe now is the time to finish it."

"I'm not sure I like surprises," Leyandrii said.

"You'll love this one," Guerlaire replied, his eyes twinkling.

Leyandrii groaned. "Do not embarrass me."

"As if." Guerlaire glared at her. "This is to remind them how amazing and powerful you are. It will in no way embarrass you."

"It better not," Leyandrii muttered.

Asher steepled his fingers and waited for them to stop bickering. Leyandrii laughed when she saw his severe expression. "Sorry, Oren. Guerlaire, tell us what you found in Terolia."

All laughter vanished as Guerlaire reported on the spread of *Mentiserium,* the rise of the Ascendants and their persuasive speeches, and their ability to target attacks, even if it was limited by the use of crystals.

Asher nodded. "That explains why they've tried to retrieve the crystals you confiscated. They need them to use their magical powers."

Leyandrii frowned. "That is not how they should be using their magic. That is twisting the natural flow."

"We need a way to defend against it," Guerlaire said. "We need to train more people to create shields."

Leyandrii shook her head. "No, no. That just twists the magic's purpose even more. If the ability isn't inherent, then it shouldn't be possible. Creating physical shields is very rare."

"Leyandrii's right. My shields were a lot weaker in Terolia, because I didn't have any wild magic to bolster me. I struggled just to protect Chryll and I."

"It is a rare skill and uses up an enormous amount of magic. It is difficult to sustain a shield for a long time." Leyandrii stared at Guerlaire. "Dear heart, you'll have to destroy any crystals they have. It's the only way to defend against them."

"And how am I supposed to find them?" Guerlaire asked.

"I don't know. We'll have to work on it. There must be some sign, some resonance of building magic that I would be able to sense." Leyandrii rubbed her temples. "They are not natural. They are an abomination being used for terrible purposes. The Land must recognise such a weight. There has to be a way I can find them."

"Then we should destroy the crystals we have in storage," Asher said.

"Yes, I will help you with that," Leyandrii said.

"Actually," Guerlaire said with a grin, "I might have a use for them."

"I'll be glad to get rid of them," Asher said. "Did you find out why they want slaves and where they are taking these people?"

Guerlaire shook his head. "We disbanded any meetings we came across so they didn't have a chance to take anyone. But the Families need to be more vigilant. They need to protect their own people." Guerlaire paused and met Leyandrii's gaze. "I thought maybe you could call a conclave and explain the situation to the Mederas."

"Conclaves are rare," Leyandrii replied. "They also take time to arrange. Getting all six Mederas in one place is no mean feat."

"We cannot scale to cover the deserts; the Mederas need to be informed," Asher said.

"Very well. I will begin the process. But I warn you, it will take months to track each family down, let alone get an agreement on the place to meet." Leyandrii thought it would be nigh on impossible, but she would try. "Is that enough for today? I seem to be the only one gaining all the work."

Asher smiled. "But you are the one most suited to the tasks. I have begun working on extra ranger assignments. We will be running a bit thin in the garrison and may need to bump up some of the second-year cadets. We have some smart youngsters coming through that we can utilise. The sooner they get experience, the more effective they will be."

"And use the first-years," Guerlaire suggested. "Give them more on-the-job training. They can learn by shadowing."

Oren nodded thoughtfully. "Yes, that is feasible. I'll look at the plans for next year."

Leyandrii was glad when the meeting ended and she could whisk them back to the palace, though her plans for a rest were curtailed when her assistant, Reba, placed a pile of reports on her desk.

"My Lady, these are now overdue, and you have to read them today." The poor woman was flushed in the face, her dark brown hair escaping the usually neat bun.

Guerlaire blew Leyandrii a kiss and disappeared down the corridor, no doubt to work on her surprise. She shuddered at the thought of what mayhem he could find creating her gift.

"Whatever has happened?" she asked as she made herself comfortable.

"I'm so sorry, my lady, but the courier only just arrived. He was delayed by bad weather, and these missives need a reply. He has been waiting all morning, and he is quite agitated."

"Well, tell him to calm down. He will have his letters soon." Shaking her head, Leyandrii cracked the seal on the first request and absently accepted the mug of kafinee Reba handed her.

22

BIRLER

RANGERS ACADEMY, SUMMER 1121

Spring had turned into summer, and Birler mused over the fact that his first year at the academy was almost over. He had settled into the routine and found he enjoyed it. A sense of purpose and contentment filled him as he soaked up whatever the academy was prepared to teach him.

He even enjoyed the drills, sparring, and, especially, Apeiron.

Returning to the barracks after drills one evening, he found an angry mob of boys waiting for him. He glanced around the room, but Tagerill and Serill were nowhere in sight.

Tyrler stepped forward with a smirk on his face. "I have tried to tell you the nice way, but you do not have the intelligence to understand me, so this is a message you can't ignore. We—he gestured at the grinning boys behind him—"are here to make sure that you"—Tyrler poked Birler in the chest—"understand what we mean. If you want to live, you should go back to whatever slum you came from. You are not welcome here."

"I have every right to be here," Birler replied, backing towards the door.

A hard shove in his back sent him stumbling forward, and Tyrler swung at him. Birler jinked back, and the blow passed by harmlessly. Tyrler swore, flushing bright red. Hands grabbed for Birler, and he twisted out of his jacket.

"There's nowhere for you to go. You should leave while you still can." Tyrler paced him. "No one's coming to help you."

"I'm not leaving." Birler glanced around the room—still no sign of Tagerill. He should have been right behind him with Serill. He caught sight of Parsill braced against the wall by two boys, an arm across his throat, a black eye blooming.

Tyrler laughed. "He'd be here, wouldn't he? If he thought anything of you. You are nothing. A Descelles wouldn't waste his breath on you. Leave, you loser, or we'll make you. We don't need the likes of you here. Leave, or we'll make sure Serill regrets it, too."

Birler stared at him. "You have no idea what you are dealing with," he said.

"I know exactly what I'm dealing with," Tyrler said as he flicked his knife out and swiped it at Birler. Birler jumped back, but not before the blade sliced his shirt and skin. He watched the red bloom that spread across the material, though he hadn't felt it cut.

He inhaled and steadied, moving into the steps for *Acceptance*. Whatever happened here, he would trust in the Lady. She was all he had. Exhaling, he faced six boys who wouldn't give him a chance. He blocked the first strike, and a knife bit his skin as he spun. His blood splattered across the wall as he focussed on his target, ignoring the sting. He punched one of the cadets in the face, but left himself open, and a burn ran across his ribs, followed by another, and then he was overwhelmed by sheer numbers.

Tagerill erupted into the barracks. He cast about, searching. "What did you do?" he demanded, seeing bruised faces, swollen knuckles, and smears of blood on the floor. His stomach sank. "Where is he?"

"Where's who?" Tyrler asked a little breathlessly as he stepped forward.

Serill skidded in behind Tagerill. "He'd better be alright, or you won't live to regret it," Serill snarled. Tyrler blanched at the expression on his face, and he took a step behind the other boys as Serill advanced.

"And whatever is left of you, I will destroy," Tagerill said, his calmness all the more terrifying.

"He left," Tyrler said.

"To go where?"

Tyrler sneered. "Back where he came from."

"And where might that be?" Tagerill asked, holding himself rigid.

"The slums, of course. You told us that."

Serill struck, and Tyrler yelled as blood gushed from his nose. Tagerill grabbed Serill's arm. "Go get Asher."

Serill hesitated and then ran.

"I'll have you both expelled," Tyrler mumbled, trying to staunch the blood.

"You'd better hope you live to try," Tagerill threatened. "What did you do?"

Tyrler cowered away, and Tagerill glared at the other boys.

Parsill shakily rose from one of the beds. "He beat him up with his bully boys."

"Say another word, Parsill, and I'll have your father gutted," Tyrler threatened.

"I'd like to see you try," Parsill replied. "You disgust me, all of you. You shouldn't be allowed to wear the uniform."

"Where is he?" Tagerill asked, taking a step towards the door.

Parsill shrugged and winced, holding his side. "I got him out of the barracks. After that, I don't know where he went. I was trying to hold this lot back so he could get away."

Tagerill cursed as he headed for the door.

"Tagerill." Parsill held his eyes. "He was hurt bad," he said. "He won't have got far."

Tagerill ran down the path towards the academy gates. How far was not far? He somehow thought it would be farther than the academy. Where would Birler go? He suddenly realised how little Birler had ever said about himself or where he came from. The all-encompassing harbour had been all he had said, and they had never pressed him, afraid of what he might reveal. He was always there but often silent, and when he did speak, it was to utter a pithy comment that made them stop and think.

Tagerill's throat tightened at what his friend must be going through. They had failed to protect him. They hadn't realised he needed protecting from their own. *Lady help us,* he prayed. *Help us find him in time.*

Serill caught him as he was trying to undo the gates. "Tagerill, Asher isn't here. I couldn't find him. I left a message with his writer." He stared at Tagerill, his face pale, his eyes wide. "I told Healer Demeren that Birler had been injured and we were trying to find him." He swallowed. "He gave me a field kit," he said, holding a sack up, "and a crystal." He brandished a clear communications crystal in his other hand.

Tagerill finally got the gate open. "Where would he go, Serill? If you were hurting, lost, afraid, where would you go?"

Serill paled. "Home," he whispered.

"But where is home? Where would he go?" Tagerill cast about hopelessly, almost in tears.

"The harbour, the sea. It's the only place he talked about," Serill said, his voice firming. Tagerill took off, with Serill on his heels.

They searched the harbour, the docks, the back alleys, and even the stinking streets with widening eyes and a growing horror. They ended up staring at the sea and breathing in the clean, salty air to clear the stench. Looking at each other, they shuddered as they realised how lucky they were.

"You can't live on those streets," Tagerill said, appalled.

"He wasn't living," Serill said slowly. "He was dying."

"But how did he end up at the academy, then?" Tagerill frowned, perplexed, watching the surf foam and reach, spread over the sand and recede.

"The Lady," Serill breathed. "He said the Lady told him where to go."

Tagerill turned away from the sea. "The temple," he said, his voice ringing with conviction. "He wanted to go to the temple on pass day, but he couldn't because he didn't have permission."

They turned together and ran up the long hill back into the city. They didn't stop until they reached the temple gardens. They paused briefly at the gate to catch their breath, their sides heaving, but they were soon rushing up to the open temple door. They burst in and halted, looking around in desperation. It appeared empty and silent.

"Look." Serill pointed at the floor. A trail of blood led them to the altar, and round the back, they found him huddled on the steps at the feet of the Lady, a bundle of blood-soaked rags, one arm reaching towards her. Only the Lady knew how he had got this far.

Tagerill knelt and carefully rolled Birler over into his

arms. His breath hissed out in shock, and his stomach quailed at all the blood. Birler was unrecognisable; his skin was pale where it wasn't bruised, and his eyes were swollen shut. He was far too still. Tagerill tried to find a pulse, and he shivered at the icy touch of Birler's skin.

Serill tugged at Birler's bloody shirt. Opening the field kit, he found a pad and pressed it hard against the slashes across Birler's chest. He reached for another pad for Birler's ribs.

"He's too cold," Tagerill said, his voice empty.

Serill gripped the communication crystal in his bloody hand. It shook as he called Healer Demeren, and he nearly burst into tears as Captain Guerlaire rushed into the temple with a healer at his back.

Guerlaire and the healer took over, with Guerlaire cradling Birler, much as Tagerill had tried to do. The healer piled blankets over them and then instructed Tagerill and Serill to sit on either side of Guerlaire and trap the heat as he worked.

Birler finally stirred. "I'm here," he whispered, his voice faint, but they all stiffened as the temple around them shimmered in response.

"He's alive," Guerlaire said, and the temple steadied. He smiled wryly at the cadets. "Leyandrii worries," was all he said, and they stared at him wide-eyed.

The healer leaned back. "Will the Lady let us move him?" he asked, glancing around the temple.

Tagerill held his breath as Guerlaire considered and then flicked a concerned glance at the altar; the temple was not really steady—it still shimmered—and Tagerill half-expected the Lady to appear.

Guerlaire's face firmed as he made his decision. "Whatever is best for the boy."

The healer looked at him. "We need to get him to

Demeren. I've done all I can here."

Guerlaire nodded. "What do you suggest?"

"If you are careful, you could carry him. Otherwise, we need to wait for a stretcher."

"How careful?"

"I've got the wounds padded, but they need stitching. If you can keep him as still as possible, they should hold."

"I will transport him," Leyandrii said from behind them. Her eyes glittered, but her expression was determined. "I should have come as soon as you found him."

"Leyandrii, I've got him," Guerlaire said. "You know it's better not to draw attention to him."

"He can't die. I'll transport both of you." She glanced at Tagerill and Serill. "All of you."

The temple shimmered and was replaced by the treatment room in the academy healerie.

Tagerill and Serill clutched each other and stared at the Lady with wide eyes, and she gave them a smile and gestured to the door. "Wait for us in the outer room. You can keep Parsill company. We won't be long."

They left without argument.

Healer Demeren helped Guerlaire lay his burden down before shooing him out. Leyandrii placed her hand on Birler's forehead as the healer went to work.

Guerlaire left the room and joined the cadets hovering over a blond-haired boy propped up in one of the beds. Guerlaire inspected him. The boy's face was pale, and his bare chest was wrapped in bandages. He moved carefully—broken ribs by the look of it. Birler would have good company while he recuperated, at least.

"This is Parsill Ferrantes of Stoneford. He tried to defend Birler," Serill said from the other side of the bed.

"Who did this?" Guerlaire asked.

Parsill gulped and told him the truth. "Tyrler Clary and his friends."

"I see."

"What else has been happening at the academy?" Guerlaire asked and kept the cadets talking until Leyandrii joined them. They exchanged glances, and Leyandrii gave him a slight nod. Guerlaire exhaled.

"Birler is sleeping now," Leyandrii said as she approached the bed and cast a reassuring smile at all of them. "He is in good hands and will recover, though he'll be keeping Parsill company here in the healerie until the end of term." She leaned over Parsill and caressed his cheek. Parsill's eyelashes fluttered. "Sleep, Parsill. You'll feel much better when you wake. Thank you for assisting Birler."

Once Parsill slept, Guerlaire escorted Leyandrii towards Commander Asher's office.

As Tagerill and Serill hesitantly followed, the reality of the situation hit them. "This is my fault," Serill moaned, his body starting to shake.

Tagerill wrapped an arm around him. "Don't be an idiot. Of course it isn't."

"If I hadn't blamed Birler when I was expelled, they would never have gone for him."

Tagerill sighed. "They were doing the rounds; they were determined to get both of you out."

"But why?"

"I don't know. I guess we'll have to find out so they don't do it again."

"You are correct, Tagerill," Guerlaire said. "Unfortunately, there are some people today who seem to think that their bloodlines are the only ones that should survive." Blue sparks crackled around Guerlaire, and Leyandrii stroked his arm, drawing the energy away.

Guerlaire ducked his head as his cheeks heated. That he needed Leyandrii to help him control his anger was embarrassing. Leyandrii tutted. She glanced over at Tagerill and raised an eyebrow.

"I'm fine," Tagerill said, raising his hands as if to keep her away from him.

They arrived at the office, and Commander Asher asked, "Did you find him?"

"Yes, Demeren has him," Guerlaire replied as he hovered by the chair Leyandrii sat in. "Asher, what are you going to do about Clary? It's getting out of hand."

Asher tapped the onoff, and multiple orbs lit up the room. "Tyrler has declared self-defence, that Birler went for him. He has several witnesses."

"Then why is Birler the one in the healerie?" Guerlaire paced, careful not to think too hard about what he was doing. The boy's survival was paramount. A slow burn started in his chest that he knew he would not be able to contain. He had failed Leyandrii, and he had failed Birler. He didn't fail often—nor did Leyandrii. He knew she would take this personally.

"They say he was not himself, that he attacked them for no reason."

"And how likely is that?" Guerlaire snapped. "You know the boy, Asher. You need to speak to Parsill for the details. He's in the healerie, too; he came to Birler's defence. He's a witness."

"I'll speak to him, though I doubt it will have little bearing. Cadet Clary will only be an echo of his father. What are you doing about *him*?"

Leyandrii sighed. "His father hasn't done anything wrong. There is nothing I can do."

Asher snorted. "He is touting a group called the Ascendants. Some prophets from the deserts. Surely, that is treason against you?"

"How so?" Leyandrii asked. "I don't force choice. I only provide a peaceful world for people to live in."

"Then why are they so determined to overthrow you?"

"Because people always want more." Tagerill's voice came from the doorway.

Asher raised an eyebrow. "Don't loiter, cadet. Come on in. What do you mean?"

Tagerill entered Asher's office, followed by Serill. "It was something Birler said months ago. He asked how long it would last. Nothing good ever lasts, he said. People always want more."

Guerlaire grimaced. "He's right about that."

"Leyandrii, you need to curb them before it's too late," Asher said.

Guerlaire shifted restlessly. "Easier said than done."

Leyandrii rested her hand on his arm, and he stilled.

"If you can't curb them, how am I supposed to? I can punish them for attacking another cadet but not for their beliefs."

"You should expel them; they almost killed Birler." Serill's shocked voice came from behind Tagerill.

"But they didn't. Clary will say it was Birler's fault and that it got out of hand. His father will back him."

"Even though you know different," Tagerill said

"Yes," Asher said, and he heaved a sigh. "Even though I know different."

"That's not fair. Why should they get away with attacking someone, ganging up on him?" Serill was beginning to spark with anger. "If I even laid a finger on Clary, you would expel me."

Asher watched him. "He won't get away with it. He will be dealt with. But it won't change his views."

"It's not the way of our world," Tagerill said.

"I know it doesn't seem fair, but I won't force anyone to submit to my will," Leyandrii said. "I want people to choose their own way of life. Within that, they are responsible for the choices they make. Unfortunately, not everyone considers others in the choices they make."

"What about Birler's rights?" Serill demanded.

"He will recover, graduate, and become a ranger, much like yourselves," Asher said. "It is fortunate it's almost the end of term."

"Fortunate?" Serill exploded. "What will it take? One of them killing us? That's what they would prefer."

"Hush. Don't say such things," Leyandrii said. "Birler will be fine. I will consider how to manage the Clarys, and I will deal with the Administration. It is not your responsibility; it is mine."

Guerlaire moved towards her. He reached for her and then dropped his hand to his side.

"All will be well," Leyandrii said.

Serill bowed, mesmerised by the sight of her. "Of course, my Lady."

Leyandrii smiled and waved a hand, drawing the sparking magic out of the air. "Why don't you two go and work off some of your excess energy? It will make you feel better."

Asher nodded, and Tagerill and Serill reluctantly left the room.

Tagerill turned back at the door. "Birler will need time to recuperate. He can come with me to Greens. My pa would come and get him. He'd help a friend of mine."

"Thank you Tagerill. I think that is an excellent idea. Birler will be ready to travel by the end of term." Leyandrii smiled, her face calm and serene, and as Tagerill left, a warm flush spread over his cheeks.

23

BIRLER

GREENS, VESPIRI, SEPU 1121

Birler lie on the sofa in an elegant morning room, feeling a little awkward, if he were being honest. The manor house around him was a hive of activity, with voices rising and fading as the staff managed the bustle of the family arriving home. From what he could remember of the journey, considering the time it had taken to get from the main road to the house, it was located on a large estate. The carriage had been travelling through tree-lined tracks for quite some time, though he had dozed most of the way; he was always tired.

When they finally pulled up at the house, Tagerill's father had carried him inside, ignoring Birler's protests that he could walk. He had a vague impression of grey stone and crenellated walls but little else.

And now he had been told to rest whilst everyone rushed around him. He closed his eyes. Resting was a good idea, even if he had rested all the way here. He didn't have the strength to face Tagerill's obviously vigorous family. Having met Tagerill's father, he had an idea where it came from.

He woke to a tongue slobbering all over his face. "Yuck,"

he said, pushing the dog away and rubbing his sleeve over his face. He was covered by a light blanket that hadn't been there when he had fallen asleep.

"Sorry!" A younger version of Lord Warren dragged the dog away, and Birler saw it was huge, more like a small horse than a dog. Its coat was a smooth blend of brown and black brindle-coloured fur. "This is Barron, and I'm Penner, Tagerill's eldest brother. Welcome to Greens. My mother will be in shortly. Is there anything you need?" Penner grinned as he watched Birler try to absorb all his words. "Tagerill will be back soon. He was just helping with the horses."

"Thank you. I'm fine," Birler replied.

Birler flushed under Penner's gaze; it was obvious he didn't believe him, but he dragged the dog out and returned with a glass of water. "Here, you're probably thirsty, just too polite to say. If you don't speak up in this house, you won't get."

Penner stood over Birler whilst he took a deep gulp. Birler had to admit, he was extremely thirsty, though his hand shook with the effort to hold the glass. Penner took the glass, which suddenly seemed too heavy for Birler to hold, and Birler relaxed back against the cushions. He scrunched his face as tears threatened to rise, and Penner left.

Birler opened his eyes at the touch of a cool hand on his face. Marian's brown eyes watched him, and he realised it must be Tagerill's mother, Lady Melis. He instinctively tried to sit up, but she placed a hand on his shoulder.

"Stay put. There's no need to rise. Though, if you can teach Tage such instinctive manners, that would be a good thing." Her rich voice was comforting. She smiled at him, her eyes twinkling, and he smiled back as he relaxed. She was a more mature version of Tagerill's sister, Marian, with more rounded curves and a firmer face, but the resemblance was striking, and Birler thought Tagerill's mother was very beautiful.

"Your bed is almost ready. I can see the journey was too much for you. They should have taken a break. My boys tend to forget not everyone has their constitution."

"I-I'm fine, really. I just keep falling asleep," Birler said, smiling at the thought of Lord Warren being called a boy.

Her soft laugh soothed his fears of offending. "You can sleep as much as you need, and when you are ready, Greens will be waiting to welcome you. You've arrived to see the estate at its best. Tagerill will be eager to show you it. I understand you don't ride, but Tagerill will teach you."

Birler wasn't too sure about that, but he smiled wanly in agreement. A rustle at the door behind her had Lady Melis rising, and Birler realised with horror that she had been kneeling on the floor. "Ask Lord Warren to join us, would you?" she asked the maid and turned back to Birler. "Warren will take you up to your room. Be welcome in our home, Birler."

Lord Warren ignored Birler's protests when he arrived, intending to carry him upstairs. "Don't argue," Warren said, noting Birler's flushed face and over-bright eyes. "You can walk when you're ready. That is not today. Save your strength for later." As he scooped Birler up, he hardly noticed Birler's slight weight.

He was aware of Birler gazing around him as they mounted the stairs, taking in the large paintings adorning the walls, with coloured paper filling the gaps. Many doors lined the upper corridor, and the first one they reached, Warren shoved open with his shoulder. Golden sunlight streamed through the large window, leaving a vibrant orange stripe across the pale brown wall. The bed was a welcome sight, with warm blankets folded back, a blatant invitation to rest.

Lady Melis followed them with a nightshirt in her hand. "Warren, help him into this. I'll go and get Sallar; he's running a temperature."

Warren took the shirt and waited for Melis to leave. He turned with a smile as she closed the door behind her. The boy's eyes *were* too bright. He ignored Birler's feeble protests. He'd had four children; he could manage one sick boy quite easily. He recognised the defensive wounds on Birler's arms immediately and frowned at the extensive bandages around his chest. The boy's skin was hot and still had signs of faded bruising. Although Guerlaire had warned him, he hadn't quite realised the extent of Birler's injuries.

Birler was lying in bed, exhausted, his face flushed and drawn when the healer arrived.

"This is Sallar. She'll soon have you feeling better," Warren promised as he watched her efficiently check him over. Warren raised Birler at the healer's request, and she poured a draught down his throat. Birler swallowed, gagged, and then relaxed in his arms, and Warren gently laid him down. The boy looked frail and defenceless, and Warren's heart clenched as an unexpected rush of protectiveness over-came him.

Lord Warren stood in front of the empty fireplace in the parlour, and Tagerill squirmed under his father's intense inspection. "What happened to him? Guerlaire said he was recovering from a fight and took some injuries. I thought he meant a sparring match. That boy didn't just lose a fight."

Lady Melis sat in the chair opposite. "Who is he, Tagerill?"

Tagerill dragged a hand through his hair. How to answer when he didn't really know himself? "He's my friend," he said first, as if that was all that mattered.

Warren and Melis exchanged glances.

"And?" his father prompted.

Tagerill sighed. "I don't really know much about him. He's from the streets of Vespers. I don't think he has a home, a family, or if he does, not one that cares. He's never mentioned them." He looked at his mother. "Maybe you'll be able to get him to tell you. He doesn't talk about his family."

"How did he get into the academy, then?" His father's face scrunched up in bewilderment.

"He just turned up a month into training. Just him and his basics. He owns nothing except a bow that the weapons master gave him."

"The weapons master gave Birler a bow?" Lord Warren repeated.

"Yeah, and permission to use the range whenever he needed to."

"Why?"

"Because he's so good," Tagerill said. Lord Warren raised a sceptical eyebrow. "He is. Birler will show you when he's better. He will be alright, won't he?" Tagerill turned to his mother in worry.

Lady Melis nodded. "The journey was too much for him. Sallar said he needs sleep and good food; the rest will follow. It just takes time to heal."

Tagerill breathed out a sigh of relief.

"What happened to him, Tagerill? That was no sparring accident." His father's voice was sharp.

"Tyrler Clary and his friends ganged up on him in the barracks. They don't think he should be at the academy. Birler was unarmed, but Tyrler and his friends had knives.

Serill and I were delayed on the field; it was our turn to help put away some equipment. By the time we arrived, Birler was gone." Tagerill clenched his jaw so tight his teeth ached. "Parsill managed to get him out of the barracks and held them back long enough for Birler to escape, but Parsill got three cracked ribs because of it."

"Parsill Ferrantes of Stoneford?" Warren asked.

Tagerill nodded. "Serill and I searched the city, even though Parsill said he wouldn't make it far. We didn't know where to look for him. He only ever mentioned the harbour, so we went down there, though it felt too far." Tagerill paced restlessly. "My friend Serill remembered he liked the Lady's Temple, so we went there." Tagerill paused, his gut roiling as he remembered the scene in the temple. "He was bleeding out by the altar at the feet of the Lady. Serill had a field kit from the healerie, so we tried to staunch the blood, but there was so much of it, and he was so cold." Tagerill swallowed, and his father gripped his arm. "I prayed to the Lady for help," he said, with tears pricking his eyes. Warren hugged his son carefully as Tagerill finished. "And then Captain Guerlaire arrived with a healer."

Warren looked at his wife over Tagerill's shoulder. "Guerlaire," he said.

"Leyandrii," she replied, holding his eyes. He nodded.

Warren released his son and gave him a weak grin. "Well, we'd better make sure he recovers, then. I want to see Birler with a bow."

Tagerill smiled, relief making him tremble. "It'll be worth it," he said. "You should see him with a sling."

Warren shook his head. "A sling?"

Tagerill laughed, a little more like himself. "Yeah, he's lethal."

A week passed before the healer would allow Birler out of bed. He was heartily fed up with sleeping by then, even if the bed was the most comfortable one he had ever slept in. There was even an onoff in his room. Birler couldn't believe he had one in his room; they were so expensive. Much safer than a naked flame, of course, but still, he had never rated a candle, let alone an onoff. He had wasted a lot of time just playing with it, trying to figure out how it worked.

His arms had scabbed over, and they itched like crazy. The healer had been clear: leave them alone or be bandaged up. He left them alone—most of the time.

When he was awake, someone was always with him: Tagerill's mother or Tagerill himself. Even Lord Warren spent a chime chatting about the estate, asking about Birler's sling and where he had learnt to use it.

Birler thought about that conversation. Lord Warren had been digging for something; he didn't know if he had found what he was looking for. He had answered truthfully about what he knew, which wasn't much. He didn't remember making his first sling; he just had in response to a rather persistent gang of lads who wouldn't leave him in peace. They had afterwards, giving him a wide berth whenever they crossed paths.

One overcast day, a rather shaky Birler was escorted down the stairs by Tagerill and his brother Penner. He wasn't sure why he felt so weak. The Lady had healed the worst of his injuries, but it seemed his body hadn't received the message.

They plonked him on the sofa where he'd been when they had first arrived. "You need to eat," Tagerill was saying. "Then we can go outside. I can show you the stables and the nursery and the plantations and …"

"Give him a chance, Tage." Penner laughed. "It's his first day up. If he overdoes it, he'll be sent back to bed."

Tagerill smiled sheepishly. "I'm sorry. It's just there's so much to show you."

Tagerill's love for his home was clear in his expression; he would, too, if this had been his. Tagerill's family were close. Even though Marian and Versill were away, they were still very present, as the family talked about them all the time. To be loved so, Birler's eyes teared up at the idea.

Tagerill stared at him, worried. "What do you want to eat?" Penner left them to decide what to have for their morning meal.

Later that day, Warren was flabbergasted to find his youngest son in the library of all places. Tagerill never sat still long enough to read anything. He was even more amazed when he realised his son was listening to Birler read and correcting his errors. He backed out of the library unnoticed, not wanting to interrupt.

Another week passed, and Tagerill showed Birler around the estate. One of the first places Tagerill showed him was the Lady's Grove, a small copse of lime trees surrounding a simple grey stone table. Birler fell to his knees before the altar and gave heartfelt thanks to the Lady for saving him. He apologised for not visiting sooner and promised he would return to the temple in Vespers. Birler smiled as Tagerill stopped hovering and joined him. He felt a soft caress on his cheek and relaxed as a blessing descended around them.

Birler reluctantly allowed Tagerill to drag him away, but he would make sure he visited again. Back at the estate, they climbed onto the wooden fence penning in the horses, and

Tagerill pointed out which ones they could ride, promising to teach him to ride in a week or so.

"How long can we stay here?" Birler asked one day as they walked through the plantation of saplings growing behind the mansion house.

"As long as you need to," Tagerill said promptly. "But we have to be back at the academy for start of term by Novu 1."

"How long does that give us?"

"Another month or so," Tagerill said.

Birler stiffened as he realised he didn't really know how long that was. They hadn't explained the calendar to him yet.

Tagerill was chattering on. "When were you born?" he asked, jumping to catch an overhead branch. He missed and spun when he realised Birler had stopped walking. "I was born Octu 14, on Lady's Day."

Birler stared at him, mute, as his stomach dropped. He didn't know. He had never celebrated his borning day.

Tagerill's grin faded. "It doesn't matter; you can share mine."

Birler nodded slowly as a warmth spread through his body. Octu 14, Lady's Day. A small smile crept over his face.

Tagerill smiled in return, relieved. "C'mon. I'll race you," he said, and then slowly ran through the ranks of trees back towards the house. Birler chased after him. They arrived, breathless and laughing. "Do you want to practise some archery? You can teach me how to hit a target."

Birler flexed his shoulders. Yes, practice sounded good. "Alright, what bows have you got?" he asked, and Tagerill gently eased him back into the rhythms of life.

24

GUERLAIRE

CHAPTERHOUSE, VESPERS

Guerlaire, accompanied by a taciturn ranger called Royer, travelled to the Chapterhouse by way of the cadets' barracks and blithely stole a bright first-year cadet called Nialler. The lad was prodigiously gifted, and Guerlaire recognised talents he could use.

Walking through the city streets, Guerlaire grinned as the golden towers of the Chapterhouse came into view. "Did you know that the four bells were all cast in Stoneford and then transported all the way down the East Road?"

"Yes, sir, and that it took three months. I prefer the lower -toned bell; it doesn't resonate so much," Nialler replied. "Those higher bells hurt my ears."

Guerlaire laughed. "Indeed. Sometimes, the smaller bells are a bit strident."

Leading the way through the corridors, Guerlaire hurried down the steps to his workroom, and as if on cue, the bells chimed, one after the other from highest to lowest, marking the second chime in the afternoon. Royer took guard at the top of the stairs. There was no other entry.

"Right," Guerlaire said as he closed the door, muting the

chiming bells. "What we discuss today is to be kept a secret. I don't want anyone to ever find out how we achieved this. This is a gift for Lady Leyandrii, and it has to be kept unique and special, a symbol of her absolute authority. Can I trust you to never speak of this work?"

Nialler grinned, his thin face alive with curiosity. "Yes, sir. Never a word."

"Tell me about yourself while I find the plans."

"Not a lot to tell. Born and raised in Vespers. Never travelled anywhere."

"We'll have to do something about that," Guerlaire muttered as he rummaged in the bottom of a trunk.

"M'father taught me numbers and letters; he kept the books for a tradesman. Wanted me to be the same, but I found it boring. Adding columns of numbers all day wasn't enough for me."

Guerlaire found his plans and spread them out on the table. "I can assure you, this will not be boring," he said as he weighted the corners, and Nialler peered at the design.

Nialler leaned closer and traced the design. "This cannot be possible," he said in a low voice.

"Not usually, but I have plenty of magic to help us. I need to ensure the core structure is sound and can hold the weight. The magic will do the rest."

"Have you measured the distance?"

"Once. But I'm hoping you will help me reconfirm all the numbers. We only have one go at this, so we need to get it right." Guerlaire grinned at Nialler's absorption. The cadet's nose was almost touching the parchment as he followed the curves, tracing Guerlaire's calculations.

"The lower end will be attached to the Chapterhouse?" Nialler asked.

"Of course. Leyandrii rises above us all."

Nialler nodded. "We may need to reinforce the tower.

Depends how much stress the weight will place on it, though I suppose the magic may take some of the pressure?"

Guerlaire pursed his lips and concentrated on his sword. He thought the question, and a soft burble filled his mind. His sword was laughing at him.

"I think we can assume the magic will cater for the weight," he said.

"On an ongoing basis?"

"Let's assume so."

Nialler nodded. "Then, first, we should confirm your measurements. No point recalculating everything if there is a discrepancy in the base numbers."

Guerlaire nodded and placed the coil of measuring strings and angle dividers on top of the plans. He tucked his notebook and charcoal stick in his pocket. "I have all the dimensions in here." He patted his pocket. "We can check my numbers."

Nialler grinned, his grey eyes sparkling. "Then let's get to it, Captain." He picked up the measuring string and angles, led the way to the door, opened it, and reached the top of the stairs before Guerlaire had even moved.

Guerlaire shook his head and followed.

Watching Nialler contort himself into the tightest corners to ensure the measurements were as accurate as they could be instilled in Guerlaire a measure of awe he had never experienced before. This young cadet, in his late teens, with no experience beyond Vespers, was demonstrating initiative, genius, and pure dedication to a project he had only just been seconded to. The lad was in a world of his own, muttering under his breath, commanding Guerlaire about as if he were his skivvy, and Guerlaire had to glare at Royer quite a few times to get him to stop laughing.

"Hold it up, Guerlaire," Nialler snapped, Guerlaire's captaincy long lost in the dust of Nialler's requirements.

Guerlaire knew when to watch and listen, though. Nialler had measured every possible angle one could think of, some of which Guerlaire was positive they wouldn't need.

The Chapterhouse bells chimed eight, and Guerlaire's stomach growled. His ears vibrated as the highest bell chimed, and he shook his head and glanced around. They had been fortunate that they had taken the measurements at the palace first because, by the time they reached the Chapterhouse, trailing their piece of string, the roads had quietened down as sensible people went for their supper.

But not Nialler. He had the bit between his teeth, and he was going to measure the Chapterhouse to death and beyond.

Chimes passed, and Guerlaire watched Nialler with some awe as he showed no sign of stopping. "It's getting too dark to work," Guerlaire said. "It's time to stop for today. We can continue tomorrow morning if necessary."

Nialler glanced up and then around him. "Oh, I hadn't noticed," he said, straightening, and then he winced as his bones cracked when he stretched.

Guerlaire grimaced. He would have to keep a closer eye on this young recruit. He obviously didn't know when to stop. "It's time to eat. You can come back with me."

"Oh, no, I can eat at the garrison."

"You'll have missed last meal in the mess hall. The least I can do is feed you after all your hard work. But remember, not a word to Leyandrii. It's a surprise."

"Um, will we see Lady Leyandrii? What do I say if she asks?"

"She won't."

"But …"

"Don't worry. She'll already have eaten."

Nialler looked a bit dubious, but he wound up the string as they walked back towards the palace.

"Um, I just wanted to say thank you," Nialler said, keeping his gaze on the ground.

"For what?" Guerlaire asked.

"For letting me be involved in your project. The summer recess can be really long."

Guerlaire frowned, realising that term was over and Nialler hadn't, in fact, gone home. "Why are you still in the garrison?"

Nialler exhaled, his shoulders drooping. "My pa washed his hands of me when I accepted the Lady's scholarship. He said if what he offered wasn't good enough, then I was on my own."

Guerlaire wrapped an arm around Nialler's shoulders and side-hugged him. "I'm sorry."

Nialler shrugged. "Not your fault."

"And your mother agreed?"

"She died when I was eleven. Since then, it's just been me and my pa."

Guerlaire was glad when they reached the palace, and he directed Nialler where to go to wash up. "Bring him to the kitchen once he's ready," he instructed Royer, who gave him a quick nod.

Guerlaire strode through the corridors, cudgelling his brain for the details of the scholarships Leyandrii had put in place.

"Love?" he thought.

"Another late night?" Leyandrii asked, amusement colouring her voice.

"Yes. How many scholarships did you set up for the ranger cadets?"

"Two. One male, one female."

"And did they include travel and clothing allowances?"

"Of course."

"I just met Nialler, your male cadet. He is a genius, and we need to give him additional support."

"We do?"

"Yes. He needs tutoring in the Chapterhouse as well."

"As well? He won't have time to complete his cadet chores, let alone scholar work as well."

"Oh, I assure you he will. He is dying to learn more. He is using half his brain, and we need to make sure he reaches his full potential. He is stuck in the garrison for summer recess. Enrol him in the Chapterhouse until term starts."

"Where are you?"

"In the kitchen. About to make sure he eats something."

"Ah, one of those."

"Oh, yes."

"I'll be down in a bit."

"Don't ask him what he's working on, and no peeking."

Leyandrii's laugh pealed in his mind. *"You didn't! Oh, you did; you nabbed him for your secret project, didn't you? Your brain not up to the challenge after all?"*

"My brain is perfectly fine, thank you." Guerlaire ignored her after that, though he couldn't help smiling, as his mind was full of her amusement.

He wheedled some soup, cheese, and bread out of the cook and sat at the kitchen table, waiting for Nialler. He made his own sandwich and took a bite.

Royer escorted the lad into the kitchen and then departed with a wave.

Guerlaire grinned and pulled out the chair next to him. "Sit, help yourself."

Nialler had reverted to the demure, silent cadet, and Guerlaire concentrated on coaxing out the brilliant young man hidden inside. They were both onto their second bowl of soup, deep in discussion about the methods of navigation, when Nialler suddenly stiffened.

"Oh, don't stop on account of me," Leyandrii said with a

smile as she poured herself a mug of kafinee from the jug warming on the stove. She leaned over to kiss Guerlaire and then slid into the chair opposite. Smiling at Nialler, she said, "Did I just hear you expounding on the Tandril weight displacement method? I thought that was disproved by Fortin in 1115?"

"No, not at all. Fortin misinterpreted Tandril's calculations. His whole thesis is based on an erroneous assumption. He didn't check his facts."

"You must always check your facts," Leyandrii murmured, watching Nialler as he explained how Fortin had gone wrong. Arguing data, Nialler was in his element, but as soon as he finished, he folded back into himself.

"You make an excellent point. I don't believe Fortin's thesis has been overturned. You should write your own thesis, explaining his error. Otherwise, other scholars will use his thesis for the basis of their own work and they will all be wrong."

"I'm not a scholar, my Lady."

"But you could be for the summer."

Nialler flushed and crumbled his bread. "I … I can't afford the fees."

"If you didn't need to worry about the fees, what would you study?"

"The mechanics of buildings and structures. How and why things work the way they do," Nialler said without hesitation.

Leyandrii nodded. "A noble topic. Understanding why the world around us behaves in the way it does is enlightening." She leaned on the table and smiled. "Dear Nialler. You will only waste your time hanging about the garrison. Go to the Chapterhouse, enrol in the courses you want, and I will pay your fees. All I ask is that you study hard, but also that you stop to eat and make friends as well. Life is not all work.

Understanding people and how they think is also part of the puzzle."

"Really?" Nialler gasped. "You really mean it?"

"Of course I do. I will advise Commander Asher that you will be reassigned to the Chapterhouse during recess. Term time, though, you are his."

Guerlaire grinned at Nialler's joyful expression.

"Oh, my Lady, how can I ever thank you?"

"By doing your best. That's all anyone can ask. But please do refute Fortin's work. We need people working off the correct data." With a smile, Leyandrii rose and left the room.

"Let's get you back to the barracks," said Guerlaire. "I'll meet you at the Chapterhouse in the morning, and we can enrol you in the courses and work on my numbers."

Nialler bounced to his feet. "Yes, sir."

It was unlikely that the lad would sleep a wink, but Guerlaire had no doubt he would be focussed and content, working through all the measurements they had collected. Between Nialler's genius and the power swirling in his sword, Leyandrii's bridge would be spectacular. He could not wait for her to see it.

25

WARREN

GREENS, OCTU 1121

The leaves had begun turning from the myriad shades of greens to the browns, ambers, and reds as the end of the year approached in Greens. Warren was crouched on the ground, inspecting the bole of a juvenile tree, when he was interrupted by his son Penner.

"Tagerill and Birler are down at the range," Penner said with a small smile.

Warren straightened from his crouch and observed his eldest son. "They are, are they?"

"It's a sight to see."

Warren laughed. "You mean Tagerill has hit something?"

Penner laughed with him. "He has, actually, but that is not what I meant."

Warren eased his shoulders and joined his son. They walked back through the trees and round to the archery range. Warren stopped short in surprise. Birler was teaching Tagerill and some of his men how to use the bow. The boy stopped one man and demonstrated the pull. He made the man do it; then he took his place and smoothly nocked and released an arrow. He turned back to the man before it hit the target, gesturing. The arrow thunked into the centre, next to the others already there. The man tried again. Birler straightened his arm, and the arrow caught the edge of the target. Birler grinned and patted the man's back in congratulation. He moved on to Tagerill.

"Just wait till you've got a sword in your hand," Tagerill growled as Birler pushed and prodded him into the correct position.

Birler gave a crack of laughter. "Concentrate," he said. "Feel the air and go with the flow; it should be instinctive, not forced." Tagerill sighed, trying to release his tension. His shoulders dropped as he thought about Apeiron and acceptance, and he released his arrow. It thunked into the target.

"Yes!" Birler crowed in delight, thumping his back. "See, I told you you could do it."

"Your turn," Tagerill stepped back, rotating his shoulders.

Warren raised his eyebrows in surprise.

Birler laughed. "Last time, then. You're the one who needs the practice." He raised his face to the breeze, adjusted his stance slightly, and nocked his arrow. The men all stopped to watch as he released. He nocked the next arrow and smoothly released, grouping them all in the centre of the target.

Tagerill shook his head. "I don't know how you do it."

Birler laughed and walked down the range to retrieve his arrows. He slotted them back in the quiver and returned.

"Try your sling. I know you made one," Tagerill said.

Birler shook his head. "This is an archery range, not for slings."

"Show us." The men around Birler joined Tagerill in trying to persuade him.

Birler gave in. "Alright, just one target." He loaded his fingers with the smooth stones he had found the previous evening. In quick succession, he whipped them down the range. The men heard a whistle and then a thump, thump, thump as they hit the target.

One of the men trotted off down the range and dug the stones out of the target with his knife. He returned and handed them to Birler. "I would've never believed it, young master, if I hadn't seen it myself." He gave him a salute before leaving the range and returning to his work.

Warren laughed under his breath. "I think young Birler will be one to watch, don't you, Penner?"

"Definitely. I suggest he'll even be the making of our Tage."

"You may well be right," Warren said, watching his son and his friend leave the range.

Birler awaited Tagerill's borning day approach with interest. He had never experienced one before, at least not one that he remembered. He realised from an overheard comment that gifts were involved, and he racked his brain as to what he could give someone who already had everything, especially when he had precisely nothing to his name.

The day dawned clear and sunny, though there was a fresh bite to the air, heralding the approach of the end of the year. He was amused to find that he no longer feared the approach of the colder months. A roof over your head changed your whole perspective, and he had other things to worry about, like finding something to wrap his gift in, for example.

"Lady's blessings on your borning day, Tage," Birler whispered, giving his friend a hug, and he stuffed his gift into Tagerill's hand.

Tagerill grinned in delight as he unwrapped the sling.

"This is great. Thank you. Lady's blessing, Birler, on your borning day," he said in return and handed Birler a flat package.

Birler smiled as Tagerill stretched the sling, glad he hadn't provided any stones. Tagerill would have been trying it out there and then. He ripped open the paper, revealing a copy of the Lady's almanack. He had his very own copy! His face split into a huge grin. "Tage, thank you, but it's not really my borning day."

Tagerill shrugged. "It is now. I told everyone today was your borning day, too; you can't change it now."

"You did what?" Birler flushed with mortification. Tagerill had lied to his family, and Birler wasn't sure if he could continue the lie. After everything the Descelles had done for him, the thought of misleading them left a bad taste in his mouth.

Tagerill laughed. "Everyone has a borning day; why not you, too?"

"But I don't know when I was born!"

"Of course you do; it's today, same as mine. C'mon." Tagerill dragged him into the family parlour and pushed him into his seat.

Birler joined the family in a prayer of thanks to the Lady and relaxed as they began to eat. He let the camaraderie and love flow around him. He felt like they truly wanted him to be a part of the celebration.

Warren read out the messages from Versill and Marian that had arrived, wishing Tagerill a happy day and teasing him that he would need a walking stick soon at the grand old age of eighteen.

Birler felt Penner's glance on him and grinned back at him.

"How old are you today, Birler?" Penner asked.

The excitement Birler had been feeling drained out of

him, and he sat mortified. How old was he? He didn't know that either. He looked at Melis in mute appeal, and she stepped into the breach. "Why, you're seventeen, aren't you?" She smiled at him and then tilted her head as she observed her son. Tagerill wouldn't meet her eyes, and her penetrating gaze gentled as it returned to Birler.

Birler nodded. He didn't know what else to do.

"Congratulations, Birler," Penner said gently.

After breakfast, the family laughingly dragged both Tagerill and Birler down to the stables. Warren smiled as the stable master brought out a glossy black stallion. "Happy borning day, Tagerill," they all chanted as Tagerill whooped and flew around, hugging them all, even Birler, though he had not known about nor contributed to the gift. Tagerill ran a possessive hand down the stallion's neck and rubbed his nose. He was overjoyed. "How did you keep him hidden?" he demanded.

Warren laughed. "George brought him over this morning. What are you going to name him?"

Tagerill considered for a moment. "I don't know; I have to think about it."

Melis dug her husband in the ribs. "Ouch," he said, rubbing his side. He nodded at the grinning horse master, who disappeared and came back leading an elegant creamy brown mare.

"Happy borning day, Birler," they chanted, and Birler froze.

"What?" he gasped, staring at them wildly as his heart thrummed in his chest in sheer panic.

Melis laughed. "She is for you. We thought about a stallion, but you being a novice, a mare is more docile to begin with. When you're ready, we can swap her for another if needed."

Birler's eyes bulged. "Y-you can't give me a horse; you

don't even kn-know me." He was beginning to gasp in air as tears welled. He didn't know where to look. "I don't know anything about horses. I c-can't afford to look after her." His chest hurt as he tried not to cry.

Warren grabbed Birler's arms as if he thought he might run away. "Birler, calm down. She is a gift, and you will learn how to look after her. Tagerill will show you, and the academy will house her. You don't need to pay for her, as it's covered under the fees. All second-year students have a horse."

Birler shuddered. "Fees?" he asked, horrified. He hadn't thought about fees, even though he knew nothing came for free; he had trusted the Lady.

Warren jerked his head, and everyone else melted away. "You must know the training is not free," he said calmly.

"I was just doing what the Lady told me to," Birler said, staring at him, trying to hold back the tears.

"Then the Lady will be covering your fees, won't she?"

Birler stiffened, trying to control his breathing. "How do I ever pay her back?"

"By working hard and doing your best. That is all she wants for you," Warren replied. "And you have been doing very well."

Warren rubbed Birler's back as if he were a nervous horse, trying to reassure him. "I'm so sorry, Birler. We never meant to upset you. We just wanted to celebrate your borning day, and the mare seemed like an ideal gift." He drew Birler back towards the mare. "What will you call her?" he asked, placing Birler's hand on her neck. She whuffled against his chest as Birler smoothed his hand down her silky skin. Her hide was warm and soft under his palm. Her liquid black eyes watched him, and she nudged him in the chest. Birler ran his hand down her neck again, and a blanket of calm descended over him, soothing his panic.

He looked at Warren, his pulse still a bit jittery. "She is really mine to name?"

Warren smiled. "She is yours completely. You will learn to look after her and to ride. George here will begin teaching you, but you will continue at the academy. Learn well, Birler; that is all we ask."

Birler nodded. "I'm sorry." His voice was muffled against the horse's mane.

"For what?"

Birler shrugged. "For overreacting," he said, his eyes downcast.

"I am sorry, too, for springing her on you like that. We should have been more considerate." Warren watched him. "And now we've apologised, shall we go and join Tagerill so he can show us his gift and we can help him enjoy it?"

Birler nodded. He stroked the mare one last time, almost reluctant to leave her.

"She is yours," Warren repeated. "You can visit her whenever you want."

The smile that spread over Birler's face was reward enough, and Warren exhaled carefully. He wrapped an arm around Birler's shoulders and gave him a hug. "Come on. Let's find the others."

Tagerill was showing off the stallion's paces in the home corral. He looked over in relief as he saw his father and Birler approach.

"Isn't he gorgeous?" he asked, his eyes glittering with excitement.

Birler climbed up the fence and sat on the top rail beside Penner. "He is amazing. What did you decide to call him?"

"He's stuck between Midnight and Raven," Penner said with a laugh.

"Midnight is a bit of a mouthful. I like Raven, or Inky,

maybe. His coat shines like ink," Birler said thoughtfully, staring at the glossy coat.

The stallion snorted, and Tagerill laughed. "Inky, it is, then." He glanced at his father, who was leaning against the fence with an arm around his mother's shoulders. His father nodded. He smiled again in delight. "What are you going to call your mare?"

Birler smiled. "Kafinee."

Tagerill gave a bark of laughter, and Inky shied. He soothed the horse's neck. "Sorry, Inky, blame Birler."

Over the next week, George only had time to lay in the basics of how to ride a horse and how to care for them before they were preparing to return to Vespers. Birler would have to learn on the road, which Lord Warren said was the best way. The night before they left, Warren and Melis called them both into the family parlour.

"We wanted to tell you, Birler, that you are welcome here anytime, whether Tagerill is with you or not," Lord Warren said with a smile.

"Yes, we want you to treat our home as your home. You will always be welcome," Melis said, standing beside him.

Birler gaped at them. "You've been so kind," he stammered. "I couldn't accept anything more."

"You will because we insist." Warren looked at Tagerill. "You will make sure he understands. We expect to see you both on the next pass day."

Tagerill's grin said it all.

"Tagerill, remember he hasn't ridden much. Make sure you stop every five miles or so and stretch, or else he won't be able to move tomorrow." Warren grinned at Birler, his blue eyes glinting. "I find *'Understanding'* usually works best."

Birler smiled in appreciation as Tagerill promised to stop for breaks.

26

GUERLAIRE

LADY'S PALACE, VESPERS

Guerlaire waited in heightened anticipation, with Nialler and Royer beside him, as Leyandrii stepped out of the palace's main entrance and stared up at the scintillating twist of light and colour that stretched between the tallest silver spire of her palace and the tallest golden tower of the Chapterhouse, joining the symbol of Leyandrii's rule with the centre of learning and development.

Guerlaire's heart was fit to burst as Leyandrii's surprise and awe filtered through their bond and he experienced every emotion with her. Her jaw dropped as she craned her neck and followed the glistening strands as they twisted above her, with light dancing and refracting through the crystal threads.

"How?" she whispered as her gaze followed the impossible bridge. She walked down the drive, fixated on the glowing structure.

Guerlaire laughed, exulting in her happiness. "For you, anything," he declared. "A token of my love and esteem but also a representation of what you mean to your people."

"But … how?"

"I found a use for all those crystals I confiscated and the magic you made me siphon off into my sword."

Leyandrii's smile grew broader. "You did? How clever!"

"And a lot of help from Nialler."

"Extra studies, no doubt," she said as she continued down the drive, determined to see the complete bridge. "I hope he got extra credit as well."

"Oh, he passed without even trying," Guerlaire replied, and Leyandrii laughed.

Leyandrii paused, glancing around, until she caught Nialler's excited gaze. "It is amazing," she said to him.

"It was Captain Guerlaire's idea and design. I just helped to confirm the measurements."

"But the data is the foundation, and without correct numbers, you cannot build anything," Leyandrii said.

Nialler's smile bloomed. "Exactly so, my Lady."

Leyandrii swooped in to give him a hug and a kiss, and before he could protest, she released him, grabbed Guerlaire, and swung him around. "I cannot believe you managed to keep this a secret from me."

Guerlaire laughed. "You love it?"

"Love it? I adore it! It is the most exquisite thing I have ever seen. And you made it for me." Tears overflowed from her brilliant eyes, and Guerlaire drew her into a hug.

"I wanted to show you how much I love you," he said into her neck.

"Sweetheart, I know how much you love me, every single day. I don't need any symbols or … or bridges, but I love it all the same."

Guerlaire gave her a wicked grin. "At least it will give the Administration something else to talk about."

Leyandrii's infectious laugh pealed out, and everyone grinned until their cheeks ached.

27

TAGERILL
VESPERS, NOVU 1121

Tagerill and Birler arrived in Vespers in high spirits. They had taken three days to travel what usually took two, but Birler was still mobile, so Tagerill felt the slow pace was worth it. Inky didn't; he was prancing about, straining against the reins. Tagerill took him for a gallop down the road and back just to work some of his jinks out.

The man Lord Warren had sent with them agreed to hold their horses whilst they dived into the Lady's temple to pay their respects.

The temple shimmered as Birler entered, and he smiled. They knelt at the steps, and Birler rested his hand on the white stone. Even Tagerill felt the thrill race around the temple. He watched Birler carefully. What was it about this unassuming boy that the Lady liked so much? Come to that, what was it *he* liked about him so much? He promised the Lady he would look out for Birler like a brother, and he felt the promise lock into place deep inside him. The Lady's happiness glissaded around them, and they both stood a little breathless at her welcome.

Tagerill glanced at Birler, sure that he looked as starry-eyed as Birler did. "Well," he said, "that was some welcome."

Birler laughed. "She knows we're back."

"That, she does," Tagerill agreed, following Birler back out to the horses.

He watched Birler remount. His father had been right; Birler had picked up the tricks of riding a horse because he had to, and to be honest, Kafinee was an absolute darling. She would do anything for Birler. *He lucked out*, Tagerill thought, but then Birler was owed a lot of good fortune. *May he be rolling in it*, he thought fervently.

Tagerill's admiration for Birler only deepened as he showed no sign of anxiety as they left the temple. His father had warned him to keep an eye on Birler, and he had sworn he would, his father hadn't needed to tell him. Birler had been determined to return to the academy; he wasn't about to let Tyrler dictate his life, and Tagerill fully agreed with him.

They walked their horses up the street and stopped, stunned, as a fragile structure, which sparkled and glistened in the sun, came into view. It twisted and turned, sparkling in a myriad of colours, and reached impossibly into the sky, a bridge between the Lady's palace and the Chapterhouse. Tagerill's jaw dropped. "What is that?"

Birler chuckled. "Wasn't there a rumour that Captain Guerlaire was working on a project that would take our breath away? I would suggest this is it."

"But what is it?"

Birler shrugged. "Looks like a bridge to me."

"But what is it for?"

Birler burst out laughing at Tagerill's awed expression. "You'll have to ask the captain. Come on." Birler led the way through the streets, under the stunning edifice and into the academy stables. The stable master gave them their stalls—

fortunately, next to each other—and they hauled their saddlebags off and dumped them on the floor outside the stall. Lord Warren's man added two more bags before giving them a cheery wave as he left.

Tagerill poked his head in the door, checking to see if Birler had managed to unsaddle Kafinee alright. He grinned at the sight of the mare with her back leg hocked, enjoying a good brushing. "She'll have you there all day." He laughed. "We need to get cleaned up and report in."

Birler straightened and waved away the cloud of horse hairs floating around him. "Should she shed this much?" he asked, frowning.

"She's getting her winter coat; it'll get better soon." Tagerill picked up his saddle. "C'mon. We'll clean this lot later."

Birler threw his brushes in the bucket and grabbed the tack, pulling the half door shut behind him. Kafinee whuffled in her hay net, making him grin. After disposing of the tack, they returned for their bags and headed up to the office block.

"We're not in the old barracks, then?" Birler asked as they walked.

Tagerill glanced up at the bridge, unable to take his eyes off it. "No, the newbies will use those barracks. We move up to the main building. This term, we get assigned to the Justice, the palace, or the Chapterhouse. Rotate each term, and we have three terms this year." Tagerill made a face. "Along with looking after the horses, weapons practice, training, and learning whatever else they throw at us, we have to spend one day a week shadowing an official. We won't have time to breathe."

Birler smiled at his tragic tone. "Never mind. I'm sure you'll find some time to get up to mischief."

They entered the office and reported their arrival. The

adjutant made a notation on his pad and handed them each a sheaf of papers. "Barracks, assignment, cohort, and schedule. Drop your belongings off and report to the main hall," he said in a bored tone.

Birler and Tagerill compared barracks and were relieved to find they were together. They were on the second floor. A room with six beds greeted them. It looked like one of the beds had been taken, so someone had arrived before them. They dumped their stuff on their chosen beds and made their way to the hall.

They were waylaid by Tagerill's sister, Marian, who grabbed her brother in a hug. "I just wanted to let you know I'll be back in the Elothian Wastes for the next few months." She rolled her eyes. "Some crazy people want to start expanding up there, so we have to go and break the trail. Don't get into any more trouble while I am away," she said with a mock frown.

Tagerill immediately took offence. "I don't get into trouble," he began.

"I haven't got time to argue with you, Tage. I just wanted to say goodbye. Taurill and Severen are waiting for me. Versill is out east in Stoneford, so you two are on your own. Be good!" She kissed him on the cheek, flashed Birler a grin, and was gone.

Tagerill scowled. "As if we need them looking after us." He turned towards the door and chuckled. "At least we won't have them hovering over our shoulders."

The hall was buzzing with voices as they entered, though only half the seats were taken. Serill pounced on them as they cleared the door. "Thank goodness. I was getting worried." He grinned at them. "I'm so glad to see you both. There was a rumour you weren't coming back, Birler."

Birler slid into an empty pew. "Don't see why not."

Serill flushed, looking at his hands. "Because of what

happened last term." He looked earnestly at Birler. "I never meant what I said, honest. I was just so angry—at myself more than anyone else."

"Don't be daft. We said we would forget it."

"I know, but I can't," Serill said, his shoulders dropping. "I should never have doubted you."

"Serill, stop it. You were there when I needed you. That's all that matters."

"I'll never doubt you again. I swear it," Serill said fiercely. The vow locked into place as he looked earnestly at Birler.

Birler held his hands up. "I believe you. Now, can we drop it?" he asked, looking around the hall. "What's up? Do you know?"

"Apart from Guerlaire's bridge?" Serill asked. There's a new watch system being introduced by the Lady. She's asked some of the lords to become Guardians of Vespiri."

Tagerill stared at him. "But *she's* the Guardian."

Serill shrugged. "That's what I heard. Maybe Asher will explain more."

They looked up expectantly as Commander Asher arrived, flanked by his adjutant and Captain Guerlaire, the commander of the Lady's Guards.

Asher stood behind the lectern. "Welcome back, cadets. I am pleased to see that you have returned for another year of training to become the best of the best, to protect our Lady and our people.

"You'll be pleased to know that your days will now be even longer. With your horses to care for comes additional responsibility. You will also be sent out on assignments to put what you have learnt into practice. I think you will find that, eventually, you will be away more than you are here, but more of that later."

A ripple of surprise spread through the room, and the commander paused to let it die down. "You will be placed on month-long assignments to gain a greater understanding of Remargaren, first here in Vespers, in the Chapterhouse and the Administration, and later in the outer regions. After all, you cannot protect what you are not familiar with.

"Work hard. Study well. This is a year of change, and change drives opportunity, so be prepared. This is a year to hone your skills so you are ready to protect Vespiri and Remargaren." He looked around the room at the eager faces before him and smiled. "You will see that we have accepted recruits from the other regions this year, opening our academy to all Remargaren. Those who graduate will be assigned to their home regions.

"Today, settle in. Tomorrow, your new schedules start. I look forward to another successful year. Support each other, grow together, and we will provide our Lady with the resources she needs to protect our people." Asher stood back from the lectern, and his adjutant stepped forward to dismiss them back to their barracks.

Tagerill led the way back to their room. Parsill poked his head through the door and grinned. "I'm in here, too, along with Edril and Samis. He waved the other lads in. They were tall and broad-shouldered like Tagerill. Smiling easily, they dumped their bags on the empty beds.

"Edril from Melila, Terolia," the taller of the two said. He had curly black hair and the sun-blasted skin of the people who lived in the desert. "This is Samis; he's from Nikri on the borders with Birtoli." He gestured at an olive-skinned boy whose hair was just as black and curly.

Birler raised his eyebrows. "Birtoli? What brings you here?"

Samis grinned, his black eyes sparkling. "I thought it would make a change from fishing! But seriously, the Emperor wants closer relations with the Lady, so he sent a few of us up to the academy."

"Well, welcome. It's a bit colder up here—for both of you," Birler said.

Samis scowled. "And dull. It's always cloudy and grey. Birtoli is vibrant and light by comparison. The rain is cold, too. At home, it's warm and infrequent."

"At least you get rain. Terolia is parched," Edril said as he sat on his bed. "We could do with some of this rain."

"Do you not travel with—a Family, isn't it? Aren't all Terolians nomads?" Serill asked.

"Not all. I live in a village some ways south of the border of East Watch. It's a lot warmer. My friend Adil is somewhere here as well. We'll no doubt find him later."

"If you have time. It sounds like this year is going to be packed," Parsill interjected with a laugh. "What with looking after a horse as well, we won't have time to sleep!"

"If my sister can do it, then we can," Tagerill said comfortably, and the conversation devolved into finding out more about each other as they unpacked and settled in.

Birler scowled at his bags. "When did I collect so much stuff?" he asked, trying to fit it into his cupboard.

They soon found their routine, rising at dawn to care for their horses and run around the perimeter. Then came Apeiron, followed by weapons practice. After a huge lunch that even Birler now devoured without blinking, it was on to lectures on a variety of subjects, ranging from the geography of the bordering kingdoms to the structure of the Administration in Vespiri.

Birler and Tyrler avoided each other. Although Tyrler cast him evil glances, he never approached Birler. Apart from that, Birler was generally accepted and found himself enjoying academy life. He loved looking after Kafinee. She adored him, and Birler absorbed her affection hungrily.

He was clearing out her stall, lugging the sack of dirty straw to the manure heap, when he heard Edril burst out laughing behind him. He lurched round, his arms full, and bumped into Kafinee, who had been following closely behind him.

The Terolian leaned over the partition, watching Kafinee. "She must have Darian bloodlines somewhere in her family," Edril said. "She acts more like a Darian than not, the way she follows you around."

Birler grinned. "She doesn't quite have the lines of Deren, though, does she?" He dumped his load and led her back, with Kafinee nudging his shoulder. They had all admired Deren, the sleek stallion Edril had brought with him, and were rather jealous of the obvious link they had. Darians bonded with their riders for life, and once accepted, rider and horse could communicate silently.

"Maybe not, but she has his intelligence for sure. She is a clever horse, and she likes you. You could probably train her to do anything you wanted."

"Do you think I could train her to respond without reins? I was thinking, if I need my bow, I'll need my hands."

"Of course. We'll help, won't we, Deren?" He nudged his horse, and the black stallion whickered.

"What about first thing tomorrow morning? We could start then?"

"Sure. It won't take long," Edril agreed and returned to grooming his horse.

Edril and Birler worked with Kafinee all week, and the conversation between Deren and Edril made Birler feel awkward. He was sure they were all talking about him. "What?" he demanded when Edril kept chuckling.

"Deren was just saying you ride funny."

"What's that supposed to mean?" Birler asked, ready to take offence.

"He doesn't understand why you can't hear Kafinee when we can."

"You can hear her as well? That's not fair."

"Only through Deren, but don't worry. She is very protective of you. You won't come to any harm with her."

Birler smiled as he rubbed her nose. "I love you, too," he murmured in her ear. Her ear flicked in his face, and then she rubbed her head against him. Edril had removed Kafinee's bridle, so Birler grabbed a handful of her mane and mounted smoothly. He had brought his bow with him today, and he was cantering past the targets, practising his archery. The bow occupied his hands, and he felt more balanced. Once they reached a rhythm, he never missed, and he could practise guiding Kafinee with his knees. Kafinee was steady and smooth. From an archery perspective, it was like he was standing on the ground.

After another week, he tried kneeling on her back without the saddle, but they lost all coordination, and Birler ended up flat on his back in the dirt. Kafinee trotted up and whuffled his hair.

Tagerill came running up and stood over him with Kafinee, both watching him with the same resigned expression. "You could kill someone doing that you know," Tagerill said, a smile glimmering in his eyes as he offered his hand. Kafinee wandered off and cropped the long grass at the edge of the path.

Birler reached for his hand, allowing Tagerill to pull him to his feet. "That's the general idea," he wheezed, brushing the dust off his clothes.

"Stop showing off and come join us in the sparring ring. Pallinten has a demonstration going."

"So that you can show off?" Birler laughed. He called Kafinee, and they walked towards the training area.

"If you practised with the sword more, I wouldn't be showing off."

"I have been practising." Birler shrugged. "You keep

saying I need more muscle." He looked at his arms. "But, no matter how hard I try, it makes no difference," he said mournfully.

"That's why you practise. Take Kafinee back and join us in the ring."

Birler rolled his eyes and led Kafinee away.

When he reached the sparring ring, there was quite an audience. First-years were crowding around the sparring master as he spoke. Tagerill and another lad his size—Birler thought his name was Lorill—were sparring in front of them. It seemed the master was criticising their technique. Birler joined them and climbed onto the railings to watch as Tagerill forced Lorill across the ring and the sparring master called out, "Break!"

Both lads stopped, breathing heavily. Lorill grinned. "I almost had you there."

"In your dreams," Tagerill replied, walking over to Birler.

"Cadet Birler, in the ring, please."

Birler rolled his eyes as he climbed down, drawing his sword. Tagerill took his place on the fence as Lorill joined him. They grinned at each other and watched expectantly as a lithe young woman joined Birler in the ring.

The sparring master critiqued the two new combatants as they circled. "Now, not everyone has brute force like the cadets you've just observed. But that doesn't mean you can't fight. There are other skills that can be brought to bear. For example, Cadet Cleo will show us that just because she doesn't have the muscles those young men have"—the sparring master smiled at the slighter-built cadets in the group—"it doesn't mean she hasn't got power."

Birler heard the master's words and gripped his sword tighter. One day, he thought, just one day, he would show them what he could do with a sword. He sighed internally. He knew it wouldn't be today. He was glad it wasn't Tianer he was up against; she would have flattened him without a blink. He set about trying to minimise the damage Cleo was going to do to him.

Cleo lunged, and Birler moved into *Understanding* as he parried, driving his strength into his arms to contain the blow. She swung low, and he managed to block, twisting her sword away as he moved out of her range. The swords slid their length, and the screech of steel vibrated in the air.

"He's not doing badly," Lorill said, watching Birler critically. "He's definitely improving."

Tagerill nodded in agreement and watched Birler until Cleo outwitted him and he ended up flat on his back in the dust, her sword at his throat.

Cleo laughed at him and helped him up. "You're getting better. That was much more rewarding," she said as they left the ring.

Birler climbed onto the fence. "See?" he grumbled. "A slingshot is much better. They can't get near enough to hurt you."

"They would when you run out of stones," Tagerill said with a grin. "Then what would you do?"

"Run," Birler replied.

28

BIRLER

VESPERS. YEAR END 1121

Birler and Serill gladly accepted Tagerill's invitation to spend the Year End with his family in Vespers—a two-day pass of freedom away from the daily grind of the academy, only available to second-year cadets. The first-years were grumbling at the unfairness of it all. Not that it really meant anything to Birler; he had never celebrated Year End before, so he hadn't missed it.

Arriving at the Descelles townhouse early on Year Ends Eve, their breath pluming in the frigid air, their cheeks red and eyes sparkling with vigour, Tagerill, Serill, and Birler dismounted.

Men ran to take the horses as they pulled their saddlebags off, and Birler rubbed Kafinee's nose in thanks before she was led away. He turned towards the steps as Tagerill's mother, Melis, appeared in the doorway with outstretched hands. It hadn't even been two months since she had seen them last, but Melis engulfed Tagerill as if he had been away for years.

Birler stared at them for a moment before glancing away and inspecting the imposing grey stone building with ranks of gleaming windows. He gulped at the sheer size of the building. Serill stood wide-eyed and silent beside him. When Melis pulled Birler into an equally heartfelt embrace, Birler's eyes prickled with tears. He blinked them away as he hugged her back, overwhelmed by her generous welcome.

Tagerill disappeared into the depths of the house with a yell of "Versill!" and the thud of his saddlebags landing on the flagstones in hallway.

Melis laughed and rolled her eyes. "Tage is home. Serill, welcome. Come in and tell me what you've been up to." She led the way into the dim interior, and Birler gaped at the elegant hallway dominated by a dark wooden staircase curving up to the upper levels.

Fronds of evergreen and holly were arranged in tall vases. They filled the air with their resinous scent, and Birler took a deep breath as he gawped. Liveried servants relieved them of their bags, and Melis led them into a light and airy reception room where Tagerill was hugging an equally red-headed man with broad shoulders who gave some indication of how Tagerill would look in a few years' time: Tagerill's second-eldest brother, Versill, who was dressed in the grey and black uniform of a Lady's Ranger.

Versill grinned at them as they entered, offering them a firm handshake when they were introduced. Versill was the Descelles he had never met until now, having been away on duty. His voice was deep and vibrant like his father's, and Birler liked him straight away.

Melis listened to the babble with a huge smile on her face as they all tried to tell her everything at once.

"One at a time. There's no rush," she said with a laugh, fending them off. "Sit down, all of you. You're like giants towering over me."

As she sat, a maid brought in a tray loaded with china. Versill leapt to his feet and proceeded to pour everyone a cup of tea, and Birler watched, wide-eyed, as he handed round the delicate cups and saucers. When offered milk or lemon, Birler stared at Versill in horror, paralysed by ignorance. Versill quirked an eyebrow and poured in milk. Copying Serill, Birler balanced his saucer on his lap and took hesitant sips. The taste was quite pleasant, though scented; unusual, he thought, as he sipped again. Not as strong as kafinee, but refreshing.

He tensed as Melis said his name and looked up in concern, wondering what he had done wrong. Melis smiled in reassurance. "I was just saying your room is ready upstairs. Tagerill will show you where to go and freshen up. Dinner is at seventh chime; Warren will join us then." She pinched her lips. "If Guerlaire has finished with him by then. And then we will join the evening service at the Lady's temple at ten."

Birler nodded, sensing she was expecting a response.

"Relax, Birler. Don't look so worried. This is a time of celebration. Enjoy it," she said as she rose, and he flushed, staring down into his cup. A soft hand lifted his chin. "You are among friends. Nothing you do will upset us. Don't fret so." She took his cup, and Tagerill grabbed his arm and tugged him out of the room after Serill.

"Thank you, ma'am," Birler whispered before he followed.

Once upstairs, Birler rotated as he stared around the room he was sharing with Serill. More sweet-smelling greenery was draped over the picture frames on the wall. His bags had been unpacked, but he only had his clean uniform hanging in lonely splendour in the cupboard. He felt even more out of place than he had in Greens. Greens was much more relaxed.

"Serill, please make sure I don't do anything stupid," he said, his voice low as he gingerly sat on his bed.

Serill grinned at him. "Don't be daft. You'll be fine."

"What happens at Year End?" he asked, staring at his hands.

His bed dipped as Serill sat beside him. "It's a time when we thank the Lady for the year gone by and ask her blessing for the year upcoming. Some people have parties or balls; others spend time with their families. The temples offer a service of thanksgiving for all comers, usually late in the evening. It normally finishes in time for everyone to return home and open their doors to the new year and welcome it in. I'm sorry, Birler. I never thought; we should have explained it all before we arrived."

"I could have asked."

Serill hesitated. "Have you never celebrated Year End?"

Birler shook his head, his eyes downcast.

"Then this year will be extra special. Tagerill's family wouldn't have invited you if they didn't want you to share it with them, so relax and enjoy it. Once we graduate, who knows where we will be for the next Year End? We could be in a place that doesn't even celebrate it!"

"There aren't gifts, like borning days, are there?" Birler raised his eyes as sudden fear gripped him and his stomach cramped. "I haven't got anything."

Birler leaned into Serill's sudden embrace. "No, Birler. Being with friends is the only gift we share, and that is a gift you have in abundance."

Birler relaxed in relief. "What year will it be next?"

"Eleven twenty-two."

"Eleven twenty-two," Birler repeated.

"And the current year is eleven twenty-one," Serill said gently, just in case.

"So if I'm seventeen, then I was born in … in eleven oh four?"

Birler was conscious that Serill took care in how he

answered. "Yes. If you are seventeen, then you would have been born in eleven oh four."

Birler nodded, his eyes distant.

They were interrupted when Tagerill stuck his head through the door. "Aren't you two changed yet?" Serill grimaced at him, and Tagerill frowned and slid into the room, closing the door behind him. "What's wrong?"

"Nothing," Birler said, straightening up out of Serill's arms.

"This is Birler's first Year End."

Tagerill's eyebrows rose into his hairline, and he opened his mouth to make a witty comment, but then he snapped it shut as he saw Birler's flushed face. He gave Birler a lop-sided grin. "Well, we'd better make it special then. You need to get ready. My father just arrived."

"I've only got my uniform," Birler whispered, staring at Tagerill's fine-frilled shirt and velvet trousers and waistcoat. He'd never owned clothes as fine as Tagerill's.

"Same as me, then," Serill grinned, thumping Birler's shoulder. "You go have a wash first; I'll follow, so don't take too long."

Birler nodded and then grabbed the towel on the end of his bed and dashed to the bathing room.

Serill caught Tagerill's arm. "Tage, don't make it special. Birler is uncomfortable as it is. He had no idea what Year End was. He's scared of embarrassing himself. Keep it simple; keep it real for him."

Staring at him for a moment, Tagerill slowly nodded. "I keep forgetting where he came from. He is so natural, and he fits in so well. You'd never know." He heaved a deep sigh. "I'll see you downstairs. Don't take too long." And he was gone.

Once Birler returned, Serill dashed off for his wash and returned to find Birler shining their boots.

They dressed and descended the stairs, following the sound of voices. Onoffs lit the hallways, casting a warm golden glow, and Birler's rising tension ratcheted. To be able to afford so many onoffs, Tagerill's family had to be richer than he had thought. His unease increased.

Warren's deep laugh welcomed them into the drawing room, and Birler relaxed a bit as he saw Tagerill's father standing in front of a roaring fire with Versill, resplendent in his ranger's dress uniform.

Warren extended his hand in welcome. "Birler, it's good to see you again, and this must be Serill. Welcome to our home."

"Thank you, sir," Serill said, shaking his hand.

"Ah, and here's Tagerill at last. We are complete," Warren said with a grin as his youngest son escorted his mother into the room.

Birler stiffened, and embarrassment swept through him as he realised Tagerill had changed back into his cadet uniform because of him.

Warren flicked him a swift glance, though he smoothly continued. "You all look so smart in your uniforms. I can't wait to see you all once you've graduated. Not much longer, is it? Where did the time go?"

Melis smiled as Warren passed her a glass of wine. She raised it. "To our cadets and rangers," she said.

"Cadets and rangers," they all murmured before taking a sip of the sweet, golden wine.

"Shall we?" Warren asked as he escorted his wife into the dining room, and a mirage of glistening silver, sparkling crystal, and white linen cloth greeted them. The boys sat where they were told, and Birler stared around the room with wide-eyed apprehension. He fumbled through the meal by discreetly watching Warren, whom he had been sat next to. Tagerill and Versill kept up a flow of small talk, describing what they had been doing, and Birler nodded whenever he was called upon, his attention on the rows of cutlery and the unusual dishes.

He flushed when Warren murmured, "Honey-roasted carrots with sesame seeds." He had no idea what it was and only took one, even though it smelt delicious. Warren scooped some more onto his plate. "You don't eat enough, Birler. Thank the Lady, there is plenty." He made sure two slices of roasted meat found their way onto Birler's plate.

"I can't eat that much," Birler murmured. "It makes me ill." However, he did add carrots to his growing list of food that he had tried for the first time.

"As long as you eat *enough*. Year End is a time for feasting. We're all expected to groan in a food stupor afterwards."

Birler chuckled, and Warren continued. "It fortifies us to leave our lovely, warm homes and walk through the cold night air to the temple for the service of thanksgiving. We can walk it off then."

Thank the Lady, Birler thought devoutly, already weighed down by all the food he had eaten. He was glad when they finally rose from the table after a heavy fruit pudding steeped in brandy had finished him off.

He stood by the fire in the drawing room, his face flushed and his stomach heavy, though he had enjoyed every morsel he had eaten. The food had been delicious.

Serill crossed the room, looking just as stuffed, and joined him. "We were eating for nearly two chimes!" he said in disbelief.

"Feels like it," Birler replied, rubbing his stomach.

Tagerill joined them. "Best meal of the year," he said, his grin stretched across his face.

Birler flicked him a glance. "You didn't have to change," he said, his cheeks burning hotter at the knowledge that

Tagerill had realised he and Serill didn't have a change of clothes.

Tagerill's grin deepened, and he looked down at his uniform. "I hate dress clothes. This is much more comfortable. All those frills." He shuddered.

A half-chime later, they were all bundled up in warm woollen cloaks and scarves and walking down the road towards the Lady's temple, down by the Chapterhouse. Warren and Melis greeted fellow worshipers as they walked. The walk did ease the digestion, and Birler felt much better once they arrived at the temple.

There were a great many people approaching the temple door, and their party stood off to one side, letting the congestion ease. Birler stiffened as Tyrler hissed behind him in a low voice, "So selfish. You're just a wharf rat, and still, you won't listen. You'll be the ruin of the Descelles. Their downfall will be on your head."

Birler spun in shock at the viciousness of the words and met Tyrler Clary's hard eyes. An equally severe-faced older man called Tyrler away, and Birler shivered as the man's black eyes slid over him, mentally peeled back his skin, and found him wanting. The man dismissed him, and Birler's breath escaped in a low moan.

Tagerill was beside him in a moment. "What's up? You look like you're about to puke. Did you eat too much?"

Birler managed to shake his head as he clamped his mouth shut. Fortunately, their party was called together, and they entered the temple. They shuffled into the narrow wooden pews, and Birler's anxiety eased as the temple shimmered around him in excitement.

The Lady's blessing percolated through him, and he relaxed. His lips parted in wonder as a choral arrangement was sung, with the choir's voices blending with and echoing the temple's joy, and he was snared once more.

Warren cast him a thoughtful glance, but left him in peace. He walked over to greet Leyandrii and Guerlaire as they entered: Leyandrii resplendent in a pale blue gown, her blond hair piled elegantly on her head, Guerlaire hovering attentively. They paused to speak to the father before taking their seats, and Warren returned to his family.

Tagerill pointed out all the local dignitaries to Serill, who was staring around wide-eyed, at all the affluently-dressed worshipers. The little father nodded to Leyandrii and stood to one side of the Lady's altar and welcomed everyone as the singing voices faded.

Leyandrii rose and took his place. "Welcome, one and all. May you all be blessed with peace and good health this Year End. Join us as we celebrate the end of one year and welcome in the new." Birler smiled as the warmth of her regard settled over him. Leyandrii continued speaking, her voice filling the temple and, Birler knew, reaching out across Remargaren. Her voice soothed his jitters, filled his heart, and promised a great future.

As the service progressed, Serill leaned across to Birler and nudged him in the ribs. Birler turned towards him, but he was ensorcelled by Leyandrii and didn't see him at first. Slowly, his immediate surroundings penetrated his thrall, and he felt someone's gaze boring into his back. It made his neck prickle, and he slowly turned and met Clary's black eyes. He moved his gaze to Tyrler, who was smirking next to him, and then he deliberately turned his back on them.

Leaning over Tagerill, Warren murmured, "Ignore them." He rested his arm across Tagerill's back and gripped Birler's shoulder in support. Tagerill looked at them in suspicion, but at his father's glare, he kept his mouth shut.

After the service, Birler found himself flanked by Warren and Versill as they left the temple. Tagerill and Serill escorted Melis in front of them as they headed home. "How did you attract Dominant Clary's ire?" Warren murmured as they followed the cheerful exclamations preceding them.

"I'm not sure," Birler admitted. "I've never met him. His son Tyrler is a cadet with us, and he's taken me in dislike. Apparently, the likes of me shouldn't be a cadet."

"What rubbish!" Versill exclaimed. His voice was loud in the still night air, and Tagerill jerked an inquisitive glance over his shoulder. Melis drew his attention forward, but Birler knew Tagerill was straining to listen.

"He is short-sighted and opinionated," Warren said. "But he is a powerful voice in the Administration, so you would do well to avoid him."

Birler twisted his lips. Warren would have no argument from him, but the Clarys seemed to search him out, and Tyrler's vicious words before the service burned there way through his brain. The Descelles were so nice; they didn't deserve to be dragged into his problems.

Warren must have divined some of what he was thinking because he suddenly hugged Birler. "Don't let them spoil such a special night. We are blessed by the Lady, and it's time to welcome in the new year. This is a time for celebration." He looked up as they turned into their street. "And here we are home, just in time."

Footmen took their outer clothes for them, and maids waited with trays of steaming mugs. As the scent of cinnamon and spice warmed the air, Birler relaxed into the welcoming atmosphere and joined the celebrations, not wanting to ruin the night for anyone else.

The cadets rose late the next morning, as the celebration had continued into the early chimes. After a quick meal, they collected their belongings and their horses. With many good wishes and demands for them to return the next pass day, they reluctantly mounted and set off for the garrison.

Tagerill accosted Birler as soon as they turned at the end of the street, and Birler was glad the journey through the city streets was not long. "What were you talking about with my father on the way home last night?" Tagerill demanded as they rode.

"Nothing important," Birler replied.

"Rubbish. Versill was quite indignant. He wouldn't get upset about nothing."

"It was nothing, Tage. You only make it larger by acknowledging it."

Serill cast Birler a sharp glance and thinned his lips.

Tagerill badgered him all the way to the garrison until he wheedled it out of him, and he glowered as they passed through the academy gates.

"Tage, please, it's nothing," Birler said. "I'll avoid him. I'm insignificant; he'll soon forget about me."

Tagerill exchanged a glance with Serill and didn't reply.

BIRLER

RANGERS ACADEMY

Birler sighed and rolled over on his back. He watched the clouds chase each other across the sky. "What a perfect day," he murmured.

Tagerill and Serill were stretched out on the grass beside him, making the most of a rare free chime. They were relaxing by the pond behind the sparring rings. The early spring sunshine was unexpectedly hot, and they were sprawled on the grass, their jackets discarded, shirts undone, and collars flapping in the breeze.

"Mmm," Tagerill replied, drowsing in the sun.

A gentle breeze fluttered over Birler's skin, following its own quest and as light as a kiss. Birler closed his eyes. It was quiet; not even the sound of someone sparring disturbed the idyllic scene. He heard Tagerill snore and smiled.

The next thing he knew, he was erupting out of icy cold water, choking out the mouthful he had inhaled in surprise. He stood waist deep in the muddy pond, glaring at his friends as they folded over with laughter.

"Gotcha!" Tagerill shouted, as he burst out laughing.

"Your face," Serill said as he leaned against Tagerill. He was laughing so much that tears streamed down his cheeks.

"You bastards," Birler swore as he climbed out of the pond, his boots sinking into the gloopy mud. Tagerill and Serill backed off, still laughing. "I'll get you," he threatened, shaking his fist.

"You can try," Tagerill taunted.

Birler reached into the back of his waistband, and Tagerill backed up further.

"Balls," Tagerill said and ran. Serill hesitated and then saw the sling and ran after him. Birler paused long enough to pick up a few small stones, not big enough to damage but small enough to sting.

He chased them across the training grounds, through the barracks, and up towards the large barn. Tagerill flung a look over his shoulder and veered towards the large building that housed the covered sparring rings.

Birler loaded his sling. He whirled it above his head and released it. Tagerill's yelps followed him into the barn. Serill paused as if he were going to try and reason with Birler, but then he changed his mind and darted for cover. He just wasn't quick enough, and Birler's stones caught his backside. He yelled and dived behind a straw bale.

Birler hunted for some more stones, his cheeks aching he was grinning so much.

"Cadet Birler?"

He swung round and stiffened to attention, conscious of his still-dripping clothes.

"Keeping in practice, I see. Live targets as well. More challenging, I hope?" the adjutant asked, a slight smile on his face.

"Yes, sir," Birler replied, trying to hide the sling still in his grip.

"Good, good. Commander Asher would like to see you

immediately, though I would suggest you change into more suitable clothing." The adjutant nodded and walked away, chuckling under his breath.

Birler scowled at the barn and turned to follow, his boots squelching as he walked.

He stripped off his wet clothes and dived into the shower to rinse off the mud. Then he slicked his hair back and roughly dried himself off before dressing in his only other uniform. He wiped his boots clean, but there was nothing for it; he forced his feet back into the wet boots, shuddering at the feel of the soggy, cold leather.

With a wicked grin, he piled his wet clothes in Tagerill's bed and the towel in the middle of Serill's bed and then headed off towards the commander's office.

Guerlaire observed the cadet standing at attention before Commander Asher. He didn't look like the same boy he had dragged in from the temple a year ago. He had filled out, and he looked healthy. His deep blue eyes were sparking with life and vitality. He was a young man learning the skills of his trade.

His reports were excellent. He had knuckled down and learnt to read and write. The masters said he had caught up with the others in record time. It hadn't been intelligence he lacked; it was opportunity. His weapons skills were off the chart, all except the sword. Even then, it wasn't that he was bad; he just still didn't have the strength behind him, but Guerlaire could see that he would in time.

Commander Asher was outlining his assignment. Leyandrii had been insistent; it was time for Birler to extend his horizons. Birler was assigned to the Chapterhouse to shadow the scholar-dean's assistant.

Starting the next day from eighth chime to five, he was the scholar's.

Birler settled in the Chapterhouse easily. The more he saw, the more envious he became. To have had the opportunity to study and learn here would have been his dream if he had known such a place existed.

Keeping his distance, he watched the scholars in awe as they debated any subject that was tabled. They eventually coaxed him to join in, and the thrill of people listening to what he had to say and respecting his opinion was a novelty that never tired him. Not that they always agreed with him, but he enjoyed the arguing and the process of learning.

He was seated in the library, researching the ownership of the harbour wharves and surrounding areas in preparation for a debate he wanted to raise about basic rights and living conditions, when a young scholar sat opposite him.

She was silver-robed as he was, but his eye was drawn to her delicate face, framed in honey-gold blond hair. Emerald green eyes watched him, and she had a slight smile on her face, which grew as he stared.

Birler blushed from being caught staring, but she looked so familiar, and then he knew. His eyes widened, and his stomach fluttered. No, it couldn't be.

"I hear you are quite the debater. A supporter of the man in the street. It is quite refreshing to hear there is someone who sees past all the finery and considers what lies behind." Her voice was light yet rich and warming; it caressed and shivered through him, and he was positive he knew who she was.

"There are not many who speak up, my Lady."

"Hush. 'Scholar' will do."

"What are you doing here, my L … uh, scholar?"

"Why, the same as you, scholar. I'm here to learn."

His eyes flickered around the room. "You're not alone, are you, my … scholar?"

Leyandrii smiled. "I'm quite safe."

"Don't they realise who you are?" Birler stared at her, aghast.

"I'm in disguise," Leyandrii replied with a gentle wave of her hand. She looked at him. "I should have known you would see through it." She rose and walked round the table to peer over his shoulder. "What are you researching?" She frowned as she looked closer. "That's the harbour, isn't it?"

"Yes, I was looking to see who owned it all. Surely, they should have some responsibility for the condition of the housing? They collect the rent, after all; they should have an obligation to provide at least the basic amenities."

"Do they not?"

Birler was very aware of Leyandrii standing beside him. His body sang in response, and he wanted to fall to his knees in awe, but he concentrated on answering her question. "I take it you haven't been to Harbourtown recently?"

"No, I don't believe I have. Would you escort me? I believe it is time I did."

"It's not safe, my, uh … scholar."

"Of course it is; I have you. Now is a good time, I think. Come, show me."

Birler escorted her out of the Chapterhouse, unable to refuse her request. They walked down the long hill towards the harbour. He had grown this last year with good food and exercise, and Leyandrii barely reached his shoulder. She was as delicate as a flower, yet her roots reached deep into his soul, entwined, entrenched. Her presence resonated throughout his body.

"Relax, Birler. We are quite safe. Tell me what is wrong with Harbourtown; no one has raised it as a concern before."

Birler scowled. "What's right with it? You'll soon see. I

always wondered why no one helped us. It never occurred to me that you wouldn't know. I mean, you created all of this. You see all your people."

"Not everyone all the time. Only if they ask. I am not here to enforce anything on anyone. I provide a peaceful world where we can all live together. It's up to you what you do with it."

Birler couldn't prevent the bitter laugh from escaping. "Some would call that idealistic."

"And what is wrong with that?"

"It is not reality. Everyone wants the same thing, to live peacefully, but some people want more than others, and it skews the balance. They take more and give nothing back, leaving those they took from destitute and desperate. Not everyone is equal."

"But why did they give up what they had in the first place?"

"I don't know. Maybe the other person was stronger, cleverer, or even deceitful. But once lost, it's very difficult to regain, and no matter how hard you work, you end up with just enough to live on, and each generation, it worsens as people take advantage of you until you end up living like this." Birler spread his hand before him, and Leyandrii wrinkled her nose at the pervading stench rising from the streets before her.

"Until you plucked me out of these streets, I didn't know there was a different way of life just out of reach. I knew there had to be something, but it was as unattainable as reaching the moon, so there was no point in trying. There are no temples here, no running water, no basic amenities, which is why the air is so putrid."

"But this is not even half a chime from the city. How can it be? You have to pass it to get from the harbour to the city."

"The harbour road skirts the area. The barns block the

sights, and salty air masks the smell. We don't go into the city; we would be hounded out as thieves or beggars."

Leyandrii picked up her robes and ventured deeper. Her face was expressionless as she peered down disgusting back alleys and into dilapidated buildings.

"My Lady, it is not safe to go any further. Street gangs roam the alleys. They would see us as a rich target."

"Street gangs?" Leyandrii looked up at him with a tiny frown on her exquisite face.

Birler shrugged. "What do you think happens to us if our parents die?"

Leyandrii grew still.

"Although your temple is beautiful, my Lady, I always thought your money would be better spent on a home for the street kids or a chapterhouse to teach us to read and write so we would have a chance to regain the right to walk in the city. A purpose, even. There are many here who would serve you, who would contribute if they had the chance." Birler fell silent, afraid he had said too much.

He led her away from the depressing streets and down to the sea. They stood on the beach and watched the grey water swell into waves that crashed down onto the sand with a satisfying roar, rushing up the beach and then swirling back into the sea. The clean sea air flushed away the putrid stink.

After a moment, Birler asked, "Why did you choose me? You plucked me out of those streets, gave me a chance. Why?"

"You asked."

"I didn't."

"Yes, you did. You were so loud and demanding, and yet, I couldn't find you to begin with. That was why I built the temple—for you." She turned her back on the sea and looked back up to the storage barns. "This area is dead and dying. There is no hope or vitality. That's why I can't see it. No one is reaching out, no one calls, except for you."

Birler stared at her, stunned. "You built the temple for me?"

Leyandrii smiled at him and then reached up and patted his cheek. "It worked, didn't it?" She looked around and inhaled the fresh, salty air. "Thank you, Birler, for opening my eyes. I will investigate further. Please continue your research and send your findings to Commander Asher. He will forward them to me. Make sure you include your opinion and suggestions; I would value your input. I can assure you I will hold them accountable." Her eyes gleamed emerald green, her disguise forgotten in her pre-occupation.

"Of course, my Lady."

They began the long walk up the hill, skirting the muddy puddles gathering in the cart tracks. A haulier steering his wagon down the road almost twisted his head off staring at them as they passed. "Um, my Lady? I think your disguise has slipped."

Leyandrii chuckled, and her appearance shimmered, though she looked no different to Birler. When they reached the Chapterhouse, a frantic ranger was berating the gate-house guard. "Oh dear." Leyandrii wryly twisted her lips. "I seem to have upset Elliar. I wonder if we can slip in the back entrance."

"This way, my Lady, we can go in the goods entrance."

"Excellent. It is better for her that she doesn't know I ventured out."

"Better for her?" Birler cocked an eyebrow at her. "Do you usually deliberately lose your guards, my Lady? I doubt Captain Guerlaire will be impressed."

"Don't you start." She rolled her eyes. "I had *you*, didn't I? I was perfectly safe. And here we are, back safe and sound. No one need know."

"My Lady, please, it is not safe for you to roam Vespers without your guards."

Leyandrii frowned at him. "Hush. I'm a scholar, and anyway, Birler, *you* are my guard. Escort me back to the library, and I will be found by Elliar."

"Yes, scholar."

Leyandrii laughed. "What a good boy you are."

They made it back to the library unseen, and Birler returned to his books, though it was a long time before he read anything on the page in front of him. His sympathies lay with Elliar. No wonder she had been frantic. He knew how he would feel if he lost the Lady on his watch; it didn't bear thinking about.

Birler duly wrote up his research and handed his report into Commander Asher's office with a note that Lady Leyandrii had requested to see it. He hoped it would get passed on.

Two months later, the next assignment found Birler at the Administration building. Birler waited in the ante-chamber until Dominant Vincent was ready to see him. He understood that Vincent was responsible for finance, and he was interested to learn what that meant. He only had a vague idea that it must have to do with how the Administration paid for everything.

He regretted not having more time in the Chapterhouse; the information available there was alluring. He knew Serill spent every free chime possible researching whatever took his interest, and Guerlaire had officially made him his assistant. He was often joined by a cadet called Nialler. Skinny and dark-haired, Nialler was clever with his hands, always dismantling things, trying to understand how they worked, and improving designs as if commonplace. Birler sighed. He would never be in Nialler's league; his mind worked on a different level.

He was musing on the idea that somewhere there was enough money to run a whole kingdom and wondering how he could get the Lady to divert some of it to where it was needed when the door finally opened, and an elderly gentleman stood staring at him. His grey hair was swept off his narrow face, and his clothes were elegant and well-tailored. Birler stiffened to attention, and the man waved him down. "You don't need to salute me, young man. I assume you are Cadet Birler? Here to solve our country's problems?" Hard grey eyes at odds with his soft voice inspected him.

Birler relaxed. "I don't know about that, sir. Understand them, maybe?"

Vincent gestured him into his office. "Well, if you understand them by the time you've finished, make sure you tell me before you leave, understood?" he said with a gentle cackle as he shut the door.

"Yes, sir." Birler halted at the sight of the Dominant's office. Manuscripts, folders, and books were piled everywhere. The air was musty and dry; a bit like Vincent, Birler thought. His nose twitched; he thought he might sneeze.

"You can sit over there." Vincent gestured to a dark corner, and Birler peered over the stack of papers and realised there was a desk underneath it all. "We'll call you my aide for the duration; that way, no one will complain when you accompany me."

"Accompany you, sir?"

"Yes, yes, you can't learn if you don't hear, now, can you? I'll expect your opinion on what was discussed, so make sure you pay attention."

"Yes, sir."

"You can move that lot onto the floor. I must get it all sent to the Chapterhouse at some point."

"What is it, sir?"

"The ratification documents for the new watches."

Birler stared at the pile with interest. He reordered the piles of paper so he had space to work, but he left them on his desk like a barrier. He didn't think they should sit on the floor.

"Umm, sir? What exactly do you need me to do?"

"Watch and listen. Don't speak unless I tell you to. You're my first cadet, so we'll see how it goes." Vincent placed a pair of glasses on his nose and peered over them. "I assume you can read?"

"Yes, sir."

"Good, then read this and tell me what you think." Vincent handed him a folder and returned to his desk. He was soon lost in a pile of papers, muttering under his breath.

Birler looked at the folder. It was titled, "Justification – B4TC". He opened the folder and scanned the contents. He was frowning over what an optical extension unit could possibly be when Vincent's office door opened and a tall man entered unannounced.

"Vincent, this is unacceptable. You can't refuse my request."

Vincent peered up at the man. "I can refuse any request that I deem pointless, not worth the money, or an unjustified expense."

"Which this isn't, so approve it now," the man demanded, slapping his paperwork in front of Vincent.

"I can also have you barred from my office if you don't abide by the scheduling rules. And that would mean you wouldn't get any budgetary support at all, so I advise you to go and make an appointment with my secretary."

"I'll escalate this to Clary."

"You do that," Vincent said as he refocussed on the work on his desk, ignoring the man.

The man stiffened with anger, but he did storm out of the office, leaving the door wide open. Birler rose and shut the door.

"Thank you," Vincent said absently as he turned a page.

Birler smiled. He wasn't that engrossed in his work after all. "May I ask a question, sir?"

Vincent looked up. "Of course, my boy. What is it?"

"This report you asked me to read—it doesn't say where they want to build whatever an optical extension unit is."

"That's two questions, and very pertinent. Write them down. When you respond asking them for further information, you'll want to list the information we require."

Birler gulped. "You want me to respond to this, sir?"

"Yes, yes, that's what I said, and go ask Simmond for some kafinee, would you? Get some for yourself if you want any."

Birler rose and went in search of Simmond, whom he found in the outer chamber. "Dominant Vincent would like some kafinee," Birler said as he stopped by Simmond's desk. His desk was one of four, squashed into the small office space, all populated by harried-looking young men. Simmond was no exception. He dragged his hands through his sandy-blond hair and glared at Birler. "He expects too much. I can't do all this and run around after him."

Birler smiled. "If you tell me where to go and what he likes, I'll get it for him if you like."

"Would you? I'm never going to get these reports out if he keeps interrupting me."

Birler nodded, amused that Vincent's aide thought his work was more important than Vincent's.

"Down the corridor, second door on the right takes you

to the kitchen. He likes his kafinee with milk, not too weak, two sugars."

Birler hesitated. "Would you like one?"

Simmond stared at him and then slowly smiled. "A kafinee, no milk or sugar, would be perfect."

Birler left, and he soon returned with a tray. He balanced it and left Simmond's kafinee on his desk and then entered the office. Placing Vincent's on his desk, he returned to his own. Then, after taking a sip of his own kafinee, he jotted notes on the pad that had been placed on his desk.

Vincent drank his kafinee and then closed the report in front of him. He stared across the room with a frown on his face. "If someone asked you to fund the demolition of a building, only to build the exact same building in its place, what would you think?"

After taking a brief moment to think, Birler replied, "Either something is drastically wrong with the original building, and I would want to know what, or they have no intention of knocking the building down and intend to pocket the money instead."

Vincent's gaze sharpened, and he smiled. "Very good," he said, "which proves my point that we should view the site before and after the work to ensure the money was used as expected."

"Don't you do that already?" Birler asked, leaning his chin on his hand as he watched Vincent.

"We don't have enough people. It's not feasible, especially in the watches on the borders. Takes too long to get there."

"Maybe random checks would keep people in order?" Birler suggested, frowning in thought. "If there was a chance you might check, most people would do what was approved."

Vincent eyed Birler with interest. "That is not a bad idea. You finished with that report?"

Birler handed his notes over.

Vincent skimmed through them. "Yes, yes, excellent. Write it up. Use this as an example of the format"—Vincent handed him a paper—"finish it with a request for information by Apru 1, or the application is denied. Make a copy for our files and then put it in that pile over there. Here's another one for you to review." He gave him another folder and returned to his own work.

They worked diligently all afternoon, and Birler handed his letter and the copy to Vincent when he had finished. Vincent paused, checking over his work, and then handed him a sheaf of papers. "Give these to Simmond; he'll get them sent out."

Vincent observed him over the top of his glasses and nodded. "Be back here tomorrow at ninth chime."

30

BIRLER

JUSTICE BUILDING, VESPERS

Birler found he enjoyed working with Vincent. He might have been a crusty old man, but that was a result of having spent years responding to ridiculous requests. Birler was amazed at what came across his desk. His routine was adjusted to rising at dawn and running the perimeter, followed by half a chime of Apeiron, and then caring for Kafinee before changing and heading to the Justice building. The only times he saw Tagerill and Serill were first thing in the morning and in the evening.

Serill talked nonstop about working in the Chapterhouse. He was helping Captain Guerlaire catalogue all his discoveries and notes. "Can you believe that Guerlaire is actually the first person to step onto some of this land? No one has ever been there before. Do you think we would ever have the chance to go with him?" Serill asked, his eyes bright and his expression eager.

"You'd have to ask him." Tagerill grinned and lay on his bed, and then his face dropped. "Marian's back. She is up at the palace. They are having a ball this evening to celebrate the approval of the new watch system, and my father is here. Do you think we'll ever get invited?"

"To the palace? Unlikely, wouldn't you think?" Birler replied.

"But think of all the lovely ladies—lots of opportunity to twirl them around in your arms," Tagerill smiled, his dimple flashing as his smile deepened at the thought.

"Not much point, as I don't know how to dance," Birler said.

Tagerill jerked upright. "What? We can't have that." He turned to Serill. "What about you?"

"I know enough, thank you. I don't need your help," Serill replied, backing away from Tagerill.

"Then you can help me teach Birler; everyone needs to know how to dance. It's easy, really. I know. We'll sneak out next Lady's Day. There is a dance at the meeting hall next week. Good practice."

Birler shuddered with horror. "If you think I am going to dance in public, you're wrong."

Tagerill laughed and slapped him on the shoulder. "All dancing is in public, but no one watches unless you are really good, so you'll be safe."

Every spare moment, Tagerill taught Birler how to dance. He was a ruthless teacher and a persuasive rule-breaker. By the time the day of the dance came around, he had even managed to get Parsill and Serill to go with them as well.

"We won't get in trouble," Tagerill assured them. "They won't even know we went."

"But what if they do?" Serill was in a panic of indecision now that the time had arrived.

"Then we take the punishment; it will be worth it. Birler needs to go to at least one dance."

"Look, no one needs to get into trouble for me. Just Tage

and I will go. No need for you all to get into trouble, too." Birler gripped Serill's arm and shook him.

"No, I am coming, too," Serill said, straightening his shoulders.

"We won't get into trouble," Tagerill soothed. He looked around their small barrack room and grinned. "You know, I think this is the first time in ages we've been out of uniform. I hardly recognise you, nor will anyone else."

Birler grimaced. "Come on. Let's go before *I* change my mind." His stomach was fluttering—he was eager to try out his new steps and terrified at the same time.

They made their way through the shadowy grounds and slipped out the gate when the guard's back was turned. "How do we get back in?" Serill whispered as they scuttled down the street.

"Don't worry so. I have it all arranged," Tagerill reassured him, his eyes glittering in the glow of the street lamps. Wispy strands of mist drifted low to the ground, swirling around their legs as they hurried down the road. "This way; it's the other side of the market square."

"Who comes to dances, anyway?" Birler asked.

"Lots of lovely ladies; they like dancing. Mainly those from the offices and shops."

Parsill snorted. "You hope."

Birler stopped in the middle of the street. "But how do you get them to dance with you?"

Tagerill rolled his eyes. "You ask them, you idiot!"

Parsill laughed. "Don't worry, Birler. We'll look out for you." He tugged Birler down the road towards the sound of music and voices. A jaunty jig was playing.

Birler gulped. "I can't dance to that."

"You sit those ones out," Tagerill replied.

"Which ones should I dance to? How do I tell?" Sweat

trickled down Birler's neck; this was far more complicated than he'd thought.

Tagerill groaned. "Will you all stop worrying? You'll be fine! Relax. Enjoy it. It's supposed to be fun."

Tagerill dropped the requisite coins in the jar and breezed into the dance hall. Birler hadn't even considered that they would have to pay for entry. He gazed around the brightly lit hall. Wooden stools lined the walls; some were taken, but most people were on the dance floor. At the opposite end of the hall, a group of musicians stood on the stage: four men and a woman. Birler recognised a guitar and drums. One man was seated and had a wooden instrument under his ear, and he was pulling a stick back and forth; the sounds he made were amazing. The woman stood at the front and played a thin pipe. As Birler watched, they dropped into a slow waltz, with the trill of the pipe rising above the other instruments. He drifted to a halt and stood there, mesmerised.

"This, you can dance to," Tagerill said, tugging Birler deeper into the hall. They skirted the dance floor while Birler watched the couples twirling around with ease. It seemed rather busy and very colourful.

"Watch me." Tagerill stopped in front of a young lady. "My name is Tagerill. Would you like to dance?" he asked, extending his hand. The lady rose immediately, accepted his hand, and eagerly followed him onto the dance floor. Birler watched them twirl away and swallowed.

He drifted nearer the musicians, watching the dance floor. Both Parsill and Serill were dancing, and he looked around rather desperately. He spotted a young woman seated on one of the wooden stools, alternating between staring at her hands and watching the dancers. "Would you like to dance?" he asked, unable to keep the quiver of uncertainty out of his voice.

She looked up at him and smiled as she placed her hand in his. "I'd love to," she said.

He took her in his arms and carefully counted his steps. The girl chuckled. "Relax," she said, "I won't break."

"Sorry. I'm new to this." He smiled back at her. She barely reached the middle of his chest. He was looking down on a head of brown curls.

"You're doing great. I appreciate you asking; people don't tend to as I'm so short." She grimaced at him.

He laughed. "What's that got to do with being able to dance?"

"That's what I say, but most men don't like short partners. Ouch," she said as he stepped on her toes.

"Sorry."

"You're not the first, and I'm sure you won't be the last."

They twirled, trying to avoid the other dancers, and when the tune changed, Birler led her off the floor. "I only know the waltz," he said, grimacing in apology.

"I can show you the steps to this dance if you like. It's quite easy. Watch that couple there." She pointed at Tagerill and his partner. "See how he twirls her out and in? This is an eight-count song and every second eight-count you spin your partner."

"But how do you know when it's the right eight count?" Birler asked, watching them sway and twirl.

"I'll tell you. Come on." She dragged him back onto the floor, positioned his arms, and whispered instructions. "Push now." She moved away, extending her arm as he released her and pulled her back in, and they continued. "Again, push."

"This is great. What's it called?"

"'The Return.' They'll play it again later; it's quite popular."

"I can see why."

They left the floor, hot, flushed, and laughing. Tagerill

paused beside them. "Having fun?" Birler's grin was all he needed to see. "A drink is included in the price of entry when you want one," he said and was gone.

Birler looked at the girl. "Would you like a drink?"

"Yes, please. I'm Celia."

"Birler."

Celia smiled up at him, and as their gazes met, her smile wavered. Birler took her arm and led the way to the drinks station.

"What would you like?" he asked over his shoulder.

"Lemon water, please."

Birler returned with two ice-cold drinks, and they sat against the wall and gratefully took the chance to cool down.

"I haven't seen you here before," Celia said.

"It's my first time; I'm only just learning to dance. I have two dances now, thanks to you."

"My pleasure."

Another waltz began, and he smiled an invitation. She stood immediately as if she were scared he would change his mind.

They glided around the room. "You're good, you know, Celia said, her hand smoothing over his back.

"You make it easy," Birler murmured into her curls. Her hand slid more tightly around his waist, bringing them closer. Her cheek warmed Birler's chest, and he smiled. He caught Tagerill's wink, and his smile grew. He was disappointed when the evening ended. Celia had felt lovely in his arms.

"Birler, say your goodbyes. We need to go," Parsill hissed.

Birler looked down at Celia. Her face was flushed pink, and her light blue eyes sparkled with pleasure; she made a pretty picture. He couldn't believe she had been left sitting out. "Will you get home alright?"

"Oh yes. I'm here with some girlfriends. We always walk home together."

"Good. Thank you for dancing with me, and I hope your toes recover."

Celia laughed. "You didn't step on them once the last time."

"True. I'm improving."

Serill waved at him, urgently beckoning.

"I have to go. Maybe see you another time? Though, I'm not sure when I will be able to come again."

"I'm here most weeks. If you can come again, I'll teach you another dance."

"Deal." He looked down at her, sure his face was as flushed as hers. "Good night." He kissed her on the cheek and made his way over to Serill.

"Come on. We're late." Serill hauled him out of the door.

"You move fast." Parsill slapped him on the shoulder. "I could hardly get a word out of my partners."

Tagerill grinned at him. "See. Told you it was fun."

"I'll never doubt you again," Birler replied as they hurried down the dark streets.

Tagerill tugged out a rope from under a nearby tree root and slung it over a bracket on the wall. He boosted the others over before following, climbing up and coiling the rope behind him.

They made it back to their beds unseen, hurriedly undressed, and climbed into bed. "I can't believe we got away with it," Serill breathed.

"Shut up and go to sleep. Dawn is not that far away," Tagerill replied, snuggling under his blanket.

Birler stared at the ceiling, luxuriating in the buzz rushing through his body. *Celia,* he thought and fell asleep with a smile on his face.

Four reluctant cadets stumbled out of bed at dawn the next morning. Birler winced as the muscles in the backs of his legs twinged. "You didn't say dancing would hurt," he complained as he limped towards the training field.

"Apeiron will help with that," Tagerill said with a gleam in his eyes. "Anything to do with the ladies uses different muscles, you know."

Parsill chuckled as they ran. By the third lap, their muscles had warmed up, and Birler stopped complaining.

31

LEYANDRII

LADY'S PALACE, VESPERS

Early summer sunshine flooded Leyandrii's study in the palace as she welcomed Commander Asher and gestured to the chair next to Guerlaire. As he made himself comfortable, she sat behind her desk.

"So, our cadets progress and graduation approaches. Have you plans for their continued development?" she asked.

"Of course," Oren replied. "We will be sending them further afield. They need to know there is more than Vespiri in the world of Remargaren."

"Good. As our regions expand, my rangers need to grow with them."

"And what about the Administration? Clary continues to spread false rumours. Your denial of his seat as leader of the Administration rankles. I think his personal embarrassment must be driving most of that."

"That's his own fault for spreading the word of his appointment before I ratified it. Maybe he thought once it was announced, I would be reluctant to cause any discomfort. He was mistaken."

"We need to watch him," Oren said thoughtfully.

"I haven't stopped," Guerlaire said with a grimace.

"No, of course not, but his ambition continues."

Guerlaire exhaled. "I'm convinced Clary is behind much of the recent unrest, but proving it is difficult. Even when it's his wagons or men involved, he manages to squirm out of any responsibility by saying he is not culpable for the actions of those who hire his resources."

"Well, he didn't get away with his recent attempted coup," Leyandrii said. "Clary's actions have only reinforced my decision, and I have decided to devolve the Administration's power to the watches. I will confirm the lords as legally responsible for the welfare of the people within their territory. The lords will have a seat at the Administration's table and contribute to the decisions. Their word will be final."

Oren stared at Leyandrii. "I didn't think you'd do it," he admitted. "The administrators are going to be upset."

"The administrators have been lax. They had their chance, and now they will be held accountable by the watches. They will re-dedicate themselves to Vespiri as part of the investiture if they want to remain in the Administration. Be ready, Oren, because you will be an integral part of this. You understand how the Administration works. You'll need to help our new Guardians navigate treacherous waters."

Oren huffed out a laugh. "Not likely. With the likes of Warren Descelles and Daven Ferrantes leading the way, they are more strategically savvy than I'll ever be."

"Then you are in good company," Leyandrii said with a grin. "I have the scholars working on the agreements now. The investiture will be in Novu."

"That's not long," Oren said, raising his eyebrows.

"I can't afford to wait. There is too much going on." Leyandrii rose and paced around her study. "I'm still trying to get the Mederas to agree to a conclave. There is always one who can't make the date. It is so frustrating."

"Maybe it's time to accept a quorum," Oren suggested.

"Maybe," Leyandrii replied, wrinkling her nose. "And how is Birler doing?"

"Just as bright and running Vincent ragged," Oren said with a chuckle. "He was complaining to me the other day. The lad never stops coming up with suggestions that he then has to consider."

Guerlaire smiled. "Serill has really stepped up this year as well. He has been a great assistance in the archives. I can leave much of the cataloguing in his hands, freeing me up to focus on the unrest these Ascendants are causing. I've also got Nialler investigating the crystals. We managed to find a few for him to experiment on so he can find out how they are being used. This is a good year for the cadets. Some strong candidates."

"I think they may need to be," Leyandrii said as she sat back down and clasped her fingers together. "I think we should continue to broaden their experiences for the rest of the year. They need to be able to deal with any situation that gets thrown at them."

"I agree," Oren said.

Leyandrii nodded as she stared off into the distance. What was she doing wrong that so many people were rebelling against her rule? It wasn't as if she were actually ruling, just keeping the people's chosen administrators on course. Why would that cause unrest? Unless it wasn't her they were rebelling against. Or were they even rebelling? Was it someone else's agenda? Of course, if *one* person had discovered *Mentiserium*, then there might be more, and if that were the case, it would explain much.

She had tried so hard not to interfere, but issues kept cropping up. Like Harbourtown. She still needed to speak to

Jarvaine about the conditions there. She groaned. That was another meeting she needed to get scheduled.

Refocusing her gaze on her office, she realised that both Guerlaire and Asher were staring at her with expectant expressions.

"My apologies. I was just considering how *Mentiserium* could be playing a part here. What if those who are causing unrest are not actually aware of what they are doing?"

Guerlaire nodded. "That is a possibility. How do we know if it is in force? Can we remove it?"

"Use your sword. It will detect other magics. Once you identify someone who is affected, you can remove the persuasion by sweeping it out of their mind and then encouraging a mind block, a mini shield, so they cannot be affected again."

"You mean I have to enter their mind?" Guerlaire asked.

Leyandrii chuckled at Guerlaire's horrified expression. "You just skim their mind, not enter it. We'll practice it later."

"That is not scalable," Guerlaire said. "I can't release each person individually, especially if I'm in the middle of a fight."

"I'll work on it, see if I can find a way to mass release them, though, if these Ascendants have already affected that many people, we may be too late."

"You need to check the Administration and protect them if needed," Oren said. "We need to be able to trust the administrators to do what is right for the people."

"A very good point, Oren. I will consider it," Leyandrii replied. "Have all your officers been taught how to shield?"

Oren frowned. "Yes, but I am not convinced they are practising continuously. It is difficult to do their work and concentrate on that at the same time."

Leyandrii sighed. "Something else I need to think about. There must be an easier way to protect my own guards."

Guerlaire reached over and squeezed her hands. "You'll think of something. I find thinking of you strengthens my shield."

"I wonder if that is it," Leyandrii said. "I could imbue my image with protection. I'll think about it. One problem I think I've solved is the faster way for you to travel. If we empowered a marker stone or something in one place, and if there was another marker at a different location that you could connect to, then you could use the magic to travel faster between those points."

"A marker stone?"

"Yes, you know, it would be a point of focus for the magic, and then that would be a way for you to travel between the points of magic."

"A waystone."

"If you like. I could show you how to activate a waystone elsewhere, a point where you can transport yourself from one place to another without having to rely on me."

"That would be useful and a way to transport more people."

Leyandrii smiled. "I knew we would come up with a way eventually, though you'll have to be in a place to create the waystone before you can travel to it."

"I can start now." Guerlaire grinned at her. "Wherever I go, I can create one."

"Don't create too many. We don't want to overload the land with points of concentrated magic. One per watch would be enough."

"And anyone can use them?"

"If you know how to open the waystone and you can find it and another to travel to, then, yes, anyone could use it if they can cope with the magic."

"What do you mean by cope?" Oren asked.

"Well, it takes a lot of energy to power the waystone. I

mean, to transport a person from one place to another is not insignificant. So, you will be affected by an influx of magic as you travel. If you are familiar with magic and can control it, then you should be unaffected."

"And if you are not?"

Leyandrii shrugged. "It will be unsettling, and you'll probably feel a bit ill with having all that magic wash through you."

Guerlaire nodded. "Then we need to be discreet to begin with. We don't want anyone accidentally entering one, nor do we want the Ascendants finding them or learning how to use them. I want to be able to creep up on them without them knowing."

32

GUERLAIRE

LADY'S PALACE, VESPERS

Seated in his office in the palace, Guerlaire glanced at the report on his desk and jotted down a few notes in his pad. Lafferty, the manager of Clary's warehouses, was turning into a mine of information. That Clary used such a man to run part of his business baffled Guerlaire, though it played into his favour. The man had no idea he was being watched, had even less security, and Fonor had managed to pilfer documents on a regular basis. Fonor and Marian, two rangers he had added to his team, were sharing the rotation.

He checked one of the files spread out on his desk and frowned. Leaning over, he tugged a map of Remargaren closer. The central portion was well notated, much of it his work, but it was the northern and southern reaches that hadn't been fully populated. The Elothian borders with Deepwater and Stoneford were still largely unmapped, even though the watches had taken on the burden of surveying the area.

He looked up as the door opened, and he waved Chryll and Fonor in.

"Finally," he said with a grin. "I thought you'd managed to get lost."

"Wouldn't be difficult in this warren," Chryll replied as he squeezed his bulk into a chair.

"Get used to it, because you'll be billeted here at the palace for the foreseeable future."

"Doing what?" Fonor asked with a quiet strength in his low voice as he took the other seat. Half the size of Chryll, he had a wiry constitution and was the same age as Chryll and Guerlaire. "Watching Lafferty is boring. Yesterday, Marian was suggesting we do a daylight raid, just to relieve the boredom."

"Let's wait for the others," Guerlaire said with a grin. "Then I'll only have to explain once."

"Others?" Chryll asked.

"The rest of the strike team, and here they are," Guerlaire said as a slender, ginger-haired man, with a spray of freckles across his cheeks and nose entered the room. "Eren, please come in." He was followed by two more rangers: a slender young woman with dark brown skin, black hair, and eyes, and a stocky man with a thatch of blond hair and vivid blue eyes. "You know Calene and Denir, don't you?"

Chryll rose and held out his hand. "Of course. Long time since we last worked together," he said as he shook their hands.

Eren grinned. His bright blue eyes sparkled with intelligence, and he inspected Guerlaire as he moved to stand by the wall, making room for the others. "This is going to be cosy," he said as he leaned against the wall.

"I won't keep you long," Guerlaire said as the others found a place to stand. He glanced around the room. "The six of us have a new mission. We need to find out and stop whatever the Ascendants are planning against Leyandrii and Remargaren."

Eren huffed his breath out. "You're not expecting much, are you?"

"Will six of us be enough?" Fonor asked with a frown.

Guerlaire held his hand up. "I know we seem too few, but until we know what the Ascendants are planning, I want us to remain hidden. Too many of us would be noticeable. As we discover more, we can expand as needed, but for now, I want us to get in and out unseen. We need to infiltrate and discover what is going on without the Ascendants knowing we are there. And whenever we find evidence of any crystals, we need to figure out how they are using them and then destroy them."

"Crystals?" Calene asked, wrinkling her nose. "In Stoneford, we used them for communication. They are good over short distances, like between guard posts."

"I don't think that is what the Ascendants are using them for." Guerlaire waved his hand at Chryll. "Last time we experienced them, they were being used to focus magic to attack us."

Calene huffed out her breath. "Really? Crystals don't last long. They burn out after a while and need recharging." Her eyes widened. "If they are being used as a focus, that would explain why there are so few crystals on the market and why the prices are ridiculously high."

Denir leaned forward, and Guerlaire raised an eyebrow. Denir and Calene were younger than the others, but he knew they were perfectly capable; otherwise, he wouldn't have chosen them.

"Remargaren is huge," Denir said. "How do you intend on deploying us?"

"We'll always be in pairs, but to begin with, we work as a team until we know what we are dealing with. Everyone needs to practise their mind shielding; none of us can be exposed to *Mentiserium*, and you'll need to know how to remove and block it in others. Whereever we can undo any Ascendant control is a bonus."

"That doesn't address travelling over distance. It takes two days just to get to Deepwater," Denir said.

"Leyandrii will transport us, to begin with, and once we arrive, I'll create a waystone," Guerlaire said. "It's like a portal for us to step through to return. You have to know where another waystone is located in order to travel to it. We'll be practising visualising the locations for a couple chimes so you know what to expect and to make sure everyone can cope with using them. They are magical constructs, so you might be affected. And then we'll be on duty." Guerlaire tapped his map. "I have reports of some strange behaviour on the Elothian borders, and Leyandrii says it's a dead zone. Something is blocking her connection to the land, so we need to investigate."

Guerlaire looked at his recruits and grinned. This was going to be such fun.

"I don't like that expression." Chryll groaned and pointed at him. "You are going to get us in so much trouble."

"We get to use magic and be sneaky. What's wrong with that?" Guerlaire asked. His grin widened.

Eren laughed and slapped Chryll's shoulder. "You're part of Guerlaire's super-secret strike team, and you thought we wouldn't get into trouble?"

Fonor rose. "Marian is going to be so pissed at missing this, but if there's trouble looming, let's make sure we're prepared to deal with it. Meet me in the sparring ring in ten. Let's get warmed up and practice shielding. Guerlaire can try and breach our shields while we spar."

"And then we get to play with the waystones," Guerlaire said, rubbing his hands with glee. "I've already created a couple in the palace grounds. Let's see who pukes first!"

"Ew!" Calene screwed up her face in disgust.

Once Guerlaire was satisfied that each member of his team could defend against his mental strikes, he led them over to the rose garden, where he had created a waystone. Pointing at the rock, he said, "This is the rose garden waystone. You visualise the garden and step into a waystone, and it will bring you here. If you move closer, you'll feel the chime." He waved Chryll forward.

Chryll rolled his eyes and stepped towards the rock, and a soft chime resonated through him. He shivered. "That is so weird," he said.

Guerlaire laughed and waved the others forward. "It's magic; of course it's weird. A waystone is only active if you hear the chime. There is another waystone by the back entrance of the palace. I don't want too many people seeing us repeatedly disappearing and reappearing or knowing about the waystones. They are our secret.

"You can only travel to a waystone when you can visualise its location. Do not try travelling to a location you have never been to. You could get lost or even trapped within the waystone."

Denir shuddered. "Do we have to use them? Can't Lady Leyandrii move us around?"

"When possible, she will, but she won't always be available, and we need to be able to return whenever we need to."

"That's a good point, I suppose," Denir said with a grimace.

"Everyone got this location memorised?" Guerlaire asked. "Then let's walk over to the other one, and we'll use the waystone to return to the rose garden."

Once Guerlaire was sure everyone had the second waystone location memorised, he grinned at them. "Visualise the rose garden and step into the waystone." He stepped over the rock and disappeared.

Guerlaire stepped out into the rose garden and moved to the side. He wasn't surprised when Chryll rushed out of the waystone almost immediately. Chryll would never let Guerlaire out of his sight if he had his way. Guerlaire tugged him out of the way, and Fonor, Calene, Denir, and Eren appeared one after the other.

He grinned. He knew he'd selected the right people. They hadn't baulked at entering the waystone, though they all had pale faces—even Calene was a sickly brown—and wild eyes.

"That was the weirdest experience," Eren gasped, bending over and grasping his thighs.

Guerlaire rubbed his back. "How do you feel?"

"Queasy," Eren admitted as he swallowed hard.

"I'm gonna vomit," Denir said as he turned away and retched.

"No, don't," Calene screeched and covered her ears as she turned away. "You'll make me vomit, too."

Guerlaire's super-secret strike team were all rather green in the face. Eren leaned against Fonor and groaned. "I shouldn't have had such a heavy lunch."

Fonor chuckled, not looking much better. "If he makes me do that again, I know I'm gonna puke."

"We won't normally be travelling through the waystones in quick succession," Guerlaire said, observing them all with a frown. He hadn't been affected when travelling across the palace grounds, but they were all incapacitated to some degree after only one journey. "Well, that's not good. You're not going to be able to defend yourselves if you're all puking everywhere. Let's take a break. You get your stomachs under control, and I'll go and speak to Leyandrii."

Chryll held up his hand. "I am not sparring anymore."

Guerlaire chuckled. "Take a chime and freshen up. We'll meet in the palace library and go over the maps. We all need to know where we are, wherever we go in Remargaren. Whichever territory you are weakest on, that's your homework. Memorise landmarks until you know them all. I don't want anyone getting stranded if something goes wrong."

Calene grinned, her expression brightening. "Do you think we'll get to go to Birtoli? I've never been."

"Me, neither," Eren said.

Guerlaire glanced at the rest. "How about you?" When everyone shook their heads, he frowned. "Really? None of you?" Staring off into the distance, he scowled. "We'll fix that tomorrow. We meet at sunrise. Leyandrii will transport us there, and we'll waystone back."

Eren clapped his hands together. "A group outing! Make sure you bring your lunch."

Fonor snorted under his breath and slapped Eren on the shoulder. "Waystone, remember? No travelling on a full stomach!"

33

GUERLAIRE

LADY'S PALACE, VESPERS

At dawn the next day, Leyandrii stood beside Guerlaire and smiled as his team assembled in the rose garden. Each carried a sack over their shoulder and a sword on their hip.

"I'm so sorry you were affected by the waystone," Leyandrii said in greeting. "Magic can be quite potent if you are not used to using it. The more you practise, the more your bodies will acclimatise to the effects. I will give each of you my blessing and see if that helps to balance your body's reaction."

"Leyandrii will transport us to Astille in southern Birtoli," Guerlaire said. "It is remote enough that we shouldn't be seen, and it will give you an idea of the climate. If we go to Molinti, Emperor Pierien will hear of it and expect us to visit, and we need to practise travelling."

Fonor groaned under his breath. "Let's have a bet. Whoever lasts the most journeys without puking gets to spend a day on the beach."

Guerlaire laughed. "And are you going to pay for that person to get a day off?"

"No, you are for putting us through this torture."

"That seems fair," Leyandrii said. "Now, let me bless you before you leave. Hopefully, that will help." She approached Chryll, went up on tip-toe to kiss his cheek, and whispered her blessing. She chuckled when he blushed, and she patted his shoulder. Fonor was nearly as tall. He bent his head so she could reach him more easily, and she whispered in his ear, making him flush as well. Eren grinned at her, but his grin faded to a more introspective smile as her blessing percolated through him.

"Dearest Calene," Leyandrii murmured as she kissed Calene's cheek, and tears gleamed in Calene's dark eyes. Then there was only Denir left, and he bent his head as Leyandrii went back up on tip-toe to reach him. "Bless you, Denir."

Guerlaire cleared his throat at the sight of their shining eyes. "Right. Next stop, Astille. We'll return shortly."

Leyandrii stepped back and waved her hand, and all six of them disappeared just as the sun rose from behind the palace, bathing her garden in golden sunlight.

Guerlaire spun around, checking his surroundings, and noted that the others did the same. Standing on the sandy beach, he raised his face to the sun as it warmed his skin, and he inhaled the moist, herb-scented air. The sea sparkled, a bright turquoise spreading out behind him and a gentle incline rose in front of him. The incline led to dunes covered in tall grasses, which rippled in the slight breeze.

"It's so beautiful," Eren whispered.

"I've never seen anything like it," Denir muttered, inhaling deeply. He frowned. "What is that beautiful smell?"

"Samphire, probably," Guerlaire said. "It's a herb that grows near the sea. I'll create the waystone by that large rock between the two dunes. Leave your things here. We'll do a couple of journeys and then have a rest." While he went to create the waystone, the others dug out blankets to put on the sand and dropped their bags on top.

"So, visualise the rock and the dunes; this will be the Astille waystone. Once you're comfortable that you can see it in your mind, return to the rose garden and then back here. Leyandrii is expecting to see each of you at least twice before she'll leave."

Chryll groaned. "I hope her blessing works, or I'll be puking over her shoes."

"Please don't," Guerlaire said with a grin. "Off you go."

Chryll scowled at him, but he stepped forward, shivered as the chime sounded, and he disappeared.

"That looks as weird as it feels," Eren said as he followed him.

"Are we likely to collide if they come back?" Fonor asked, eyeing the rock.

"I guess we'll find out," Guerlaire replied, settling on his blanket and digging in his bag for his water.

"I'm so glad you are concerned," Fonor said and then stepped forward.

Guerlaire grinned and lay back on his towel, enjoying a moment of lazy peace before his team returned. He wished he'd been able to convince Leyandrii to come with him. It was beautiful and relaxing.

Denir's groans had him rolling over on his side to inspect him. The ranger was bent over, gripping his thighs and breathing in deeply. His face paled to a sickly green.

"Journey there was fine; now I'm going to be sick," Denir said as he swallowed desperately.

Calene appeared and then Fonor.

"Inhale this balmy air. I'm sure you'll feel better," Guerlaire said.

"Says the person lazing on the beach," Calene said as she took a deep breath. "Though I feel fine this time."

"Me, too," said Fonor in surprise. "Chryll was trying to persuade Leyandrii to come with us."

Eren appeared, turned around, and stepped back through the waystone.

"He wants the day off," Calene said with a grin and followed him.

Guerlaire watched them all pop back and forth. Only Denir appeared to be affected, and after two trips, he sat down on his blanket and drank some water. "I'll be fine if the trips are spread out. It's doing them back to back that I'm struggling with."

"Hopefully, that won't be necessary. At least we know Leyandrii's blessing does help. I wonder how long it will last?"

Leyandrii appeared with Chryll, and laughing she sat beside Guerlaire. "Chryll convinced me we should all have a day on the beach. I am inclined to agree."

Eren appeared in time to hear her. "Do you mean I'm wasting my time?"

"Practice is never wasted," Leyandrii said as she slipped off her shoes and stockings. "I'm going to paddle." She hitched up her skirts and walked into the gentle surf. "The water is so warm," she called as she turned and grinned at them all in delight.

Everyone stripped off shoes, jackets, and weapons and followed her into the water. It didn't take long for the paddle to turn into a water fight, and the air was filled with shrieks and laughter.

Later, they lay on blankets and spread their sodden clothes out to dry in the sun.

The soft breeze caressed Guerlaire's bare skin as he stared out over the glittering sea. Leyandrii leaned against his chest, and her damp hair was cool against his skin. He inhaled her scent, roses and salt and thought he was the luckiest man alive.

Chryll and Fonor lay on the beach next to them, chatting in soft tones. The others had gone to explore the deserted beach. This was an unexpected, peaceful interlude, one that was a gift and should be treasured for the wonderful memory they would all have.

Guerlaire wished they could do it more often, but tomorrow, they would be back trying to discover the Ascendants' plans and preventing any further disruption.

34

—————

BIRLER

GRADUATION, AUGU 1122

The weeks passed, assignments changed, and the day of the cadets' graduation dawned bright and clear. Tagerill was hopping about the barracks in excitement. "I can't believe we finally made it. Where do you think we'll be sent?" He didn't give them a chance to answer. "I hope we get somewhere interesting. I am so fed up with listening to people drone on about wheat stocks and milk deliveries."

"You'd be worried if they didn't arrive to fill your belly," Parsill said with a laugh as he crouched on the floor and tied his boots.

"Maybe, but I don't have to be the one who makes sure they arrive," Tagerill grumbled.

"I shouldn't worry; I'm sure Asher knows you well enough not to assign you back there," Serill said, his voice soothing. He looked up as Birler and Edril entered. "Where have you two been? You're not even changed."

Birler grimaced. "We got called to the office. It seems Kafinee and Deren managed to get out of their stalls and go on a date."

Tagerill laughed. "And he managed to keep it from you, Edril?"

"We've had words, I can assure you," Edril replied, trying to keep his face straight.

"When will they know if she's with foal?" Serill asked.

Birler hissed his breath out. "In a few weeks."

Edril clapped him on the shoulder. "Be happy; you could get a free Darian out of it. Men pay a lot of money for a Darian."

"But we don't know where we're going. I need a horse now, not some future possibility."

"She'll be fine," Tagerill said with a grin. "She won't show for months yet, and if she does, you can take her to Greens. My father will lend you another whilst she, um, whilst she does what she needs to."

Parsill and Serill burst out laughing at Birler's pained expression. "Get changed, or you'll miss your own gradua-tion," Serill said once he had calmed down.

Samis peered out the door. "They are ringing the bell; we'd better get going."

Birler and Edril shed their clothes and hurriedly scram-bled into their new rangers uniforms. "Go. We'll follow." Edril shooed the others out and sighed with relief. "They would just slow us down with their fussing," he said as he rubbed a cloth over his boots.

"Is everything straight?" Birler asked, tugging his new dark grey jacket down and smoothing the lapels. He adjusted his collar.

Edril cast a glance over him. "You look fine. How about me?"

"You look good. Don't forget your cap."

Edril grabbed it, and they hurried out of the barracks to join their comrades seated in ranks of chairs on the training field. Behind them, family and friends filled the rows of chairs set aside for them, rising on a wooden structure to give them a clear view over the people in front.

The stands were filling quickly, and Birler knew Warren and Melis Descelles were in the masses somewhere. He had been invited back to Greens to celebrate with them before they were all sent off on assignment. He had deliberated about whether he should go or not, but Tagerill wouldn't accept any answer but yes, and he had given in; after all, he had no one else to celebrate with.

Birler joined his friends, grinning across the rows at Nialler, who was graduating top of their year. He found his seat next to Tagerill, his stomach buzzing. Smoothing his jacket, he tried to relax. He had made it; he was a Lady's Ranger. He would get paid to protect Vespiri, and now that he had some status, the Clarys should leave him alone.

Tagerill nudged his shoulder. "Look, Ma and Pa are in the third row up on the end." He was waving frantically, trying to get their attention. Birler twisted around and joined him. Melis spotted them, tugged her husband's arm, and waved back.

Commander Asher stepped up to the lectern and raised his hand for silence. He was a commanding presence in his long black robe edged with light grey. "Welcome, welcome to the graduation of the class of 1122. This has been a year of change and challenges, as most years are, and our graduates today are our hopes and our future. They will take Vespiri and Remargaren into the years ahead and protect us as we continue to grow.

"I am especially pleased to be announcing the graduation of some of the first ranger cadets from Terolia and Birtoli and look forward to the day when Elothia begins to submit their candidates for admittance. Remargaren is growing as our territories develop, each to its own needs and each with its own problems. But if we work together in harmony for the good of all, then Remargaren will continue to be a place of hope, our home.

"These new rangers seated before us will help us protect that home for the good of all. In the name of Lady Leyandrii, the Guardian of Remargaren, join me in celebrating our new rangers and their achievements." He led a round of applause.

"And join me in thanking those masters who endeavoured to teach these young men and women much of what they will need to know to navigate the complex waters of our future." He indicated the men and women seated behind him.

The cadets all clapped furiously.

"Let us begin to call forward our new rangers so they may be acclaimed and begin their new lives."

He began calling out names, and the cadets rose in turn, walked towards him, paused as he placed the pin on their lapel, and then walked back to their seats. Birler didn't remember rising from his chair or shaking the commander's hand, though he fingered the pin as he sat back in his chair. He was a Lady's Ranger.

The next thing he knew, they had crossed the grounds to the covered sparring area where the reception area had been set up, and Melis was giving him a warm hug. "Congratulations, Birler. Well done. We're so proud of you and Tagerill."

Warren stopped hugging Tagerill long enough to embrace Birler. "Well done, lad, well done. You are coming back with us to Greens, aren't you?"

Birler smiled, as a warm feeling spread through him. "I'd love to. Thank you."

"Good. I spoke to Guerlaire and he agreed."

"Guerlaire?"

Warren grinned at him. "Who else would I ask? I haven't

had a chance to speak to Leyandrii. What's this I hear about Kafinee?"

"Good news travels fast, I see. Yes, she could be in foal with a Darian, which should be interesting."

"Well, it will be a first for our stables. George will be ecstatic, I'm sure."

"It will be alright to ride her for now, though, won't it?"

"Of course, though, once she's about six months in, we ought to rest her. Let's see how she goes."

Birler nodded, relieved. "This is going to be the longest two weeks, waiting for our assignments."

"Make the most of it," Tagerill butted in, and his father rested his arm across his shoulders. "We probably won't get much of a break for ages after this." Tagerill gestured at Serill. "Pa, you know my friend Serill."

Warren shook Serill's hand and smiled at his parents, trailing behind him. "You must be very proud," he said as he offered his hand to Serill's father.

"That we are. This is a right treat for us all, coming up for the ceremony."

"You work in the nursery at Marchwood, don't you? How are the saplings coming this year?"

Melis rolled her eyes at Serill's mother. "Men! All they can talk about is trees. I'm Melis, Tagerill's mother."

"Anna." Serill's mother blushed. "Don't they all look so smart in their uniforms? It's been a hard two years, but it was worth it all to see them now."

Melis smiled. "That, it was. We are so proud of them all."

Serill herded his parents away with a grin and a grateful flick of his hands. Warren turned back to the boys.

"You will all come home for the investiture. Once all the legal stuff is finished, Leyandrii intends on having a formal ceremony to confirm the Lords of the Watches. I have already stipulated that I expect all my children to attend, and that includes you, Birler, so be warned: you will drop whatever it is you are doing and come home."

"Yes, sir," Birler replied with a grin. His happiness faded as a harsh voice spoke over the top of him.

"Warren, you shouldn't be associating with the likes of him," Gilbert Clary said, interrupting them. "Tyrler told me that young Tagerill had been led astray, but for him to deceive you as well, he should be ashamed of himself."

Warren turned towards Clary, gripping Tagerill's shoulder as he stiffened beside him.

"Gilbert. Congratulations. Is Tyrler the last one you're putting through the academy?" Warren asked as he smiled at the large man who stopped beside him. Gilbert Clary scowled at Birler, drawing his black eyebrows tight, hooding his eyes. Birler ignored him and turned his back on him to speak with Melis. Warren's lips twitched. Birler couldn't have done anything else to infuriate the man more.

"No, Russell is next," Clary ground out, staring at Birler's back.

"Ah, you'll have a veritable army by the time you've finished."

Gilbert squinted at him, trying to decide if Warren was being insulting. His face hardened, and he jutted out his chin. "At least my boys know what's right. They wouldn't drag home nameless scum. Standards are dropping, and I'll tell Asher so as well."

Warren's voice deepened. "Be careful what you say about my family, Gilbert. I will not tolerate you slandering them or their friends. All the young men and women graduating today are the Lady's Rangers. They have all graduated on their merits as equals. Treat them as such."

Gilbert reared back, but he clamped his mouth shut and

bit his lip as he met Warren's determined eyes. He turned away, scowling.

"Pa."

"Not now," Warren said as he squeezed Tagerill's shoulder. He turned to Melis and Birler with a bright smile. "Are we ready? I believe Marian and Versill are awaiting us at the house. They are joining us for lunch before we leave for Greens."

Melis tucked her hand in Birler's arm and smiled back. "Yes, I was just saying what a crush it is; no need to stay here any longer."

"Fine, let's go then. I'll just have a word with Commander Asher, and then I'll be with you."

Warren caught up with them as they left the garrison. "Sam and the men will bring your bags and the horses to the house. Asher will send your assignment to us at Greens," he said, smiling at Birler. "So, let's go and get some lunch. I'm hungry, so you two must be starving."

Tagerill laughed. "We've been up since dawn; of course we are."

It didn't take long to reach the Descelles house, and Birler flushed at the warm welcome and hugs he received from both Marian and Versill.

Birler joined in the friendly banter around the table. The Descelles treated him like he was one of the family, teasing him the same as they did Tagerill. The anxiety caused by those cold words Gilbert Clary had said at the reception faded, and Birler concentrated on enjoying himself.

Warren relaxed as he saw the closed expression on Birler's face replaced by a happier one, and he concentrated on ensuring it stayed there, not allowing any of them to raise the subject of the Clarys. Warren leaned back in his chair and observed the table with a grin; four rangers all batting the conversation back and forth, opinionated and humorous. They all got on so well. He smiled at Melis, who was watching him from the other end of the table, and she nodded.

Warren cleared his throat, and they all turned to him. "I have a proposal to make." He looked around their expectant faces and laughed. "Your mother and I have a proposal to make," he corrected himself. "We want to make it official. We want to offer Birler a place in our family, to give him our family name." He sat back and watched the reactions. Birler's mouth dropped in shock. Tagerill was ecstatic as he rose to his feet, and Marian and Versill were laughing in agreement. Warren breathed a silent sigh of relief. They had thought their children would support them, but you never knew.

"Of course! What a great idea! He's already family anyway, aren't you, Birler?" Marian leapt to her feet and rushed around to hug him.

Tagerill pounded Birler on the shoulder. "Welcome to the family, mate. Didn't I say you'd like it here?"

Melis stood. "Give him a chance to speak. Birler, would you like to join our family? We can be a bit rowdy at times, but you would be most welcome. We already see you as our son. We love you very much. We would very much like to make that official."

Birler gaped at her, at a loss for words. He paled as his mouth snapped shut, and his eyes filled with tears. Warren suddenly doubted they were tears of joy. Melis walked around the table and drew him to his feet, hugging him. "Oh, Birler, please say yes."

"You can't want me. I'm no one. I have nothing. People hate me."

Warren stiffened at the hint of despair in Birler's voice.

"*We* don't," Melis replied. "*We* want you."

Birler shook his head and gripped the edge of the table, his knuckles whitening. "You would regret it. I'll only bring you trouble. I can't do that to you." He swallowed. He looked like he might throw up.

Tagerill frowned at him. "Don't you want to be part of my family?" His lips thinned as he stiffened.

Birler gripped his shoulder. "You're my best friend. I don't want to ruin that."

"You wouldn't." Tagerill looked at his father. "I don't understand. Why doesn't he want to be with us?"

"I c-can't join your family. I have a father somewhere; at least, I think he's still alive."

"But he doesn't want you. You said so."

Birler flinched at Tagerill's thoughtless words, and Warren stood.

"Maybe we should have spoken to Birler first," Warren said, his voice soft as he rubbed Birler's back. "Birler, I am sorry; we were so excited at the thought of you joining our family that we never thought. We ought to give you time to think about it. Tagerill, enough. Leave him be. Birler, the offer stands whenever you're ready. For now, let's get ready to go home." He hustled his children into getting ready for the journey and left Melis to reassure Birler. The boy looked like he might faint.

By the time they were ready to leave, Birler had recovered some of his composure, though he was still pale and subdued. Warren was sure he was in no doubt of their desire to claim him, but he still refused to accept their offer.

There was much teasing about Kafinee when she was brought around, which eased the awkward moment when everyone regrouped. Warren handed Melis up into the carriage, Birler and Tagerill mounted their horses, and

Marian and Versill waved them off. Tagerill kept glancing over at Birler, but he kept quiet, clamping his lips tight.

Birler stared at Kafinee's ears and wished he could curl up and die. He had never felt so embarrassed and uncomfortable in all his life, and it was all his own fault. Tagerill would hate him; he could see he was upset. How they would get through the next two weeks was beyond him. The topic was bound to come up again. He stiffened his resolve; he couldn't become a Descelles. He was a wharf rat, good for nothing and unwanted. They would become the laughingstock of Vespiri if he accepted, and he couldn't do that to them. He was nobody, and no one wanted him. The words repeated in his head as they rode.

Behind him, Sam drove the wagon with their bags piled high. His stomach dropped. He had no home now. Where would he go? He couldn't stay at the academy anymore. Where did rangers live? Hysteria rose within him as his heart sped up and his stomach tightened. *Don't panic,* he thought. *See where your assignment takes you. Worry about it then.* Kafinee jinked as his grip on her reins tightened. He relaxed his hands and patted her neck in apology. He vented a deep sigh and rubbed his temple; his head throbbed.

They stopped for the night at a small inn off the East Road. As soon as they had eaten, Melis glanced at Birler's face and sent him off to bed. He'd only picked at the food and went gladly—anything to avoid talking to them. He climbed into bed, but he couldn't sleep. His head ached, and the tears wouldn't stop. He pretended to be asleep when Tagerill came up, but he stared into the dark long after Tagerill's snores drifted on the night air.

Melis took one look at his heavy eyes the next morning and engulfed him in a hug. "Oh, Birler, we're so sorry. Please don't worry. We don't think any less of you. In fact, we love you more. Your head aches, doesn't it?"

Tears stung Birler's eyes, and he angrily brushed them away.

"Come on, sit down, drink some tea. It will help settle your stomach. I'll get you something for your head." She returned with a glass of clear liquid. "Drink it." She stood over him while he did and then smoothed a gentle hand over his hot cheek. "Now, no more worrying. We won't mention it again. We'll all forget it ever happened."

Birler stared blindly at the tablecloth. The promise made him feel even worse, but he tried to smile and eat some toast, which kept clogging up his throat. He choked it down with his tea. Tagerill was unusually quiet. He ignored Birler but made a healthy breakfast.

Once they arrived in Greens, Birler lingered over settling Kafinee, reluctant to return to the house. He didn't know what to say. He had hurt Tagerill; he could see it. Tagerill was so open and uncomplicated. He rested his head against Kafinee's neck. Why couldn't he be the same? No, he had to make it confusing and ruin everything. Kafinee nudged him, and he sighed. He would be late for dinner.

He walked back to the manor house and up the steps. Large wooden doors stood open and led to the imposing staircase. His room was ready, Melis had said. Stopping in the bathing room, he washed off the dust and horse hair. His room was waiting, as promised, with his bags already unpacked and a change of clothes laid out on his bed. Pausing by the window, he stared out over the fields that led up to the tree line. Exhaustion dragged him down, his head ached, and the thought of facing the family again upset his stomach.

His mind spun with regret and what-ifs. He couldn't do it. He couldn't cause the people who meant so much to him so much trouble. Clary had been clear many times. If the Descelles continued to fraternise with the likes of him, they would regret it. Maybe he should leave now, but to go where? His assignment would be sent here. He had to wait and survive two weeks of Tagerill's aloofness.

35

TAGERILL

GREENS, VESPIRI

Two days later, Warren dragged his son into his study. "What's going on with you and Birler, Tagerill?"

Tagerill stared at him in surprise. "Nothing! I thought he'd be grateful. What's wrong with him? Our family is heaps better than what he's got already."

"Tagerill, I'm disappointed in you."

"Me?" Tagerill was outraged. "I'm not the one who rejected us."

"He didn't reject us. He wants to be part of our family so badly it's making him ill. You are the one doing the rejecting, and it's not helping him."

"I'm not."

"Oh? Then what *are* you doing?"

Tagerill squirmed in his chair. "Why did he say no?"

"He thinks he is protecting us."

"Protecting us? From what?" Tagerill asked, a bewildered expression passing over his face.

Warren glared at his son and tapped his knuckles against

Tagerill's skull. "What do you have in there? Use your brains. Why do you think Birler would think he needs to protect us?"

Tagerill stared at his father. "We would give *him* protection. He would have our family name. He is more at risk on his own."

"Exactly. He knows people hate him. He knows Clary, for one, has already said that he is worthless, that he will bring disgrace down on Greens."

Tagerill stilled. "He thinks he will bring his disgrace with him? But he isn't a disgrace. Birler has more honour in his little finger than the Clarys have in their whole house."

"Maybe you should tell him that."

"But he knows I respect him."

"Does he? You've hardly spoken to him since we've been home."

Tagerill flushed. "How do we get him to change his mind?"

"You show him that you are his friend no matter what. You reassure him that he is always welcome here, that this is his home. You teach him about the Descelles and our family honour. You teach him we *are* his family and family love everything about you, the good and bad."

"I have to do all that?"

"We'll help you. Your mother and I will teach him that families protect each other, that we look out for each other. We are not just responsible for him; he is responsible for us, too, just as Penner, Versill, Marian, and you are."

"But won't that make him even more reluctant?"

Warren smiled. "Very good; You're finally thinking. We have to teach him that love goes both ways. He's thinking he is the only one gaining in this bargain. He thinks he has nothing to give us but trouble. But you know better, don't you?"

Tagerill nodded. "Do you think he will change his mind?" he asked in a small voice.

Warren sighed. "I don't know; it may take some time. Don't expect him to have a change of heart before you leave, much as we would prefer him to."

"What if he won't accept us as his family?"

"Then that is his choice. We can't force him."

Warren struggled not to laugh at Tagerill's horrified expression.

"But he belongs with us. He's my brother."

"Then treat him like one," Warren said as he rose and left his son staring after him.

Tagerill found Birler in the stables, grooming Kafinee. It looked like he had been there all day. "She'll disappear if you brush her much more."

Birler looked up, startled, and Tagerill cursed himself at the sight of his strained face. He grabbed Birler by the shoulders and pulled him into a rough embrace. "You fool, what are you doing?"

Birler stood in his embrace, his arms hanging limply at his sides. Tagerill eased back. "You're my best friend."

"I didn't think you would speak to me." Birler's voice was emotionless, as if he'd already given up.

"I was upset. You know I want you to be my brother more than anything. It means I'm no longer the youngest," he said with a grin. Birler didn't smile back.

Tagerill heaved a sigh and eased the brushes out of Birler's hands. "We need to talk. Come on." He tugged Birler out of the stables and led the way towards a huge oak tree. "I'll race you to the top," he said, pushing Birler towards a thick branch near the bottom. "I bet I get there first."

Birler reached for the branch and began climbing; the

effort warmed him, and stirring him out of the miasma of misery he had been drifting in. His face had some colour by the time he reached Tagerill, and he grinned in triumph as he joined him in the vee at the top.

"It's such an amazing view from up here," Tagerill said, all laughter gone from his voice. "You can see all of Greens, from the nurseries to the plantations. You can see the cycle of life in action from up here. Over and over through the centuries. From a small seed to a tree like this." He slapped the branch they were sitting on. "It's a bit like families; your parents nurture and love you from a baby, give you chances and opportunities to learn and develop. What you do with them is your choice. You either reach for them with both hands and make the most of them or you ignore them and waste your life."

Birler watched him in surprise, but he hadn't finished.

"Greens has been here for centuries, and it will be here for centuries more, long after you and I have died. Penner's kids will take up the responsibility, continue the nurturing, the loving, and the growing. I sometimes wonder who they'll be and what they'll be like, fortunate to hold the future of Greens in their hands." He laughed off his deep thoughts. "But you and me, we'll be forgotten, just a passage in history. Lucky enough to be here for a brief moment, grasping the opportunities in our hands. Don't waste them, Birler, on what *might* be. Make the most of what is." He looked up at the sun, shielding his eyes. "And on that note, we'd better go in for dinner. I'm starving."

Birler grinned as relief melted away his tension. "Me too," he replied, and they began climbing down.

Warren breathed a sigh of relief as the dinner table relaxed into the more usual banter. The strained silence had been unnerving. Birler looked much happier, and Tagerill was teasing him about Kafinee.

The evening was spent with Tagerill teaching Birler how to play chess. "It's all about strategy, thinking one step or even two ahead of what your opponent will do in response. It's about planning and being prepared." He looked up as his father stopped beside them, his gaze wandering over the board.

"It's also about knowing when to defend and when to sacrifice," Warren said. "Just because it's a pawn, it does not mean it's not important. They are not there just to be sacrificed; everyone has their part to play." He smiled at Birler. "Look to your pawns, son." He left them to it, and Birler watched him go, digesting his words. Then Birler looked back at the board and moved his pawn to safety.

Early the next morning, Tagerill was eager to be out; he had energy to burn. "Let's go for a run and then go down the archery range. We haven't practised in ages. Even you need to practise sometimes," he said as he poked Birler's shoulder.

Warren rose from the breakfast table and glanced across at his son. "I'll be in the nursery with Penner. Why don't you take Barren with you and run up to the Ancestor tree? Birler hasn't met him yet."

Tagerill's eyes brightened. "It's been a while since I've visited. That'll be a good ten-mile run. Straighten out the kinks."

They were laughing and breathless by the time they reached an old, gnarled tree. Barren flopped on the ground, his tongue hanging out as he panted, his big brown eyes staring at Tagerill in adoration. Thick branches twisted and turned, spreading out from the base. The tree split into two sturdy trunks that thinned as they rose into the sky, each festooned with branches that intertwined as one. Moss and lichen covered the knobbly bark, making it glow a soft green in the sunlight. The lower branches were thicker than Tagerill's leg, sturdy and strong.

"We call it the Ancestor tree because it's been here since our records began. I'll show you the entry in the family book later. The very first Descelles planted it in the year 642. It turns 480 years old this year. My father brought me here when I was two, just about toddling. He lifted me up onto this very branch, and he explained its history. I still remember that day. Sit here, and I'll tell you."

Birler sat astride the low branch, his feet dangling just above the mat of leaves decomposing below him. As he gazed up through the branches; the soft green light bathed his face. A few patches of blue peeked through the leaves, but not very many. The tree was dense, the foliage thick. Barren rose with a grunt and padded off to sniff around the tree roots.

Tagerill started to speak, his voice quiet and distant, and Birler listened. The rustling of leaves was a soft backdrop, reminding Birler of the sound of sifting sand as a gentle wave caresses the beach. "My father said no one knows what type of tree it is; it was never recorded when it was planted. I suppose everyone knew then, so they didn't think to write it down. But it's the only one of its kind in Greens.

"Everyone knows him. He's been here so long he's a landmark. He *is* Greens. All parents bring their children to introduce them to him, and they carve their name in the bark."

Birler frowned. "Why?"

"To show we belong." Tagerill stood on the branch next to Birler and pointed. "Here's my name. Marian is above, then Versill and Penner, and Pa. Next to Pa is my mother. Pa brought her here when they were joined."

He took out his knife and began to carve. "It's like a tradition, passed on through the generations. It connects us all together, ties us to each other and to Greens. We are all joined in looking after Greens." He paused in his carving. "Which is what the Lady is extending by confirming the watches," he said, enlightened. "She is enshrining what we are doing with her blessing." He smiled down at Birler. "She's good."

Birler nodded in agreement.

"Did you know the Clarys only date back to 942? Mere upstarts in the scheme of things. And they call themselves purebloods. Purebloods of what, I wonder," Tagerill mused. "They come from the East, on the borders with Terolia. Gilbert's nephew, Mayer, holds East; that's why Gilbert went into the Administration, I think. He didn't want to be second best to anyone. He cut his ties with East, fell out with his nephew, last I heard, and built his own place on the borders of Marchwood. Clary doesn't understand what family means.

"Families mean different things to different people," Tagerill continued, his eyes dreamy as he sat back down beside Birler and dangled his legs over the thick branch. "I don't think you've had much of a chance to understand what a family is supposed to be."

Birler stirred, but he didn't know what to say. "I don't remember my mother," he admitted in the end.

"I'm sorry, Birler." Tagerill rubbed Birler's back in a gesture of sympathy. "Families are more than having 'a mother' or 'a father'. It is how we react to each other. It's the strings that bind us together that are important, the constant two-way flow of love, support, and respect. The strings that keep us connected will always tug us home."

"Strings?"

Tagerill grimaced. "It's how I think of it. I'm not very

good with words. I just want you to understand that being part of a family is not just taking what you need, like Clary does, but giving back as well. It goes both ways. We all sustain each other, we all contribute, and we all benefit. It's what makes us strong."

"So you are saying I don't have a family?"

"Well, not a very good one. You have no ties to your father, do you? All he did was take, as far as I can see. What did he ever give to you, apart from life?"

Birler considered him. "Nothing."

"Exactly. If he were family, he would care for you, nurture you, and love you. And you would want to protect and care for him. He cut your ties long ago and left you to fend for yourself."

Birler shuddered at the memory of those not-so-distant fraught years.

"Those strings, those ties, that's what knit us together as a family. We all weave them together tightly all the time, drawing us all closer together. We belong to each other. Don't you want to belong, Birler?"

Birler stared at Tagerill until his vision went blurry as tears arose. He blinked them away and gripped the branch beneath his legs as he wavered.

Tagerill rested his hand on Birler's arm. "Whatever you think, Birler, you are my family. You are tied to me, and I to you, and when you realise it, you can follow the thread; it will always lead you back to us." He pointed above his head. He had carved Birler's name in the bark below his own.

Birler tried to smile. "You don't understand, Tage," he said, his voice strained. "It's not that simple."

"It is, and I do understand. Better than you think. Don't let others take away your choices through their lies and deceit. Find out the facts for yourself and make your own decisions. You worked at the Chapterhouse; you know how to do research. We have a whole library here, remember?" Tagerill challenged him. "Family is about what you can give, who you are inside." Tagerill place his hand over Birler's heart. "I know you are good, honourable, loyal, an amazing archer, and that's just for starters. You would bring so much to any family lucky enough to have you." Tagerill straightened and shook himself. "My, I think it's time we practised those archery skills. Come on. I'll race you back." He slid off the branch and darted away, not giving Birler a chance to respond to anything he had said.

Birler stood up on the branch and traced the letters of his name. The bark warmed beneath his fingertips, and he rested his head against the trunk. His tears fell, silently absorbed by the tree. To belong, that's what Warren and Melis had offered, and he had turned them down. He had cut the ties he had begun to weave into the Descelles family, and that was the emptiness aching inside him.

Tagerill waited at the edge of the tree line, watching Birler. His face tightened at his friend's distress. His father was right; Birler wanted to belong. He had been blinded by his own anger. He had tied his knot in triplicate, secure and lasting. Only Birler could break it. He turned away and jogged across the open fields, giving Birler time to catch up.

36

GUERLAIRE

LADY'S PALACE, VESPERS

Guerlaire frowned at the handful of crystals he had put aside so he could investigate how the Ascendants were using them. The problem was that he didn't have time to experiment; he was too busy with the strike teams, disrupting anything related to the Ascendants. He rotated a cylindrical crystal in the palm of his hand and felt the frisson of energy it contained.

It was not beyond the realm of possibility that someone could harness multiple crystals to amplify their innate power. The question was how. If he knew how they were used, he would have a chance of stopping them.

Exhaling, he stopped procrastinating and slid them into the pockets of a wrap and rolled it up. He knew a couple of rangers who did have time to experiment; after all, they had figured out how the communications crystals worked and how more than one person could be pulled into a conversation from different locations.

Nialler and Parsill were too bright for their own good. He only hoped they didn't destroy the Chapterhouse with their experimentation.

Rising, he left his office and walked to the waystone in the palace gardens. He stepped through and came out at the waystone he had created inside the cloisters of the Chapterhouse. It was a much safer way of travelling, especially when he worked late into the night. He found both Nialler and Parsill deep in the Chapterhouse, crouched over their work tables, examining the communications crystals.

It looked like they were busy creating different-shaped crystals, but the shards they were working on were so small that it was unlikely they would see any results. It seemed like sacrilege to shatter crystal, but if you didn't experiment, how would you learn?

"I bet if we create more crystals, they will augment the others," Parsill said. "That can be the only reason they need so many. Combined, they must increase the power."

"There may be more than one reason," Nialler said, carefully smoothing the edge of a crystal. "Where did you learn to cut crystals?"

Guerlaire entered the workroom. "It seems I've arrived at an opportune moment," he said, and both lads looked up and peered at him. Guerlaire tried not to laugh at their myopic expressions. "I have some new crystals for you to experiment on."

Nialler dropped what he was he was working on, his face brightening. "Thank goodness. I thought I was going to go blind with the tiny fragments we've got left."

Guerlaire unrolled the wrap, revealing the crystals. "A new problem to solve. I want to understand how multiple crystals can be used to amplify a person's innate power. And once we know how it works, I want to know the easiest way to dismantle it so it no longer functions and it's difficult to fix."

Nialler pursed his lips. "Theoretically or in practice?"

"In practice."

Nialler's eyebrows rose. "Really?"

Guerlaire grinned. "The array I saw had about six large rings. We've only got enough for one tiny ring. I doubt you'll do too much damage."

"You've seen one? Could you draw it?" Nialler asked.

"I've included a diagram of what I can remember, but I only saw the briefest glimpse."

Parsill tilted his head. "Umm, you may be surprised with the results. If the person has plenty of magic, like yourself, I doubt you'd need too many crystals."

"I'm not available to be your guinea pig, so you'll have to find someone else. You don't need anyone too powerful; you just need to demonstrate the theory. Try heating water or something else non-violent."

"We'll find someone," Nialler promised as he reached for the diagram.

"We don't want to damage the Chapterhouse," Guerlaire said. "If you think your experiments are too strong, please take them outside."

Nialler waved his hand, his gaze already glued to the diagram. "Of course," he said absently. "Is this a wire mesh they are sitting on? That would make sense, as it would help conduct the energy. The question is, which are the most efficient fittings?"

"Parsill, please make sure you are being careful," Guerlaire said, suddenly doubting his decision. "Nothing with fire."

Parsill grinned. "Don't worry. I'll keep it sensible."

Guerlaire nodded and left them to it.

Parsill moved around beside Nialler. "Copper wire for the fittings?" he suggested.

"It might be too delicate, but we should certainly start there. Other metals might be better conductors. Maybe we should test them and see which performs best.

"I've never been able to use any magic. Have you?" Parsill asked.

"No, not so far."

"We'd be stupid not to try," Parsill said, his eyes bright. "And if we can't do anything, we'll ask Serill."

They both failed dismally. Neither could create a ball of light, heat water, generate a flame, or move a quill.

"We're a good baseline," Nialler said, trying to remain upbeat. "We knew we didn't have any magic."

"Let me find Serill," Parsill said, wrinkling his nose. "His magic is more obvious. I heard that Birler can see it crackling around him. Maybe he can access it more easily than we can. I'll go and see if Serill's in the archives. I heard he was working for Guerlaire over the break. You see if you can source any wire."

It wasn't long before Parsill returned, followed by Serill, who glanced around the room. "What are you up to down here?"

"Learning about crystals," Nialler replied, waving one in the air. "What about you?"

"Earning extra credit by cataloguing different types of moss and lichen from Elothia."

"Sweet," Nialler said. "We're trying to replicate a crystal booster."

"A booster for what?" Serill asked, coming closer to the workbench.

Nialler gestured at the mini crystal array he'd arranged on the table. "To boost magic."

"Really?" Serill stared at them.

"Yes. We want to see if you can channel magic on your own with one crystal or with all of them."

"I don't have magic you can just call out of thin air," Serill protested.

"Do we need to make you angry?" Nialler asked. "Isn't

that when you usually feel the need to go and destroy the sparring dummies? That's excess magic, isn't it?"

"I'm not sure," Serill replied, rubbing the back of his neck. "But I don't think anger is the key. I would suggest high emotions and magic are not a good mix; that's why we have to get rid of the excess."

"Oh. Good point. I suppose so," Parsill said, his shoulders slumping.

"Guerlaire wanted to enhance innate magic, so let's just try." Nialler peered at Serill. "Can you create a ball of light in your hand?"

"I don't know how."

"Just try. See if you can sense that energy within you and push it into a ball of light in your hand."

Serill rolled his eyes and held his hand out. He concentrated, wrinkling his nose. Nothing happened.

Nialler went down his list, and Serill couldn't heat the water, create a flame, nor move a quill.

"Alright, hold a crystal and try again."

Nialler noted down the lack of results with a frown. "Next, place your right hand flat on all the crystals; see if you can draw on any energy from them to help you."

When Serill failed again, he exhaled. "Maybe it's me? I don't have any magic."

"We are just going to have to pin Captain Guerlaire down," Parsill muttered. "We know he uses magic."

"Tomorrow, we try with the fittings," Nialler said. "The experiment isn't over yet. I'll go and get the wire, and we'll see if that makes any difference."

By the next day, Nialler had created the fittings and the spider's web to hold the crystals.

"When did you have time to do that?" Serill asked, inspecting the fine mesh.

"Last night. I was up until third chime, finishing it off. Let's see if it's any easier with the wire fittings and base."

Serill placed his hand on the crystals and snatched his hand back. "It vibrates."

Nialler placed his hand on the crystals and shook his head. "They don't vibrate for me."

"Try the ball of light again," Parsill said eagerly.

Serill tentatively put his hand on the crystal array again, and then he scrunched up his face as he concentrated. He shivered. "That is so weird," he muttered.

"What is?" Parsill asked.

"It's vibrating through my body." He focussed again, and his hand began to glow. He gasped and released the crystals, and the glow faded. "Did you see that?" he said, his face flushing with excitement.

"See if you can do it again," Nialler whispered.

Serill repeated the action, and his hand glowed a deep pink as if there were a light within it.

Parsill and Nialler took turns to try, but they couldn't create a similar glow.

Nialler chewed the end of his quill "I wonder why the magic picks one person and not another?"

"That's a question for Lady Leyandrii," Parsill said, pushing the cup of water in front of Serill. "See if you can heat the water."

Serill frowned in concentration, but nothing happened.

"Keep trying," Nialler said.

Parsill shivered. "Is it getting colder in here?"

Nialler looked around him and stiffened when his breath plumed in the air. "It is. What are you doing, Serill?"

"Trying to heat the water as instructed," Serill said with a huff.

Nialler peered at the water in the mug; it was a sludgy

consistency, and his eyebrows rose as he swirled it with his finger and realised it was freezing cold. "It's ice."

Serill sat back with a grunt and rubbed his temples. "Well, that's a fail then."

"No, don't you see? You must have been drawing the heat from your surroundings, though I have no idea where it went."

"Not in the water," Parsill said with a grin.

Rubbing his fingers together, Serill smiled. "I don't feel cold."

"So, you've drawn the heat into your body but couldn't dispel it," Nialler said. "I think being able to use magic is a combination of an innate ability to feel the magical energy, knowing what to do with it, and using crystals to give you a boost."

"And there are very few people who have all three requirements," Parsill said with a crease between his brows as he thought his way through the puzzle. "Which is why there are so few people using magic."

"There must be some people who have enough innate magic that they don't need the crystals," Serill said. "Like Lady Leyandrii and Captain Guerlaire."

Niall nodded. "I think that's enough for today. Serill looks tired. Let's leave it for now. This is a good start. Let's go out and celebrate." He grinned. "We can write up our report for Captain Guerlaire tomorrow. There are plenty more experiments we can try after we get his advice. Maybe he can help Serill access his magic so we can remove lack of knowledge from the equation."

The next morning, when the others arrived, Nialler was frowning at the crystal on the bench. "I wonder what else they can do?"

Parsill hefted a crystal. "We'll only find out through trial and error, I suppose."

"It's a shame, but we are going to have to shelve our experiments." Nialler pulled a piece of paper out of his pocket. "I've been assigned to Retarfu in Elothia."

"The assignments are in, and you didn't say?" Parsill asked, his voice rising in outrage.

Serill grabbed his arm. "Let's go check. Much as I enjoy working in the Chapterhouse, I would like to see some of the world. I am a ranger first, then a scholar."

Parsill grinned. "We'll be back!" and he tugged Serill out the door.

37

BIRLER

GREENS, VESPIRI. SEPU 1122

Birler was mortified the day Melis sat him at the dining room table in front of a single placement of different-sized cutlery, china, and crystal glasses. "It's nothing to be embarrassed about if you take the time to learn. No one will be able to make you feel uncomfortable if you know what is expected. Who knows where you will be assigned, Birler? You need to be prepared as much as possible."

Birler's flush died down as he considered her words. She was right, as usual. He diligently spent a chime learning about finger bowls, napkins, and when to use the correct cutlery.

The next evening, he had a chance to put all that he had learned into practice as the dining table was festooned with china and sparkling crystal.

"What's the occasion?" Tagerill asked as he sat and dipped his fingers in the lemon-scented water bowl.

"I thought that as you'll both be away for your birthday, we could celebrate it tonight," Melis replied, allowing Warren to seat her. Birler watched, storing away Warren's actions and the way Melis responded.

The dining room table had been reduced to accommodate the five of them and was more intimate as a result. Penner grinned at Birler. "Who'd have thought Tagerill would make nineteen?"

Birler laughed as Tagerill threw his napkin across the table at Penner.

"Boys, not at the table," Warren growled.

"And Birler's eighteen. Where did this last year go?" Melis said, looking around the table.

Warren smiled at her. "Where it usually goes, I expect. I had a letter from Versill this morning. He's been assigned to Molinti, so he'll stop here next week—unfortunately after you lads have gone, but we'll be pleased to see him."

"Why doesn't anyone get assigned to Greens?" Tagerill stopped eating long enough to frown at his father.

"Who said there wasn't anyone? We are expecting Tianer to arrive with Versill. She will be stationed here."

"Oh good. You'll like her." Tagerill grinned, leaning back as the plates were cleared and the next course served.

"I'm surprised Serill hasn't written with his assignment. I wonder where he'll be," Birler said, selecting another fork.

"Maybe it will come tomorrow." Warren looked around the table. "A toast. Happy borning day, Tagerill and Birler."

"Happy borning day," everyone chanted.

Birler laughed and raised his glass. He chinked Tagerill's and took a sip. He was growing to like the pale, golden wine Melis served with every meal.

Courses came and went, and Birler savoured the different flavours. Conversation flowed, and he absorbed the comfort of a loving family without realising it.

Finally, Warren rose. "If everyone has finished, we'll move into the parlour."

Birler looked down at his plate, surprised he had

managed four courses without error. He caught Melis's eye and grinned. He rose and held her chair for her, and she laughed as she patted his cheek. "You'll do," she said.

There was another surprise awaiting them in the parlour. Two long, cloth-wrapped bundles lay on the table.

"We thought it was time you had a weapon suited to your situation," Warren said with a smile, handing first Tagerill and then Birler a smaller package. They eagerly unwrapped them to find a pair of finely wrought daggers: Tagerill's ornately decorated, Birler's engraved with a single tree.

Birler sat tracing the engraving in wonder and looked up, his eyes shining.

"Those were from Guerlaire. He sent them with a note; you can read it later. This is from Greens, from our own armoury, so we know you will always be able to protect yourself." Warren handed his son and then Birler long, cloth-wrapped bundles.

Birler knew what it would be as soon as he held it. The weight was unmistakable, and his vision blurred as the gleaming sword was revealed. The edge would be sharp, he knew. The steel shone, leading up to a twisted hilt. The junction with the blade was covered by a disc engraved with a single tree and an elaborate G entwined around the trunk. He turned it over and saw that his name was engraved on the blade, just under the hilt. It was more than he should accept, but he knew it was meant for him. Greens was as stubborn as he was. His head was bent over the blade when Warren gripped his shoulder. Birler looked up, his welling tears making his eyes gleam. "Thank you."

Warren smiled. "Greens salutes you on your borning day. We wish you many more."

Tagerill carefully sheathed his new sword. It was a huge broadsword meant to be strapped on his back, the first of its kind he had ever owned. He recognised the sword. He had been coveting it since he was a child. It came with a history, one he swore to uphold now that he was old enough and strong enough to wield it.

He looked across at Birler and grinned—one more tie to Greens. His father had given Birler the honour blade—the blade that his grandfather many times removed had used to first swear the family to the Lady. It made sense, seeing how Birler was utterly and completely the Lady's. He would tell him the story later.

The day their assignments were due finally dawned, and they waited nervously for the courier to arrive.

"Well, go on. Open them. We all want to know where you're off to," Melis said once the courier had been fed and watered and the papers handed out.

Birler slid his fingers under the red seal and broke the wax. The paper crackled as he unfolded it, and the Descelles waited anxiously as he read the contents. Excitement fluttered in his chest as he read. He looked up and laughed at Melis's expression of hope. "East Mayer," he said. Far enough away from Vespers and the unsavoury politics for him to be able to breathe.

"That's the other end of Vespiri, like Tagerill!" Melis exclaimed. Tagerill's posting was to the Watch Towers up past Stoneford.

"At least we're in the same area. Maybe we can catch up?" Birler said.

"Of course we can. We do get time off, you know," Tagerill said, catching Birler's eyes, knowing perfectly well that it was unlikely their time off would coincide.

"Good experience," Warren said. "It's on the borders of Terolia. Take the opportunity to learn more about them. It may be useful."

Tagerill looked at his father with exasperation. "You didn't say that about my posting," he complained.

Warren laughed. "The Watch Towers are up past Velmouth. Unless you find an unknown trail into Elothia, you're not going anywhere except Velmouth."

"Or Stoneford," Birler interjected with a grin.

"Maybe Stoneford," Warren conceded.

Melis stood up. "Well, this is cause for celebration, our last night all together. A toast"—she raised her glass—"to our boys. May they be successful in all they do. Tagerill and Birler."

"To Tagerill and Birler," Warren and Penner repeated as they raised their glasses.

Birler flushed as he raised his glass in response. He loved this family; they were so generous. He could never cause them any harm.

Warren rested his arm across Birler's shoulders. "Remember, you're always welcome here. This is your home. Don't forget."

"I won't," Birler promised, his eyes bright.

"And Kafinee can stay here when her time comes. George can't wait to look after her."

"Thank you." Birler hadn't been surprised when George had confirmed that Kafinee was with foal.

Melis joined them, worming her way under Warren's arm, and she held her other arm out to Tagerill. "We expect to see you when you when you have time, separately or together. Make sure you come home."

"Always, Ma." Tagerill gave her a lopsided grin.

Melis hugged him. "Make sure you do. No excuses." She glared at Birler.

"I know, I know. I'll try to," he said, careful not to promise something he couldn't do.

"Good," she said, hugging her boys close.

Birler hugged their love tightly and stored it deep inside. He still couldn't understand why this family had taken to him so firmly. They knew nothing about him except that he was homeless and unwanted. Pain flared through him; that his own father didn't want him cut deep. Not that he wanted to live with him; it was the desertion that hurt most. The lingering stigma meant he couldn't embrace the unconditional love the Descelles offered him.

He couldn't repay their trust by bringing their name into disrepute. He just couldn't. The need to protect them from any type of slander stiffened his resolve. Smiling, he joined in the plans, though Tagerill cast him concerned glances; he wasn't fooled.

The next morning, Birler and Tagerill prepared to leave. Warren and Melis lingered in the hallway as George brought the horses around to the front of the manor house. Birler checked Kafinee's girth strap and smoothed his hand down her warm neck, all the while inhaling her comforting scent. Kafinee had become as important to him as any chance of a family. She was a constant and she was his. Warren had taken pains to reassure him of this.

Birler glanced up as Warren descended the steps from the mansion. Melis followed him and went to hug Tagerill. "Birler, you ought to read this. It came in last night." He handed over a piece of paper and Birler skimmed it.

"Clary?" Birler stared at Warren, his face paling.

"I'm afraid so. His nephew, Mayer, is the Lord of East Mayer, but they fell out years ago, so I didn't think it would be an issue. If he's got an estate on the borders, you are bound to run into him. You need to be careful."

Birler blew his breath out, his stomach clenching. "I'm not sure I can be. If he knows I'm there, he'll deliberately cause trouble."

"I know. Just keep your temper. You can't allow him to rile you. If you retaliate, you'll give him the upper hand."

Clenching his jaw, Birler nodded and then exhaled. "I'll try."

"Treat it as another assignment. Practice keeping your temper against all provocation. It will drive him crazy. Remember, you are a Lady's Ranger. You represent her at all times."

Birler stiffened. "Yes, sir."

Warren hugged him and moved over to Tagerill, pulling him out of Melis's embrace to give him a hug of his own. "Be careful. Just because it's remote, it doesn't mean it's safe. Those passes are notorious for smugglers and bandits."

"I know, Pa. Don't worry so."

Warren glared at his son. "I'm serious."

"I know, and I'll be careful."

Warren gave him a final hug and boosted him up into his saddle. He stood with Melis on the steps, gazing down the road long after they had ridden out of view.

"I don't feel good about this," Melis said after a long, drawn-out silence.

Warren sighed and tightened his arm around his wife. "I know. Something is brewing, and our children are going to be in the centre of it."

"Our children?" Melis asked with a sad smile.

"All of them," Warren said, turning her towards the door.

38

BIRLER

GREENS, VESPIRI

Birler and Tagerill made good time down the track towards the East Road. It was a muddy road that was deeply rutted by passing wagons and bordered by ranks of tall trees, their multi-hued leaves glistening in the weak sunlight after a recent shower. They intended to get as far as the ford that crossed the Vesp River, which wended its way south through Deepwater and formed the border between Marchwood and East Watch, and camp there for the night. A village had sprung up around the ford, catering for travellers, so they should get a good meal there.

"I wonder what Serill ended up with. I thought we would have heard from him by now," Tagerill said.

"He'll stay at the Chapterhouse, don't you think? Guerlaire will want him."

Tagerill snorted. "Doubt it. He'll get the least-expected option. It's all about making us grow and develop, remember?"

Birler laughed. "Well, whatever he gets, I'm sure he'll land on his feet."

"Yeah, and it'll be better than up at the Watch Towers."

"You don't know that. They are the Lady's creation, so you'll be helping her. It's your chance to find out what they are really for. You should be pleased."

"But it won't be exciting," Tagerill replied as they rode out of a tunnel of trees into brilliant sunlight.

It was the slightest vibration on the air that alerted Birler and had him twisting into Tagerill and sweeping him out of the saddle. They landed in a heap as their horses bolted. Birler already had his sling whirling, releasing his stones in the direction the arrows had come from. Solid thunks reassured him he had hit something as he dived behind a fallen tree. Tagerill followed, cursing under his breath. "We haven't even left Greens. Who could possibly be attacking us here?"

"Bandits, maybe?" Birler said as he hunkered down beside Tagerill, listening carefully. It was silent except for their heavy breathing. Birler dug out another handful of stones from his pocket, regretting that his bow was still strapped to his saddle and long gone with Kafinee. Fortunately, his habit of always picking up stones was about to pay off.

"We can't stay here," Tagerill muttered and eased himself around the bole of the tree. He jerked back as arrows thumped into the trunk.

Birler released his stones in response. "Two remain to the right. Unknown number in that copse to the left."

"I'll just stick my head out again, shall I?" Tagerill growled.

Birler grinned. "They won't be able to resist."

Tagerill peered around the end of the tree again and jerked back as Birler cursed. Blood seeped through his collar. "It's just a scratch," he said, seeing Tagerill's concern. His grin was strained. "They refused the bait."

"They won't resist this." Tagerill leapt to his feet and

rushed the two bandits to his right. Birler frantically provided cover and followed him.

"Are you crazy?" Birler hissed as he reached the protection of the trees.

Tagerill grinned. "They were after you. At least now we can move." He crouched over the bodies. "These are no bandits," he said, his voice cold as he recognised the men's colours. "We need to find Inky and Kafinee and get out of here." He stiffened as a voice shouted across to them.

"Tagerill, our fight isn't with you. Leave, and you won't get hurt."

Tagerill hissed out his breath. "Go home, Tyrler. You're out of your league here."

"You'll regret it, Tagerill. I've warned you before. If you throw your lot in with that scum, you'll come off worse."

Tagerill stared at Birler. "South is Dalehurst. There is a courier station there. We could get help from them."

"He's right, Tagerill. You should go. This is my fight," Birler said, gripping his friend's shoulder.

"Don't talk such rubbish. As if I'd leave you. You're a ranger and my brother. I'm not leaving you anywhere."

"Whatever the outcome here, there are going to be repercussions. If we kill Tyrler, his father will take it out on your family."

"*Our* family," Tagerill corrected him. "And they started it. They must take the consequences. Let's try to circle behind them and lead them south."

Birler glowered at him, and then he grabbed a bow from one of the fallen men, tugged an arrow out of his quiver, and followed.

They crouched in a ditch and watched Tyrler regroup his men. Birler took careful aim and released his single arrow. Tyrler howled as it went through the meaty part of his thigh.

Tagerill tugged Birler away. "That should keep them

occupied," he said viciously and dragged his friend into the trees.

They made their way south into Deepwater before reaching the East Road, which passed through thickly forested hills until they reached arable fields. They skirted the fields, choosing cover over speed, and dropped into another ditch to catch their breath as they scanned the open terrain between them and the courier outpost, a collection of one-storey wooden buildings off the East Road.

"C'mon." Tagerill led the way and ran for the building, with Birler on his heels. They burst through the door, surprising the ranger on duty.

"Ranger Tagerill Descelles, sir. We were ambushed in Greens just north of here. Bandits. Lost our horses."

"Bandits? This far west? Are you sure?" The man was huge and broad-shouldered, with thick blond hair tied back in a queue. He barely fit in the chair behind the desk. A heavy broadsword was propped behind him against the wall.

Tagerill shrugged. "There were about ten of them. We took out half of them and ran. We left the bodies about here." Tagerill pointed to a spot on the map tacked to the wall.

The man scowled. "That doesn't make sense. The patrol is due back in a chime. I can divert them to check the area and see if they can find your horses."

Tagerill groaned. "My father will lose it if the horses turn up at Greens without us."

The ranger grinned in sympathy. "I can send a courier with a message if you want. Meantime, are you alright?" He had spotted the blood on Birler's shirt collar.

Birler shrugged. "It's just a scratch."

The ranger cocked an eyebrow at him, his blue eyes bright. "We'll just make sure, shall we? Come on through; we have a field kit in the back office. No point in taking a risk.

Descelles, write a message to your father; that will stop him from sending out men looking for you."

Tagerill nodded and sat as directed. Birler reluctantly followed the ranger into the back office and took off his jacket and shirt. The arrow had grazed his neck. The ranger sat back and stared at him. "You were lucky," he said briefly, and Birler grimaced.

The man cleaned the wound, smoothed a salve over it, and taped a covering over the cut. Birler shrugged back into his shirt and jacket. "Thanks. I'm Birler."

"Anter," the man replied, rinsing his hands. "Let's get this message sent off, and then you can tell me what happened." He peered out the door and gave a sharp whistle. A young lad came flying around the corner in response. "Saddle up. You're going to Greens. Urgent," Anter said. He turned back to Tagerill. "You done?"

Tagerill handed him the note, and Anter shoved it in a courier bag without looking at it. "For the attention of Lord Warren?" he asked.

"Yes, sir, m'father."

Anter nodded and strode out the door. "Billie, for Lord Warren, and if two horses turned up at Greens unexpectedly, bring them back with you," he instructed as he boosted the young lad up in the saddle.

"Yes, sir!" Billie wheeled his horse and cantered down the road.

"He's a good lad. He does all the local runs for us; he'll be back in a few chimes. We only have so many men, so we're training up those lads who are interested," Anter said as he turned his sharp blue gaze on Birler. "Birler, why don't you explain how you almost got killed?"

"I'm headed for East Mayer, Tagerill for the Watch Towers above Stoneford. We just got our assignments from Commander Asher. We left Greens this morning, intending to get as far as East Ford, and we were about fifteen miles or so from Greens when we were ambushed, and we dived for cover."

"You mean you knocked me off my horse," Tagerill interjected.

Birler grimaced. "I heard the arrow; it was instinctive."

"We were pinned down behind a log. Tagerill was baiting them, and I was trying to pick them off with my sling. One of them got me instead." Birler shrugged and then recounted the attack. "I managed to get an arrow into who we thought was their leader, and we ran for it. And here we are."

Anter exhaled loudly. "There shouldn't be any bandits around here. We'll have to reinstate road patrols if that's the case." He frowned at the map in concern. "I'll have to report it to Lord Benoir at Marchwood. Make sure you inform Lord Mayer at East Mayer."

"Maybe it's a random ambush?" Tagerill suggested. "An opportunistic strike. Though, what we have that they wanted, Lady knows!" he finished with a grin.

"Well, hopefully, either Billie or the patrol will find your horses, and you can be on your way," Anter said. "While we wait, mug of kafinee?"

Birler smiled. "That would be great. Thank you."

Anter returned with two steaming mugs and a bowl of sweetener. "Help yourself," he said, handing them the mugs. He returned to his desk and took a sip of his kafinee. He rotated his massive shoulders and leaned back in his chair, watching the rangers. "What's been happening in Vespers? Anything interesting?"

"The Lady has confirmed that there will be six watches; the investiture is in a couple of months. The Dominants are not pleased. Now that the Lady has given power to the people, they've changed their minds. They think the Administration should hold all the power."

"They are never pleased, as history tells us. It's said there was much protestation when she created the other territories, so it shouldn't come as a surprise," Anter said with a grin.

Tagerill gave a snort of laughter. "They seem to have forgotten it was their suggestion."

"I expect they wanted to be its rulers. Though, personally, I think the Lady chose well. She understands what her people need, and it isn't more of the Administration, that's for sure." Anter heaved a sigh. "It's a shame there is always someone trying to cause problems, but I guess that's what gives us a job."

"How long have you been posted here?" Tagerill asked.

"About six months. Due to rotate soon. You don't normally stay longer than six months at any post. I'm originally from Marchwood, so not far from home this time, which makes a change. Furthest I've been is down in Birtoli. Nice down there, much slower. Very clannish, though; the elders are funny old birds."

"I've never been anywhere but Vespers and Greens," Birler said with a wry grin. "East Mayer is the furthest I'll have travelled. What is Lord Mayer like?"

"Nothing like his uncle, you'll be glad to hear. He knows his land and his people. He's a good lord, so you shouldn't have any problems."

"That's a relief. Do you know much about the borders?"

Anter grinned. "The Terolian Families, you mean? Once you've proved yourself, you'll be fine. They tend to be insular, and they'll probably ignore you to begin with, so don't take offence. It's how they treat everyone. If you're in the Family, they'll die for you; if you're not, they aren't interested."

Birler nodded. "I know a couple of rangers who are from Terolia. Hopefully, that will help."

Anter looked at him in interest. "That's right. This last

year, they opened up the academy, didn't they? How did that go?"

"It was great," Birler said. "We should know more about the other territories. We all live in the same world, after all."

"The purists didn't like it, but they never do," Tagerill said.

Anter nodded, watching them thoughtfully. He cocked his head, stiffened, and then stood up to peer out the window. Striding to the door, he said, "Patrol's back."

Tagerill and Birler followed. It seemed like there was a garrison of men and horses outside the office, but it resolved itself into a unit of rangers led by one formidable-looking woman the equal of Anter.

"Anter, we found a body just off the East Road. No markings. No obvious wounds. Looks like a failed ambush." Birler grinned as he recognised the woman who dismounted. Saer had consistently beaten him in the sparring ring until she had graduated. She had been a year ahead of them.

Anter gestured to Tagerill and Birler. "These lads were ambushed this morning. I was going to send you off to check, but it looks like you already found them. Was there anyone else in the vicinity?"

"We only saw a group with Clary's boy headed back to Vespers, claiming they had been ambushed. Some were bruised up a bit." Saer raked them with a sharp glance and then relaxed. She tilted her head. "Birler, was this you?" She gestured behind her at the loaded horse.

He stepped forward, swallowing at the sight, but then he stiffened. "Yes, I'm afraid so. I was just trying to incapacitate. I didn't mean to kill him."

"Impressive," she said, giving him a nod. "A killing shot like that is difficult." She turned back to her troop. "Offload him here. We'll send in a report. They can decide what we should do with the body."

"You didn't come across two loose horses? A black stallion and a brown mare?" Tagerill asked.

Saer shook her head. "Only those three." She indicated the three chestnut horses, one carrying the body. She smiled grimly. "Clary had three horses with double riders, though I don't think they were yours."

Tagerill heaved a sigh. "I expect they went back to Greens. My father will freak. We haven't even got to our post yet, and we're already in trouble."

"Saer, take them around the back; use the shed for now."

Saer nodded. "Gellan, you heard the man. Take them round to the shed." She looked at Tagerill. "Being ambushed is hardly your fault," she said. "You're still alive. I would say your father would be pleased." She gave him a grin and followed her men around the building.

"The horses will be too tired to go on today; they'll have done forty-plus miles," Tagerill said, glancing at Birler.

"You can bunk here for the night and continue tomorrow," Anter reassured him. "We can lend you horses if needed, but let's see what your father sends from Greens."

Tagerill and Birler were deep in conversation with Saer and her men when the clatter of horses arriving drew everyone back out of the barracks. Tagerill strode up to Sam, one of George's assistants in the stables, who was leading Inky. "Are they alright?"

"Yes, young master; otherwise, m'lord wouldn't have sent them on."

"Good." Tagerill breathed out a sigh of relief. His lips thinned as he saw the unit of men following. "We don't need an escort!" he exclaimed as he saw the captain of his father's guards.

"It seems you do," the captain replied. "You're lucky

your father didn't come himself. We're to escort you to your new postings. I've two other horses for you to ride tomorrow. Inky and Kafinee need the rest."

Tagerill looked back at Birler. "I'm sorry, but my father does overreact sometimes."

Sam huffed. "Overreact? Your parents had quite the shock when your horses arrived without either of you. And you'd only just left as well."

"Well, it'll be a bit crowded but you can stop here for the night and get an early start," Anter suggested, looking around at the men and horses. "Gellan, take them round to the stables."

Once the horses were settled, Sam and the captain returned. "Your father gave me this for you." Sam handed over the letter and accepted a mug of kafinee from Anter.

Tagerill read the contents and grimaced. "He says he will deal with Clary."

"You told him?" Birler was horrified.

"Of course I told him. He attacked us; he can't be allowed to get away with it."

"He was after me, not you. You shouldn't be dragged into this."

Tagerill exhaled. "How many times do I have to tell you? You are family; of course we are involved."

"What's this?" Anter asked, sitting beside Birler.

Birler flushed. "There are some at the academy who believe only families of pure blood should be allowed to be cadets or rangers."

Saer raised an eyebrow. "They're still going on about that? Who do they class as purebloods then?"

"Those with a family name you can trace back at least two centuries."

"We'd soon run out of bodies, then. There aren't enough old families to man the defences. What would they do then?"

Birler shrugged. "I think they want to lord it over everyone. They seem to have taken a dislike to me and some of the other cadets who don't have a family name."

"You're a ranger now; it's got nothing to do with them," Tagerill said, his eyes flashing with anger. "You graduated on your own merits."

"Clary doesn't agree, and you know what he thinks," Birler pointed out.

"You know better than to believe anything he says. You know my father; he stands against that type of talk. He would never treat you so. You're family; it's up to you to make it true."

"It doesn't give him the right to take your life, to set a ranger on another ranger," Saer interjected. "That breaks the vows you took to protect each other and the people of Vespiri. Clary ought to be cast out. He's not fit to be a ranger." A murmur of agreement went around the hut, and Birler realised everyone was listening.

He flushed in embarrassment. "I don't want to make it worse. Accusing Clary, getting him cast out, would only make it worse for the Descelles."

"Hiding from it won't solve the problem," Anter said firmly. "It needs to be dealt with. They are not trustworthy or honourable. If you don't deal with them, the very people you are trying to protect will get hurt, and you will never forgive yourself."

Birler's shoulders drooped. "I never asked for any of this."

Tagerill gave him a hug. "No, and they'll regret targeting you. You've more honour than they will ever have, and they'll soon learn."

Saer grinned. "And look on the bright side—it looked like you wounded young Clary, so he will be paying for it for a few weeks yet. It will be interesting to see how he explains that away."

Birler grimaced. "It was the only way to distract them. I knew he would panic if I took him out."

Saer gave him a keen glance. "You mean the leg wound was deliberate?"

"Birler hits whatever he aims at," Tagerill said. "If he wanted Clary dead, he would have been."

"Tage, don't."

Saer whistled. "I doubt he realises how lucky he was."

"No, he'll just be angry that I managed to hurt him. Maybe I *should* have killed him." Birler rubbed his face. "But I didn't want to start out killing one of our own, even if he has betrayed me. It's not his fault; it's what his father has taught him. He's only acting on his father's orders."

"He should be acting on his commander's orders, not his father's," Anter growled. "And so I'll tell him if I ever see him. If I ever catch him betraying another ranger, he won't know what hit him."

Birler looked around the room at the nodding rangers. He felt warmed by their support, but the thought that they would all spread this story far and wide horrified him. "I'm not sure this is something we ought to be spreading about. It doesn't do the rangers' reputation much good."

Anter considered him before glancing around the room. "You're probably right. Lads and lasses, be careful who you tell. We don't want to tarnish our good name with idle gossip," he said.

The next morning, Tagerill was still trying to convince their escort to go home. The captain ignored him, and Tagerill resorted to whining. "It's going to look great, a ranger turning up with an armed escort. They're going to think I'm a right weakling."

Sam laughed. "They are following your father's orders,

and if that means tying you to your saddle, we will do so, so don't think about trying to lose us."

Tagerill gave up, and Birler was secretly relieved. He half-expected Clary to retaliate straight away. A bit of protection wouldn't go amiss, and Anter had said the same. Birler was more worried about what Lord Mayer would say when he found out Birler had deliberately injured his cousin.

The guards took up the rear, with Sam following Tagerill and Birler, and led Kafinee and Inky, both of whom tried to get to their riders, and offended that they were riding other horses.

Saer led her unit on a roving patrol, sweeping in front for trouble. Fortunately, none was found, and two days later, Birler arrived at East Mayer in one piece. He swapped over to Kafinee, handing his borrowed horse back to Sam with thanks.

Tagerill clutched Birler in a desperate hug; this was where they parted. "I thought it was bad when Versill left home, and then Marian. I'm going to miss you, Birler. Take care of yourself, for the Lady's sake."

"I will. I'll be alright."

"I'm so used to you being here; it will be weird without you," Tagerill said.

"Take care of yourself, Tage." Birler's gut tightened now that it was time to say goodbye. They had spent two years in each other's pockets. It would be lonely without the irrepressible Tagerill around.

"Remember, you have to come home for Pa's confirmation. He'll be gutted if you don't come."

"I'll come home. I promise." Birler watched Tagerill ride down the road with his entourage. It was time for him to embark on his life as a Lady's Ranger. He squared his shoulders and turned down the road that led to East Mayer.

39

BIRLER

EAST MAYER, VESPIRI

Birler rode down the track to Mayer's Landing, the home of the Lord of East Mayer, accompanied by one of Saer's roving rangers. She had agreed it would be less conspicuous, and they had cleared the area already, so she waved goodbye and led her unit back to their allotted route.

Laurel was from Ridgewood, a small village to the north of Deepwater, on the border with Elothia. He was older than Tagerill, thicker around the waist, and if not for having met Anter and Saer, Birler would have said he was a big man. He had been with Saer for the last year and regaled Birler with some of their more hair-raising exploits. Who would have thought they could find so much trouble? But Birler appreciated the stories, as they made the miles pass quicker.

The road curved around a bank of wiry trees and opened into a gently rolling vista, in the middle of which stood a large stone house surrounded by outbuildings and corals. The openness was unnerving; there were a few trees dotted about, but they were not the type Birler was familiar with. The rolling hills were a patchwork of green grass and fields of reddish soil. Woolly white sheep were dotted like bright stars against a verdant night sky.

As they neared the house, Birler realised there were leggy goats and mules as well, all studiously cropping the lush grass.

A stocky, black-haired man stood waiting for them on the veranda that encircled the house, and he smiled in greeting as they pulled up by the steps. "Rangers, welcome. Courier or passing through?"

Birler grinned. "I'm Birler; I am posted here. Laurel is passing through."

The man nodded. "Take your horses around the back and get them watered. I'll meet you there."

Birler and Laurel rode around the back of the house, and a bustling stable yard opened before them, with the clang of metal from the smithy providing a counterpoint to the high-pitched voices of the stable lads.

The stocky man from the veranda arrived as they were dismounting. "I'm the steward. You can call me Archie. Where you from, Birler?"

"Vespers. Here are my papers." He handed Archie his orders as he led Kafinee over to the water trough, her head dipping immediately. Archie glanced over the papers and handed them back. "They look fine."

Birler unstrapped his saddlebags and handed her over to the stable lad with a grin. The lad led her away, whispering sweet nothings into her flicking ear.

"She'll be spoilt, don't worry, a pretty mare like that. Come on in, and we'll get you sorted out."

Laurel stood by his horse as he, too, drank from the trough. "I'll head back now, Birler. Good meeting you. Stay safe." He flicked a salute as Birler nodded and followed Archie into the dim building.

"This is the main manor house. The barracks are in the

north wing. You'll room there, though you ought to know we have another barracks over in Berbera, as we tend to cover the border. Half your time will be spent over there, I expect. Lord Mayer will explain more."

"What do you need defending against around here?"

Archie grinned at him. "You're thinking we're exposed, aren't you? With it all being so open?"

Birler flushed as he nodded.

"Most of the land is arable; it's the livestock we need to protect against thieves. We have roving patrols; no point being dug in in one position. Most are hit-and-run raiders from over the border, those who aren't prepared to barter in the market like most civilised folk. It doesn't happen that often; only if the Families clamp down and banish folk."

"Banish?"

"Yeah, if a person betrays the Family, they lose the right to live with them. They are cast out, become homeless. They tend to get a bit desperate 'cos no Family is supposed to help them."

"That's a bit harsh, isn't it?"

"The Families have rules they live by. Break them, and the punishment will follow." Archie shrugged. "Works most of the time."

"Until it doesn't," Birler breathed.

"It's their way of life. Not for us to say it's wrong."

"True. Do you have much of a bandit problem around here?"

"Not really. That's more up north. Smugglers' routes go through the Stantons—more places to hide. Here, our fields bleed into open desert. We tend to get waifs and strays looking for work in the fields. It's more about managing disputes and land grabs than anything else." Archie paused by a door. "This is you. We've usually got two other rangers here. Frener is over in Terolia, and we're expecting another to arrive any day. The three of you will rotate, one here, one in Terolia, and the other acts as courier.

"This is a large watch. We have a lot of land to cover, and we're also responsible for managing the border, so there's plenty to do. Dinner is at six in the main dining hall. We all eat together when Lord and Lady Mayer are home; otherwise, you eat as your shift dictates. Take the time to freshen up. My office is on the ground floor, by the entrance. I'll have the maps ready for you. Lord Mayer will speak to you in the morning; he is down at the harbour today."

Birler blinked. Harbour? He didn't realise East Mayer had a coastline, let alone a harbour. He dumped his saddlebags on the bed and propped his bow in the corner. Unbuckling his sword belt, he dropped it on the bed and stretched. His neck jabbed, and he shrugged out of his jacket. He peeled the bandage off and grimaced at the slimy mess. After grabbing his shirt and the pot of salve he knew Melis had tucked into both his and Tagerill's saddlebags, he went in search of the bathing room.

Feeling much better for a shower, he wrapped his towel around his waist and, twisting awkwardly, inspected the wound in the mirror. He slathered the ointment on the angry-looking graze. Hopefully, it would calm down in the next day or so. If not, he'd have to find a healer on his travels. He scrubbed his shirt in the sink, but the bloodstains were stubborn.

He made it back to his room unseen and changed into fresh clothes. He hung his jacket up, intending to give it a good brushing. The shirt, he threw on the floor. Hopefully the washerwoman would have more luck.

After unpacking his bags, which didn't take long, he wandered through the building, peering in doorways and smiling in apology when he startled the staff. Eventually, he reached Archie's office.

Archie looked up from the paperwork on his desk. "That was quick!"

"Not much to unpack."

"Those are the maps," Archie said, pointing at a stack of folded papers. "I suggest you speak to Captain Devis. He can give you details of the roving patrols and the borders."

Birler picked up the maps. "Thank you." He went to find Devis. By the time he arrived, he regretted removing the bandage. His shirt rubbed his neck, making it sore, and he knew he would have another ruined shirt. He eased the material away from his skin and tapped on the office door.

A deep voice bade him to enter, so he did. "Ranger Birler reporting for duty, sir," he said as he entered the cluttered office. Piles of paper covered the floor and the shelves. Behind the desk sat a portly man, red-faced and sweating.

The man squinted at Birler. "A ranger, eh? Took your time. We've been short for weeks. Courier bag is over there; the list is on the top. Get as many as you can done today, eh?"

Birler picked up the list and the bag. There were at least ten locations, none of which he recognised. Well, at least he would know them soon.

"Are any urgent, sir?"

"If they were, they're not anymore," Devis replied, unconcerned.

"Very good, sir." Birler retreated. He caught a young maid in the corridor. "Excuse me. Could you tell me where the healer is located?"

The young girl blushed as she met his eyes and bobbed her knees. "It's attached to the stables, round the back."

"Thank you," he said, wondering why she was so flustered.

He found the healer and peered into the room, where a young woman sat at a bench writing notes in a file. "Excuse me? I'm looking for the healer?"

The woman looked up and gave him a keen inspection. She wasn't as young as he'd first thought; her face was lined, and her brown eyes were bright. "That would be me," she said, slipping off the stool.

"Ah, I need a bandage if you have one."

She tucked a stray brown curl behind her ear. "What for?"

Birler sighed and eased his shirt. "For my neck. I have to go out riding, and my shirt is rubbing."

"Let me see." The woman pointed at a low stool. He sat and eased his shirt away from his neck.

"Take it off," she said, collecting some instruments.

Birler took his shirt off and sat back down.

"How did you get that?" she asked from right beside him. Her fingers were cool against his sore skin.

"Stray arrow."

"On the way here?"

"We were ambushed south of Deepwater."

The woman tutted and efficiently cleaned the wound. She dusted it with a power and taped a bandage over it. "The salve is good for minor wounds, but wounds like that, we need to dry out. Keep it covered when you are outside and for at least the next two days. Best to leave it uncovered after that, give it a chance to breathe. It will heal quicker."

"Thank you." Birler shrugged back into his shirt.

"You're welcome. What I'm here for."

"I'm Birler, just arrived today from Vespers."

The woman arched an eyebrow. "Ah, one of our new rangers? They've been expecting you for weeks. I'm Damaris." She held out her hand, and he shook it.

"Anything I should be wary of?" he asked as he picked up the courier bag again.

The woman shrugged. "Just the usual. Always carry water with you. It gets hot this time of year, even though you expect it to be winter. Especially when you are over the border, the desert creeps in real quick. Avoid swampy areas if you can. Bogflies can cause nasty rashes and make you ill. Always go around them—worth it in the long run."

Birler nodded. "I appreciate the advice."

Damaris looked at him thoughtfully. "Seeing as you're asking and you're new, I recommend you take this: it's a barrier salt." Damaris handed him a small cloth bag. "Dilute two spoonfuls in water and drink it all. Gives you some protection against the sand flies. Get the lads to put some in your horse's water as well. They should anyway, but make sure."

"It won't affect her foal, will it?"

Damaris turned back to him in surprise. "Your horse is in foal? Why is a ranger riding a pregnant mare?"

Birler shrugged. "She's my horse, and I only just found out. She's only a month or so gone. Early days yet."

"It should be fine. Better to protect her than not."

"Thanks." Birler left with the salts. He mixed his up in his room and drank it all, shuddering at the sour aftertaste. Then he sat over his map, marking the locations of his deliveries and planning the most efficient route. He strapped on his bow and sword, made sure he had his daggers and his water canteen, and went to dose Kafinee before they left for the first delivery.

He cinched in the girth and patted her neck. "Ready to start work?" he murmured in her ear, and she flicked it in his face. Birler laughed and secured his full canteen under the flap. He checked his map and his bearings. First stop, Hoxton, which looked like a small group of dwellings in a dip, according to the map.

He found it easily enough; a track off the road to Mayer's Landing. He named it harbour road as the map said it led all the way to the tiny stretch of coastline that East Mayer did indeed have. He dismounted and rapped on the flimsy wooden door. After a short wait, a man with thinning brown hair and watery eyes peered out. His gaze flicked around the yard and back to Birler.

"Delivery for you, sir." Birler held out the paper.

"Th-Thank you," the man stuttered, his gaze flicking around again before coming back to rest on Birler. His knuckles gleamed white as he gripped the edge of the door.

"Is everything alright, sir?" Birler looked around more closely. The dwellings were in a state of disrepair, and the man looked thin and unwell. "Do you need help?"

"N-No, we're fine." He pulled the door shut, and Birler held his hand against it.

"You're not alright," he said, keeping his voice low. "What has happened?"

The man licked his lips and shuddered, his eyes wide. "Please, we're fine." He pushed the door shut.

Birler stood looking at it for a moment and then turned away and remounted. He rode away, deep in thought, circled the dwellings, and climbed the rise behind it. He dismounted and crouched down, watching the road.

Not half a chime later, two horsemen rode up to the house and barged inside. Birler heard the crash of furniture, and then one of the men came out, dragging a struggling woman. He groped her body suggestively, and she screamed. Birler had his bow in his hand without thinking as the second man came out, dragging a small child, who was crying copiously. Birler shifted his sight to the man holding the child. He was threatening something. Birler didn't wait, and as soon as he released the first arrow, the second followed, and the woman grabbed her daughter and rushed back into the house.

Birler rode back down the hill, his sword ready. He swung his leg over, slid out of the saddle, and stood over the man rolling in the dust. The other man lay in a motionless sprawl, and Birler was relieved to see he was still breathing. He had only meant to disable him, not kill him. The man stilled as Birler's sword rested against his throat. "Who are you, and what do you want with these people?"

"You'll regret this," the man spat.

"I think you'll find *you'll* regret it more if you don't answer my question."

"The lord of this land expects payment from those living off it."

"I am quite sure Lord Mayer does not go around treating his people in this manner."

"Dominant Clary, not that fool prancing about in that big house."

"That 'fool', as you term it, happens to be the lord of these lands, not Dominant Clary," Birler said calmly, his heart fluttering in his chest.

"Not for much longer," the man groaned, holding his leg.

Birler rested his foot against the man's leg and grasped the arrow, his mind racing as he digested the man's threat. "What do you mean?"

"Nothing." The man tensed as Birler leaned over him.

"Is Clary planning to attack Lord Mayer?"

"I don't know!" The man stiffened as Birler's grip on the arrow tightened. "Please, I don't know. He doesn't tell me his plans. I'm just the help."

"What *do* you know? What does Clary charge? And for what?"

"Clary expects a tithe of all goods and a tax for the dwellings and each person. Don't!" The man hissed his breath out as Birler twitched the arrow.

"And how much does all that come to? Everything these people earn?"

"Two obols a month."

"Two!" No wonder the people were so destitute. "How long has this been going on for?"

"About half a year, ever since Clary moved into his estate."

"And where is this estate?"

"East of here, between Jaren and Ramila."

Birler looked up as the man peered out the door. "Have you got some cloth to bind this wound?"

The man nodded and darted back indoors, and he returned with a length of cloth. Birler took it and firmly yanked the arrow out. The man passed out. He bound the wound tightly, tying it off.

"They'll come back and burn our home down," the man whispered from the doorway.

"Lord Mayer will protect you; he is the Lady's Guardian. She will protect you if you ask."

"She hasn't so far."

Birler looked up. "I'm here, aren't I?"

"But you won't stay. He'll send someone else."

Birler leaned back on his heels and considered him. "I'll take these men back to Mayer's Landing. Captain Devis will send a patrol to keep an eye on you."

"You'd do that for us?"

"Of course." Birler looked at him in surprise.

"Lady's blessing on you, sir."

Birler nodded and then checked the other man. He was relieved that he was just unconscious; maybe he had passed out from the blood loss. Heaving the men over their horses, he wrapped the stirrups around them to keep them in place. The man came out with a frayed piece of rope and helped tie them on before he rushed back into the house.

Birler rode back to Mayer's Landing, trailing the two loaded horses. He caused quite a stir as he rode into the yard, and Devis came striding out of his office, his face redder than usual.

"You can't go around shooting people," he gasped as the men were unloaded.

Birler cocked an eyebrow. "What, even when they are threatening to rape innocent women and children?"

Devis spluttered. "Take them to Damaris," he ordered. "You come with me and explain." He grew angrier as Birler reported what had happened. "You mean you only got one delivery in? You are a courier, not a one-man army."

"I'm a ranger," Birler replied, "here to protect the Lady's people, not to deliver mail."

"You are here to do what I tell you," Devis said with some heat. "Wait until Lord Mayer hears of this. You're confined to your barracks until he gets here."

"What about the family at Hoxton? They need protecting against Dominant Clary's men."

"That is up to Lord Mayer, not you."

"You would leave them exposed? He's already taken everything they have. They're barely existing."

"They are not my responsibility!" Devis shouted. "Now, get out."

"If they are not your responsibility, then what is? Aren't you here to protect your lord's people on behalf of the Lady?"

"Don't you dare tell me what I should be doing. Get out."

Birler left in disgust. He paced his room, trying to control his anger. Should he have done things differently? If he had been at the homestead when the men had arrived, they might have attacked him, and he would have had to fight two of them instead—and then he might have killed them. He sighed. Maybe he had been a bit hasty, but still, the family were being threatened. And more concerning, they were still at risk.

He looked up as a lean, young man peered in his door as he introduced himself. "Lieutenant Casper, roving patrol. Where was that family you said needed checking on?"

"Hoxton," Birler said with relief.

"We'll keep an eye on them," the lieutenant said and was gone again.

Birler lay back on his bed, staring at the ceiling. Bored, he got up and unfolded his maps. He spent the evening poring over them until he knew he had them memorised. He looked up as a shadow darkened his doorway.

Archie stood studying him. "Didn't take you long to cause trouble, did it?"

Birler grimaced. "I wasn't expecting to come across innocent people being threatened in their homes."

"Come with me. You need to eat. Confined to barracks doesn't mean you have to starve." His eyes narrowed at the mess on Birler's bed. "What are you doing, anyway?"

"Memorising the maps you gave me."

"I see." Archie shook his head. "Come on." He led the way to the dining hall. "We have men on various shifts, so there is always food available at all times of the day and night."

Birler nodded. "Good to know."

"When Lord Mayer is home, the meal is always at sixth chime. He's late tonight." Archie picked up a tray and selected his food. He waited for Birler and led the way to the long table down the middle of the room and slid onto the bench. "So, you're from Vespers, you said?"

"Yes, born and bred in Vespers. I joined the cadets when I was sixteen. Just graduated."

"So, ah, this is your first posting?"

"Yes."

"Don't you think you might have been a bit hasty?"

Birler toyed with his food. "I've thought about it, and no, I don't. If I had interrupted them, I would have had to fight them hand-to-hand. I probably would have killed them. Using the bow, I could disable, not kill."

"If you had ridden away and not engaged, then no one would have got hurt," Archie suggested.

"Except the woman and her child. They would have been raped."

"The men deny they were going to rape them."

"Just threatening it for fun, were they? Maybe you should speak to the woman and see what she says."

"I will," Archie replied.

"What did they say their reason for being there was if they weren't threatening that family?"

"They said the family owed Clary some money; they were there to collect it, and the man refused to pay it."

Birler snorted. "So, they deny they were collecting taxes from Lord Mayer's tenants."

"He said you forced it out of him under duress."

Birler laughed. "Convenient. Aren't you concerned that your lord's tenants are the ones being fleeced? Have you been to Horton lately? Or any other of the dwellings around here?"

"Times have been hard recently," Archie said mildly.

"So, that makes it acceptable?"

"No, of course not, but you cannot assume the worst when you know nothing of the situation. You are new here."

Birler sighed. "The people are desperate, and the Lady uses what she has to hand." Birler looked at Archie. "Especially if those who should be acting are not."

Archie nodded. "Fair enough. We'll see what the Hoxtons have to say."

Birler grimaced and ate his food.

The next morning, Birler leant on the railing outside the barracks, watching tiny brown birds fluttering their wings in the dust. They were making small depressions and flipping the sand over their bodies, their wings a blur. He smiled at their antics.

The sun was just rising in the clear blue sky, not a cloud to be seen. The Lady's moon faded as red and orange streaks replaced the steel grey dawn. He needed to find a temple; the need to pray in the Lady's calming presence was an overwhelming urge, and he could use her guidance right now.

He hoped Lord Mayer returned today; he was already bored with being cooped up in his room. Hopping over the railing, he concentrated on emptying his mind and began the motions of Apeiron, feeling his tight muscles relax as they warmed. His skin was gleaming with sweat when Archie cleared his throat behind him. Birler turned smoothly to face him and came to a close.

"What are you doing now?" Archie asked, his tone resigned.

"It's called Apeiron."

"Apeiron?"

"Helps align the mind with body," Birler explained.

"Well, go shower the body. Lord Mayer wants to speak to you."

Birler grinned and went for a shower.

40

BIRLER

EAST MAYER, VESPIRI

Birler arrived at Lord Mayer's office within half a chime of the summons, showered and smartly dressed in his ranger's uniform. He waited patiently as Mayer scrutinised him. He took the time to observe the lord in turn.

Lord Mayer wasn't as tall as Clary or as imposing, but he was an intense man. His sharp brown eyes took in Birler in moments, though he pretended to inspect him for much longer. "For such an unassuming man, you cause a lot of trouble, don't you?" he said in a clipped voice.

"Not intentionally, sir."

Mayer's eyes gleamed. "I understand I have you to thank for unearthing Clary's latest ploys to undermine me."

"I did, sir?"

"You know damn well you did. You will accompany me when we go visit him later today and set him straight."

"Yes, sir. Umm, I should say that he doesn't like me, sir."

"Why am I not surprised?" Mayer grinned. "Don't worry. I know all about my brother's prejudices. They are not mine."

"No, sir."

"Good, and then you can return to your duties. No point in having a ranger bored to death in my watch. Who knows what trouble you'll be kicking up next."

"Yes, sir."

"Very well. We leave in a half-chime. Be ready."

"Yes, sir." Birler left.

Birler was waiting with Kafinee when Lord Mayer arrived. Mayer leapt up on his horse and was leading the way down the road before his men had assembled. Birler rode behind him. They passed the turning for Hoxton and continued up the road before turning off towards Jaren.

Mayer critically viewed the dwellings in Jaren and the nervous people who watched him pass. Mayer's lips grew thinner as he passed the dilapidated buildings. Dominant Clary's estate came into view another five miles past Jaren.

Birler stiffened as they approached the mansion. It was an old house with ornate cornices and statuettes decorating the palisades. It was much more pretentious than Mayer's Landing.

"My uncle was always a show-off," Mayer said as he observed the mansion. "The house was impractical to live in, though; that was why my father built the Landing: a working base. Suits Gilbert, of course; makes him think he is the Lord of the Watch, living in the family seat." He waited as Lieutenant Casper sent one of his men up to the door.

A stooped man answered the door, looked down the drive, and nodded abruptly before disappearing back inside. He left the door open. Mayer waited some more.

Birler unsheathed his bow in one smooth movement and had an arrow nocked and aimed as a man peered down over the wall running around the roof of the house.

"Stand down, Birler." Mayer's voice was soft, and Birler lowered his bow, though he remained tense. "Ah, finally, Chambers. Took you long enough. Where is Gilbert?" Mayer said to a thin, dark-haired man who stood at the top of the steps.

"He's not here, my lord."

"When did he leave?"

"Couldn't say, my lord."

"It disappoints me that I need to remind you that this is my watch. You are not at liberty to threaten or collect taxes from my people. If Gilbert isn't here and you don't know how to get hold of him, then I assume you are acting on your own initiative?"

"No, my lord."

"Then on Gilbert's?"

"Yes, my lord."

"And what are his orders?"

The man was silent.

"Seeing as you can't get hold of him and you don't know his orders, I suggest you make a decision now. You can either stop obeying his orders or I'll call down the Justicers on you. And once they start trawling through all your activities, I expect you'll find my uncle will drop you like a hot coal and deny that he ever instructed you so."

There was silence.

"Do you feel like paying the price for Gilbert's greed?"

"No, sir."

"You will return whatever you have collected to the people you collected it from. My men will accompany you to make sure your apologies are appropriately worded. And then I suggest you close this estate and find other employ until such time as Gilbert comes to ask my permission to settle here. Understood?"

"Yes, my lord."

"If I have to deal with you or your men again, I will not be so lenient."

"Understood, my lord."

"Good." He looked at Casper. "See to it."

Casper nodded and rapped out instructions to his men, who fanned out and dismounted. Chambers scowled down at them, but with an eye on Lord Mayer's departing back, he led them inside.

Mayer rode back down the drive, and Birler followed, glancing back at the man on the roof.

"He won't do anything," Mayer said.

"How do you know?" Birler asked.

"They don't move unless Gilbert tells them to. None of them have any initiative, not like you. No, if Gilbert were here, it would be a different story. He is impulsive, hot-headed. Doesn't always think things through."

"You knew he wasn't here?"

Mayer smiled. "Of course. You don't leave a viper in its nest unwatched, now, do you?" They rode back towards Jaren, and Mayer stopped in the middle of the road. "Archie, could you get one of your lads to find out who has been scaring these people? They are cowering in their houses, and it is not because of me."

"Yes, my lord."

"This shouldn't have happened right under our noses."

"Casper can't be everywhere, my lord," Archie replied.

"Casper? What about Devis?"

Archie didn't reply. Mayer glared at his steward and rode on. He unexpectedly turned down a narrow track that sunk below the fields. "You'll like this, Birler," was all he said as he led the way. He gestured to a small copse of trees surrounding a stone slab. "The Lady's Copse," he said grandly.

Birler smiled with pleasure. "It is, indeed," he murmured

and slid down from Kafinee. He knelt before the stone table and bent his head as the air shimmered around him, and Mayer smiled in acknowledgement.

"I hear you, my Lady," Mayer breathed.

As Mayer patiently waited for Birler, his men watched in surprise at their lord waiting on someone else. They discreetly observed Birler.

"Apologies, my lord, for keeping you waiting." Birler's voice was soft, and his eyes were luminous as he mounted Kafinee.

"Not at all," Mayer said with a grin. "She sent you. We should give our thanks." He turned his horse and retraced their steps to the harbour road, and this time, they returned to Mayer's Landing.

"Thank you for the company, Birler; you can return to your duties now. I believe you are supposed to be our courier this month?"

Birler smiled. "Yes, sir."

"Good, good. See you at dinner, then." Mayer dismounted and entered his house, calling for Devis.

Ranger Lorill arrived a few days later, a solid and reassuring ranger and one Birler thought of as a friend. He gauged the watch within a chime, and that evening, they caught up on academy gossip and everyone's postings.

"Serill is at the palace in Birtoli. I'll bet that's a cushy job." Lorill grinned at Birler.

"I've never been there. Hopefully, I will get to visit one day," Birler said.

Lorill flicked him a glance. "You do know the rumour mill has it that it's your fault Devis is out of a job? Of course, Casper is pleased to be promoted, so you've got lots of support there."

"I didn't realise I needed support," Birler said.

Lorill scowled. "You shouldn't, but there are some of

Devis's cronies causing ill will, so be warned. I scotch it whenever I hear it, but just so you know."

Birler sighed. "It's never simple, is it? I was just protecting the people, as the Lady wills. It only happened because others weren't doing their jobs."

"I know. That's why I scotch it. They are idiots."

The next day and all the following month, Birler criss-crossed the watch, happy to be out in the countryside with Kafinee, delivering and collecting mail, messages, and instructions. He discovered many shortcuts and cross-country trails, met most of Mayer's people, and knew many by name, and even some of Lord Benoir's people in the adjoining Marchwood Watch. He brushed by the Terolian border but never crossed it. The sea still drew him, and he often spent a few minutes in the harbour, staring out into the open expanse, listening to the rush of water over the pebbles. He found the soft clacking soothing.

The investiture for the new watches was set for Novu 14th, Lady's Day. Birler was accompanying Lord Mayer and his wife to Vespers for the investiture. He was looking forward to seeing Tagerill and his family, and when he returned from Warren's confirmation, he was due to take his turn in Terolia, and Ranger Frener would rotate back into East Watch.

Birler had to grin when he heard the Mayers had been invited to stay the night at Greens. Warren was taking no chances; he was determined that Birler would be there.

As a result, they left East Mayer early so they would only have to rest one night before reaching Greens. He half-expected Tagerill to be waiting for them on the East Road, and he wasn't surprised when he was.

"How long have you been waiting?" he asked as Tagerill pulled Inky in next to him behind the carriage after introducing himself to Lord Mayer. The guards rearranged themselves, and they set off again.

"About a chime."

"You should have come up to the house. Lord Mayer would have fed you. After all, you're giving us a bed tomorrow night."

Tagerill's dimples flashed as he laughed. "By the Lady, it's good to see you, Birler. How's it been?"

"Great. I'm enjoying it. How about you? What's it like at the Towers?"

"Boring! Fortunately, I spend half my time at Stoneford and the other half patrolling the passes. I was even in some action last week. We caught some smugglers. Could have done with your bow behind us."

"You mean you haven't been practising?"

"Me? Practice? You're having a laugh."

At that, Birler did laugh, glad to have his friend back by his side. "I'm with Lorill, and I'll meet Frener next week when I go into Terolia for a month. Who else is with you?"

Tagerill rolled his eyes. "Some old bloke called Darll, a really weird guy called Ellaer and a woman called Livell. They're all a lot older, but they know their stuff. At least Parsill should be at the confirmation; it will be good to see him. His father is nice. Well liked."

Birler grinned at his easy dismissal of his fellow rangers.

With Tagerill's company, the miles passed by quickly. They stopped overnight at the inn at Woodrow and then pushed on the next day to arrive at Greens just as dusk was falling. The excitement built in his chest as they rode up the drive. He was home. He could feel it. Greens reached out and embraced him as they reached the large mansion.

Tagerill's expression filled with anticipation as he saw his parents standing on the steps to greet them. They formally greeted Lord and Lady Mayer and welcomed them to their home, and Lady Mayer laughed as Melis swooped in on Tagerill and then Birler, closely followed by Warren.

"It's so good to have you home. You frightened us to death when your horses turned up without you."

Mayer turned on the steps. "What's this?"

Melis glared at the boys. "Didn't Birler tell you? They were ambushed on the way to you."

"No, he didn't tell me," Mayer said slowly, inspecting his ranger. "It seems Ranger Birler has not told me a lot of things. Including his relationship with Greens."

Birler stiffened beneath Warren's arm, and Warren squeezed his shoulder. "Never mind. He can tell you later. Let's all go in. You must want to freshen up and have some dinner. How's Kafinee doing, Birler?"

"She's great, not even showing yet."

"Good. Keep an eye on her. I have a stallion that needs the exercise when you have to rest her. Kafinee will be cosseted here."

Birler grinned. "She gets cosseted wherever she goes."

"Your room's ready, Birler. Go on up with Tagerill." Melis patted him on the cheek and turned to Lady Mayer. "When will they stop growing? They get taller every time they come home," she said with a smile. "Lord Mayer, your room is this way." Melis led them down the corridor.

"Call me Henry, please," Mayer said with a grin, "and my wife is Gemma. It's very kind of you to invite us to stay, though now I have an inkling I know why."

Melis laughed, her voice fading as she led him away. "I'm Melis, and you know Warren already. We'll introduce you to our eldest son, Penner, at dinner."

Birler dropped his bags in his room, took off his jacket, and raced to the bathing room. He hurriedly changed, hoping to have some time with Warren before the Mayers joined them. He peered into the drawing room and found Penner already waiting. "Penner, how are you? Has your father been down yet?"

"Our father is down in the cellar discussing wine with Lord Mayer. Why?"

"I hoped to have a few minutes to speak to him before Lord Mayer got hold of him."

"What have you been doing that you need to explain?" Penner asked with a grin.

Birler made a face. "Crossing swords with Mayer's uncle!" he said, keeping his voice low.

"What? Pa told you to avoid him."

"I didn't know it was him behind it at the time."

Penner grinned. "Might have known you couldn't keep out of trouble for five minutes."

Warren's voice came from behind him: "Henry was just telling me."

Birler spun in surprise. "Pa, I didn't mean to." He tensed as he realised he had called Warren 'Pa', but it had seemed so natural, just as natural as Greens feeling like home, and by the pleased expression on Warren's face, he didn't mind, either.

Warren's smile lit up his face. "Son, it sounds like you did what the Lady asked of you, and you can't do more than that." He hugged Birler and grinned across at Penner.

"But when Dominant Clary finds out, that's another thing he'll chalk up against me."

"I'm afraid when it comes to Clary, no matter what you do, it won't make any difference. I'm proud of you, son. You didn't kill them; you took time to take the right action. Your mother would have been upset if you were hurt."

Lord Mayer's voice came from the doorway. "And it was my action, not yours, that closed him down."

Birler's stomach clenched. "He won't see it that way."

"Don't borrow trouble, Birler. He'll have enough to manage soon enough." Warren looked up as Melis arrived with Tagerill. "Excellent. Shall we go through? Henry, have you met Penner, my eldest son? And you already know Tagerill and Birler."

Dinner was a great success. Tagerill was excited to be home, and Birler was keen to talk about East Mayer, how different it was to Greens and how friendly the people were. Mayer basked in Birler's compliments about his watch, and Warren glowed over the fact Birler had called him Pa. Melis sat back and watched the table with a small smile hovering over her mouth. When Birler called Warren Pa again as he and Tagerill were vying for his attention, her smile matched Warren's.

"I'm afraid dinner can get a bit rowdy with so many of our boys home at once," Melis apologised to the Mayers.

"Not at all. It brings back memories of me and my brothers," Henry replied with a grin.

"You have a large family?"

"Three of us, though they are off in the guards. East Mayer takes all my time now."

"Birler seems to have taken well to your watch."

"Indeed. The way he talks about it, he knows more about it than I do!"

Birler looked across the table. "Did you know East Mayer has a harbour? I didn't realise it had a coastline."

"Only a small one." Lord Mayer grinned.

"Still," Birler said fairly. "It's better than none. Marchwood takes up the the rest of the coast."

"And in a month's time, you will know all of Terolia," Lord Mayer teased.

Birler grinned, his eyes bright. "Only the borders, sir."

"You are being stationed in Terolia?" Warren asked.

"Yes, in Berbera. I'm relieving Frener."

Warren nodded. "We still expect you home when you get a chance."

"I'm off at the end of Decu. See if you can get the same time. We can travel back together," Tagerill said.

"I should be back from Terolia by then. Might fit well," Birler agreed.

"You'll be due some time after a solid month in Terolia," Lord Mayer agreed, straight-faced, and Birler laughed.

After dinner, they moved into the parlour and Tagerill and Birler got the chess board out. Lady Mayer sat with Melis. "You're very lucky in your sons," she said a little wistfully, watching them set up the board, while joking back and forth.

"I know," Melis agreed. "We have another son and daughter in the rangers; they will meet us in Vespers. It will be the first time we've all been together in months. With them posted all over the country, it's difficult to co-ordinate them," she said with a laugh.

"All the more memorable when you do, then," Lady Mayer said.

Warren passed Mayer a glass. "Try the '89. It has a lovely aftertaste."

Mayer took the glass. "I'm being spoilt. My cellar is very poor compared to this."

"You should stock up on the '18 whilst you're here. Give it five or ten years, and it'll be amazing," Warren said, sitting opposite, and the conversation slipped comfortably to wine.

The next morning, they were back on the road, Warren eyed Kafinee, though as Birler said, she wasn't particularly rounded.

George reassured him. "She's fine, eating well. I would

suggest that when they return at the end of the year, we should rest her then."

Warren focussed on organising the rest of them and handed Melis and Gemma into the carriage. "Did you give the boys their clothes?"

"Yes, they are packed in their saddlebags. They'll be fine," Melis replied, making herself comfortable.

Warren corralled everyone into order, and the cavalcade finally left for Vespers. "It's worse than moving an army," he muttered to Mayer as they rode down the road in front of the carriage.

Mayer laughed as his men formed up around the carriage with Warren's. "You know, once all this confirmation is done, we should schedule a quarterly meeting. We ought to get together regularly to co-ordinate the watches."

"Good idea," Warren agreed. "You should suggest it. We can rotate the host so the burden doesn't fall on one watch all the time."

41

MELIS

LADY'S PALACE, VESPERS. NOVU 1122

Upon arriving in Vespers, the Mayers said farewell and continued up to the palace after the Descelles arrived at their townhouse. Once the bustle of arrival died down, Melis collapsed into a chair in the sunny parlour and looked at Warren. "Did Birler call you 'Pa' yesterday?"

"That, he did, twice," Warren replied with a grin.

"Should we say anything?"

"No, let him approach us in his own time; he'll tell us when he's ready. We keep rushing him, and he is not to be rushed."

"He was so pleased to be home. I think he's missed Greens."

Warren laughed. "We should have left it to Greens. She'll snare him in the end."

"She will." Melis tilted her head and asked, "Not worried East Mayer will tempt him away?"

"Never. I think our Birler is thorough in all he does. Wherever he goes, he will find out all that he can. But he'll always come home to Greens."

"Good."

They were interrupted as Tagerill and Birler clattered into the room. Tagerill was holding up a frilly shirt with a horrified expression on his face. "Ma, you don't expect us to wear this, do you?"

Melis laughed. "It is a formal state occasion; of course you will wear it. Everyone else will be dressed the same."

"But it has frills! It's for girls."

"Rubbish. It's a dress shirt," Warren said. "They won't let you in the palace unless you are properly dressed."

"Yuk! Let's hope state occasions are few and far between," Tagerill muttered to Birler as he turned away. His mother's laughter followed them up the stairs.

"It's only for one night," Birler consoled him.

"That's one night too many."

Birler endured Melis's inspection as they prepared to leave for the palace later that evening. He had never worn such fine clothes before, and even though Tagerill complained continuously, he thought they both looked very handsome in black trousers and white shirts overlain with green fitted jackets. Birler laughed at Tagerill's scowl as his fingers strayed to stroke the soft ruffles at his wrists.

"Cheer up," Melis advised him. "You'll chase away all the pretty girls with that face."

Tagerill brightened at the thought and climbed up into the carriage with his parents. Birler sat back, staring at the Descelles in all their finery, from Melis, elegantly gowned in green silk, to Penner in his elaborately frilled shirt. He wondered how he had managed to end up here; it was a far cry from his life two years ago.

Torches lit the road up to the palace, attended by men in

opulent white and gold livery. Warren and Melis led the way, with Penner behind them. Birler took a deep breath and followed Tagerill out of the carriage and up the steps. The carriage pulled away behind them to make way for the next one.

The palace was resplendent in swathes of white and gold banners and the golden glow of many torches. They were directed inside and joined a mass of people in the large reception area. They followed Warren, who threaded his way through the crowd, acknowledging greetings left and right. Birler stuck close to Tagerill, gazing all around him.

"Stay with your mother," Warren said as he veered off to the side, and Birler saw him speaking with Commander Asher.

Melis stopped next to their seats to one side of the main dais, which had six elaborate chairs upholstered in red velvet. In front of them was a kneeling pad on the floor in the centre. Penner, she instructed to sit at the far end, leaving two empty seats, then Tagerill, Birler, and herself. Birler sat as directed and watched the room with enormous eyes. Elegant, silk-clad women drifted past on the arms of even more elaborately bedecked men. It seemed everyone was trying to outdo each other.

Birler leant towards Melis. "Who are they trying to impress?" he asked, staring around the room.

"Themselves, I think," she murmured back. "That lady in the enormous pink turban is the wife of the ambassador from Terolia."

Birler blinked at the elegantly-robed woman. "They have ambassadors?"

"Don't be blinkered by popular gossip; all countries have representatives," Melis whispered. Her voice grew cooler. "And that lady in blue is the wife of Dominant Clary," she said as the woman circulated through the throng to find her seat.

Birler watched the woman, studying her face. She looked too young to be Tyrler's mother. He averted his gaze as Tyrler appeared beside her, along with two other young men. Tyrler's brothers, Birler assumed. He made a note of where they were seated and then continued exploring the room.

He nodded as he caught Lord Mayer's eye and smiled as the man came towards them. Lord Mayer's way was blocked by a large man who poked his shoulder. Birler rose but looked down as Melis caught his arm. "It is not your job to protect anyone today except me," she said in warning. "Lord Mayer can look after himself."

Birler sat and squirmed in his chair. "It doesn't feel right, leaving him to manage on his own."

"He managed all these years before you went to East Mayer. He is quite capable, you know. You are not responsible for everyone."

Birler flushed. "I know. I can't help it."

Melis patted his arm. "Don't worry. You'll get used to it. You have to learn to temper your response and be more discreet. You don't want everyone in the room to know what you intend to do."

Birler looked at her in surprise.

"I haven't been joined all these years to a master strategist without learning some of it, you know." She looked around the room. "Ah, discretion is the watchword, remember," she said as she rose, moving slightly in front of Birler.

"Is he such a coward he has to hide in your skirts?" Dominant Clary sneered as he towered over Melis.

"Not at all," Birler said as he rose. "I appreciate you coming to apologise personally."

Clary's face turned puce. "You will pay for attacking my son and his friends. It is unacceptable behaviour, even from one as low-born as yourself. But then I suppose I shouldn't have expected any better."

Birler gave him a distant smile. "Such low expectations seem to run in your family. I doubt anyone could achieve it as well as you do."

Clary spluttered. "You can dress him in all the finery you want, but you can't take the gutter out of a rat." He leaned toward Birler, his face tight with anger. "Filth like you have no right to be here, and I will see that you are removed."

Melis grasped Birler's arm as she raised her chin, her eyes cold. Tagerill and Penner flanked them. "You demean yourself, sir, with your crudeness, which is uncalled for and insulting to my family."

"Your family is craven if you shelter the likes of him. You'll be the laughingstock of Vespers."

"I think you overestimate your influence," Warren said from behind him with ice in his voice, "and underestimate the distaste people have for your crass behaviour. I believe you should look to your own reputation before you consider mine and find a more gentleman-like behaviour before *you* are removed."

Clary stiffened, his glare scorching Birler before he turned to face Warren. He hesitated as he saw Commander Asher beside him, watching him with a raised eyebrow.

"Is this how you treat guests of the Lady?"Asher asked, a fleeting expression of distaste passing over his face. "I was sure the report was mistaken; after all, you have your position to consider."

"My position is quite secure, I can assure you. You should look to yours," Clary snapped as he barged through them.

"The Lady needs to do something about him. He is getting more reckless and intolerant," Warren murmured to Asher.

"Sometimes, it's best to keep your enemies close. At least

you can see what they are up to," Asher replied, watching Clary force his way through the milling people. He turned back to Birler, who was frozen in Melis's grip. "Birler, come walk with me. I have some people I want to introduce you to." Asher smiled at Melis and eased Birler away. "I'll bring him back before the ceremony," he promised, aware of the tension in all the Descelles. "Remember, this is a party." He grinned at them as he dragged Birler away.

Birler gave Warren an anguished glance and went with the commander. "I'm sorry, sir. I didn't mean to cause a scene."

"You didn't. I think you'll find that Clary chose the wrong day to show off. Ah, yes." He stopped by the dais, where a young man in a severe military-style uniform with lots of gold braid stood speaking to Captain Guerlaire. "Your Grace, this is the ranger I wanted to introduce you to, Ranger Birler of Greens. Birler, this is His Highness Crown Prince Olwyn of Elothia and his wife, Princess Aisha."

Birler bowed deeply. "Your Royal Highness, Princess."

Olwyn smiled. "Ranger Birler, we've heard much about you."

Birler straightened, and Prince Olwyn laughed as he failed to hide his surprise.

"I'm just a ranger, Your Highness," Birler said.

Prince Olwyn shook his head. "I see you need to learn to receive a compliment. If you are ever stationed with us, we'll have to work on it. We look forward to it."

"As do I, Your Highness," Birler murmured in reply, smiling tentatively at the young woman beside him. She gave him a reassuring grin, and Asher dragged him away.

"No flirting with royalty," Asher muttered.

"I wasn't," Birler protested, flushing, and Asher laughed.

"That's better. Relax a bit, Birler. Don't give Clary the satisfaction of knowing he upset you."

"It was more that he upset Lady Melis. I didn't want him to spoil her day."

"As long as you are happy, she'll be happy. It's the sight of you fretting that would concern her."

"I shouldn't be here. I just bring them trouble."

"Warren can handle it. He will shortly be the acknowledged Guardian of all of Greens Watch; he's quite capable, you know."

"But he wouldn't have to handle it if I wasn't here."

"You need to learn the politics of the situation. Clary wants what Warren has, so he'll chip away at every opportunity. Warren taking you under his wing gives him another target, but Clary would have found something else if not for you. It is Warren's choice. Don't let fear of Clary control Warren's or your actions. Watch how Warren handles Clary and learn. You couldn't learn from anyone better."

He pulled Birler into an alcove. "Lady Cynthia, you wanted to meet one of my rangers. This is Birler. He graduated this year. Birler, Lady Cynthia is one of the academy's sponsors. Her late husband was my predecessor."

Asher bowed and abandoned Birler, leaving him to make the best of the situation. Birler recovered and bowed, taking the opportunity to observe her. "My lady," he said as he straightened. She was elderly, her hair white and rigidly coiffured, her face lined and creased, but her blue eyes were sharp as she peered at him over her beaky nose. "You don't look old enough to be a ranger, boy. How old are you?"

"Eighteen, ma'am."

"And where are you from?"

"Vespers, though I'm currently assigned to East Mayer."

"And what do you think of the Lady's new watch system?"

"I think she is very wise and the people will love her for it."

"Enough to stop these dissenters?"

Birler shrugged. "The watches will drive a sense of community; neighbours will look out for each other. People only want to live their lives in peace and raise their families. The Guardians will bring the Lady closer to them."

Lady Cynthia nodded. "Idealistic, I like it, and you would protect the Guardians to achieve this?"

"Yes, my lady."

"What do you think of East Mayer? It's on the borders, isn't it?"

"Yes, I like it very much. The people are really friendly. I am due to go over into Terolia when I return."

A soft chime interrupted them, and he raised his head. Lady Cynthia's eyes narrowed as she watched him. "You'll do. Tell Melis I approve. You'd better get back to your family."

Birler rose and bent over her to kiss her hand. "It was a pleasure meeting you, my lady."

Lady Cynthia laughed. "A sweet-talker. Get you gone." She was still chuckling as he left. Birler returned to the Descelles, slightly mystified, and missed the malicious glares directed at him by the Clarys as he passed by.

Versill and Marian greeted him as he arrived back at their seats, and Melis fussed over him as he sat beside her. "Are you alright?"

"Oh, yes, the commander introduced me to Crown Prince Olwyn and Lady Cynthia."

Tagerill snorted beside him. "You met Lady Cynthia, and you came out alive? She's worse than the Clarys."

"I thought she was really sweet." Birler frowned at him.

Melis gave a puff of laughter. "You'll have to instruct Tagerill on how to manage his grandmother. I'm surprised Asher introduced you."

Birler grimaced. "Commander Asher said she has an

interest in the rangers. She said to tell you she approved, not sure what of, but the chime interrupted us, and she sent me back here."

"Chime?"

"Yes, to start the ceremony."

Melis exchanged glances with Warren and patted Birler's arm. "About time. They won't get many more people in here."

Birler watched the stage as the room quietened and Guerlaire led Lady Leyandrii onto the dais. She wore a shimmering green gown that writhed and danced around her slender body as if it were alive. Lady Marguerite, dressed in soft grey, took a seat to the side of the dais beside Crown Prince Olwyn. A tall, stern-faced man stood behind her. Melis named him as Taurill, Marguerite's escort. Marguerite bounced in her chair as if unable to remain still, her auburn hair crackling around her glowing face. Taurill leaned forward and murmured in her ear, and she glanced up at his face and grinned unabashedly.

Leyandrii glared at her before sweeping her gaze around the room, and then she raised her hand, and the room quietened. "Thank you all for joining us on this day of celebration. Vespiri comes into its own today as we confirm those who will protect and lead our people into the future. Those who will bring our Administration's vision to fruition. You are all here to witness those prepared to take that responsibility and ensure that our future is secure, just as others will do the same in Elothia, Birtoli, and Terolia." There was a stir of surprise through the room.

"It is my honour to invest in these lords of Vespiri the future of our land and its people, to hold and protect so that we may flourish and prosper. Lord Warren Descelles, please stand forward."

Warren stood and strode up to the dais. He knelt before the Lady and stared up into her face.

"Warren, the Guardians created Remargaren in the hopes of building a peaceful and prosperous world. Do you accept responsibility for the land known as Greens, which extends from the Guardians Mountains to the River Vesp and is now known as Greens Watch?"

"I do."

"Warren, do you swear to honour Greens Watch, to protect and nurture it's people, to guard their right to live within your watch?"

"I so swear." Warren's voice was firm.

"In sight of the Land, do you swear to nurture and propagate the natural resources given to your care?"

"I so swear."

"Before me, and at the behest of my Administration, do you swear to uphold the rules of the land and to join in the protection of Remargaren should it be needed?"

"I so swear."

"As Guardian, do you swear to honour and protect the rules of Remargaren?"

"Guardians protect and, in turn, are protected. Keep the line. All honour to the Lady," Warren replied. His voice rang out across the room, and the audience rippled.

"And so, in the presence of your peers and with the blessing of the Guardians who created our world, I declare that Warren, son of William and Elsa, be known as Lord Warren of Greens Watch, his to keep and honour for so long as he shall live, to pass through his descendants in perpetuity. Rise, Lord Warren, and accept my blessing."

Warren rose, and Leyandrii kissed him on either cheek. *"Your oath binds us, Warren. Lady and Land, we are entwined, and you will guard us well."*

Warren stiffened as a palpable burden descended on his

shoulders, bracing as it settled into place, and then he smiled. Leyandrii smiled back at him, her face alight with a luminous glow, which slowly extended to embrace Warren and coalesced around his right hand, leaving a metallic golden gleam on his fourth finger. He turned towards the audience and said, "I, Warren of Greens Watch, greet you in the name of the Lady and am honoured to stand Guardian to Greens Watch, Vespiri, and Remargaren."

"Lord Warren of Greens Watch. We see you," the audience chanted their response.

Warren smiled at his family, his blue eyes alight as he sat in the chair, now shimmering in a deep green cloth. Melis watched him with pride, her eyes brimming with tears. Birler offered her his hankie, and she took it with a small laugh. "Thank you, Birler," she said, her voice thick with emotion.

Leyandrii's voice rang out. "Lord Ricard Landeros, please stand forward."

A slim man, neat and trim, with dark hair swept off his alert face and tied in a queue at his nape, stood forward. He gracefully knelt before the Lady, his grey eyes bright.

"Ricard, the Guardians created Remargaren in the hopes of building a peaceful and prosperous world. Do you accept responsibility for the land known as Deepwater which extends from the River Vesp in the west to the Stoneford Ridge in the East and is now known as Deepwater Watch?"

"I do," Lord Ricard replied.

And so it continued; Lord Daven Ferrantes accepted Stoneford Watch, Lord Henry Mayer accepted East Watch, and Lord Philip Benoir accepted Marchwood. There was a stir as one chair remained unclaimed.

Birler saw Clary watching with a hopeful expression on his face. He was expecting to be tapped for whatever was left.

"Oren Asher, please step forward."

Birler's eyes widened as his commander stepped forward and knelt before the Lady.

"Oren, do you accept responsibility for the land known as Vespers, which extends from the coast on the West to the Guardians Mountains in the East?"

"This is absurd! The administrators rule Vespers and Vespiri." Clary was on his feet, his colour heightened. "You cannot just parcel the land out to whomever you please."

Leyandrii paused and spread her hands. "Dominant Clary, if you listened with your heart as well as your ears, you would realise that Vespiri is not, nor will it ever be, for sale. Guardians hold the lands in trust for the people, as you hold the power of the Administration in trust. I hope you are using that power for the good of our people, Administrator?"

"The Administration is not in question here," Clary blustered.

"Oh? Are you sure? If you don't want your actions questioned, I suggest you be seated." She stared at him until he sat.

Smiling at Asher, Leyandrii continued with the ceremony, and once he had completed the catechism, Leyandrii raised her arms and clapped her hands above her head. "It is done. Lady, Land, and Guardian entwined, may it be done well," she intoned, and the dais was engulfed in a brilliant golden light which exploded into a shower of sparkles that sprinkled the witnesses. "Let us celebrate!" Leyandrii held her hand out to Lord Asher and led the way into the ballroom.

Melis and their children clustered around Warren, exclaiming over the ceremony and admiring his ring. Warren swept them into the ballroom ahead of him and joined the other lords and their families in celebration.

42

BIRLER

LADY'S PALACE, VESPERS

Warren kept his children firmly in check, ensuring all remained in his orbit and away from the Clarys. Birler watched in awe as Warren swept Lady Leyandrii onto the dance floor and away from the watching Guerlaire. When Lady Melis tapped his arm, Guerlaire was quick to smile and lead her onto the dance floor.

The room ebbed and flowed around him, and Birler watched with interest who socialised with whom. He was concerned to see two distinct camps forming: the administrators observing the new Lords of the Watches with disdain, though hesitant to blatantly shun them. He was surprised they were not trying to ingratiate themselves.

Lord Asher paused beside Birler. "Ranger, I expect a report of your observations first thing in the morning."

"Yes, sir," Birler responded automatically before blushing. "Uh, congratulations, my lord."

Asher's eyes twinkled as he smiled at him. "Don't think that changes anything. I am still your commanding officer. First thing, don't forget."

"First thing, sir."

Asher moved on and was replaced by Tagerill frowning after him. "What does he think you observed that the rest of us haven't?" he muttered.

Birler chuckled. "The only thing *you* observed was that pretty young lady seated with your grandmother."

"Do you think you could ask her to dance? Then you can bring her over here."

"Why don't you?"

"M'grandmother likes you."

Birler looked at him. "She's your grandmother. What was that you were saying about strings? She's tied to you, isn't she?"

Tagerill choked. "She's from my mother's side, not part of Greens."

"Excuses," Birler grinned, though he did make his way around the room and was shortly bending over Lady Cynthia's hand. "My lady. How did you enjoy the ceremony?"

Lady Cynthia cast him a sharp glance. "Very well. Sit and tell me your thoughts. Cherry, move up, my dear. Cherry is my great-niece on my son's side, visiting from Stoneford. Cherry, this is Ranger Birler."

Birler smiled at her. "Pleased to meet you."

Cherry blushed, and the elderly lady began questioning Birler. His respect for her grew as she teased out all the nuances that he hadn't realised he'd noticed. Lady Cynthia nodded, satisfied. "Just as I thought. Off you go. I'm sure Cherry would like to dance if you ask her."

Birler rose, offering his hand, and Cherry lost herself in a confusion of half-sentences that Birler took for acceptance as she rose and took his hand. He spun her onto the floor and set to reassure her that he meant no harm.

"You are from Stoneford?" He said, finally trying to get her to respond.

"Yes." Her voice was soft.

"My friend Tagerill is posted to Stoneford. Maybe you've met him? He's a ranger like me."

"I-I don't know."

"He's sitting over there, the man with the red hair. Would you like me to introduce you?"

Cherry flushed. "Oh, I wouldn't like to impose."

"Not at all," Birler said as he steered her over to the other side of the room. "Tagerill, may I present Cherry of Stoneford. I thought you might have some common ground to discuss." He grinned as he handed her over.

Cherry's blush deepened. "Thank you, Birler, for the dance."

"It was my pleasure," Birler replied as Tagerill spun her off, hoping he would have more luck breaking through her shyness.

Birler turned and was confronted by the young woman he knew was Lady Clary. Her face was cold and severe, her eyes glittering shards of blue ice. "Dance with me," she said.

"My lady, I don't think your husband would want me to dance with you."

"I'm not interested in what you think. I'm telling you to dance with me."

"Of course, my lady. It would be my pleasure." Birler bowed and led her onto the floor.

Lady Clary inspected him. "You're not what I expected. You seem polite, well mannered. You dance well. What did you do to alienate my husband so well?"

"I don't know, my lady."

"He won't stop until you're dead, especially as you hurt his son. He doesn't like to be embarrassed."

"Even though his son attacked me?"

"With Clary, it is all about face, and you seem to be able to make his mask slip."

"You don't agree with his methods?"

"It has nothing to do with me. I am only his wife."

"Then why are you warning me?"

Her eyes glittered with anger. "To make a point, and because I like you." She patted his cheek. "Take care, Ranger. It would be shame for that pretty face to get spoilt." She left him on the edge of the dance floor and made her way back to her table. Birler watched her go and met Clary's eyes across the room. His face was livid, and he took an unconscious step towards Birler.

Lady Marguerite tucked her hand in Birler's arm and dragged him onto the dance floor. "You do like to live dangerously, don't you?" she said, looking up into his face.

"My lady?" Birler glanced round the room frantically.

"Relax, Birler. You dance very well. I wanted a turn. Dominant Clary won't dream of interrupting us if he knows what's good for him."

Birler's arms convulsed around the lithe young woman, so full of vitality and simmering power. He could feel it swirling around them. "What are you doing, my lady?"

Marguerite chuckled. "You are wasted as a ranger, Birler. I am trying to lower your anxiety levels, though you keep resisting." She smiled up at him, her eyes vivid pools of aquamarine. "You won't be able to resist me forever, you know."

"I wouldn't dream of it, my lady."

Marguerite pouted. "If Leyandrii hadn't found you first, I might stake my claim."

"But I have, so you can't," Leyandrii's voice intruded, and Marguerite burst out laughing.

Birler stumbled, and Marguerite held him up. *"Not fair, Leyandrii. Go away."*

The Lady chuckled in the depths of his mind, and Birler was relieved when Taurill came to claim Marguerite. He took a deep breath and retreated to the Descelles' table.

Warren was waiting for him. "What did we say about avoiding the Clarys?" he asked, raising his eyebrow.

"I didn't have a choice. She accosted me."

"What did she want?"

"I think she was using me to get back at Clary because she was angry about something."

"Well, she succeeded. What did she say?"

Birler took a gulp of wine, unable to stop his hand from trembling. "She warned me that Clary won't stop until I'm dead; it seems I manage to get under his skin."

Warren's face tightened. "And Lady Marguerite?"

"She accosted me, too. Honest, I wouldn't dream of asking her to dance."

Warren's lip twitched. "You seem to be a magnet for beautiful women. I am sure Tagerill will be asking for tips."

Birler's face heated, and he looked down at the table. "I think Lady Marguerite was protecting me against Clary. I saw his face; he was furious. But what was I supposed to do? Embarrass Lady Clary by refusing to dance with her? Wouldn't that have been a worse slight?"

"Possibly, though Clary won't see it that way."

"Whatever I did would have been wrong," Birler said, his shoulders drooping.

"In this situation, yes, but I think you took the best route. Causing a scene would have been worse, though, of course, that doesn't mean Clary won't achieve one before the night is out."

Birler closed his eyes. "Don't." He shuddered at the idea.

Warren clapped his shoulder. "Cheer up. Here comes Marian. She must want a dance." Warren grinned as his daughter hauled Birler off, a martial light in her eye. The family had closed in around Birler. Clary would find it difficult to find a way through.

Birler was aware that Warren kept a discreet eye on him all evening. The fact that Clary's inexplicable hatred of him had tarnished Warren's evening galled him. Determined not to cause Warren any more grief, Birler concentrated on dancing his way through an impressive list of partners, and if not dancing, he engaged in conversation with an equally impressive list of dignitaries. Birler enjoyed the give and take, the delicate balance of asking the right person the right question and leaving them thinking they had found out something he didn't want to share. He moved from one possibly sticky situation to the next with surprising ease, and the evening passed in a glow of pleasure and delight.

It was towards the end of the evening that Clary made his move. Warren was occupied by Dominant Selby and his wife. Melis and Penner had been drawn into a conversation with her mother, Lady Cynthia, and Birler was seated alone at their table, watching the room. Marian was dancing, and Tagerill had coaxed Cherry back onto the floor. Birler could see she was smitten. Versill was nowhere to be seen, but he must have been around somewhere.

Birler leaned back in his chair, idly exhausted. His feet ached; the night seemed to go on forever. He had the beginnings of a headache, the result of managing all the manoeuvrings of various dignitaries trying to find a way in to Lord Warren. He had been very careful not to promise anything, though there were a couple of feelers he thought Warren would be interested in.

He stiffened as a wave of hatred rolled over him, so strong it was like a physical presence entrapping him in its cloying reach. Looking up, he met the stormy eyes of Lord Clary across the table. Clary didn't speak, but his frown deepened, and a wave of despair engulfed Birler. He gripped the table to keep himself from grabbing the nearest knife and slitting his own throat.

Birler's eyes locked onto Clary's. After the initial shock of the mental intrusion passed, Birler realised that Clary was somehow trying to control his mind, and he pushed the suggestion back at Clary in disgust. Clary flinched, hissing out his breath, and a suffocating cloak of dread descended around Birler, holding him in place. Birler struggled to control the panic that rose within him, though his body responded to the threat. He launched to his feet, his face a mask of indifference as his brain calculated his response. He reached for the glass on the table. A soft hand stayed his response, and he stilled the beginning of his move.

"My dear Lord Clary, I fear you have miscalculated." Leyandrii's voice was low. "You stand a dead man before me. Is that your intent?"

Clary staggered as he released the persuasion he'd attacked Birler with and focussed on Leyandrii. "What?" His voice was slurred from the effort.

"Did you not think I would notice such a blatant use of magic within my palace walls? You forgot your own protections in your eagerness to defeat those of my ranger. You are exposed, and if I had not stayed his hand, you would have been dead."

Clary stilled and looked around him. His face lost all expression as he realised he had gained an audience. His gaze returned to Birler, and he swallowed at the sight of Birler's taut face before scowling at Leyandrii. "Your interference was not necessary."

Leyandrii smiled, though it didn't reach her eyes. "I believe you will find that was your last attack on one of mine." She swirled her hand as she drew away Clary's magic, and the air shivered.

Clary swayed, and his eyes widened as he stared at her. "How dare you! You will regret—"

"How dare *you* misuse what is gifted to you," Leyandrii replied, her hair rising around her as she held Clary's angry eyes. "It is time you took your family home, Dominant Clary. You have outstayed your welcome."

Hesitating, Clary's mouth worked, though no sounds came out, and then he stalked away.

Leyandrii tucked her hand into Birler's arm. "Walk with me, Birler." She led him out of the room and into a small ante-chamber. Birler accompanied her, encased in a shell of indifference. His mind was busy calculating positions, reactions, and responses. Leyandrii sat him in a chair and stared into his luminous eyes, untold power swirling in the depths.

"You need to learn finesse, Birler. It doesn't have to be all or nothing; there are degrees of response. I know his attack was unexpected, but you did well to restrain yourself." She smoothed her fingers over his temples. "Look at me, Birler," she whispered, and his gaze focussed on her instead of his internal calculations. "Stand down, Birler."

Birler took a shuddering breath, and his eyes widened as awareness flooded through him. He stiffened, and his mouth tightened. "I would have killed him," he said, his voice flat.

"Yes, I know, but it is not necessary for you to kill him. I have dealt with Dominant Clary."

Birler rubbed his forehead; the ache behind his eyes had become a physical pain. "What did he do?"

"He attempted to use his magic to control your emotions. It's a form of *Mentiserium*, a magical persuasion that can influence a person's behaviour. He wanted you to take your own life. I see I will need to teach you how to shield against such mental attacks."

"I don't understand."

"Clary had you locked in a stasis of panic. He tried to

control you so you would end your life; only, your response was not what he expected because you were conflicted as to what you should do. His persuasion was nulled by your need to defend yourself. Given time, I think you would have broken his mental hold and attacked him. You are full of surprises, Birler. But now is not the time to discuss them. I believe your family are looking for you, and they are worried." She smiled at him. "You have chosen well. You are tired, Birler. It is time to go home and sleep."

Birler stared at Leyandrii as a soothing wave of approval flushed through him, warming his bones and melting the icy grip of panic. Exhaustion followed on its heels.

"Come, before Warren tears my palace apart." Leyandrii helped him stand, and he wobbled. The ante-chamber door flew open and Warren paused at the threshold, with Guerlaire close behind him.

"Is my son unharmed?" Warren demanded.

"He's fine. Take him home, Warren. He needs to sleep. Clary tried to use his magic to force a mental stasis lock on him, and he is exhausted."

"Clary did what?"

"He miscalculated." Leyandrii scowled. "He won't be able to do anything like that again. Take your family home, Warren. We'll talk more tomorrow."

"Of course, my Lady." Warren caught Birler as he staggered, wrapping a supportive arm around his waist.

"Go out the back way. Your carriage is waiting. Guerlaire will assist you."

Guerlaire stepped forward and took Birler's other arm. Between them they supported Birler out of the palace. Birler slept all the way back to the townhouse and didn't wake until late the following day.

· · ·

Birler opened bleary eyes and recognised his room in the Descelles townhouse, though he didn't remember returning to it. As the memory of the previous evening percolated through his sluggish brain, he shot upright, only to be brought up short as a thumping headache reverberated around his skull. He groaned and swallowed against the rising bile. He only just made it to the basin, where he threw up repeatedly.

Icy shivers incapacitated him, and he collapsed to the floor. He was mortified when Melis exclaimed above him. Strong hands helped clean him up and returned him to bed. A cool draught was forced down his throat, and he descended back into darkness.

A shaded lamp greeted his eyes the next time he awoke. His empty stomach growled, and he raised a shaky hand to his head. The clamping vice of the headache had gone, leaving a faint ache.

"How are you feeling?" Melis was seated beside him, all her finery absent.

"Washed out," he admitted.

"I'm not surprised."

"I didn't embarrass you, did I? I don't remember coming home."

"Don't worry, Birler. You did well. Warren brought you home."

"He did? I remember Clary trying to force me to do something. I would have killed him but for the Lady." Birler covered his eyes. "At the investiture, too. I couldn't stop. It was like someone else was telling me what to do."

"I know. It's alright, Birler. The Lady defused the situation. She was concerned about you. She said you would have a horrific headache, so she made you sleep, and that's why you don't remember."

"I didn't spoil the night, did I?"

"Stop fretting, Birler. You'll bring another headache on. You are liable to suffer headaches for a few days, I'm afraid. Don't make it worse. You didn't embarrass us or yourself, and you didn't spoil the night. If you carry on, I'll send Warren in to speak to you, and he's only just gone to bed himself."

Birler sighed back on his pillows. "Sorry."

"Don't be. You have nothing to be sorry for. Now, are you hungry? Cook has some soup simmering for you. I'll go and get you a bowl."

"How long have I been asleep?" he asked as Melis returned with a tray. He was sure it was no longer the day after the investiture.

"Two days. Be careful." Melis made a grab for the tray as Birler lurched forward.

"Two days? I was supposed to report to Commander Asher the day after the investiture."

"Don't worry. He knows where you are. You have to report before we return to Greens. That's the only reason Warren and I are still here. Penner and Versill went home yesterday, and Tagerill returned to his post in Stoneford. He travelled with the Ferrantes. Eat your soup."

The soup settled the queasiness in his stomach, and Birler relaxed back against his pillows, his eyelids drooping.

"Sleep, Birler. You can report in the morning." Melis smiled. "Lady Leyandrii wants to speak to you as well before you leave. I think she wants to make sure you understand what happened and how you can prevent it from happening again."

"That would be good," Birler mumbled.

Melis watched him relax into sleep and smoothed his dark hair off his forehead. She leaned forward and kissed his cheek. "Sleep, my son."

"Night, Ma," he breathed drowsily.

.   .   .

The next morning, Birler met an equally heavy-eyed Warren at the breakfast table. They sat across the table, and Birler cast a glance over the two settings. Everyone else must have eaten already. Gleaming china and elegant cutlery mocked him. What was he doing here, seated amongst all this finery? He tarnished the room just by sitting in it.

"How are you feeling?" Warren enquired, buttering some toast. He watched Birler as if he knew what was coming.

"Much better, thank you. Better than you, I think?" Birler replied with a smile.

Warren smiled ruefully. "Commander Asher and Lady Leyandrii have taken advantage of the fact that we're here for a few days." He rubbed his face. "I don't think I've ever been to so many meetings."

"How are you going to deal with the division between the Administration and the watches?"

"Noticed that, did you? What else did you notice?"

Birler twisted his lips. "Apart from everyone being awestruck by Guerlaire's bridge? A concerted effort to win over Prince Olwyn and that there is a belief that the Dominants have discovered some new way of protecting Vespiri and the Lady won't allow them to use it. There are many outlandish thoughts on what that could be, but no one really knows. They are all guessing. But they are very open to believing it will be better than the Lady's rule for some reason." Birler frowned in thought. "Why are people always looking for something other than what they already have?"

"Human nature, I guess."

"But they are assuming the Dominants only have their best interests at heart."

"As they should. That is their position in power, to manage Vespiri in the people's interest."

Birler stared at Warren. "But what if they don't? Not all Dominants are so transparent. Many want power for themselves. Why doesn't the Lady stop them?"

"It may be obvious to you, but hearsay and opinion don't make proof. So, be careful what you say. The Lady cannot remove the people's chosen officials without good reason. If she did, that would only make the situation worse, and she would be seen as the one depriving people of choice. What she can do and what she has done is to dilute their power. By giving it to the watches, the Dominants will have a more difficult time influencing people, and as for making Asher the Lord Captain, well, the Lady is very clever. She is protecting Vespiri from within."

Birler's stomach roiled. The likes of Clary and Selby wouldn't give up that easily. They had been busy ingratiating themselves all night. And as members of the Administration, people would listen to them, thinking they knew what was best. How had they become so corrupted?

"Once you've reported to Asher, we will leave for Greens, and you need to return to East Watch. They are expecting you by the day after tomorrow at the latest."

"Lord Warren, I can't stay here. I can't impose on your hospitality anymore. I only bring you trouble."

"It's too late for that. You are bound to us, Birler, as we are bound to you."

"He sees me as your weak point. He'll continue to attack you through me if we are connected."

"Then he'll find he has made a grave mistake."

Birler ground his teeth. "What about Lady Melis and the rest of your watch? What if I bring down havoc on you?"

"Then we will deal with it. Birler, stop it. I know you think you're acting with our best interests at heart, trying to protect us, but what does that say about us? We welcomed you into our home with open arms. Would we turn you away because of a little difficulty? There will always be a Clary; someone will always want more than their allotted share. Does that mean we let them dictate our choices?"

Birler flushed, looking down at the pristine cloth on the table.

"I name you my son; the Lady blesses us. Accept us, Birler. You won't regret it, and we would be honoured to welcome you into our family." Warren watched Birler struggle and smiled. He rose and walked around the table, pulling Birler up out of his chair. "Welcome to the family, Birler," he murmured as he hugged him. "Greens is ecstatic."

Birler surrendered and hugged him back, feeling his acceptance lock into place. "I won't let you down."

"I know, son."

43

SERILL

MOLINTI, BIRTOLI

S erill sat on the sandy beach and inhaled the balmy Birtolian air. Muscles that were tense from navigating Emperor Pierien's court relaxed as the warmth of the sun bathed his skin. He concentrated on rolling up the sleeves of the loose shirt he wore.

As soon as he had escaped from the palace, he had changed out of his formal uniform. Cut-off trousers and sandals were all you needed in this heat. Gentle waves lapped the beach, a few yards away from his bare toes.

If all assignments were like this, he wouldn't be complaining. Birtoli was a beautiful country. The land stretched south from Marchwood and was surrounded by water on three sides. White sands and clear blue seas tempted everyone off the land.

Skiffs and sailing boats dotted the waters, and many were pulled up onto the beach. Rafts anchored offshore served as platforms for divers. Behind him, even more boats were moored at the jetty. Bronzed sailors sluiced down decks and repaired nets. Even though everyone was busy, there was a calmness, no sense of urgency.

He lay back, tucking his arms behind his head, and stared up at the equally blue sky. Grey and white birds hovered high above, rising with the thermals, their eerie calls drifting on the air. He had never known such peace. His eyes drifted shut, and he drowsed as the gentle waves swished over the sand and a warm breeze caressed his skin.

Emperor Pierien and Empress Olini were the perfect hosts, encouraging him to explore their beautiful lands and offering a boat to take him around the coastline. It would take at least two days to sail down to the horn and the more remote islands to the south.

He had wanted to explore, so he was going to take them up on the offer. Samis was going inland to Aguinti for a few days and had asked him to accompany him, and the natural harbour in Plinii was supposed to be beautiful. Once he returned to Vespiri, he expected Guerlaire to ask him to work in the Chapterhouse. Guerlaire hadn't been happy when he'd been reassigned to Birtoli, but Lady Leyandrii had stepped in.

Her rangers were not only Vespiri's resources. They were here to help everyone, and they couldn't do that if they didn't know the other people. She had been right. The Birtolian way of life was so different from Vespiri's.

The heat in the middle of the day was extreme and would burn his sensitive, pale skin if he wasn't careful. Most people napped during the hottest part of the day, and the towns came back to life in the cooler evenings.

The other difference, of course, was the abundance of fish and other aquatic creatures he'd never heard of. They made a tasty change from meat and vegetables. And the variety of sweet fruits that filled his mouth with lush juices were definitely his favourites.

His skin tingled, and he sighed as he sat up, scattering sand around him. He needed to find some shade and maybe have a nap. He hoped Tagerill and Birler were having as much fun as he was.

Tagerill peered down the narrow pass and signalled for the guards behind him to follow. Grey rock rose high above him, with crevices stuffed with greenery and golden lichen alleviating the sheer grey cliff face.

A narrow canyon wound through the ridges, and the soft mud underfoot muffled the sound of their passing. However, if the fine drizzle misting around him got any heavier, the mud would soon become a sludge, sucking and squelching at their boots.

Tagerill had found it easy to settle in as part of the Stoneford patrols. He was one of three rangers in the watch, and they rotated, leading patrols or staying behind to help guard the keep. The other rangers were both much older than him, and they had both rolled their eyes at his enthusiasm. One good thing, though, was that they had plenty of tales to share over an ale in the evening when the nights were drawing in and the heat of the log fire tempted them inside.

Tagerill was leading a patrol that had been tracking a posse of about eight bandits for two days. The bandits had attacked a merchants' caravan, killed them all, and absconded with their goods. Lord Ferrantes, Parsill's father, had been livid and instructed them to track the bandits down and make sure they didn't attack anyone else.

Leading the other tracking parties were Venter, a short, thick-set ranger, dark haired and intense, and one of Lord Ferrante's sons, Adain, who had proved to be a highly competent tracker. Tagerill thought it likely that Adain would find the bandits first.

The third ranger, who had remained to guard the keep,

was Laer. She had proved to be a worthy opponent in the sparring ring. He had recognised her skill and learned a lot. Laer had been free with her advice, and Tagerill was not about to ignore it. She was tall with tresses of golden hair, blue eyes, and a knack for subterfuge which Tagerill fell for every time. It was very frustrating!

Tagerill preened a little that he had been assigned to lead a unit. He was finally being given some responsibility, and he wasn't going to mess it up. He had six men with him, including Lieutenant Evin, who typically led the unit. Tagerill twisted his lips. Lord Ferrantes liked to rotate his commanders and gave them all experience at leading, apparently.

A soft curse up ahead had him halting and pumping his fist. The unit was silent behind him, and pride flashed through him at how well trained they were. Everything about Lord Ferrantes and the way he ran Stoneford impressed him.

Careful not to jostle his sword, he crept forward and peered around the bend.

One of the bandits, a thin, red-headed man, had come to a halt as his load had become unbalanced and slid precariously to one side. The heavily laden mule had stuck in its hooves and refused to go any further.

Tagerill just caught the low conversation as one of the other bandits came to see what the hold up was. "We can't wait for you. You should have checked the load before we left."

"If it had been loaded right, there wouldn't be a problem," the other man replied.

"It's your problem now. Meet us at the campsite as soon as you can."

"You can't leave me here on my own!"

"Keep your voice down. Do you want to alert everyone where we are?"

"There's no one else here."

"Then what's your problem? Sort it out and follow." The bandit hurried off, and the man continued cursing under his breath as he undid the ropes and all the bundles fell into the mud.

Tagerill eased back and whispered, "One man. Take him down but don't kill him. We can use him to lead us to the rest."

Lieutenant Evin nodded and passed the word. "I'll be right behind you," he whispered, and Tagerill grimaced, but there wasn't really room to go two abreast.

Unsheathing one of his daggers, he peered around the rock. The man had his back to Tagerill and was busy stacking the bundles. Once he had his hands full, Tagerill rushed him. Something alerted the man, and he spun, but hampered as he was, his head snapped back when Tagerill punched him in the face. Tagerill followed him down into the mud to bash him again, but the man was unconscious. He'd hit his head as he'd fallen.

Fear had Tagerill searching for a pulse. He hadn't intended to kill the man. "Shit," he muttered when he realised the man was out cold.

"Send a scout on to follow the others. We need to know where the campsite is," Tagerill ordered. "Observation only. We'll reload and try to catch them up."

A couple of the men hurriedly tied the bundles onto the mule. "You're going to have to take his place," Evin said. "You're the only redhead here, and his clothes should fit you."

"One of the lads could wear a hat," Tagerill suggested, though it was a half-hearted suggestion. As soon as he'd realised the man was unconscious, he'd known he would have to take the mule. They didn't have time to try and rouse him.

Evin shook his head. "You'll give us the element of surprise. Long enough for us to surround them."

Tagerill exhaled and then unbuckled his weapons belt, stripped out of his jacket and shirt, and pulled on the dead man's clothes. They were thin, worn, and soaking wet. Tagerill grumbled under his breath and drew a line at the trousers.

He tied the scratchy scarf around his neck, trying to ignore the rancid odour, and then belted his weapons back on.

"We won't be far behind you," Evin said, handing him daggers, "but once you exit the canyon, we'll have to drop back until our scout confirms the campsite location."

"Let's hope I can track them most of the way. The mud is pretty churned up, so they must have at least six to eight mules."

"Yes, these may be the main band. The question is whether any others are going to be at this camp, so be careful, Tagerill."

"You're asking me to walk into a camp of bandits, and you want me to be careful?"

Evin grimaced. "You know what I mean."

"We should have brought an archer with us. At least he could have picked some off and reduced the numbers," Tagerill said, wishing his brother were with him. Birler would have evened the score in a moment. He huffed his breath out. Birler would have told him in no uncertain terms not to be an idiot, and he definitely wouldn't have let him enter the camp unprotected.

"Wish me luck," he said, wrapping the reins around his hands and tugging the mule down the trail. He followed the churned-up mud out of the canyon and down the hill, joining a larger track, which, fortunately, was still made of mud. If it had been stone-lined, he would have lost the trail quickly enough.

There was no traffic, probably because he was in the middle of nowhere, headed over the Elothian borders. He kept his gaze on the trail as he plodded down the road, occasionally glancing around.

Spindly trees leaned at a steep angle, trammelled by the winds that came off the mountain ridges, dark silhouettes looming up on either side of the track.

Chimes passed, and Tagerill plodded onwards. Night would descend soon; the bandits would expect to reach camp before full dark. It couldn't be much further. Tagerill's stomach fluttered at the thought. He hadn't seen a hint of Lieutenant Evin or his men; they must be further back than he hoped or much better at concealing themselves than he realised.

When the tracks veered off into the scrub, Tagerill sent up a silent prayer to the Lady to watch over him. His father would not be impressed when he found out about this escapade. He tugged the tired mule after him as he pushed through the low bushes. His trousers were soon soaked as the shrubbery held the water, and the mule swiped at some of the leaves.

A low whisper coming from within the brush made him hesitate. "There are eleven of them. Straight ahead, take a left at the river. About one hundred paces, there was a look-out. He's been dealt with; try not to raise the alarm. Camp's on the left. Slow down and give us time to surround them. Your marks are the two closest to you. Quarter-chime."

"Got it," Tagerill muttered.

The faint hint of woodsmoke on the evening air was the first sign Tagerill was nearing the camp. He continued down the hill towards the gleam of the river. Turning left, he followed the riverbank until he tripped over the lookout, who was sprawled in the grass. Cursing under his breath, he dragged the body into the shadows and tugged the mule onwards.

The mule must have sensed, or more likely smelt, its friends or food because its ear flicked and it quickened its pace. For once, the mule was leading. He hunched his shoulders and kept the mule between him and the camp.

A sharp voice came out of the shadows. "Blimey, you took yer time."

"I'm 'ere, ain't I?" Tagerill kept his voice low and gruff, his face averted.

"Tie yer mule up and get some grub. We've got an early start."

Tagerill didn't answer, just pulled the mule towards the picket line. At least six men were seated around the campfire, no doubt eating. That meant at least another four were on the perimeter. He tied the mule up, scowling at the way the animals were being treated. None of the loads had been removed, and they were left to crop the grass beneath their feet.

He hunted for the water bucket and couldn't find one.

Unable to find any reason to loiter further, he unsheathed a dagger and slid it up his sleeve before walking nearer to the fire.

"Hey, yer not Corun. How did 'e get 'ere?" A thin man rose to his feet, pointing his mug at Tagerill.

Taking a deep breath to steady his nerves, Tagerill grabbed the man closest to him. He had thrown his plate down and was twisting to his feet. Sliding his dagger into his hand, Tagerill gritted his teeth and thrust it up under the man's ribs. The bandit clawed at him even as his eyes rolled whitely and his body fell. Tagerill let him drop as one of the other bandits lunged for him.

Voices rose in confusion.

"Who is he?"

"Is he alone?"

"What do you want?"

Tagerill parried a sword swinging at him and lunged at the other man. This bandit was more aware and faster on his feet. A blade glinted in the man's hand, and his teeth gleamed in the firelight as he beckoned Tagerill forward.

Flashing a glance around the campfire, Tagerill was relieved to see Evin's men had arrived and no one was creeping up on him from behind.

The bandit attacked in his brief moment of inattention. Tagerill twisted out of reach of the blade and circled. Metal rang as blades collided, puffs of breath plumed in the chill air, and low grunts marked when they struggled to hold a wrist or release a hold.

The man was fast, darting in and out, and Tagerill's focus was on keeping that blade out of his body.

"Who sent you?" the man demanded, managing to get inside Tagerill's guard and slicing his blade across Tagerill's unprotected stomach.

Tagerill hissed his breath out, ignoring the sting as he jumped back and stumbled over a body lying on the ground behind him. He fell heavily, winding himself, and the bandit landed on top of him, kneeling on his arms, pinning him in place, his blade at Tagerill's throat.

"Who sent you?"

"Who do you think?" Tagerill wheezed, barely able to breathe.

"Selby?"

"Yeah." Darkness was beginning to creep over Tagerill's vision. He tried to twist out of the man's grip, but the blade bit into his skin, and Tagerill stilled. Cold, muddy water seeped through his clothes, chilling his skin, and he shivered.

"That bastard. Does he think to double-cross us? He'll pay extra for that."

"Wants a better cut," Tagerill said, prevaricating blithely. Lord Ferrantes would be interested to know Dominant Selby was involved in smuggling.

"I'll show *him* a cut and his fancy friends. Maybe send him your head as a reminder. Think he'd like that?" The man jerked, his blade biting deeper into Tagerill's skin, and then he toppled over, and Tagerill gasped for breath.

"You alright?" Evin asked as he crouched beside Tagerill.

"What took you so long?" Tagerill gulped in air.

"Seemed like you were having a nice chat. Didn't want to interrupt."

Tagerill stared at him in horror. "A chat?"

"Now we know Dominant Selby is involved." Evin clapped him on the shoulder. "Good work."

Tagerill groaned as he sat up and checked his throat. Blood smeared his fingers, and Evin grunted an apology.

"Might have left it too long. Sorry." Evin offered a wadded piece of cloth to press against his throat. "Doesn't look too deep. He get you anywhere else?"

Tagerill checked his stomach. Fortunately, the cut was barely a scratch, though it bled freely. Evin offered another pad.

Tagerill was soaking wet, covered in mud, and bleeding. He'd bet a month's pay that Birler wasn't having to put up with this shit.

44

BIRLER
EAST WATCH, VESPIRI

Birler arrived in East Watch late in the evening, a week after Lady's Day and the investiture. Mayer's Landing was quiet and dark, though a silent patrol rotated around the settlement. The sky was a sparkling cloth of bright stars, and the waning moon lit the rolling landscape with a soft glow. The night air was fresh, but nowhere near as icy as it had been in Vespers.

Birler reported to Captain Caspar and went to drop his bags off in his bunk. After a quick shower and a change of clothes, he ventured into the main building, looking for Archie or Lord Mayer. He found them in the dining hall, where a tall thin man dressed in black robes was organising a chair at the front. Birler grabbed a tray of food and slid in beside Lorill.

"Hey, glad you're back at last," Lorill said with a fleeting smile. "We thought you might have been assigned elsewhere."

Birler snorted. "Unlikely. Lord Mayer would have had words, I'm sure."

"You're just in time. We have entertainment tonight. A

travelling minstrel come to tell tall tales, no doubt," Lorill said.

"Where did he come from?"

"Who knows? Across the border, I expect." Lorill shrugged, unconcerned, and drained his mug.

Lord Mayer stood and clapped his hands. "We are pleased to welcome Ser'ander to our table, and he has graciously agreed to entertain us tonight. Please, everyone, show your appreciation." Lord Mayer led the applause, and Birler raised his mug in salute when Lord Mayer caught sight of him. He flashed him a smile and sat down.

Ser'ander took his place at the front. His voice was rich and deep, at odds with his thin frame. His black eyes glittered in the lamplight as he told his tale. His voice vibrated as he wove a word picture of golden sands and burning sun, red mountains and sparkling coastlines. He urged them to visit this beautiful place.

Birler glanced around the dimly lit room, picking out the faces of those he knew well. There weren't many, and even they were beginning to look unfocussed. The traveller continued speaking, his voice becoming more sonorous. Was he trying to put everyone to sleep? Birler shifted in his chair, nudging Lorill. "Don't doze off; it would be rude," he said.

Lorill jerked upright and blinked.

Frowning, Birler caught the gist of the man's story and stilled. The man was expounding on life in Terolia and how everyone should visit—not only visit but support the Ascendants who would show them the true way of life. The Ascendants would lead them to glory, and everyone in the room would benefit.

Was this an example of the *Mentiserium* that Lady Leyandrii had explained to him? Birler shored up his mental shields. They firmed immediately as he had been practising during the journey from Vespers. He never wanted to experience such a mental assault ever again. "I'm sure Terolia is lovely," Birler said, raising his voice. "But everyone has a job here already. What would you be expecting us to do in the desert?"

The traveller glared at Birler but continued speaking, his voice unchanged. Birler glanced across at Lord Mayer, who was frowning as he watched the minstrel. Rising, Birler walked around the table, stopping by Mayer's chair. "My lord? Is everything alright?"

Mayer blinked at him. "I'm not sure."

"I think you ought to stop this story, my lord. It's sending everyone to sleep. Shouldn't it be uplifting?"

Mayer looked around the room. His men were in various stages of slumping against each other.

Birler rapped the hilt of his dagger hard on the table, making everyone jump. "Unless everyone is intending on being conscripted, I suggest you all leave now."

Lord Mayer jerked to his feet and blinked around the room.

Birler stared at the thin man in the black cloak. "I think your story is finished."

"My Lord Mayer, I've only just begun." The man glared at Birler. He made a gesture with his hand, and Birler ignored him.

"And now you are finished. The practice of *Mentiserium* is banished in Vespiri, and unless you want Lord Mayer to restrain you, I suggest you leave."

The man gaped at him. "You wouldn't dare. I have done nothing wrong."

"*Mentiserium?*" Lord Mayer said from behind Birler's shoulder.

"It is a form of persuasion. They make people do things they wouldn't normally do, like desert their posts and follow this man into the desert. It's what Lord Clary tried to do to me at the palace."

A murmur grew in the audience as Birler's words reached them and they realised that was what the man had been suggesting they do.

"Lorill, Caspar, escort our guest to the cells. I think we need to understand what is going on here." Lord Mayer's voice was sharp.

"How dare you. You asked me to entertain you. I am but telling a story," the man blustered.

"Not just a story, I think," Birler said, watching the struggling man as he was led away. "Did he say where he was from, my lord?"

"No, I assumed he was a travelling minstrel. We often get them visiting; they make for good entertainment on a winter's evening."

"I think we need to know where he came from," Birler said, narrowing his eyes in thought, "and where he's been. We need to go check the border towns."

Mayer stared at him. "But what would they want people for? There has been no news of people massing anywhere."

"If they get enough of your guards to desert, you would be defenceless if someone wanted to take over your lands," Birler suggested.

Mayer blanched. "But who …?" he began and cut the words off.

"Maybe you ought to be more wary of strangers, my lord."

"You weren't affected. Why was that?" Mayer asked, staring at Birler.

Twisting his lips, Birler replied, "I experienced *Mentiserium* recently, and I recognised its effects. Lady Leyandrii taught me how to shield; I can teach you and your men, if you like."

Mayer was silent for a moment. "I see," he said, his voice soft. "Very well. I will take you up on that offer. Afterwards, you and Lorill had better do a sweep from Livia up to Ramila and check that all is well. I will look to my defences."

"Yes, my lord."

"How did we ever manage before you came, Birler?" Mayer asked with a quirk of his lips.

Lord Mayer and Lieutenant Casper soon picked up how to shield their minds, so Birler left them to teach the rest of the enclave. He and Lorill left the following morning, crossing the Terolian border at Berbera. The rolling hills soon petered out into golden sand dunes over a distance of about ten miles. Birler was amazed at the transformation. Succulent, spiky green plants replaced the wiry bushes and trees. Palm trees renowned for their oil were scattered along the dusty trail leading into the town of Berbera.

Birler thought Berbera looked more like a sprawling village, a collection of red stone buildings jumbled around a marketplace. More temporary dwellings made of palm leaves and bamboo poles skirted the edges and provided shelter to a transient population.

They found Frener behind a two-roomed dwelling which had a stable tacked on the back. He was brushing down his dust-coated horse. A fire pit was dug into the sun-baked ground, and a trellis arched over the open area, providing some shade.

Frener's face was creased with weather lines. The sun had dried out his skin and deepened it to bronze, with the lines flashing white as his expression changed. His hair was black though the tips had been bleached by the sun. He wore a dark brown robe that covered him from head to foot. He stopped brushing his horse and straightened to reveal alert brown eyes that assessed his unexpected visitors.

"Ah, the relief. I've spent months waiting for one, and then two of you arrive." His voice was gravelly and deep, his teeth very white in his tanned face.

Birler grinned. "Always the way. I'm Birler. This is Lorill. I'm your relief, though Lord Mayer sent us to do a sweep from Ramila down to Livia. There are reports of people using a magic called *Mentiserium* to persuade people away from their homes. We need to check how far they've infiltrated. Have you seen any signs of it being used?"

Frener tilted his head, inspecting him. "Not that I am aware of. How familiar are you with the Terolians?"

Birler shrugged. "Not at all. I was hoping to have time to meet them and learn more, but we have to get sweeping. I was going to check if Adil is home. He was a cadet with us."

"I suggest you start tomorrow. Tonight, meet at least one Terolian before you go blundering in. And learn a few tricks before you go; otherwise, you won't last two minutes out in the desert."

"We weren't intending to go into the desert, just along the borders," Lorill said.

Frener laughed. "It's all desert. Easy to lose your way without a guide."

He dropped his brushes into a bucket and indicated the other room. "We sleep in there. Put your bed rolls down there for tonight. The only comfort you get here is a good meal. They have a way of slow-cooking the meat because it is so tough, but it's worth the wait, I can assure you. While you're eating one, they start the next." He squatted by the fire pit and raked the coals over what Birler realised was an earthenware container buried under the ashes.

"I'll go and find Adil. He won't refuse a free meal." Frener flashed a white grin at them and left.

Lorill let his breath out in a whoosh. "Well, I can see that this visit is not going to go as expected."

Birler grinned. "It never does. Let's make sure we find out everything we need to know tonight. I get the feeling we won't get another chance."

Peering into the other room, Birler found it empty except for a simple bedroll and a lamp. He dumped his saddle bags in a corner and flipped out his bedroll and blanket. He leaned his bow against the wall with his quiver and thoughtfully strapped his daggers on. His sling, he kept shoved in the back of his waistband, with the small bags of stones within easy reach, though he could see replacing them would be difficult; he should have collected more to bring with him.

Lorill followed suit, staring around the dark room with concern. "It's a bit dank, isn't it?" He inspected the bowl of water in the corner, but it just seemed to be water. "What do you think that is for?"

"Something to do with the heat, I expect. At least it's cooler than out there."

"Yeah, but does it have to be so basic?"

"You can decorate when it's your turn."

"Too right," Lorill murmured as he returned to unsaddle his horse.

Birler spent the time with Kafinee, grooming her gently, smoothing his hand over her rounded stomach. He would have to give her up soon, and he wasn't looking forward to being without her. Frener returned with Adil and an elderly wrinkled man he introduced as "Ael'vin, the village elder."

Adil was the opposite of Frener: slender, with deep brown skin and bright black eyes. Blue-black curly hair bounced around his face. He gripped Birler and Lorill's arms in welcome. "It's great to see you. Have you heard from Edril?"

"No, I was hoping to see him on this rotation. Maybe I'll see him if I get as far as Melila," Birler replied.

"That is deep in the desert, young man. There is much to learn before you venture there." The elderly man sat on a cushion by the fire pit and stirred the ashes. His long grey hair trailed into narrow plaits entwined with his beard, making him look even more distinctive.

"I hope you will find me worthy of learning, Elder Ael'vin," Birler replied, folding his long legs under him as he sat beside the old man.

Ael'vin gave him a toothy grin. "Ah, a willing student. So rare."

"As the Lady wills, so I listen," Birler replied. He smiled at the elder. "I would be a fool not to accept any wisdom you are willing to part with."

Ael'vin nodded. "I like this one. He'll do well." He glanced at Lorill. "How about you?"

"How am I supposed to follow that?" Lorill protested, and the old man chuckled.

Adil grinned as he sat on a bright red cushion opposite. "Stop teasing, Uncle. That Tanjia smells delicious. Frener has listened well enough for all of us tonight."

A little later, a replete Birler had to agree as he stretched on his cushion. "You'll have to teach me the recipe," he murmured, sipping his syrupy kafinee. It was a lot sweeter than he was used to, but the pungent liquid helped ease the food.

"We will when you return," Ael'vin said. "I understand you need to travel to Mistra and Livia?"

"Yes, I travel south. Lorill will sweep north. Have you seen any strangers trying to persuade your people to leave?"

Ael'vin glanced at Adil. "There have been no strangers through here, though we will watch for them. We are forewarned and will pass the warning on. Adil, you go south with

Birler. He can't go alone, unprepared. Frener, you go with Lorill."

"I was intending to." Frener smiled. "They can't learn enough in one night. Terolia is a tough land; heat and sun combined dry out everything, including us." He indicated himself with a grin. "What can be protected from the sun should be. Expose as little skin as possible. Otherwise you will burn up." He lifted his shirt, revealing unexpectedly pale skin; his face and hands were the only tanned areas. "Water is life. Never forget to check your canteen; without it, you will die."

"Always preserve your water and cover up. What else? Are there any maps?" Birler asked.

Adil laughed. "Maps are useless out here because the sands constantly move, changing the landscape."

"But how do you find places then? How would I find Mistra from here?"

"You have to use the landmarks that don't change: the sun, the moon, and the stars."

"Alright, I'll bite. How do you use them to find Mistra?"

Frener chuckled. "How do you think? The sun rises in the same place every day, as does the moon. You take your bearing on the sun's position and use that as your starting point. As you travel, the position of the sun to the fall of your shadow gives you your direction. The sun rises in the east and sets in the west. If the sun is behind you then you are travelling west. Simple."

Frener grinned. "You take your bearing off your shadow. Keep your shadow in the same position relative to the sun, and you will maintain your heading. The Telusion mountain range is located on the east coast of Terolia. If you travel towards the sun and the mountains, you are going east. In central Terolia, there is the Khama Ridge; it runs from

Fuertes in the north to Marmera in the south. Everything else moves about."

Adil laughed at Birler's exasperated expression. "There is a basic map, but it is more how places are located in relation to each other rather than a fixed position. And for those in the know, way markers guide us."

"Way markers?"

"Signs, if you know where to look for them. For example, Mistra is east of Berbera, and Livia is south of Mistra. Melila is east of both in the lee of the mountains."

Lorill's eyes crossed as he struggled to understand. "How does that help? You could miss them by miles."

"Which is why you will take a guide who does know," Elder Ael'vin said firmly. "Our children grow up learning this way of life; you can't learn it overnight."

"But we *can* learn it?" Birler asked, leaning forward.

"If you are here long enough, of course."

Birler nodded. Then he would learn. The conversation moved on to the Families and laws. "Is it true that if a person breaks the Family Law, they can be banished from all family support?"

"It is an extreme punishment," Ael'vin said slowly, "but it does happen. You have to understand that Family is central to a Terolian's way of life. Protect the children, provide a loving home, teach them to survive, honour the Lady.

"We are nomadic because resources are so scarce. If we all lived together, the water would soon run out, so we move between the oases and gather at markets to trade outside those towns that have managed to survive. We trade for food and water. There is little else we need as we roam the sands. We live a simple life."

"Why choose such a harsh way of life?" Lorill asked.

Ael'vin shrugged. "Why live in a building, stuck in one place, rooted and no longer free?"

"But you can move around; you don't have to stay in one place," Lorill protested.

"And how often do you see families in Vespiri move to a new village?"

Lorill held his hands up. "True. I suppose the watches act the same, providing protection and family, even if they stay in one place."

"The children of Terolia have always been nomadic. Sands drift, light changes, and the Family will travel." It sounded like Ael'vin was quoting from somewhere, though he didn't say where.

The scented perfume of the night-blooming plants drifted on the cooler air, sweet and unexpected, as the night drew to an end. They helped Frener clear away and then arranged to meet again at first light.

Birler stared up at the night sky. A soft glow diffused through the thin clouds, creating a halo around the moon. The starlit sky sparkled with swathes of stars, a rash of sparkles across the midnight blue backdrop. One bright star dominated the sky. Positioned just below the moon it shone lower on the horizon, but was noticeable all the same. He watched the moon, sending his prayers to the Lady before entering the small room and rolling in his blanket, glad for the extra warmth, even though he would be sweltering come morning.

He awoke when someone dropped a bundle of cloth on him. It wasn't yet light; only a predawn greyness permeated the small room. "What's this?"

Birler unrolled the bundle: a deep blue robe with what looked like a nightshirt and paper-thin trousers. He dressed without comment, tugging on the robe and tying the belt around his waist, strapping his sword and daggers over the top. Once he realised how deep the sleeves were, he tucked his daggers underneath the robe with his sling. After a few practice attempts of whipping out his daggers, he felt comfortable tucking them out of sight. He stamped his feet into his boots. He wasn't so sure about the sandals that Adil and Frener wore. He tucked his pair of sandals in his saddlebag in case he changed his mind. He watched the others with a more informed eye as they prepared their horses.

He checked his canteen one more time, reassured by its heavy weight. "What do we feed the horses on?" he asked Adil as he waited. He was only taking his weapons; all else, he had left in the dank room. He had tucked a spare canteen of water, wrapped in a clean shirt, in his bag, along with some strips of dried meat and fruit that Frener had given him.

"We're travelling from village to village, so we will get supplies as we go. If we were going into the desert, we'd take a mule loaded with their feed and more water. As it is, we won't need it." Adil flicked him a glance. "We'll head to Mistra first. Which way should we go?"

"East, towards the sun," Birler replied, shading his eyes.

Adil laughed and mounted his horse, a rangy chestnut with a white flash and socks. "Let's get going, then." He raised his hand to Frener and Lorill, who were preparing their own mounts, and then led the way out of Berbera. As they headed east, the horses walked side by side along the sun-baked track. He raised his hood and shielded his face. Birler copied him.

"We travel early and late. We'll rest when the sun is high. Speak as little as possible because the sun will dry your mouth out."

Birler nodded and clamped his mouth shut, watching the landscape change from wiry bushes and succulent plants to empty sand and sun-baked stone. Birler found the silence unnerving. There were no birds singing, no insects chirping, no voices, just the muffled clop of hooves deadened by the sand drifting across the trail. It would take just a little swirl of wind, and the trail would be lost to the sands, too.

The sun beat down on his back; it burned through his robe even this early in the day. They had only been travelling for about a chime since sunrise, and already, sweat slicked his skin. He kept his head down and followed Adil.

All semblance of a track was lost when Birler raised his face and looked around. He was surrounded by sand. The dunes rose and fell in rippling mounds, all looking the same. It was disorienting. He had no idea where they were. With an effort, he controlled his panic. If he kept the sun at his back, he would be heading west, and at some point, he would end up in East Watch.

Adil shielded his eyes as he looked east. He flicked a glance at Birler. "We'll stop in a chime. There is a small oasis a few miles further on. We'll rest there."

Birler nodded, and they continued through the never-ending sands.

Birler dismounted in the unexpected shade of a palm tree—three palm trees, in fact, standing next to an almost perfect circle of water, a deep blue pool nestled in the golden sand. Kafinee dipped her head and drank as Birler filled his canteen.

Adil encouraged his horse to lie down and rigged his awning above them.

Kafinee settled down next to them without a murmur, and Birler rigged his awning. After taking a swig of water in the sweltering heat, he carefully stoppered it and tucked it away out of sight. He settled down, lying against Kafinee. "How long will we stop?"

"Until the sun is past the end palm tree. Sleep, Birler. I'll watch."

Birler yawned, his jaw cracking, and with a laugh, he made himself comfortable and fell asleep.

The sun was midway between the second and third palm tree when Adil shook him awake. "We have company. Don't speak. Stay with Kafinee and keep your eyes down. Let me do the talking." Birler remained seated with Kafinee and observed the approaching men.

Kafinee raised her head and huffed in his ear, and his lips twitched. Four men, all with the curved swords of the Terolian Families strapped to their waist, drew to a halt. The horses gleamed black in the glaring sunlight, all the same, with long tasselled blankets under their deep-seated saddles.

The lead man leaned on the raised front of his saddle and observed them as his men spread out on either side. Deep brown skin hid beneath the bright orange scarf which twisted around his head and face. A four-pointed yellow star was tattooed on his right cheek, bright against his dark skin. Lean and muscular, his strength coiled around him, poised and ready to strike.

"You hoard all the shade," the man said.

"There is plenty to share," Adil replied.

"What if we don't want to share?"

"Then I would say we were here first, but you are welcome to share our hearth, should you be so inclined."

The man laughed and leaned back, glancing at his men. "I see no hearth."

Adil shrugged. "A hearth is where the owner says it is and is offered without stint to Family."

"And you declare right of Family?"

"All Terolia is family. I invite you to join mine for the space of time we stay here, no more, no less."

"Well said. I accept." The man swung his leg over and lightly dismounted. His elegant stallion stood at his shoulder. He placed his hand over his heart. "Tiv'erna, Atolea."

"Adil, Kiker."

"A brother in truth, and who is your companion?" The man grinned, revealing pearly white teeth, bright in his dark face.

Birler searched his memory for the familial lines; the Kiker were a sub-line of the Atolea. Family, indeed.

"A friend of mine, here to help protect Terolia."

The man's smile disappeared. "We do not need outsider help; we protect our own."

Birler rose and smoothly pushed his hood back. Kafinee struggled to her feet behind him and showered him in sand. He placed a soothing hand on her neck, and the man's eyes narrowed as he watched. Kafinee stared at him with liquid eyes, and Tiv'erna's black eyes widened.

"We offer no disrespect, only assistance. A disease has come from the west. We only wish to help you identify it," Birler said.

Tiv'erna stared at him. "Name yourself, one who dares bond with a Darian."

Birler hesitated a moment. Bonded? Tiv'erna raised an eyebrow and Birler hurried to say, "Birler of Greens, rider of Kafinee. All honour to the Lady."

There was a pause where time seemed to stop, and then the man nodded as Kafinee raised her head and stamped her foot. "Birler, rider of Kafinee. If she accepts you, then so will we." He turned to his men. "We camp here," he said and then turned back to Adil. "We offer you our hearth in return. I think you will find it is much more plentiful than yours."

Adil smiled, uncertain as to what had just happened, but he bowed acceptance. "You honour us."

"That, we do, but you are Family. Join me." As they had exchanged pleasantries, the men had begun to erect a large tent, unaffected by the heat. Birler watched them in awe.

Adil followed Tiv'erna into the tent. "You expect the Medera?" he asked, his voice low.

Tiv'erna laughed and slapped him on the shoulder. "Indeed, Adil of Kiker. I think she will be interested in your words."

Birler leaned against Kafinee and waited for Adil to tell him what to do. He had no idea who these people were and felt his ignorance keenly. He had never been so unprepared in all his life, and he could tell the sands were shifting under his feet as the Lady steered him onto a new path.

"A Darian?" he thought silently to Kafinee.

"Yes, yes, yes, finally! You've been blocking me for so long that I almost gave up. You hold yourself so tightly that I couldn't get through," Kafinee said, her voice light and breathless in his mind as she nudged him so hard he almost fell over.

"How was I supposed to know?"

"It doesn't matter. You are open to me now, and you must listen. Tiv'erna is the eldest son of Medera Yannis of the Atolea. She is the voice of the family. The mother of the children. She is coming here, and you must not offend her."

Birler was stuck on the "coming here" bit. *"She's coming here? Why?"*

"Because she chooses to. Tiv'erna is a great warrior. He would be a good friend to have. His mother is preeminent among all Medera. Her voice is heard first."

"You mean she is like the Lady to all Terolians?"

"Yes, yes, she is most important, and she is coming here."

Birler closed his eyes. *"Is there anyone else I need to worry about?"*

"Her husband, Arkan is the Sodera. It would be good if you didn't offend him, either."

"And how do I do that?"

Kafinee sighed in his head. A cool flutter of air through his mind, and he shivered as he opened his eyes. *"Treat them as you would the Lady. Treat them with respect, honour their position, and tell them the truth, always."*

"Can anyone else hear what you are saying to me?"

"Only if I so choose."

"Make sure I don't make any glaring mistakes."

"You won't."

"Don't be so sure about that."

"Oh, and get me some Baliweed, please."

"Baliweed?"

"Yes, I can smell it, and it's so lovely. It's been so long since I've had some; it would be such a treat. I deserve a treat, don't I?"

"Of course you do. I would keep you in an endless supply of it if I knew what it was."

Her chuckle followed him as he went to see what they were feeding the other horses. A slighter version of Tiv'erna was brushing down an elegant black stallion. Birler offered a hesitant hand for the stallion to greet. "He is amazing."

The lad looked up and grinned. "Don't. He doesn't need any encouragement."

Birler gently smoothed his hand down his neck. The stallion was all muscle. It would take a strong man to control him. He understood why Tiv'erna was a simmering cord of power. *"I greet you, mighty steed of Tiv'erna."*

"Greetings, Birler, rider of Kaf'enir."

Birler hesitated as he absorbed the Darian's pronunciation of Kafinee's name. *"Forgive my ignorance, but what is Baliweed?"*

The stallion snorted, dipped his head in his hay net, and phaffed some dry grass at Birler. The lad stood back, wide-eyed. Birler turned to the young man. "This is Baliweed?" he asked, holding out the grass. The lad nodded.

"Where do I come by some?"

The lad held out a woven bag.

"How much does it cost? And how much should the horses have?"

"It's yours; you are our guest. Sprinkle a handful in the hay. She will find it."

Birler smiled. "You are very kind, and Kafinee will be very happy. My name is Birler. Would you be kind enough to share your name?"

The lad grinned. "Per'ilta, brother of Tiv'erna, youngest son of Yannis."

"Per'ilta, I'm pleased to meet you. Would you introduce me to these other amazing stallions?"

Per'ilta led him to his own gleaming stallion. "This is mine. You can call him Beren. We've been bonded for five years now."

"Beren, I greet you."

The stallion nodded his head. *"Greetings, Birler."*

"The others are bonded to Tar'enne and Ven'ian; they should introduce them. It is not for me to give their names."

"As it should be," Birler murmured. "I thank you for the grace of your time and the Baliweed," he finished with a grin, shaking the bag. Birler was aware of Per'ilta's thoughtful gaze following him as he left.

"Kaf'enir?" Birler asked as he sprinkled a handful of Baliweed in Kafinee's hay, and she visibly relaxed as she rummaged for the grass.

"Yes, that is my name. I couldn't tell you until you opened to me. We are bonded properly now, as we should be." A happy mumble pervaded his mind as he stashed the Baliweed in his saddle bag, and a constant hum warmed him from the inside.

Tiv'erna was standing at the entrance of the tent, watching him. "I like a man who looks after his horse."

"It takes but a moment, and she's worth it. Your stallion is beautiful, pure power. He must take some handling."

Tiv'erna clapped Birler on the shoulder. "He would take up all my time and more if I allowed it."

"I'm sure he would," Birler agreed, following Tiv'erna into the tent. He stopped and blinked at the colourful interior.

"Just because it is temporary, it doesn't mean we shouldn't take the time to make it comfortable."

"Indeed," Birler murmured, walking over to join Adil. "What's the plan? I thought we were only stopping for a short while."

"Tiv'erna invited us to eat with him. It would be seen as an insult if we refused."

"And the Medera?"

Adil grimaced. "It is unavoidable, and maybe you should take the opportunity to meet her. It may be useful for you to claim the relationship."

"A quick lesson on Mederas wouldn't go amiss," Birler said as he sat on the rug.

"No time; she's almost here. Just be polite."

Birler rolled his eyes. "How this can go any worse, I have no idea, but I am sure it will."

Adil chuckled and fidgeted on his cushion as he watched the tent entrance.

45

BIRLER

TEROLIA

dil rose as the disturbance outside the tent drew closer. Birler stood beside him, watching the entrance with interest.

Tiv'erna held back the tent flap, and a diminutive woman entered. Her sharp black eyes swept the tent, pausing on her guests and then continuing.

"Why are we camped here? I expected to stop when we reached Mistra." Her voice was sharp, and Adil swallowed nervously. She wore a deep amber-coloured robe, accentuating her rich brown skin. Her black hair was piled on her head in an elaborate coil.

"We have water, and Mistra will still be there tomorrow," Tiv'erna soothed, guiding his mother towards Adil. "A guest of the tent, Mother. Adil of Kiker and his friend Birler of Greens."

The black eyes focussed on Adil, and he flinched. Her lips twitched, and she nodded. "Adil of Kiker, welcome to the tent of the Atolea."

"The honour is mine, Medera."

Her gaze switched to Birler. "Birler of Greens," she said,

her voice thoughtful, "welcome to the tent of the Atolea. You travel far from home."

"I thank you for your hospitality, Medera. It is my first visit to your country."

"And what do you think so far?"

"I have much to learn before I can fully appreciate the beauty that is hidden here," Birler replied, holding her gaze.

The Medera laughed. It was a rich, smooth sound that rippled around the tent, and Tiv'erna relaxed. Birler hadn't realised Tiv'erna was tense until he saw the slightest change in his muscles.

"Arkan, come in here," she called. She waited until her Sodera entered the tent. He was tall, whip thin, and dressed in dusty black robes that were swept back over his shoulder, revealing a wicked scimitar at his waist. He looked strange and threatening, and Birler's hair rose on his arms as the Sodera's power crackled off him. He took an instinctive step back, and the Medera raised her hand. "You're a guest of my tent; no harm shall come to you in my care." She tilted her head towards her Sodera and squinted at him. "But our guest is right to be concerned. You are causing some discomfort. What have you been doing?"

Arkan grimaced. "Suffering fools. Yannis! It is not to be tolerated. We need to speak before the Family. It seems some have forgotten that which they should not."

The Medera's face tightened. "Arrange it for Mistra. But first, my dear, you need to look to yourself. You cannot be frightening my guests with your excess energy. Shoo," she said, flicking her hand at him. Adil's jaw dropped as the father of the Atolea Family gave his Medera a blinding smile that shed years off his face and then ducked back out of the tent, closely followed by Tiv'erna.

Per'ilta slid into the tent carrying a jug beaded with moisture, and the Medera sat, gesturing to Adil and Birler to join her. "So, Birler of Greens, tell me what you are doing in Terolia." Per'ilta poured the water and placed the jug on the low table before taking a post by the tent entrance. Another dark-haired warrior stood opposite him. "Drink, please," she said, reaching for her glass.

Birler was pleasantly surprised at the refreshing lemon water. He wanted to ask how they managed to keep it cool, but he refrained. "I am a Lady's Ranger, as is Adil here, and I am posted to East Watch on the borders here in Terolia. Recently, we had a visitor, a travelling minstrel telling tales and stories, an entertainment for the long evenings." He paused as the Medera raised her hand.

"You have a Darian?"

Birler blinked. "So I am told. I didn't know until your son, Tiv'erna, said."

"Where did she come from?"

"Lord Warren of Greens gave her to me; she was in his stables."

"He gave her to you?"

"Yes."

"In return for what?"

"She was a gift from my family."

"Ah, continue."

Birler took another sip as he gathered his thoughts, and then Arkan entered, his black hair slicked back as if he had just had a shower. He looked relaxed and in control, no longer sparking. He had changed out of his dusty robes and wore a long black tunic and trousers lined with an ornate red and blue pattern down the edge. Yannis smiled at him as he sat at her feet. She patted his shoulder, and he leaned against her leg.

Birler cleared his throat. "As I was saying, a travelling minstrel came by the watch and began to spin his tales, only he wasn't just telling a story; he was weaving a spell which affects people's actions. He was trying to persuade them to leave the watch and travel with him into the desert."

"A spell?" Arkan leaned forward, his attention caught. He had a strong face, with sharp angles and a stubborn chin. His straight eyebrows drew down over his deep brown eyes in a scowl.

"It's called *Mentiserium*. It controls a person's mind and tells them how to behave."

"Who can cast this spell?"

"I don't know. It is supposed to be forbidden, but someone has found out how to do it and is showing others. Though why they would want to bring people out into the middle of the desert, I don't know. They wouldn't last very long."

"Did this entertainer have a name?" Yannis asked.

"Ser'ander."

"No family name or mark?"

"Not that I could see, but I wouldn't know what I was looking for," Birler admitted.

"It would have been prominent, on the right cheek. I have the mark of Atolea." The Medera tapped her smooth right cheek, where a yellow star was tattooed. An orange flame was tattooed below it. "Adil has the Kiker symbol of a yellow cross. The Kiker are related to us. Arkan wears the Solari sun." Birler observed the vivid orange sun on his right cheek. On his left cheek, he wore the Atolea Star, a mark of his affiliation with Yannis, with the orange flame beneath.

"I didn't notice a mark, though I will check when I return. He is being held at East Watch."

"Why are you here if he is there?" Arkan asked.

"We didn't know where he came from or whether he had visited any other villages. I was sent to check. To do a sweep from Berbera down to Livia. One of my colleagues, Lorill, is sweeping north from Berbera to Ramila."

"And what if you find he visited other villages?"

Birler stared at him. "Then I will find out where he has taken the people and endeavour to return them home."

Arkan held his eyes. "He means it," he said under his breath.

"Of course he means it. He is the Lady's, and she sent him a Darian," Yannis said as if that settled it.

Arkan stared off into the distance, and Yannis smiled, watching him as he checked with his own Darian. He looked up and met her eyes. "My apologies," he said with a slight smile. "We should eat. Come." He rose in one fluid movement and held his hand out to his wife. She stood, and they led the way out of the tent.

A table had been set up beneath the palm trees, under a bright yellow awning. Benches lined either side, and the family waited for the Medera to be seated. Birler glanced round and saw Kafinee had been moved to the horse's picket line, and he could feel her contentment as a young boy groomed her. He grinned as he moved to the seat beside the Sodera, with Adil sitting beside the Medera. The family took their seats around them.

Birler looked around, noting Tiv'erna's absence.

"He patrols," Arkan said from beside him as Birler looked at him in surprise. "He'll join us later."

Yannis raised her hands. "Lady bless this family. We thank you for your continued care and protection. We thank you for the food you place before us and honour those who walk your path. The Lady watches."

"As the Line protects," everyone chanted.

"Tell me about yourself, Birler. How did you become a Lady's Ranger?" Arkan asked as he poured water into Birler's glass and then his own.

"Thank you," Birler murmured. "There's not much to tell. I grew up in Vespers and joined the cadets a couple of years ago. Graduated this summer. East Watch is my first posting." He reached for a piece of flatbread. The aromas were enticing, and his mouth watered.

"Yet you say you are from Greens."

Birler flushed. "Lord Warren and his family adopted me. Unfortunately, my mother died when I was young, and my father …" Birler hesitated. "Didn't want a young child on his hands," he finished as he inspected the dishes, trying to decide what to put on his bread.

"I am sorry for your loss; family is important, especially for young children." Arkan flicked him a sharp glance. "And Lord Warren took you in instead? A good man."

"Yes, he is a good man. As you say, it is important to have family behind you."

Arkan smiled. "All honour to him for looking after you so well. How did he come by a Darian?"

"I'm not sure he knew she was a Darian. Friends of mine at the academy said she must have Darian bloodlines somewhere because she was so clever, but no one thought she was a full-blooded Darian."

"And yet you bonded."

"Bonded?"

"She gave you her name."

Birler frowned. "She didn't. I didn't know what her true name was; I called her Kafinee because of her colour."

"I did. My name is Kaf'enir."

"We will speak to her later. She must have given you her name because you couldn't be bonded otherwise. Darians are rare. Few travel outside Terolia, and even fewer bond outside the Family. The Lady's gift."

"Truly, she is special."

"I'm glad you noticed!" Kaf'enir's voice was a warm chuckle in the back of his mind.

"Lord Mayer of East Watch, how do you find him?"

Birler tried to concentrate on what Arkan was saying. "He looks after his people well and is conscientious about his duties. After all, I'm here, aren't I?"

Arkan smiled. "I've only met him once. He came to Ramila to introduce himself when he first became lord."

"Maybe you ought to meet more regularly. After all, you share a border," Birler suggested.

"We should come here more often. I like it here," Kaf'enir said.

Arkan slapped him on the shoulder. "Spoken like a true son. I will consider it. Now, tell me how you came across this *Mentiserium*. How do we stop it?"

"Hold the Lady close," Birler replied without thinking.

"That goes without saying," Arkan rumbled.

Birler grimaced. "If everyone did, the *Mentiserium* would have no effect, but it is insidious and seeps into the cracks. Once it takes root, it is difficult to resist, and worst of all, you wouldn't know you were affected. If you don't know you are affected, how do you resist it? We must warn people to be more aware and pay attention, to protect each other. To be wary of strangers and those who speak in public before crowds."

"We can help with that. It is our duty to protect our family. We will spread the word. You are not eating. Come try the bread. Wrap it around the meat; it is delicious." Arkan spooned the chunks of meat onto his bread and folded it up, demonstrating how to eat it.

The delicious concoction melted in Birler's mouth, scented spices combined with spurts of fruitiness. Birler reached for another flatbread. "This tastes wonderful."

"We are fortunate that we are with the caravan. When out on patrol, we make do with dried meats and fruit. You need time to cook food like this, so we enjoy it whilst we can."

"Do you have a home base? Where do you call home?"

"Terolia is our home, though we tend to stay in the west. Other families travel as we do across Terolia."

"But if I needed to find you, how would I do that if you constantly move about?"

Arkan chuckled. "You expect me to give up our secrets? If you need us, leave a message with Ael'vin in Berbera or Adil here. They will know how to find us." And with that, Birler had to be satisfied.

"I could find them. Don't worry so," Kafinee said.

"But it is a risk. If we can't warn them, it could be too late."

"It is no different to getting a message to Warren."

"At least I know where Warren is."

"No, you don't. He could have travelled to Vespers or be out in his plantation. He is not necessarily where you left him."

Birler sat back, surprised. She was right. Arkan cocked a brow at him and smiled as he recognised his distant expression. Birler refocussed on the table as Tiv'erna sat beside him. The patrol rotated, and as young men melted into the dark night to be replaced by voracious appetites, the platters were refilled, and Tiv'erna fell on the food with gusto.

"How far are we from Mistra?" Birler asked idly.

"About four chimes."

"Why did you stop here, then, if you were headed for Mistra?"

Tiv'erna grinned and swallowed his mouthful. "You have a Darian."

"So?"

"We had to make sure she was well cared for. Darians rarely stray from the Family. They are the Lady's gift and should be honoured as such."

"But I didn't know she was a Darian."

"That is why we stayed. She was protective of you, but she wouldn't speak to us, and we weren't sure who you were."

"And now?"

Tiv'erna flashed him a grin. "You have been accepted as a guest by the Medera."

"That could just be a distraction so you could take Kafinee."

Tiv'erna's expression grew hard. "The Medera would not dishonour a guest so."

Birler caught his breath and stilled. "Forgive me. I meant no disrespect. I am trying to understand why Kafinee makes such a difference."

"She is the Lady's gift. We are honour bound to protect her."

"But you accepted me as a guest before you knew anything about me."

"She was bonded. You were considerate. My Darian approved."

Birler stared at him, confused. The horse had approved of him?

"Of course he approves of you," Kaf'enir said. *"He wouldn't have spoken to you if he didn't. He is a mighty stallion; he would make a good sire."*

Birler tried not to roll his eyes. *"Isn't the one you've already got enough?"*

"I can look."

"And where was Deren from? Is he a good sire?"

"Oh, yes, we will see him in Melila. He is a Kirshan." Birler couldn't help smiling at the dreamy tone of her voice.

Tiv'erna laughed. "I see you have found your connection."

"Sorry, yes, it is confusing."

"It'll come with practice. You'll be holding two conversations without noticing. Always listen to your Darian. They are observant and have long memories; they will remember something you have long forgotten."

"Is there anything else I should know?"

"Never share her true name outside your family. That is the basis of your bond. You don't want others trying to corrupt it."

"Is that even possible?"

"Unfortunately, yes."

"But why would someone try to do that?"

"It would drive the Darian mad and, subsequently, the bonded rider, so never share it."

"Understood."

The meal came to an end, and everyone rose, to help stack the empty plates and clear away the tables. "We will move on in the morning. What is not needed will be stowed away tonight," Tiv'erna murmured as he escorted Birler to the picket line.

Birler petted Kaf'enir as he watched the men dismantle the tables; they were efficient and well organised. Birler stored the information away. The Terolians were not what he had expected.

Birler picked up Kaf'enir's tack and slung it over his shoulder, intending to clean it.

"Please join us by the fire," Tiv'erna said, his teeth gleaming in the torchlight. "I'll be with you shortly." Tiv'erna turned away, and Birler veered over to his saddle-bags to retrieve his wax and cloths to clean the leather. Enough to keep his hands busy.

His neck prickled, and he spun, surprising the man who thrust his knife at Birler's back. The blade sliced the skin of Birler's arm as he flung it up, its sting sharp as Birler twisted, trying to muffle the knife with his robes. The blade sliced through material and skin—if the sting across his ribs was anything to go by. He shot his right hand up into his assailant's face, snapping the man's head back. Kaf'enir squealed in anger behind him as the man struggled to hold

Birler down, his grip tight around Birler's throat as he scrabbled for his knife.

A harsh curse filled the air, and the pressure on Birler's throat eased as the man was dragged off him and pinned to the ground. "Birler? Are you alright?" Arkan stooped over him, his lean face fierce.

"Yes, fine." Birler coughed. His neck felt like it had been twisted off. He sat up with Arkan's help, breathing heavily. The ornate knife fell out of his robes onto the sand, and Arkan picked it up.

"You're not fine," Arkan said, his voice sharp. "Per'ilta, call Aranna. Birler is wounded. Tiv'erna, help Birler inside." He stood and glared down at the man pinned to the ground, "Fer'arne, what is the meaning of this? How dare you dishonour our family."

The man flinched back against his Sodera's anger, his black eyes fearfully darting around the accusing faces.

Tiv'erna tightened his grip around Birler as he stumbled.

"Sorry. Must be more tired than I thought," Birler mumbled as the tent seemed to tilt, and he staggered, his legs giving way. His mind spun in a frenzy, with images flashing through his head, sparkling bright and vivid. He coughed as a sharp stinging sensation tightened his throat. His head hurt. He coughed again, struggling to breathe. The last thing he heard was Kaf'enir screaming with fear in his head.

Birler woke to a sensation of movement and pushed off his covers. He was swaying and overheated.

"He's awake," a soft voice murmured beside him. "Drink." Cool liquid dribbled into his mouth, and he swallowed desperately. "Slowly, or you'll choke. There's plenty of it." He shivered, and the covers were tucked back around him. He slept.

He dreamt of Lady Leyandrii. She hovered above him, her expressive face taut with worry. "You're sure he's responding to the antidote?"

He wanted to tell her he was fine, but he couldn't speak.

"Positive, my Lady," a young woman replied for him.

"Good. Thank you for your care, Aranna. I'll leave Ren with him. Send her if you need me."

"Of course, my Lady."

It was dark when he next awoke. He lay deliberating for a moment, aware that he was on the ground and no longer moving. A heavy weight on his chest turned out to be a sleeping arifel. He stroked it in amazement, its silky fur soft under his fingers. The little creature meeped at him as it stirred. Images of Leyandrii's concern bombarded him. Maybe he hadn't dreamt of her after all? Then Kaf'enir was wrapping him in her concern and distress. *"Hush. I'm fine. I'm fine, Kaf'enir, please."*

His use of her name made her pause. *"I've been so worried,"* she crooned. *"You've been gone for so long."*

"How long?" Birler stroked the arifel's soft fur, soothing the agitated creature. Her name filtered into his mind: Ren.

"Many moons."

"Where are we?"

"Mistra."

"What happened?"

"You were poisoned; the knife was coated with it. You collapsed. The Sodera was furious. He's taken it as a personal insult."

"A personal insult? What does that mean?"

"Your life was threatened whilst you were a guest of the Atolea. It is called a life debt."

Birler sighed and rolled his head; it was too heavy to lift, but he needed to move. He tried to roll upright, cupping the Arifel in his hand, and got tangled in the light cover.

"Birler?" Tiv'erna's voice was close.

"I need to go …" Birler's voice trailed off as his tongue stumbled over how to phrase the need politely.

"Of course. Let me help you." Strong hands untangled him and helped him sit up. He wavered. He had no strength. "Here, use this. Don't try to get up yet."

"You shouldn't …"

"Just go, Birler, or I'll get Aranna, and she can help you."

He placed the arifel on the floor and gave in.

Tiv'erna helped him lie back down and then leaned over him, raising his shoulders enough for him to drink the offered water. The cool liquid soothed his irritated throat. "Don't you have better things to be doing?" Birler asked with a weak smile.

"You are family," Tiv'erna replied as he sat cross-legged next to him. "You should sleep."

Ren chittered in agreement.

"It sounds like all I've been doing is sleeping."

"The poison has nearly run its course. You must rest; otherwise, your movement will stir it up in your blood. I am here to make you stay still. Don't make it harder on yourself. Sleep, Birler. You will soon be well."

"Do as he says," Kaf'enir said, sounding much happier. *"Sleep."*

Ren nudged his ear with her cold nose and then disappeared, no doubt returning to Lady Leyandrii to tell her he still lived. He thanked the Lady for her concern, and a soothing warmth flushed through his veins.

Birler slept.

46

GUERLAIRE

LADY'S PALACE, VESPERS, VESPIRI

The late Novu afternoon sunshine was fading when Guerlaire called his strike team to his office. He sat behind his desk and observed the men and women crowding into his small study in the palace. With so many incidents happening around Remargaren, he had officially formalised his team. He had added Royer, a swarthy man from East Mayer. Calene had rotated with Marian Descelles and now kept an eye on the warehouses with one of Asher's men. Including Marian, a young woman from Greens with a lethal sword arm, he had a team of rangers he trusted who could respond at a moment's notice and be transported wherever Leyandrii needed them to be. It was easier for him to command instead of being one of the tactical pairs. A central commander could oversee the whole mission and adapt as needed.

Asher had suggested they keep the purpose of the team quiet and continue to house them at the palace. As far as anyone else knew, they were seconded to the palace to supplement the palace guards. Guerlaire wished it were true.

As it was, he indicated the map lying on the desk before

him. "This is Deepwater. There are reports of unrest near the village of Fulgrove to the east of the middle lake. They are threatening to dam the lake, which will cause flooding around the manor. We need to help the local guards regain control and see if we can find the instigators. According to Lord Ricard, they haven't had much rain recently, so there is no reason for the lake to flood on its own."

Chryll peered over his shoulder. His friend had squeezed his bulk behind Guerlaire's desk to make room for the others. "The middle lake would cause the most risk to the manor, so the groundsmen would inspect it regularly."

"Which rangers are posted there?" Royer asked.

"Severen and Parsill," Guerlaire replied.

Royer grunted. A sign of concern, Guerlaire thought.

"Lord Ricard has requested assistance to find out who is causing the unrest. His men will deal with the rioters. That is not our job, so don't get involved in any unnecessary fights."

"By the time we get there, it'll be too late. Anyone behind this will already have left," Chryll said.

"The rioters are still forming; they haven't struck yet."

"How did he get word here so quick?" Eren asked.

"Message came by arifel," Guerlaire replied.

"An arifel?" Eren comically raised one ginger eyebrow.

"Leyandrii made all the lords Guardians of Vespiri. They can call the little creatures. The arifels can carry messages." Guerlaire unrolled a soft cloth on the desk. Faceted crystal columns flashed in the candlelight. "These are communication crystals. They work over short distances. We can use them to keep in touch."

"How short a distance?" Royer asked as he picked one up.

"From here to the Chapterhouse. Should be more than enough for what we need within Deepwater."

Royer nodded. "And how do they work?"

"Hold the crystal in your hand. It has to make contact with your skin. Think of the person you want to talk to and then speak." Guerlaire picked one up. "Royer, have you completed your last report?"

His voice came out of Royer's crystal, thin and echoey but quite clear.

Royer rolled his eyes and replied, "Not yet, sir."

Guerlaire chuckled as Royer's voice came out of the crystal in his hand, a low vibration. "We have a limited supply of these crystals, so don't lose them. We wait until dark. Be ready to leave from the landgard in one chime. No uniforms, dark clothes only. Leyandrii will transport us to Deepwater. We need to infiltrate the rioters and find out who is in charge. Remember to shield and check for persuasions. We need to know who is behind this effort."

Denir, Marian, and Fonor each picked up a crystal. Marian inspected it closely, her glossy brown hair falling forward.

"How will Deepwater know not to attack us?" Fonor asked in his soft voice as he hefted the crystal.

"They won't, so be careful. If you are captured, surrender and say you're part of my team. Ricard knows we will be infiltrating."

"In other words, don't get caught," Chryll said with a grin as he picked up a crystal and slipped it in his pocket.

"That's your advice?" Fonor asked. "How enlightening."

Marian laughed and slapped his shoulder, her brown eyes gleaming with amusement. "Knowing you, you'll talk your way out of trouble, and they will all melt out of your way."

"Let's hope so," Fonor replied as he followed her out of the room.

Chryll chuckled and waited until the others left. He grew more serious once the door shut. "Fonor has a fair point," he said.

"I know, but there is nothing we can do about it."

A chime later, the team reassembled in the landgard, the Lady's private rose garden. Dusk had fallen, wreathing the small garden in shadows. They all wore plain black clothes, their new uniform. Guerlaire knew they were all armed with concealed daggers, garottes, and other weapons. All were different and adept in their weapon of choice. All wore swords.

Leyandrii stood beside Guerlaire, her hand resting on his arm. A deep blue cloak fluttered around her, and she tugged it closer. A dim onoff hovered above them, shedding enough light to see their faces. "When Guerlaire arrives in Deepwater, he will create another waystone. You will know its location by its chime. You must memorise its location so you can find it again. When you need to return, think of my garden, the landgard, and step into the waystone, and it will bring you home. This will be faster than waiting on me to transport you."

"Well. That will be helpful," Fonor said in his usual understated way. The others chuckled.

"Onwards," Chryll said. "Remember, split up as soon as we arrive. We are not stopping the rioters; that is the Deepwater's responsibility. We need to find the organisers. Try to be discreet. It would be better if none of us were seen."

"Shame we can't be invisible," Marian said.

Leyandrii shook her head. "It's difficult to maintain an illusion over multiple people on a continuous basis, especially when you are moving. I won't be able to match to the terrain."

Marian flushed. "Apologies, my Lady. I wasn't expecting you—"

"The darkness will be enough cover," Guerlaire said. "We need to leave."

The next moment, Leyandrii transported them and they all appeared in Deepwater, in the shadows near the manor house. The land sloped down from the manor to the gleaming waters of the lake, suspiciously close. Guerlaire peered around them, but they seemed alone.

"I'll create the waystone beside the middle lake." Guerlaire pointed to part of the building that jutted out, creating a shadowed corner. "And then I'll go and speak to Lord Ricard and warn him we've arrived. Everyone, pair up and move out. Fonor, you head for Fulgrove, see who's stirring up trouble in the village. Don't be seen."

A soft chime announced a new waystone, and once Guerlaire disappeared around the building, the rangers split up and moved off in different directions. Marian hovered beside Chryll, twisting her hair up into a knot. "We should cross to the other side. I saw a flash in the trees."

Chryll nodded and followed Marian across the soggy land bridge between the upper and lower lake.

They squelched their way over the narrow bridge. The water was already rising. Marian flitted off ahead, wending through the brush, a silent whisper in the bushes. Chryll wished he could be as light of foot, but he was too heavily built.

He caught up with Marian on the edge of a clearing, observing a small camp. They even had a fire burning. "Well?"

"Classic group of losers. Too lazy to achieve anything worthwhile and, from their discussion, would rather just beat shit up."

"Any persuasions?"

"Not so far. From what I heard, this is what they enjoy."

"And where are they intending to go and 'beat shit up'?"

"They think they are going to storm Deepwater, but they don't seem very organised."

"Who's telling them what to do?"

"That short man in the fancy waistcoat." Marian pointed at the ruffian standing on the back of the cart.

Chryll stared. That was not how he would have described him. He didn't look like he would be in charge of anything. "Let's have a chat with him."

"I thought we weren't to be seen?"

"I doubt he'll go with them. He'll set them off and disappear. Let's change his mind."

Marian gave him a feral grin and led the way.

Fonor led the way down muddy tracks, keeping to the shadows as much as possible.

Royer cursed from behind him as he stepped in a puddle. "We get all the fun jobs."

"Fun comes in all shapes and forms," Fonor replied and ducked into a leafy screen of bushes.

Royer dived in after him.

A moment later, a horse and cart rattled past, and then a second and a third.

"Guerlaire?" Fonor whispered into the crystal in his hand. "The troops are moving. Three carts from the east." He slipped the crystal into his pocket. "Come on," he said, and then he darted back out onto the track and jogged in the direction the carts had come from.

Eren glared at the lake. If the water level was rising, someone had already blocked an exit point. The only problem was he had no idea where that would be. He hesitated. And if *he* didn't know, how would any other stranger know?

"We need a map," he said to Denir and headed for the manor house.

He climbed the steps and paused in the entrance hall. Voices came from a side room where the door stood slightly ajar.

Eren pushed the door open. "Captain? Can we get a map of the lakes? The water level is already rising."

"Here." A slightly built man indicated a map on the wall. "This is up to date."

Eren crossed the room and searched the map. He pointed to a section at the eastern end, between the mid and lower lake. "Are these the only drainage points?"

"Yes, above ground, though there are tunnels below ground as well."

"And how many people know about those, my lord?" Guerlaire asked with a pointed glance at his men.

Eren winced as he realised he had just ordered the Lord of the Watch around in his own home. "My apologies, Lord Ricard."

Lord Ricard waved his apology away. "The maintenance crew, the guards. The tunnels are not a secret."

"Who would know how to block them? Assuming the above-ground channels are not blocked," Guerlaire asked.

"We've been checking them constantly. All are clear."

"I'm sorry, sir, but that can't be correct. The water level is rising. There is a blockage somewhere," Eren said.

"Who was last to check the tunnels?" Guerlaire asked. "Have they returned?"

Lord Ricard strode to the door and said to his steward, "Send for Jacko and Parsill." He returned, his shoulders slumped. "I never thought anyone would use our attempts to regulate the flow against us."

A small, tinny voice came from Guerlaire's pocket. *"Guerlaire? The troops are moving. Three carts from the east."*

Lord Ricard's mouth tightened, and he left the room to update his men before returning.

A thin, gangly man wearing glasses skidded into the room. "No one's seen Parsill for over two chimes, sir." He pushed the glasses up his nose and peered around the room. "Severen reported tunnel two was all clear and is on his way back."

"Jacko, which tunnel did Parsill take?" Ricard asked.

"Number four. I'll show you," Jacko said.

"Eren, Denir, you're with Jacko," Guerlaire snapped.

"And a guard unit," Lord Ricard added. "If the tunnel is blocked, you're going to need equipment."

"Depends what the problem is," Jacko said.

Eren waved his crystal. "We can call for help if we need it."

Guerlaire nodded. "Get going, then, because this is about to become a battlefield."

"Denir, stay with the captain," Eren said. "If he's going into a fight, Chryll will kill us if he's on his own." Eren held up his hand. "I'll have Parsill."

"Who may be injured," Guerlaire said. "Severen is on his way. He'll be with me."

"I'll grab a med kit," Jacko said and hurried out of the room.

"The gates are pretty basic," Lord Ricard said. "A way for us to regulate the flow. We can open and shut the sluice gates as needed. Hopefully, all they've done is close the gates. If they've collapsed the tunnels, we have a bigger problem."

Jacko returned. "The men are ready. Let's go."

Eren and Denir followed him out of the room and down the steps. A unit of guards waited for them.

"Lead off," Jacko said, waving his hand, and the guards

jogged off down the road. Jacko hurried after them. "I'm one of the engineers who helped build the sluice gates. I'm not much of a fighter, so I'll leave that side to you. You leave the gates to me."

"Sounds fair," Eren said, jogging beside him. "Stick with us, though, because this place is going to light up soon. There is an organised riot about to start, and we're not sure what they're after."

"Lord Ricard, probably. He's the only one of importance. He *is* Deepwater. Distract enough of us, and they'll be able to storm the manor."

Denir spoke into his crystal. "Captain? Possible target is Lord Ricard. Don't leave him unguarded."

"Understood." Guerlaire's reply was clipped.

Jacko peered over his shoulder at Denir. "Is that a communication crystal?"

"Yes, sir."

"I've never seen one. Heard of 'em. Useful gadgets."

"How far are the tunnels?" Eren asked.

"At the other end of the lake, where it joins the lower lake. Probably half a chime."

Eren cursed. "Speed it up. We might have a man down."

Silence fell for a while, broken only by Jacko's heavy breathing.

Marian grinned as she skirted the camp and silently crept up behind one of the sentries on duty. In moments, she had incapacitated the man and dragged him into a clump of bushes. She continued on her circuit, passing Chryll as he dealt with another guard. The men sitting around the camp fire were discussing what they would do once they took the watch as if it was a foregone conclusion. She counted eight men, all armed in some shape or fashion though few had swords and most had cudgels or thick sticks.

One vocal idiot stood, waving his arms as he proclaimed, "Once we're inside that mansion, we'll be rich!"

Marian rolled her eyes. These men were buoyed on the idea of gold and jewels. They didn't realise the riches were in the land and what it could provide if nurtured. She stalked the next guard, and as he turned, clamped a hand over his mouth and dragged him into the bushes. Twisting, she kneed him in the groin and punched him in the face. His eyes rolled whitely as he folded to the floor with a soft grunt.

"What was that?" One of the men stood, peering into the bushes.

"Nothing, Jed. Don't be so jumpy," the man next to him replied.

Marian watched as Chryll crept up behind the man on the cart and then she stepped out of the bushes, saying, "Lads! What are you doing here all on your own?"

"Where did she come from?" Jed gasped, taking a step back.

"Doesn't matter, she's here," another ruffian said as he leered at Marian. "She wouldn't be here if she wasn't up for some fun."

Marian smiled. "Are you offering?" she asked as she walked into the circle. She ignored Chryll's strangled exclamation from behind the cart; he would no doubt be staring daggers at her. Marian beckoned Jed and his friend forward. The other men began betting on how long she would last.

The jeering expressions were soon wiped clean as Marian strode forward and jabbed her fist into Jed's face, snapping his head back. He stumbled, tripping over the fire and screeched as he landed in the flames. Marian spun, sweeping the other man's legs out from under him. She stabbed her stiffened fingers into his throat and left him gurgling on the ground, choking for breath.

"Who's next?" She glanced around the shocked expressions and smirked at the men dragging a screaming Jed off the fire. They tried to snuff the flames licking up his legs. Although a couple of men rose, they took a step back as Chryll loomed behind Marian's shoulder. She frowned at him. "Don't spoil my fun."

"This is not a game," Chryll replied, his voice a low growl.

"No, it's a lesson, and you're blunting my message."

"What message is that?" one of the men asked, unable to take his wide-eyed gaze off of her.

Marian bared her teeth. "That attacking the hand that feeds you is not good for your health."

The ground squelched underfoot as Eren, Denir, and their group approached the southern end of the middle lake.

"Was anyone with Parsill?" Eren asked after a while.

"One of my men, Stev," Jacko replied. "He's a good lad, knows his stuff. Once we reach the end of this track, we'll have to climb down the bank to the entrance."

The unit captain rapped out a couple of commands, and two men peeled off to scout ahead. The others slowed, fanned out, and then crept forward.

"The entrance is down there," Jacko whispered as he crouched next to Eren in the dripping-wet grass at the top of a steep slope. A low, booming sound echoed over and over. "The water pressure is building. The gates won't hold much longer, and then we'll have flooding in the lower reaches if they burst."

"Entrance clear," a low voice said.

"Forward," the captain snapped, and Eren waited as the men entered the tunnel.

"This doesn't feel right," Denir murmured, rising to peer behind him. "It's too easy. They must've known we'd come to check." He drifted back towards the trees.

A blinding flash lit the sky, briefly outlining Denir, who was staring at something behind him, before darkness concealed him again. A deep boom followed the flash and vibrated over the land. The swish of knives being drawn had Eren rising, his own knives ready, but he couldn't see anyone, not even Denir.

The door clanged shut, and muffled shouts came from within the tunnels. They had walked straight into a trap. Eren scowled as the men beat against the door. Gripping Jacko's arm, he tugged him back.

"We should let them out," Jacko replied. "We need them."

"I will. Stay here," Eren whispered. After pushing Jacko behind a boulder, he vanished into the night.

Jacko shuddered as the clang of steel, fast and furious, echoed through the trees. The silence was worse until the metallic chings and grunts started again. He huddled by the boulder and tried to convince himself to go and unlock the door. The trouble was, he wasn't a fighter. He had no idea how to fight, and there would be someone guarding that door. He just knew it.

He was startled when Eren returned, dragging a body. "Help him," Eren snarled, and then he disappeared again. Jacko realised the body was Denir, and he felt for a pulse. He breathed a sigh of relief when he found it and patted him down, trying to find the problem.

Jacko prayed to the Lady that Eren would be safe. He had the feeling that Eren was the only person between him and the attackers.

47

GUERLAIRE

DEEPWATER WATCH, VESPIRI

Lord Ricard's men were determined not to allow anyone across the land bridge, and as result, the fighting intensified. The clash of weapons echoed across the still water, but the lakes were proving to be an insurmountable barrier. As Guerlaire watched, more of Ricard's guards rushed to defend the bridge.

When a loud explosion split the air and shook the building, Lord Ricard rushed to the entrance and met one of his commanders.

"It's alright, my lord. It was all noise; there's no damage," the man said. "The explosion was on the other side of the lake."

"Are you sure?" Lord Ricard asked. "What about the land bridge?"

"I think it's an attempt to draw us away, but we're not moving. We've got enough men to deal with this rabble."

"Good. Keep me informed. I'll be with Captain Guerlaire."

Fonor's voice came out of the crystal. *"Captain?"*

"Report!" Guerlaire snapped.

"We've got one of the ringleaders. He's calling himself an ascendant. He's quite proud of the fact that they've taken Deepwater and have killed Lord Ricard."

"He is mistaken."

"That is a relief, though I won't tell him. Once I got him talking, he wouldn't stop. That explosion was a signal, I think."

"Keep the ascendant alive and in our hands. Once we're in control, bring him here."

"Yes, Captain." The crystal went silent, and Guerlaire heaved a sigh of relief.

"Denir? Report." Guerlaire's relief dissipated when there was no response. "Eren? Report." A chill slid down his spine when Eren didn't respond, either.

Lord Ricard hissed his breath out. "The sluice gates."

The commander met his eye. "Where are they? I'll despatch a unit."

"Jacko and some of Guerlaire's men went to check tunnel two on the lower lake," Lord Ricard said. "If you have the men, send two units. They must have met more trouble than we expected."

Guerlaire took a deep breath and then said, "Chryll? Report."

"Guerlaire?" Chryll replied. *"Apologies for the noise. We removed the persuasions, and the men changed their minds. They set the signal off early. We didn't expect it to be so loud."*

"And the purpose of the signal?"

"They'll think they have succeeded. The rest will think the fight is over and ease off. We thought it would be easier to overpower them if they thought the watch was lost."

"Excellent. Where are you?"

"We are to the north of the middle lake. We have the leader and his men. I expect Lord Ricard will want to speak to them. Maybe send us a unit to guard them? There's only Marian and I."

"They are on their way."

Lord Ricard's commander nodded. "The fight for the lake is over. They are throwing down their weapons and surrendering. I'll send some of our men on to help." He left to give his orders.

Guerlaire rubbed his face. He ought to ask the man his name.

Lord Ricard entered his study and gestured at the chair opposite. "Sit for a moment. There is nothing else you can do."

Guerlaire sat as Ricard sent for kafinee and food. An arifel appeared, landed on his lap, and butted Guerlaire's hand for a caress. Leyandrii wanted an update. "Tell her the watch is safe and I'm fine," he murmured as he rubbed the arifel's ear.

The arifel chittered and disappeared.

He was unhurt, but others weren't faring so well. He knew it in his gut. Sliding the crystal out of his pocket, he stared at it, willing Eren or Denir to speak to him.

When Chryll and Marian strode into the study, Guerlaire was still sitting there, staring into his mug of kafinee.

"What's happened?" Chryll asked immediately.

Guerlaire grimaced. "We lost contact with Eren and Denir. They went down to the sluice gates. I'm still awaiting word."

"And Fonor and Royer?"

"They caught an ascendant. They are bringing him here."

"I'll go and see what's happened to the others," Chryll said and strode back out the door before Guerlaire could stop him. Marian hurried after him.

Eren knew there were at least two more attackers between him and the tunnel entrance, though the fact that the two scouts were missing was worrying; there could be more. He tied a piece of his shirt around the stab wound in his arm, pulling the knot tight with his teeth. He flexed his hand, trying to work out the tingles.

Maybe it would be better to draw the guard out by the entrance. If he could get the door open, then he would have some help. That would be worth the risk. He couldn't protect Jacko and Denir at the same time.

Creeping through the undergrowth, he couldn't see where the man was concealed. He must have been close by to wedge the door shut so quickly. He stilled, closing his eyes and listening intently. The low booming had stopped. Hopefully, that meant they had fixed the sluice gates from within the tunnel. The guards had stopped trying to batter the door down. He hoped they had found Parsill and the engineer.

The night was still. Water dripped, the soft hoot of an owl floated on the air, and a small creature rustled in the bushes. A louder rustle. Eren spun, and his knife sliced air and skin as a man grunted and lurched back.

"Bastard," the man said as Eren lunged forward. The man gave ground, and then they were suddenly tumbling down a steep slope, and Eren was trying to avoid stabbing himself. He smashed against the tunnel entrance and gasped as pain exploded across his back.

Struggling to his feet, he fumbled with the latch. Something had been shoved through it so tightly that he couldn't budge it. He slid his dagger behind the lock and tried it lever it off. The lock groaned, and then his blade snapped.

He stared at the broken knife and then forced the broken end behind the lock and heaved again. His shoulder screamed in agony, and black spots filled his vision. His blade snapped again, and he fell backwards.

A shining blade descended towards him, and he flung up an arm, but he had lost his daggers. He rolled, and the blade skimmed his hip—a burning strike like fire. Without thought, he rolled back over the blade and thrust his hands up to stop the downward momentum of a second knife.

Eren's life flashed before him. His mother and father, his sister—he would miss them all. His hands shook; the effort was almost too much. Pain consumed him, and he gritted his teeth, straining to push the blade back.

Then the knife was gone, and he was surrounded by people. Lots of people. Strange voices. And then one he knew.

"Eren? By the Lady, Eren? Can you hear me?" Parsill bent over him and hugged him tightly. Rocked him. Pain bloomed through his body. He was still alive.

"Parsill?" Eren gasped, his chest heaving. "Are you hurt?"

"Just a bump on the head. I'll be fine. Where are you hurt? I can see it in your face. You're shockingly pale."

"Collarbone, I think," Eren replied.

"I'm so sorry. I'm making it worse, aren't I?"

"Don't care. I'm just glad you got the door open."

"Thanks to you."

"There's a crystal in my pocket. Call Guerlaire. He'll be worried."

***

"You need a larger strike team," Leyandrii said as she coaxed Guerlaire to sit on the settee. Her concern washed over him.

The clean-up in Deepwater had taken longer than expected. The betrayal was deeper than Ricard had realised, and he had been distraught that some of his own men had helped the ascendant. Guerlaire had spent most of his time helping to clear persuasions and teaching Ricard's officers how to mentally shield.

Parsill and Severen had their hands full working through the whole watch. Guerlaire sighed. What about the rest of Remargaren?

"And you need personal guards," Guerlaire replied as he let her push him back so that he lay with his head on the cushion.

"If I consider creating my own guards, will you consider a larger team?"

Guerlaire smiled as she settled beside him. He tucked her close to his body, and her warmth soothed his tense muscles. "Yes."

He inhaled the scent of roses and knew Leyandrii was meddling with his emotions, but she had agreed to the personal guards, and that was all that mattered.

"Good. Eren and Denir are recovering. Deepwater is safe. We have our first insight into Ascendant thinking and how they intend to try and divide us, undermine us."

"Which we will prevent," he replied, concentrating on keeping his eyes open.

"Birler is much better, and the Atolea have adopted him. Sodera Arkan assures me they will track down who attacked Birler and find out why." Leyandrii wrinkled her brow. "Do you think Clary was behind the attack? He seems to be the main influence behind the Ascendants."

"It wouldn't surprise me. Clary has this ridiculous fixation on Birler, though how he knew where Birler would be is beyond me."

"Opportunistic, maybe?"

"Let's hope so. Birler seems to make an impact no matter where we assign him."

"How does he manage to fit in so seamlessly wherever he goes?"

"That boy is loaded with charm. He would make a great diplomat if he didn't find so much trouble."

"True." Leyandrii twirled her fingers in the tuft of Guerlaire's chest hair peeping out of his open shirt, and she bent to kiss his neck. "Actually, that is a really good idea. I think Birler would make an excellent diplomat. I think a trip to Elothia may be a good next step after Terolia. Make sure he meets all the key players."

"And Birtoli after that?"

"Of course."

Guerlaire smiled, sinking into her embrace, his limbs heavy, his mind drifting. What was it he had been going to say? Ah, yes. "I think that will be more of a break, if Serill's reports are anything to go by."

"By then, I am sure he will need one." Leyandrii peeked up at him from under her lashes. "And maybe we'll deserve a holiday, too."

"I am sure we will," Guerlaire murmured as he held her close and inhaled her intoxicating scent.

48

BIRLER

MISTRA, TEROLIA

It took another week of Birler tottering around the Atolean camp before he could finally stand upright on his own. He looked down at the black tunic and trousers he wore, edged in blue and red like the Sodera's. He looked like a Terolian, except for his pale skin, but given a little sun, he would blend in completely. His blue eyes were dark enough to pass for black.

His sword and bow were stacked against his saddlebags, along with his sling and the small bag of stones. He stared at them for a moment, and then picked up his canteen and went in search of Tiv'erna.

He found him sparring with another man. They were stripped to the waist, and their bronzed skin gleamed with sweat as they moved through a graceful dance, their muscles stretching as they thrust and parried. Birler sat in the shade and watched. His respect grew as the moves sped up and their scimitars flashed in the sunlight. He could not have survived for long against those stunning blows.

Apeiron was calling him, and he felt the need to stretch. His muscles were tired and tight. Slowly standing, he looked around him. Tiv'erna was focussed on his practice, and no others were present. He would do *Acknowledgement* and see how that went. He shrugged out of his tunic, folded it neatly, and placed it on his canteen. Carefully stretching, he tested the stitches in his side.

He began slowly, going through the motions, his muscles warming and stretching as he turned. His tension eased as he focussed on each muscle, aligning his body and soothing the stress. The sounds of Tiv'erna's sparring faded as he concentrated. He moved straight into *Awareness* without opening his eyes, intent on inner balance. He swivelled to a close and opened his eyes.

He took in a deep breath as he realised he had gained an audience. Laughing, he stooped to pick up his canteen; he took a long swallow and shook out his arms. Tiv'erna and his sparring partner stood watching him with their arms crossed and biceps bulging.

"What was that you were doing?" Tiv'erna asked with a speculative expression in his eyes.

"It's called Apeiron," Birler said, shrugging back into his tunic. "The disciplines of the air. It helps align the body with the mind."

"So I see. I will teach you to defend against the scimitar if you will teach me Apeiron."

Birler bowed, his hand on heart. "It would be my honour."

"Good." Tiv'erna grinned. "But enough for today. We begin tomorrow. Let me change, and I will introduce you to Mistra."

Birler returned to his tent, picked up his sling, and strapped on his sword, and after topping up his canteen, he checked in with Kafinee. She was happily rummaging for Baliweed, picketed between Tiv'erna's black stallion and an elegant white stallion, just as tall and powerful, with a long, flowing tail. Birler stopped to say hello, offering his hand and standing near enough for the white stallion to greet or ignore him. The stallion stared at him with liquid brown eyes edged with long, dark lashes before he breathed out over Birler's hand and tossed his head.

Birler laughed. "Greetings, beautiful one."

"I see you have met Arkan's Darian." Tiv'erna's voice came from behind him. "Not many get too close to him. He can be, shall we say, temperamental?"

The white stallion snorted his disdain, and Birler laughed again. He patted Kafinee's rump. "Be good," he said as he left with Tiv'erna. "Where's Adil?"

"He asked to go out on patrol. He wanted to be of use, I think, whilst you recovered. It's done him good."

"We've been here too long. We should have checked Mistra and moved on to Livia by now." Birler looked around the low stone buildings and the straight streets leading into the central market square. His neck prickled. They were being watched.

"Arkan wishes to speak with you before you leave," Tiv'erna said. "There is the matter of the life debt to be settled. Now that you are recovered, the sentence should be declared."

"Did you discover why that man attacked me?"

"That is what Arkan wishes to discuss with you."

"I didn't recognise him."

"I wouldn't expect you to, but you hold the life debt. He attacked you; therefore, you have the right to request his life in payment."

Birler shuddered. He wasn't sure he could sentence a man to death in the cold light of day. It was very different in the heat of battle when you were defending yourself. "I see your men are following us. Are you expecting me to be attacked again?"

Tiv'erna's lips twitched. "They will be most disappointed that you spotted them; they are some of our best."

"They are very good," Birler conceded with a grin.

"Just not good enough," Tiv'erna muttered, flicking his fingers out from his side. Two men smoothly fell in behind them, their wicked scimitars, a warning in themselves, strapped to their waists. Their fluid movement matched Tiv'erna's, predators in waiting, just to protect him.

Mistra was a small town: a collection of red stone buildings situated around a market square. Empty stalls marked the trading posts. Wooden structures crisscrossed the alleyways, covered in dried-out palm leaves, providing sun-pocked shade. Rickety chairs sat in the dust, awaiting the evening customers, who would appear with the cooling air. Golden sands spread out in all directions.

"Did Adil ask if anyone had gone missing?"

"The Medera did. She spoke with the village elders and passed on your warning. They say no one of that description has asked to speak here. They do not believe anyone is missing."

"But?"

"It is too quiet. There are usually more people on the streets. Even at this time of day."

Birler paused, staring around the square. It was deserted except for a shopkeeper sweeping sand out of the doorway. Even the soft swish of the broom was audible from across the square. "Is there a temple here? A Lady's temple?"

"Of course. It is to the north of the town, on the outskirts."

"Not in the centre?"

"It's in the older part; the town has expanded south around the growing market area." Tiv'erna led the way through the shaded alleys; his men watched, alert and ready.

Birler's steps quickened as the small domed temple came

into view. A stone fountain stood in the open space before it, with water tinkling into a basin. A grey stone statue of the Lady held out flowers to those passing by. The temple doors were open, its dim interior inviting, and Birler ducked inside the low entrance. His shoulders dropped as he relaxed in the subdued light, and Tiv'erna hovered in the entrance, watching as Birler knelt before the altar. The stone shimmered, and Birler patted it as he bent his head.

Birler gave his thanks to the Lady for watching over him. He grimaced as she scolded him in return. *"Enough, my Lady. I'm fine. The Atolea protect me now. I thank you for Ren's company. She was very diligent."*

"Be careful, Birler. Observe and report, no more."

"Yes, my Lady."

Birler rose and bowed to the altar before leaving. Tiv'erna leaned against the door frame, filling the doorway.

"You don't enter the temple?" Birler asked.

"We have no need of stone to find the Lady. The moon is our temple and travels with us always."

Birler was not surprised. "I find she hears me better when I visit." He made a face. "Though that is not always a good thing, of course; she was most upset with me."

Tiv'erna clearly heard the "pfft" in the air, as did his men.

"See." Birler grinned as he led the surprised men back through the streets. A subtle tug in his mind made him veer off down a shaded alley, and after following the curve of a wall, he rested his hand against a wooden door. The blue paint had peeled off in the heat, leaving warped grey planks.

Birler pushed the door open. It creaked stiffly on corroded hinges as Tiv'erna came up behind him. "Birler, what are you doing?"

"Hush," Birler replied as he knelt by the door. "We mean you no harm; we came to help. I have water." He held out his canteen.

Tiv'erna peered over his head, trying to see who Birler was speaking to.

A small child scuttled out of the shadows and grabbed the canteen. She retreated just as fast, her dark eyes wide with fear. Birler shuffled through the door and sat on the baked-mud floor. He could just make out the shapes of three children in the dim light, and a larger form lay on the ground.

The girl was trying to get her mother to drink the water, but Birler knew they were too late. "I am sorry, but she is with the Lady now."

The girl stopped her efforts and slumped, clutching the canteen in her hands. One of the smaller children began to sniffle.

"What is your name?"

"Lily."

"Lily, that's a nice name. Where is your father?"

"He left. He said he would earn money in the mines; the tall man said so."

"The tall man?"

"The man who came to speak in the square. He offered work for coin."

"When did your father leave?"

Lily shrugged. "Two full moons or more. Kayer went after him to bring him back, but she hasn't come back, either."

"Kayer?"

"My eldest sister."

"How old are you Lily?"

"Twelve."

"And are these your brother and sister?"

"Yes, Daniel and Mattie."

"The Lady wants you to come with me now. She'll look after you until we find Kayer and your father."

Lily considered him, and Birler waited. Then she sighed as she looked at her brother and sister. She didn't really have much choice. "You'll look for Kayer?"

"I promise."

She wrinkled her nose at him as if she didn't trust promises, and he smiled.

"Alright." She rose, tugging the little ones with her. Birler remained seated. The smallest was just a baby, barely tottering. She had large black eyes in a brown face, tear-stained and sad. Birler opened his arms, and the baby crawled into his lap. He cuddled her, and she snuffled against his chest. Lily stood watching him, holding Daniel's hand. Tiv'erna shifted in the doorway, and Lily reared back, dragging her brother with her.

Birler raised his hand. "He is my friend. He will protect you."

Lily hesitantly returned to the door and stared up at the big man. Tiv'erna smiled at her, but she wasn't reassured.

Birler chuckled. "Come, let us find you some food. Will you carry my canteen for me?"

Lily nodded, looping the strap over her shoulder. She firmly gripped Birler's hand as he rose with the baby in his arms. Burdened with children, he led them out of the house.

Tiv'erna instructed one of his men to find out who they were and to deal with the body before he closed the door behind Birler and followed the strange procession up the road. His gaze dwelled on Birler as they walked, and a small smile hovered over his mouth.

Surprising Tiv'erna, Birler took them to one of Tiv'erna's aunts and asked her to look after them whilst he found their family. The young woman took the baby immediately and held her hand out to Lily. "Shall we wash up and find some dinner?"

Lily stared at Birler. "You won't forget us?"

"Of course not. I'll find Kayer for you. But for me to do that, you need to stay here with Jem'ima for a little while. Is that alright?"

Lily nodded reluctantly and then hugged him around the waist. "Thank you."

"Thank the Lady, little one; she is watching over you," Birler replied, hugging her gently. He watched them trail forlornly after Jem'ima, his heart aching for them. He shook the sadness off and turned to Tiv'erna. "Who was it you said the Medera spoke to in Mistra?"

Tiv'erna blinked at him. "Umm, you'd have to ask her."

"I will," Birler said, striding off towards the Medera's tent.

Tiv'erna caught up with him. "Birler, wait. You can't just barge into her tent."

"Could you ask her, then?"

Tiv'erna stared at him for a moment and then shrugged. "Wait here," he said as he ducked into the tent. He was back out almost immediately. "Elders Ber'ander and Mis'ille."

Birler detoured to his tent and picked up his daggers to slot into his belt. Tiv'erna's eye brows rose. "What are you going do?"

"Let's go make a house visit."

"Arkan wants to speak with you."

"Later."

Tiv'erna gripped his arm. "A man's life hangs in the balance. Fer'arne is due to be banished in the morning if the sentence is not passed. A life debt cannot be delayed more than twelve nights."

Birler stilled. "What is a life debt?"

"It is a debt that must be paid with blood, as the debtor caused injury, so the injured can demand payment."

"What do you mean, paid with blood? You mean his death?"

"A life debt is a life for a life. Either a summary execution or banishment. A blood debt is punishment by whipping. If he still lives a day after the whipping, he may receive treatment."

Birler stared at him. "When will Arkan speak to me?"

"Now, if you will."

"Fer'arne is your cousin, isn't he?

"Yes. My father's brother's son."

"How old is he?"

"Twenty."

Birler closed his eyes and took a deep breath. Arkan would not be lenient; he couldn't be. He followed Tiv'erna to a smaller tent behind the Medera's vaulted canopy. Tiv'erna raised the flap, and Birler ducked in, aware of Tiv'erna's sudden tension.

Arkan was seated on a large cushion studying a map spread out on his lap. He looked up as Birler entered and folded the map up. His face was inscrutable, emotionless. "Please, sit. I am glad to see you recovered."

"I thank you for your care; your swift reaction saved my life."

"We were fortunate I recognised the aroma. Not all poisons are so obvious. But even if I hadn't, the Lady was watching over you."

"But still, your action gave her the time to reach me, and I thank you for it."

Arkan waved his thanks away.

"Have you spoken with Fer'arne?" Birler asked.

"At great length."

"And his reason for attacking me?"

Arkan sighed. "He says he just wanted to frighten you off. You were a usurper, a thief. He is convinced you stole the Darian."

"He didn't intend to kill me?"

"He says not."

"You don't believe him?"

"Let us say I doubt his word. Fer'arne is a skilled warrior; he trained with my son. He would find it easier to kill than not."

"Where did he get the knife from?"

"Fer'arne said he found it outside his tent. He thought someone was helping him."

"Why did he think that?"

"He is under the impression that he isn't the only one who believes you are leading us astray."

Birler raised his eyebrows. "Leading you astray? From what?"

"Family Law."

Birler stared at him, and Arkan's lips tightened. "I see you are as surprised as I am."

"More so. I don't even know what your Family Law is, let alone know how to lead you away from it. Who else believes as he does?"

"He won't say."

"Won't or can't?"

Arkan narrowed his eyes. "What do you mean, can't?"

"I think we are seeing *Mentiserium* in action."

"You mean Fer'arne has been enspelled?"

Birler shrugged. "From what I understand, Fer'arne is one of your most skilled fighters, a match for Tiv'erna, even. Your nephew is much loved and respected. His actions are unexpected and shocking; you would never have believed him capable of such betrayal. Yet, here we are. His hand held the knife, but I live. He failed when you said he could not have.

"The elders lied to your Medera. A man was in Mistra, offering work for coin. He persuaded the men of this town to go with him to mine the Telusion Mountains. There is a man, possibly more than one, stealing people from under your noses, leaving families destitute and bereft." Birler paused in thought. "I want to speak with Fer'arne."

"Why?"

"I need to understand what happened, and he may speak more freely to me."

Arkan stared at him and then nodded. He rose with fluid grace and led the way out of the tent and across the camp. A black tent had been erected on the very edge of the camp behind the picket line, as far from the family as possible. A guard stood at the entrance. Arkan lifted the flap and gestured Birler in. He followed, dropping the flap behind him. Birler's eyes adjusted to the dim light. A wooden pole held the tent upright in the centre, and chained to the post was a dejected young man. His eyes were sunken, his face gaunt. He struggled to his feet as he saw Arkan enter.

"Uncle," he began, but his voice died as he recognised Birler, and all colour drained from his face and left him a sickly beige as his shoulders drooped.

"Birler holds the life debt; your life is in his hands. I suggest you speak truthfully, for his is the final word." Arkan nodded at Birler and stepped into the shadows.

Birler took a moment to observe Fer'arne. He was slighter than Tiv'erna, but not by much. Curly blue-black hair framed a strong face, currently slack with horror. Black eyes stared at him, filled with self-loathing and dread.

"Please, sit," Birler said, keeping his voice gentle. The man stood awkwardly, the chains not long enough for his tall frame to stand upright.

The man folded at his word and huddled against the post.

"Do you know who I am?" Birler asked.

Fer'arne nodded.

"You understand what you did?"

Fer'arne nodded.

"Do you understand why you did it?"

Fer'arne began to nod and then stilled.

"Why don't you tell me what you did."

There was silence. The faint sound of children playing, their voices high with excitement, penetrated the tent—a reminder of life in the midst of this man's abject misery.

"This is your chance to justify your actions, to plead for your life."

"I tried to kill you. I deserve the punishment." Fer'arne's voice was low and painfully controlled.

"Do you remember who suggested you kill me?"

Fer'arne started to speak a name and gagged.

"It wasn't your idea, was it?" Birler continued as if he hadn't noticed. "I'd not even been here a day. You couldn't know who I was or why I was here."

Fer'arne shook his head.

"And you would never use poison, would you?"

Fer'arne screwed his face up in disgust.

"Terolians don't use poison, do they? It is dishonourable and cowardly to use poison. Only someone without honour would stoop to poisoning, especially against a guest of the tent."

Fer'arne closed his eyes, his face taut as he struggled against the compulsion.

"But you have honour, don't you, Fer'arne? You revere your mother and father and your family. Tiv'erna is like a brother to you, isn't he? You love your cousins and your aunts and uncles."

Tears leaked down Fer'arne's face.

"You tried to fight it, didn't you? I was a guest of the tent. Killing me would break your family's honour. You deliberately mistimed your thrust. Only, you didn't realise the blade was coated with poison. You deliberately fouled the blade in my robe so that others could drag you off me. You sacrificed your life for mine."

Fer'arne collapsed. He shook uncontrollably. Birler reached for him and drew him into his arms. "The Lady thanks you, Fer'arne, for saving my life." Birler felt the blessing percolate through him and into Fer'arne.

Fer'arne relaxed in Birler's arms and forced the words out: "It was Ger'atta."

Birler looked up and met Arkan's eyes. The compassion in the man's eyes made Birler want to weep. He watched as anger replaced compassion, and Arkan's expression snapped shut as he digested the name.

49

TIV'ERNA

TEROLIA

Once Arkan left the tent, Tiv'erna hurried to unshackle his cousin. His fingers shook as he struggled with the chains. His relief at Fer'arne's salvation overwhelmed him, and he hugged him close. His tears mixed with Fer'arne's as he rocked his overwrought cousin. He was dimly aware of Birler leaving, but he was unable to free himself from Fer'arne's vice-like grip. They had both accepted his death, had hardened themselves against further despair, and the sudden relief had undone them both.

It wasn't until Healer Aranna and Fer'arne's parents arrived that he managed to get Fer'arne to release him. Tiv'erna escorted Fer'arne to his parents' tent, where Fer'arne had a complete collapse, and Aranna ended up sedating him.

Tiv'erna went in search of Birler. He found him on the edge of the camp, staring up at the moon. His face was bathed in the silver light, still and serene. A man at prayer. Tiv'erna sat at a distance and waited, offering his own thanks.

His mind spun as he grappled with the release of all the gut-wrenching fear and tension that had built over the last week. His hands trembled, and his throat tightened with the strength of his emotions. He concentrated on breathing deeply in an attempt to regain control. The relief to have his cousin back was overwhelming, and it was all thanks to the man his cousin had tried to kill. Who was he? Quiet and unassuming, he strode through Terolia, changing lives without even trying.

A chime passed before Birler stirred, and still, Tiv'erna waited patiently. The tranquility that Birler emanated soothed Tiv'erna and he relaxed, spending the time observing Birler, from the black hair curling into his nape to the high cheekbones gilded by the moon's light. He was a slender man, neat and tidy, with lean, smooth muscles; the power was deceptive, but it was there all the same. He recognised Birler's weariness as he rose, his usual lithe movements sluggish.

"I'm sorry. I didn't realise you were there," Birler said. "You should have said."

"I didn't want to intrude."

Birler smiled. "It wouldn't have been an intrusion."

"What did you do, Birler? How did you clear Fer'arne's name?"

"It was obvious your cousin would never have betrayed his family willingly. And for poison to be used, it had to be someone outside of the Families influencing him. You would never use poison. I considered who would have most to gain to rip your family apart, for your uncle would not have been able to stand by and see his son banished or executed. They would have been banished alongside him, which would have distressed your father and weakened his authority in the eyes of the other Families.

"It wasn't enough to explain this; your father had to see

it. He was walking a fine line between favouritism and impartiality. The bane of leadership. If I could show him that Fer'arne had tried to resist, that his honour had won through, your father could forgive him."

"How could you know that Fer'arne tried to resist?"

"He is your cousin."

Tiv'erna's breath caught at the sincerity in Birler's voice. "How could you know us so well in such a short amount of time? You knew nothing of Family Law when you arrived."

"I learn fast," Birler said, his dark eyes twinkling in the flame of the torches.

"Thank you, Birler, for saving my family." Tiv'erna didn't know what else to say, but Birler seemed to understand.

"We haven't saved them yet. Tomorrow, we need to speak to the elders, and then we go to Melila."

"Melila? I thought you wanted to go to Livia?"

"Livia will be the same as here. People are disappearing, and no one has noticed. Where could they be hidden and why?" Birler rubbed his eyes. "Whatever is happening must be happening in the mountains, out of sight, and Melila is the closest village to the Telusion Mountains."

"We will be coming with you."

"You don't know how glad I am that you said that, for I am sure I would get completely lost trying to find Melila on my own."

"No, you wouldn't, Birler. Somehow, I think you will always find whatever it is you are looking for. But for now, I think all you need to search for is your bed."

The next morning, Tiv'erna and Per'ilta escorted Birler to see the elders. Tiv'erna explained in a low voice that they had been unable to find Ger'atta. The man who acted as the

Family liaison with the elders had disappeared. Arkan was quietly furious and decreed he be found dead or alive. A quietly furious Arkan was to be avoided, as was his Darian, who reflected his rider's emotions. Birler could feel the crackling anger from the other side of the camp and stayed away.

The offices of the village elders were in the largest red stone building in the market square. Birler entered the dim interior and paused beside the desk of a young clerk. He glanced up at Birler and then dropped his eyes, fidgeting with his quill.

"I'm here to see either Elder Ber'ander or Elder Mis'ille. I understand they hold open appointments today."

"Their appointments are full," the man said, closing the ledger.

"Are they? And yet their waiting rooms are empty."

"I-It's a brief interlude; it often happens."

"I'm sure, and yet I have information about some young children recently made homeless. Who should I speak to regarding that?"

"Umm, that would be Elder Mis'ille."

"Who is not available. When will she be available?"

"Not until next week."

"May I book an appointment for next week?"

"Of course. Your name?"

"Ranger Birler of Greens."

The man's quill hovered over the appointment book. "Who?" He looked up and met Birler's indigo eyes, and he swallowed. "Ah, umm, you will still be here next week?"

"Of course. If I have an appointment, I will keep it. The Lady would expect me to treat her representatives with respect."

"Eleventh chime, Decu 27?" the man suggested.

"Perfect, I thank you for your help." Birler left before the clerk could change his mind. He picked up Tiv'erna and

Per'ilta who were lounging at the door. "No luck. I couldn't get an appointment until next week. Do you think your aunt will able to hang on to the kids until then?"

Per'ilta snorted. "You'll be lucky to prise them out of her clutches. Be warned: the longer you leave them, the less likely it is that she will give them up."

"Ought I to offer some money for their keep? I don't like to assume."

"For Lady's sake, don't, Birler. The Family will look after them. The Medera would be mortally offended if she found out."

"But I am not Family, and they are my responsibility until I find Kayer."

"Of course you are Family, Birler. Yannis and Arkan already pronounced it. And anyway, they are children of Terolia. They are our responsibility, not yours."

"What does that mean, they pronounced it?"

Per'ilta chuckled, and Tiv'erna glared at him. "They proclaimed you a member of the Atolean Family, to be offered comfort and protection whenever you need it."

"Does that mean I am bound by Family Law, too?"

"Probably, though the Lady claims you first, so maybe not so much. I think they more intended it as an offer of protection. You can call on us at any time if you need help."

"Sounds a bit one-sided. What do you get out of it?"

Per'ilta rolled his eyes. "You just don't get it, do you? You've already paid your dues for life; you were almost killed on our watch. We owe you your life, and then you saved one of ours, so we owe you another life. Birler, there is nothing the Atolea won't do for you. We are proud to call you brother."

"Oh." Tears pricked the corners of Birler's eyes at the idea that these people wanted to call him family. Suddenly, he had more families than he knew what to do with.

Tiv'erna grinned. "Come on, brother. Let's get you some food. Your kids probably want to see you as well. I know young Lily was starting to get worried, and then we need to plan our trip to Melila."

Birler chuckled as they walked down the street, back to the Atolean camp, where Lily was indeed on the lookout for him. Birler gave her a swift hug and went to visit the little family. Jem'ima was agreeable to looking after the children and shooed him away when he asked if they needed anything. Daniel had found friends his own age, and the baby was happily snuggled in Jem'ima's arms. Only Lily seemed unsettled. Birler tucked Lily's hand in his arm and took her to see Kafinee.

"I leave tomorrow to go search for Kayer," he said as he settled on a bale of straw.

Lily petted Kafinee and then gave him a worried glance. "What if you don't come back, like them?"

"Then Jem'ima will look after you. The Atoleans will welcome you into their Family."

"What if we don't want to be Atolean?"

"What *do* you want to be?"

Lily leaned against Kafinee. "If I can't have Kayer, then I want to be with you."

"I'm sorry, Lily, but I don't have a steady home. I am a ranger. I travel where the Lady assigns me. I am no haven for you and your family."

"You came and found us when no one else did."

"The Atoleans are my family; they will offer you a home if I ask them. They would be willing to take you all in. Don't you like it here?"

"They'll take us far away, to places we don't know. Away from my father and Kayer. We won't have a house, a home."

"I will speak with the Mistra elders on my return. If they offer you a home in Mistra, would you prefer to stay here?"

"I don't know."

"Let's wait until I return. We can see what your options are then. Don't worry so. No matter what, we will keep you all together. And who knows? Travelling around the country could be fun. You'll learn to ride and look after horses; you'll meet lots of different people. You get to eat outside, and you can learn weapons skills if you want. I saw some of the girls having lessons the other day."

Lily's face brightened. "Kayer would love it here."

"Tell me about Kayer. How old is she?"

"She's seventeen. She is good with a blade. My father taught her so she could defend herself because she is really pretty … well, she's beautiful."

Birler grinned at the young girl before him. Big black eyes watched him from a smooth brown complexion, now that it was clean, and her long black hair was tied back off her rounded face, not yet settled into the elegant lines she would one day have. "If she is anything like you, then I can see she would be beautiful, and I suggest you learn how to use a blade whilst you have the chance, so you can protect yourself, too, if necessary. Though the Atolea will be your family if you wish, and they will protect you."

Lily blushed at the compliment, but she nodded thoughtfully, turning the idea over in her head. A soft chime resonated through the camp. "Time to eat," Birler said, rising from his bale of straw. "Let's find the others."

Lily dragged Birler to the children's end of the table, and Birler happily spent a raucous dinner with the kids, teasing them mercilessly as they argued about the benefits of a sling against a dagger. Birler ended up demonstrating his sling after dinner, and the kids all clamoured for one of their own.

Birler held up his hands. "I will show Lily how to make one, and then she will show you. You will have to find your own materials to make your sling. You should always be able to replace your sling if you lose it. I will do this on one condition and one condition only."

He glared around the children, and they watched him solemnly. Birler's lips twitched. "At no time are you allowed to aim your stones at people or animals. You practise safely, targeting wood or rocks, understood? Once you can hit them, we will move on to moving targets. Agreed?"

All the children nodded furiously. "Very well. I will show Lily, and she will show you. Now, go and play."

He sat cross-legged in the sand with Lily and patiently explained how he had made his sling. She picked it up quickly and was soon making her own. "Whenever you see smooth, round stones, pick them up. Get into the habit because you never know when you might need them. And out there, they are scarce; it's all just sand," Birler said, scanning the rolling dunes that surrounded Mistra.

"What if there isn't any wood?"

"Cloth works just as well; you just need a more defined flick of the wrist to release the stone. A wood frame is easiest to learn with, and there is plenty of wood around here. You need to strengthen your wrists before you move on to other types. This will help with your knife-throwing as well; it's all a similar motion."

Lily giggled. "My mother would've had a fit if she knew we were doing this."

"That's what mothers are for. They are supposed to worry, but she would have been proud, too."

"Yeah," Lily said, looking down at her sling, her hair sliding forward out of its ribbon. "Come back, Birler, please?"

"Lady willing," Birler replied, knowing better than to promise.

Later that evening, Birler sat with Yannis and Arkan in their tent.

"The Lady asked for a Family conclave to be called," Yannis said. "I see why now. Once we address this immediate problem, I will arrange the meeting. This is a threat that affects us all."

"Medera, I kept meaning to ask," Birler said. "Was Lady Leyandrii actually here? Or did I dream her?"

"You are family now, Birler. Call us by our names." Yannis chuckled at his surprised expression. "The Lady was here. She was most concerned about you."

Birler wrinkled his brow, unsure how to respond to that. "She knows all her rangers. She takes great interest in our work."

"If you say so," Arkan said.

Tiv'erna was a welcome distraction as he joined them, spreading out the map of Eastern Terolia.

Birler looked over the map, which was scarily bare of features. "We go to Melila and then onto Lez. But I think what we are looking for will be in the mountains themselves. Lily said her father was going to earn coin by mining; that must mean he had gone to the Telusions. Could you send word up to Ramila and see if Lorill found any signs of *Mentiserium*?" He asked. "Though, I doubt he has. Ramila is too far north, and it would be too noticeable to ship people from up there."

"Of course," Arkan replied. "We will remain encamped here until you return. We have sent out patrols to Livia and Marmera, but we won't hear back from them for a few days yet." Arkan frowned at the map. "Selir is too far east, but it might be worth checking the port. If they are mining, they must be mining for something. And who is it that is mining?" Arkan rubbed his chin, thinking for a moment, and then continued. "Those mountains belong to Terolia. The more I think about it, the less I like it. Once we confirm Ger'atta is not in Mistra, I think we will follow you to Melila. I will be more comfortable being able to offer support if you need it. I'll send word to the Kiker and the Solari just in case."

Birler breathed out a sigh of relief. Having Arkan behind him would tip the balance. He ran his hand through his hair. "Thank you. So, we'll have Tiv'erna and Nir'inne's patrols? That's eight men plus myself and Adil?"

Arkan nodded. "Birler, don't rush into anything, observation only. If you find where our people are being taken, send word and wait for us to arrive."

"Of course. We'll be careful. We don't know what we are riding into. Umm, Yannis, the children—if something should happen, you will take care of them for me, won't you?"

"Birler, as if you have to ask. You know we will. They are already part of the family."

"Lily isn't completely sure. She can't equate travelling with a home. She is willing to be converted, but she has only ever known a fixed house as home, and she feels lost and scared. I think the younger ones will adapt more easily. I have an appointment with Elder Mis'ille at eleventh chime on Decu 27 to see what they can offer them. If I'm not back by then, can someone keep my appointment? I would prefer they stay with you if I can't find Kayer, but we should offer Lily the choice."

"Of course," Yannis reassured him.

"Teaching the kids how to make slings was an interesting move," Arkan said, leaning back on his cushion.

"It will strengthen their wrists, make them ready for knife throwing. It's much the same movement. Oh and I warned them, if any of them aim at other people or animals, their slings will be confiscated."

"They will just make another," Arkan said with a glimmer of a smile.

Birler laughed. "All good practice."

. . .

The camp was a mass of men and horses the next morning as the fiery sun began its daily ascent. Birler checked both his water canteens were full and securely fastened to Kafinee's saddle. He was dressed in black travelling robes. He only had his weapons, a change of underclothes, and his travel supplies. This was a patrol. The comforts would be left with the caravan.

Birler had written up a report for Lord Mayer and despatched it with one of Arkan's riders. He had also taken the time to write to Warren and Melis, apologising for not making it home as promised. He didn't know when he would return from Terolia, but when he did, he promised to visit. Wondering if Tagerill had made it home, Birler filled his letter with descriptions of the Atolea and his admiration for the way they lived. He waxed lyrical about the Darians and the fact that Kafinee was one, too. She was fine, rounding nicely, and would soon be ready for pasture.

Leaving his letter with Yannis for forwarding, he mounted up, one of many robed riders soon lost in the patrol. The only distinguishing feature was his bow, which he was loath to leave behind, but Tiv'erna had figured out a way to strap it under his leg so it wasn't so obvious.

"Kafinee will be alright, won't she? She is nearing her time. I had intended to rest her up by the turn of the year. That's only a few weeks away."

"Stop fussing. I'll be fine," Kafinee snapped. *"Anyone would think a horse hasn't foaled before."*

"Yes, but you're carrying me, and I am not light."

"She'll be fine for a few more weeks. The exercise will do her good. Standing around would be worse," Tiv'erna reassured him.

"See? stop fussing," she said, rolling her eyes and glad to be on the road with him again.

Birler checked the position of the rising sun and smiled

as they headed directly for it. He shielded his face with his hood and followed behind Tiv'erna, glad to be in his company. Adil had bounced past him, happily comfortable as part of the patrol, unrecognisable as the young ranger who had accompanied him. Birler had to admit that he was probably unrecognisable, too; his skin had tanned, even though he had covered up as much as possible. The constant sun beating down found its way. His hair had lightened as well, though it was still dark enough for him to pass as a Terolian.

He raised his face long enough to squint around. Rolling sand dunes reached out in all directions, meeting a clear blue sky, and he tugged his hood forward and trusted Tiv'erna to lead the way. Melila was two days' travel, possibly three. It was still very hot, even though it was supposed to be cooling a few degrees in the winter months; it didn't seem to be happening this year. It felt just as hot as when he had first arrived.

Birler thought he had acclimatised to the heat, but living in camp was very different to travelling on horseback under the baking sun. He huddled in his robes and endured.

Tiv'erna called a halt as the sun reached the high point. The men erected basic awnings and tethered the horses in the shade, offering them water first. Birler helped, though he thought he might be more of a hindrance. In the end, he spent his time scanning the horizon.

"Rest, Birler. You'll strain your eyes if you stare out there for too long." Tiv'erna offered him some dried fruit, and Birler sat down in the shade and nibbled it.

"Are we likely to come across any other patrols?"

"Maybe some Kirshans, but it's unlikely; this is a big desert. We'll stop here for a couple of chimes. Try to sleep if you can."

Birler didn't think he could, but he was pleasantly

surprised to be shaken awake as the patrols prepared to remount.

They didn't see the Telusion mountains growing on the horizon until dawn of the second day. Birler looked around eagerly. Melila was supposed to be up ahead, but the sands shimmered, blurring the horizon, and he didn't see the village until they were almost upon it.

50

BIRLER

MELILA, TEROLIA

The village appeared deserted as they clattered down the main street. "Water the horses," Tiv'erna commanded as he dismounted by the well. The bucket was clanked down into the dark hole. It took a long time before a welcome splash of water was heard and the long pull back up began before the water was emptied in the trough and the process repeated.

"If we couldn't get water here, where is the next well?" Birler asked through parched lips.

"Lez, or the port, though that's another two days travel. You could survive on those tricks I showed you, but it would be uncomfortable. Fill your canteens, Birler. Don't drink too much. Little and often, remember."

"Got it. Where is everyone?"

Tiv'erna looked around, frowning. "We should have attracted some attention." He sent some of his men to check the houses. They came back, shaking their heads. "It's not often we come this far east. If you hadn't been heading this way, Birler, we probably wouldn't have come at all. The Kirshans should be patrolling this area."

"How can a whole village go missing? My friend Edril lives here. He is a Lady's Ranger, and he wouldn't have gone down without a fight."

Adil led his horse over. "Birler, there is no one here. I wouldn't have believed it if I hadn't seen it myself."

"Do you know which house was Edril's? We should check he didn't leave a message. Tiv'erna, is there a Terolian sign for an emergency? Would someone think to leave a message anywhere?"

Tiv'erna frowned in thought and then strode off down the empty street. Birler leaned against Kafinee and tried to think what he would do if he were being herded out of town. He came up with nothing. How do you explain the inexplicable?

Adil came back empty-handed. "I can't tell which is Edril's home. I thought he lived off the square, but the houses look gutted. There is nothing to identify who lived there."

"Is there a temple here?"

"Yes, to the north of the square."

"Wait here. I'll go take a look." Birler strolled along the street. It was unnerving with the dark windows watching him like empty eyes as if accusing him of being too late. The heat was intense, reflecting off the sun-baked dirt. He tucked his hands in his sleeves and felt for his daggers. His neck was prickling; he was being watched.

The simple temple stood to the north of the square, as Adil had said, its red stone worn smooth by the sand and the wind. He mounted the shallow steps and entered the dim interior, glad to be out of the glare. The interior was a shambles: wooden pews smashed, cushions ripped, pointless destruction just for the sake of it. Walking up to the altar, he knelt and listened. There was nothing. The air was still, the stone solid.

"My Lady? Your people need you. There is something very wrong here in Melila."

He spun as his senses screeched a warning, and he raised his daggers to block the strike. The metal screeched, and he stared into the face of his friend.

"Edril?" he said as his daggers caught against the hilts of Edril's.

"Birler?" Edril gasped, an expression of horror flashing across his face. "What are you doing here?"

"Looking for you."

"You must leave. It is not safe. Leave now."

"I'm here to help. Where is everyone?"

"It's too late for us; you must leave. Please, Birler, before you get hurt."

"I'm not leaving unless you tell me what is going on." Birler forced Edril's shaking arms down.

"I-I can't. For your own good, you have to leave."

"The Lady sent me to help her people. I can't leave."

"Then you are doomed like the rest of us. Melila is a trap. It provides them with more bodies. If you stay, they will find you and drag you away in the night, one by one, until none of you are left."

"Why are you here, Edril? What do they want you to do?"

"I'm supposed to signal when people arrive."

"And will you?"

"I can't help myself. I've tried. I begged the Lady for help, but she doesn't hear me."

"How do you signal?"

Edril's eyes flickered—with what, Birler wasn't sure. "I-I call them."

"Call them? How?"

"I don't know how they do it, but they communicate straight into my mind, and they just take what I've seen.

They'll know you're here, Birler, and there is nothing I can do to stop them."

"Who are they, Edril?"

"They call themselves Ascendants. They are so powerful. They use crystals to enhance their power. They can attack your mind and twist it so you do what they say. They can slice through your resistance like one of your arrows splitting the air."

"Do they physically come to Melila?"

"No, it's all in the mind. They reach out and grab what they want." Edril moaned, rocking back. "Please, Birler, leave before it's too late."

"Where are the mines, Edril?"

"The entrance is two miles south of Lez, but they are watching the approaches. They will see you coming."

"Where are the watchers positioned?"

"Inside the mountain. They use the crystals; they can see all around. They are all-powerful."

"Then they will know we are already here."

"No, they watch the mountain; they don't watch Melila. They use me for that."

"So, there are limits to these crystals. Are they like those communications crystals? Do they run out? Can they be drained? Do they need recharging?"

"I don't know. They seem to be able to use them all the time."

"How many people are in the mountain?"

"I don't know, maybe three or four hundred, maybe more."

Birler's stomach dropped. "And how many ascendants?"

"Maybe twenty. But you can't attack them, Birler. They use the power of the mind, and they are invincible."

"How do you know you can't attack them if you haven't tried?"

"I have, but they see right through me. I can't shield against them."

"Where is Deren?"

Edril folded as if in physical pain, and Birler caught him. "Edril?"

He shuddered. "You must leave now; they are calling. I can't hold them off for long; they will take your mind. Please, Birler, for the Lady's sake, if not mine, please leave. I don't want to hurt you, and they will make me." His eyes glazed over, and Birler released him. He backed away, horrified, as Edril stiffened and all expression drained from his face. He turned and raised his hands.

Birler ran.

He skidded into the square. "We have to leave!" he yelled, rushing towards the men and their horses.

Tiv'erna spun around. "What's the matter, Birler?"

"I'll tell you on the way. For now, let's get out of here. We can camp outside Melila, but we can't stay here. Shield your minds and think of the Lady. Protect yourselves, or they will attack your minds. We leave now."

He grabbed Kafinee's reins and launched himself into her saddle. "Now, Tiv'erna," he snarled as he wrenched her around, and Tiv'erna leapt into his saddle and followed, calling his men.

"Kafinee, stay linked to me. Shield your mind and think of the Lady. Stay strong. Know that I would never betray you willingly."

"I know. Trust me, Birler. I will protect you."

"Tell Tiv'erna's Darian."

"I have. But he's confused."

"Does anyone else here have a Darian?"

"No, only Tiv'erna and you."

"I thought so."

When the attack came, it was like a searing blast from a furnace and swept through their minds like fire consuming dry tinder. Men fell to the burning sands, unconscious, and Birler clung to Kafinee, horrified. Tiv'erna roared as his Darian shrieked in pain, rearing up, trying to bat away the attack. Tiv'erna clung to his saddle, but his horse fell and rolled over on him, squealing in agony before lying still.

Kaf'enir shuddered as if being hit by a ten-foot wave, and Birler braced himself, conjuring Leyandrii's face to protect them. The pressure increased. Waves of jabbing pain bombarded his temples but as he resisted, it lessened and then disappeared, leaving him breathless and his head pounding. He leapt from the saddle onto the hot sands. *"Kaf'enir, are they still alive?"*

"Yes, no, I don't know." Her voice shook with fear, and her panic buffeted his mind.

"Shh, Kaf'enir, I'm here. We're together. Can you reach Tiv'erna's Darian?"

"He is confused, stunned."

Birler scrabbled around Tiv'erna, trying to feel bones under the solid body of the Darian, checking whether Tiv'erna was breathing. *"Can you link to him? Can he open to me?"*

"I don't know."

"Try."

Birler prayed to the Lady for help; this was beyond his ability to solve, but there was only silence. He swallowed desperately; he needed to get the Darian off Tiv'erna.

"Kafinee, tell him to get off Tiv'erna; he is crushing him."

"He's not listening to me."

"What is his name?"

"It is not mine to say."

"Kafinee, this is not the time. Tell me."

"Kin'eril," she said reluctantly.

"Kin'eril," Birler commanded, and the Darian jerked. *"Get off Tiv'erna; you are crushing him. You'll kill him."*

The Darian rolled and jerked to his feet, his legs splayed and trembling.

"Thank you." Birler felt Tiv'erna's neck and found a thready pulse. *"Could you keep the sun off him? Can you tell where he is hurt?"*

"I hurt him." Kin'eril's voice was deep and warm, like a caress.

"You can help him now. Can you tell what is wrong with him?"

"His leg is wrong, and his stomach."

"You must stay open to me and Kaf'enir. Together, we can protect him. Do you understand? We are stronger together."

"I understand. I am sorry."

"There is nothing to be sorry for. This is outside all of our experience. They have a terrible magic. We will deal with it after we help Tiv'erna."

"What can I do?"

"Shade him for now. I need to splint his leg."

Birler glanced around. Horses had fled and left the carnage behind them. He spotted a pack and rushed over to get it. He found poles and an awning and rigged a small shelter over Tiv'erna. He used his sword as a splint and straightened Tiv'erna's leg, tying it rigid around his ankle and knee. He was relieved to find no bones poking through the skin, though he felt a definite break in Tiverna's shin bone.

He was surprised there hadn't been a follow-up strike and wondered if it were possible that the crystals had been drained. He hoped so. Having made Tiv'erna as comfortable as he could, he moved on to check the other men. Those alive, he dragged back to Tiv'erna and, finding another pack, extended his awning. Kafinee stood beside it, quivering. He collected every water canteen he could find and stacked them beside the injured men.

Using the little as he knew about healing, he splinted

every broken bone he found. Apart from that, he had no idea what ailed them. He hoped they had just been knocked out by the concussive wave that had hit them. He was relieved when Adil groaned. He leant over him offering his canteen. "Drink," he said as Adil sat up, holding his head.

"What happened?"

"We got struck by a mental blast," Birler said with a grimace. "It knocked everyone out."

Adil handed the canteen back and looked around. "How many?"

"How many what?"

"How many men did we lose?"

"Three, and all the horses bar two. The rest were knocked out like you were. Two broken legs and a broken arm, and Lady knows what else. They decimated us in one strike."

"Why haven't they finished us off?"

"I don't know, but we can't move anyone, so we are stuck until help arrives ... or worse. Do you think you could ride for help?"

"Not right now. Why don't you go?" Adil rubbed his temple as he frowned up at Birler.

"I wouldn't know where to go."

"What did you find in the temple to come back shrieking like a dust devil in an oasis?"

"Do dust devils shriek?" Birler asked, diverted.

"Yeah, when they get hold of water."

"I found Edril."

"What?" Adil jerked upright and then heaved, holding his stomach. "Oh, Lady, I'm going to throw up."

"Well, do it over there, then, and not in the shade." Birler shoved him out of the awning.

Adil staggered and bent over in the sand. When he finished, Birler offered the canteen. Adil crawled back under the tent and curled up around his stomach, groaning. Birler buried the mess before it began to stink.

He cast an eye over the men. They would all be as bad, if not worse, than Adil. None of them would be any help. The mines were a day's ride east. If he managed to find the entrance, maybe he could sneak in before the crystals recharged and destroy them. If they managed to attack again, anyone arriving to help would be decimated in the same way they had been. The thought of Yannis and her family riding into such an ambush made him feel ill.

"Kafinee, we are going to have to go to the mines."

"I know."

"We have to destroy the crystals before they have a chance to recharge or reset or whatever they are doing."

"I agree."

"You're not going to persuade me to go for help?"

"You know it wouldn't make any difference. They would wipe them out in the same way."

"That's what I thought. Kin'eril, you need to protect Tiv'erna's mind. They can attack him through you."

"I understand now. Kaf'enir explained."

"We'll stay linked as long as we can, but we don't know how far over distance it will work."

"Do what you need to. I'll protect my people."

"Adil, Tiv'erna has a stomach injury. He was crushed when his Darian rolled over him. Don't move him if you can help it. Get a healer to see him first."

"Yeah, I'll just conjure one up out of thin air," Adil muttered.

Birler sharpened his voice. "Listen to me. I'm going to go with Kafinee to find help. You can't trust Edril. The ascendants control him, so be careful if he turns up. When help arrives, get everyone loaded up and leave as fast as you can.

If you stay here and they strike again, well, you know what will happen."

Adil held his head. "Ascendants?"

"That is what Edril called them. Adil, you must keep the men hydrated, but watch your canteens. I found six. I'll take one with me, don't forget to offer Rill here some."

"Rill?"

"Tiv'erna's Darian. We've got to call him something." *"Haven't we?"* Birler thought, rubbing Kin'eril's nose.

Kin'eril nodded his head. *"Rill. I like it."*

Birler stared out over the desert; it was empty in all directions. *"How far are we from Melila?"*

"Not even a mile," Kin'eril replied.

"Do you think they can see us from there?"

"If we can't see them, they can't see us."

"That's something, I suppose."

Birler unsheathed Tiv'erna's scimitar and shoved it carefully into his belt. He had his daggers and his sling and stones. He also had his bow and quiver. There were only twenty ascendants, according to Edril. Maybe he could reduce their numbers before they knew he was there. "Give me your daggers," he said to Adil.

"What?"

"I need your daggers; I lost mine."

Adil handed them over without argument.

Birler mounted Kafinee. "Keep them alive, Adil."

"I'll do my best."

"Look after Tiv'erna," Birler said to Kin'eril.

"Always," Kin'eril replied.

Birler nodded and turned Kafinee away.

Adil watched him leave. "He's going the wrong way," he said, and Kin'eril snorted. Adil stared at the Darian, long and hard. "Or not," he said, staring in the direction Birler had gone, lost in the shimmering haze.

51

BIRLER

TEROLIA

Birler worked on the premise that the crystals were drained and it would take time for them or the people to recharge. The thought that what he was doing was a waste of time would drive him mad. He didn't worry about why he and Kafinee had managed to resist whatever had been thrown at them. All that mattered was that they had.

He kept a light link with Kin'eril, amused by the banter between the two Darians. Kafinee's voice was light and amused; Kin'eril's was deep, smooth, and direct. He got annoyed by her frivolous comments, and she was diverted by his lack of humour.

"Aren't you ever serious?" Kin'eril grumbled.

"Of course, but only when it's necessary. Life is too short to be miserable all the time."

"I am not miserable."

"Yes, you are," Kafinee replied. *"You never laugh."*

"There is nothing to laugh about."

"There is always something to laugh about, until there isn't."

Birler grinned, muffled in his robes, as Kin'eril's confusion embraced him. It helped pass the miles. The Telusion mountains grew in front of him, steep red peaks rising into the azure blue sky like a row of serrated teeth found on a logger's saw. He had seen one once in Greens, long and jagged; it took two men to pull it back and forth. He hoped they wouldn't bite him like the saw had bit the tree.

They turned north, travelling parallel with the mountains. Hazy clouds gathered around the tallest peak, softening the jagged edges. *"We've reached the Telusions. We're turning north, looking for the pass,"* he thought to Kin'eril.

"Tiw'erna is stirring." Kin'eril sounded excited; his relief was evident in his voice.

"Remember, keep him shielded. Don't let him move."

"I will. I promise."

"How are you doing, Kafinee? Do you need a drink?"

"I'm fine. How about you?"

"I'm good."

Birler fell silent as the mountains towered over them. Sheer cliffs rose, forming an impenetrable wall, obscuring the jagged peaks. Heat bounced off the red stone and straight into them. Waves of heat flowed over them, growing hotter as they travelled closer.

He almost missed the break in the cliffs, a dark shadow that his eyes slid over. *"Birler, there is a gap,"* Kafinee murmured as she turned towards it.

"Kin'eril? We found the pass. It's very narrow, easy to miss, barely a shadow."

There was no reply.

"We must be out of range."

"Or the mountains are blocking us," Kafinee said.

"Possible."

Kafinee walked on. The temperature cooled the moment they entered the shadows, and they both breathed sighs of relief. Birler's head ached, a result of the intense heat, or so he hoped. They passed an opening, and Birler dismounted to check. It was a cave, but it didn't go anywhere. *"Maybe you should wait here. There's no point handing you straight over, and we are trying to creep in."*

"I suppose so." Kafinee sounded dubious.

Birler sloshed some water into a leather bag and hung it around her neck. He took a deep swallow and then re-stoppered the canteen. *"If we lose contact, you should return to Kin'eril."*

"I'm not leaving you here."

"Kafinee, there is no point staying here if I'm not coming back out."

"I'm not leaving you," she said stubbornly.

"Please, think of your foal. Let something good come of this."

"I wait until it's no longer necessary to wait."

"Very well." Birler gave up arguing and hugged her, and then he slid out his bow. He left her in the shadowed cave and crept along the sandy passage, hesitating at the end as it opened into a large cavern. Huge chunks of shattered rock lay scattered on the ground and a faint path beaten into the sandy rock led between them. He followed it, keeping a wary eye on the ceiling. The path led to a narrow passageway leading down into darkness. He kept going.

Sweat dribbled down his skin as heat emanated from the rocky walls. He laid a hand on the wall and snatched it back. It was scorching. What magic was this that made rock burn? The air smelt of rotten eggs, and he covered his mouth and nose with his robe as he descended.

"The walls are hot," he said, surprise colouring his thought.

"Hot?" Kafinee's voice was soothing.

"Yes, too hot to touch."

"There are some mountains that contain fire. It rushes out the top and rains down on the land. Could this be one of those?"

"I don't know. I hope not. Whatever they are doing, it won't be good for fire mountains, I'm sure." He felt her concern as he followed

the trail. He reached a junction. *"The passageway splits into two. Both go down."*

"Which has the cooler walls?"

"I like your logic." Birler smiled as he felt the walls. *"I'm going left."* He continued down, hoping Kafinee would remember how to get him back out again. This couldn't be the main entrance. He hoped it wasn't going to be a dead end.

The tunnel began to lighten, and Birler slowed. The wall on his right ended, and he peered over the edge. He was in a gallery above a huge cavern. A sparkling array of glass rods lay in a circular pattern on the floor. Each circle graduated down a size as they radiated out from the centre. In the middle was a black stone; it absorbed all light and looked dull and lifeless. He eased back and searched the gallery. It was a dead end. There was no way down, and he hadn't thought to bring a rope. He was a fool.

He stilled as he heard voices. He strained, trying to listen. "You over … the … takes time … have to wait. You know … hoard the power." The voice drew closer.

"I can't wait. They'll get away and bring more. We'll be discovered."

"There isn't enough power to hit them again. Maybe in a chime, there'll be enough to hit one person."

"I only need to kill one person."

Birler stilled as he recognised Clary's voice; it was vindictive and cruel. He could imagine who he wanted to kill, but how did Clary know he was in Terolia? He waited for the men to move on and then retreated the way he had come.

"Clary is here. I found the crystals, but there is no way down. I'm going to try the other passageway. The crystals won't recharge for another chime, and even then, only enough for one target."

"That's a relief," Kafinee replied. *"You were right. If the crystals have to recharge at least our friends are safe."*

"But only for a while. We have to destroy them before they get back to full power."

"Be careful, Birler."

"Always."

Birler smiled as she snorted in his head.

Adil slowly worked his way around the groaning men; they were all confused and suffering. He fed them sips of water and eased them into more comfortable positions, urging them to sleep. He returned to Tiv'erna and watched his face. It was ashen, which was not good on a brown-skinned man. He felt Tiv'erna's brow; it was clammy even though it was stifling under the awning.

"Can't you wake him up?" he asked the Darian.

Kin'eril shook his head. He had thought Tiv'erna was stirring, but he had sunk back down into unconsciousness. He reached out, calling to any other Darian, hoping that Ber'enger might be patrolling ahead of Sir'erle, Arkan's Darian, but there was only silence. He stiffened as he heard the concern in Kaf'enir's voice, and then there was silence again. He stirred restlessly beside his rider.

Adil patted his shoulder. "Steady, there. Help will come."

52

BIRLER

TELUSION MOUNTAINS, TEROLIA

irler stilled as he heard more voices: a low murmur which grew louder as he crawled to the end of the passage. He peered around the end of the tunnel and froze. Below him, lines of people slumped in exhaustion and without hope, chained to each other and the walls. Empty eyes followed a single guard walking among them. Birler scanned the cavern as he searched for more guards. Another stood above them on a ledge, though he was more interested in cleaning his nails with the point of his knife.

Birler's gaze swept the cavern floor again, and he caught a sharp movement in contrast to the lethargic bodies. His eyes narrowed as he watched a young girl with masses of black hair watching the guard. She was considering making a move—with her bare hands.

As the guard turned away, Birler flicked a glance at the bored guard above them, and threw his daggers, one, two. In succession, they thumped at the girl's feet, and after a shocked pause, she pulled them out of the sand and sat on them. The guard twisted, suspicious and frowning, and walked towards her.

Birler rose. His arrow pierced the bored guard's neck up on the gallery, and he collapsed. He searched for the second guard, but the girl had slit his throat, and the people had come to life, dragging him down, searching for the keys to their shackles. The rattle of the chains being pulled through the loops was loud as Birler peered down into the cavern, then levered himself over the edge and climbed down. He moved from handhold to hollow, glad of the recent climbing practice he'd had in the trees in Greens.

"I found the people," he thought to Kaf'enir as he hurried through the cavern. He spun as a hand grabbed his arm, and he met familiar, deep brown eyes. "Kayer." She truly was beautiful, even begrimed and ragged.

Kayer's eyes widened. "How do you know …"

"Not now, I have to find the crystal chamber. Do you know where it is from here?"

"Turn left at the top of the passage and take the first left again," she said, following as he hurried away. "Who *are* you?"

Birler gave her a brief grin. "Friend of Lily's. They are waiting for you with the Atolea. The Family cares for them."

"Where's my mother? I left my sisters and brother with her."

Birler hesitated and then said, "I'm sorry, but she fell ill and died." Ignoring her soft exclamation, he continued, "They are waiting for you, so you need to head for Melila, get some water, and leave. Don't stay there; it isn't safe. There is an Atolean patrol a mile north of Melila. They were decimated by the ascendants' attack and they need help. The Medera should arrive there soon."

"Medera Yannis? But what is *she* doing here?"

"Looking after her people." Birler peered down the dark passageway and darted across to the entrance opposite.

Kayer followed close behind. "You should help your people escape whilst they can," Birler said.

"What do you intend to do? Those men will be in the crystal chamber; they congregate there all the time. Communing or something."

Birler paused. "The crystals are their source of power, and I need to disrupt them."

"I can help."

"You can't do this on your own. She can help," Kafinee murmured.

Birler considered Kayer. "Alright, can you cause a distraction so I can disable as many of them as possible?"

"Of course," Kayer said, watching him as he nocked an arrow.

Birler breathed deeply, calming himself. He thought of Leyandrii. The memory of her deep green eyes soothed him, and he smiled at the young woman staring at him with such concern. Kayer instinctively smiled back, though her smile faded as he explained what they needed to do.

"The Lady blesses us. Once you have their attention, don't linger. Run. They can control the mind, so hold the Lady close, and she will protect, but the crystals are powerful, and if you stay too long they will overpower you.

Kayer nodded, watching him, her concern deepening.

"Warn Sodera Arkan that Ranger Edril is not to be trusted. He has been enspelled by the ascendants. He is not responsible for his actions, but he is not to be trusted until we can remove the compulsion."

"What about you?"

"I will be close behind you; don't stop running." Birler inhaled deeply, steadying the rush of adrenaline that flushed through him. "Go," he breathed, peering around the tunnel. He sighted his first targets and silently kept to the shadows as Kayer strode out into the torchlight.

Reaching the edge of the array, Kayer kicked the crystals laid out on the sandy floor. She crouched, gathered up some crystals, and smashed them down on top of the others. The air thrummed with arrows, and Kayer held still, the breeze of their flight wafting her hair as they passed.

An agonised cry came from above: "Stop her!" and she tossed more crystals into the air. They made a satisfying crack as they landed and clouded over. Arrows thrummed above her, and black-robed bodies fell. One, two, three, four …

"Stop him!" another voice roared, and Kayer flattened to the ground as guards rushed into the cavern. They stumbled as a swathe of arrows cut them down, and they fell over the downed bodies. One of the men scrambled to his feet, fearfully searching for the archer.

"Grab the black crystal and run," Birler hissed as he tossed aside his empty quiver and bow and drew Tiv'erna's long, curved sword. The gems in the hilt flashed as he advanced on the guards. The screech of metal filled the air as Birler spun and twisted, and the razor-sharp edge of the sword sliced through skin and bone. He flicked a glance at the array. The girl had done as he'd asked.

As he retreated towards the exit, a black-robed man raised his arms and his voice rose in a chant. Birler threw his last dagger. The chanting faltered, and he ran down the empty passageway.

"Kafinee? We'll be coming out further north. There must be another entrance."

"On my way, Birler. Hurry."

Birler ran up the corridor, climbing upwards through a large empty cavern and back into a dark, narrow passageway. He kept running towards the echoes of stumbling feet ahead of him. He burst out into a much lighter cavern, where ragged people blocked the way, milling about, confused.

"Head for Melila. Head west. Keep the mountains behind you. Leave now whilst you can!" Birler shouted as he pushed his way through. He could see sunlight at the end of one of the passageways, and he kept pushing and shoving.

Clary's voice echoed around the cavern: "Ranger, halt! I will kill them all if you don't stop. These people, the Descelles, all of them. Everyone you hold dear."

Birler skidded to a halt; the exit to the cavern was so close. He turned, buffeted by the rushing people. "It's too late; your arrays are destroyed!" he shouted.

The people parted, clearing the space between Birler and the ascendant.

"It can be repaired. There are more crystals," Clary boasted.

Birler stiffened as someone pressed into his back. A dagger was slipped into his hand, and he grasped it. He flicked it so fast that Clary didn't have time to move. It struck him high on the shoulder, and he staggered back.

"Give me the crystal," Birler said as he spun towards Kayer. She gave it to him, and he held it up. "You need this?" he shouted as Clary straightened, holding his shoulder. Blood seeped through his fingers, the blade still embedded in his body. Clary glared at him, his face rigid with anger and pain.

"Then you'll have to catch me." Birler darted for the exit.

"Get after him, all of you! We need that crystal. I want him. Forget the others. Get him," Clary shouted, his voice shaking with rage.

Kin'eril reached for the hundredth time. He was close to giving up; his head pounded, his range was exhausted, and he hadn't heard from Kaf'enir in chimes. He should have been able to hear Per'ilta's Darian by now. *"Ber'enger, help us. Help us, please."* He almost missed the faint reply.

"Kin'eril? We come."

"Mile north Melila. Don't go into Melila."

"Mile north, we come."

Kin'eril snorted, and Adil looked up. He staggered to his feet and swayed before reaching to pat Kin'eril's neck. The heat was draining them all, as was the tension of an expected attack.

"Kin'eril?"

"Tiv'erna?" Kin'eril dipped his head and nudged his rider gently. Adil dropped to his knees beside the injured man.

"Don't move, Tiv'erna. You're hurt inside." Adil carefully lifted Tiv'erna's shoulders and dribbled some water into his mouth. Tiv'erna swallowed and opened his eyes. His forehead creased in pain, but he swallowed his groan.

"How are the men?" Tiv'erna whispered.

"Three dead, the rest concussed. Three with broken bones that Birler found, including you."

"Where's Birler?"

"He went for help, towards the mountains," Adil said with a grimace. "He's been gone for chimes."

"Kin'eril? Where is Birler?"

"They went to destroy their power so they couldn't attack us again."

"They?"

"Him and Kaf'enir. I could hear them. She was speaking to him. He is under the mountain. He found the crystals. He has found our people. He is trying to get them out, but I haven't heard from Kaf'enir for a long time."

Tiv'erna scowled at the worry in Kin'eril's voice. *"How do we help him?"*

"We can't." Kin'eril snorted. *"Tell Adil there is one of our horses just over the dune to the west."*

Tiv'erna repeated Kin'eril's words, and Adil stumbled out of the awning to go and retrieve it.

"Ber'enger comes."

"How far?"

Kin'eril sighed. *"Far."*

Tiv'erna dozed in the suffocating heat. He had never hated the sun as much as he did now. Even after the sun had dipped behind the undulating horizon, the dusk air was stifling. His body screamed every time he moved: broken ribs, strained muscles, waves of debilitating nausea. He recognised Birler's straight sword strapped to his leg and groped for his own, smiling when he found it missing. *"Did Birler steal my sword?"*

"Yes. But he left you his for you to use," Kin'eril said, trying to be fair.

"So I see," Tiv'erna chuckled and gasped as he held his chest. Pain radiated through his body, and he breathed through it, his mind drifting as his awareness faded.

It was dawn when Kin'eril lifted his head. *"They approach. Kaf'enir is exhausted; she won't be able to go any further. They are being chased. She says he intends on avoiding us."* He nuzzled Tiv'erna's shoulder. *"I will take him further if you agree."*

Tiv'erna stirred, his eyes widening. *"You would travel alone?"*

"I wouldn't be alone. I would be with Birler until he can return me to you."

"If he doesn't, I will come and get you."

"That is acceptable."

Tiv'erna gave a snort of laughter and groaned as he held his chest. *"Tell Kafinee to come here."* He said aloud, "Birler is coming. Make sure he leaves Kafinee here. She is exhausted. Saddle my Darian, Kin'eril. He will take Birler onward."

Adil stiffened, honoured that Tiv'erna had shared his Darian's name. He stood and shaded his eyes as he looked to the east. It was another half-chime before he saw the dust cloud, which slowly resolved into a man and a horse shimmering in the evening haze. He saddled Kin'eril.

Kafinee staggered to a stop by the awning and stood quivering as Birler slid off her back and hung onto her as he stiffened his trembling legs. "I said go around them," he said bitterly.

Adil grabbed him and pulled him into an embrace. "Birler, are you hurt?" A puff of dust rose from Birler's clothes; he was covered in red sand.

"No, but trouble follows us, and they are determined. We can't stay." Adil shoved a canteen in his hand, and Birler took a long swallow. Adil offered Kafinee water, and she dipped her head.

"Birler," Tiv'erna called.

"Tiv'erna! You are awake, thank the Lady. How are you?"

"Kafinee is exhausted; she can't go any further."

"We have to go on; we need help. I am being chased; I need to lead them away from you. At least they won't be using those crystals again," he said with a vicious grin. "So, you don't need to worry about another mental attack." Birler rubbed his face. "There are people flooding out of the mountains, and they will need help."

Tiv'erna grabbed Birler's leg and tried to pull him close. "Take Kin'eril. He will carry you home."

"I can't. He's yours."

"Kaf'enir won't make it. I will care for her until you return. Kin'eril accepts you. Please honour me. He will look after you. You are family. You need him."

"He's right," Kaf'enir said, her voice wavering. *"I can't go on much further without rest. Kin'eril will look after you until you return.*

I will hold him responsible for you. I will stay with his rider in his place."

Birler strode over to her and smoothed her heaving sides. *"I'm so sorry, Kaf'enir. I should never have ridden you so hard."*

"We had no choice. Live or die, we are together. Please, you can't stay. You must go warn your family."

"Birler, we will hold them off. You must leave," Tiv'erna said, his voice shaking with the effort.

Birler glared down at him. "You can't even stand. How are you going to hold them off?"

"Because we must," Adil replied.

"You're wasting time," Tiv'erna panted.

Kin'eril nudged Birler with his head, and Birler gave in.

Adil handed Birler Kin'eril's reins and then linked his hands. He threw Birler up into the saddle, and Birler shortened the stirrups. It was a lot further down to the ground than riding Kaf'enir. Kin'eril's muscles bunched under his legs.

Adil stroked the Darian's head. "Ride with the wind, my friend," he murmured.

Tiv'erna looked up at Birler. "Adil and Per'ilta will ride interference. Kin'eril will keep you advised. They approach from the north. Go."

Adil stood away, and Kin'eril leapt forward.

"Tiv'erna, can you speak with Kafinee? Can you ask her how far behind the ascendants are and how many?" Adil looked down at Tiv'erna in concern. Even that brief movement had cost him.

"Many, and we could see their dust trail," Kafinee said. "They will be on us soon."

"She says many, which could be between four and

fifteen," Tiv'erna said with a wry twist of his lips. "They are about half a chime behind him."

Adil grimaced and mounted the horse he had retrieved. He unsheathed his sword, rode to the top of the dune, and waited, a dark silhouette on the horizon, watching. The approaching dust cloud veered south, and Adil scowled as the riders went around him.

Kafinee relayed the news to Kin'eril and Ber'enger and listened as the Darians strategised with their riders. Kafinee reported that Kin'eril would lead them straight into an ambush and Ber'enger would intercept. Tiv'erna and Adil breathed a little easier.

53

KAYER
MELILA, TEROLIA

Many chimes later, Kayer herded the few slaves who had rushed out of the mountain with her into the deserted town of Melila. The unrelenting sun burned her skin and dried out her mouth. She nearly regretted leaving the cool embrace of the mountain, but glimpsing the communal well through the shimmering air as heat rose from the sun-baked stone beneath her feet, she made one last effort and lurched forward.

She fumbled for the rope with shaking fingers and lowered the bucket. The splash was pure torture, and she hurriedly pulled it back up again. Dunking her face in the water, she sucked in deep mouthfuls before offering it to her fellow sufferers.

Cool, clean water—a luxury she would never take for granted again. She wiped her face and, leaving the others to help themselves, peered around. Where was everyone? A wooden door creaked in the heat, and she shielded her eyes as she searched the dusty streets. She called out, "Hello?" but there was no reply.

Lady help them, what had happened here?

"There be no one left," a man said from behind her, and she spun around.

"What do you mean?"

He gestured towards the mountains. "They all be in there."

Kayer stiffened. How could this be possible? A whole town stripped of its people, who were forced to become slaves, and no one did anything?

"We need to leave," she said, remembering Birler's instructions.

"And go where?" the man asked. "At least we have water here."

"For how long?" She flung her hand towards the mountain. "They'll just come and scoop you all back up again."

"We'll die if we go any further. Look at us. We'll not make it any further."

Kayer inspected the people sitting around the well. They were emaciated and weak. The man was right. It was astonishing that they had made it this far. "Very well. Find some shade and hide. I'll go for help. See if you can find a canteen or something I can carry water in." She darted into a nearby house and blessed the Lady when she found a water bladder hanging from a peg in the kitchen. She grabbed a jug and mugs as well.

Returning to the well, she dropped the bucket again. "Find something to put water in and then go and hide. Stay out of sight until the Atolea get here."

She filled her canteen and a second one the man returned with. "See if you can find more. Most houses should have at least one, or a bucket. Then split up and hide."

Kayer took two canteens for herself, strapped them cross-wise over her chest, and then walked up the high street.

Birler said the patrol was a mile north of Melila, so that was where she was going.

A chime later, Kayer was regretting her life choices. She should have at least found a robe to cover her head and skin instead of rushing off. She was blindly striding out into the desert, on the word of a stranger, without any real idea of exactly where the patrol was. What an idiot!

Should she turn back? Kayer stood with hands on hips and slowly rotated in a circle. Nothing but empty, golden sand and, behind her, the ridge of red mountains reaching for the sky. At least she could follow her footprints back to Melila.

"Hey! Over here!"

Kayer spun towards the voice. A robed figure stood on top of a sand dune and waved his arms at her. Exhaling in relief, Kayer slogged her way through the deepening sand. Sweat drenched her back by the time she finally reached him.

"Is Birler here?" she asked as she looked up at him.

"No, he led them away from us," Adil said. "You from the mountain?"

"Yes. I'm Kayer. Birler helped us escape. Some folks are in the town. Many others are still trapped in the mountain."

"My name is Adil," Adil said. "The Darian heard you coming."

"Fortunate for me," Kayer replied, unhooking a canteen. "I brought water."

"Lady bless you. We have many wounded." Adil led her to the awning and knelt beside one of the injured men. "Tiv'erna? We have water."

"The Ascendants did this from within the mountain?" Kayer asked as Adil carefully raised the man's head and trickled water into his mouth. Sweat dewed Tiv'erna's forehead and upper lip, and he groaned even with that slight movement.

"Yes. This Tiv'erna. He is suffering from some internal injuries and a broken leg. Many of the others are behaving as if they have concussions."

Kayer handed one of the injured men her canteen. He took a drink and passed it on with a smile of thanks. "What can I do to help?"

Adil sighed. "Not much, maybe keep Tiv'erna company, make sure he doesn't move. He has internal injuries. Let me know if he says anything. It's Birler's Darian that's listening out for the Atolea. She'll only speak to him."

Kayer nodded and sat beside Tiv'erna. She gently clasped his hand and inspected his face. Deep lines creased his skin, and his dark brows were drawn down over his closed eyes as he suffered in silence. His body was tense, his rigid muscles trembling at the effort of holding still. As she stroked the back of his hand, his lashes flickered open, and she was snared by liquid black eyes. She could drown in those depths quite easily, and she struggled to smile. "Help is coming," she whispered. "Just rest."

Tiv'erna rolled his head.

"Don't move. You'll only hurt yourself more."

Tiv'erna's lips moved but no sound came out, and Kayer leaned forward. She pushed her hair back as it fell forward.

"Who?" he whispered.

"I'm Kayer, from Mistra. I met Birler under the mountain. He rescued us."

Tiv'erna's lashes dropped, and she exhaled as his gaze released her. His fingers squeezed her hand so softly that she could have missed it, but she caressed his hand again and left their fingers tangled.

Awkwardly, she managed to wet a pad, tucking the canteen under one arm and tilting it to wet the cloth.

Wedging the canteen between her legs, she dabbed the pad over Tiv'erna's face. He didn't stir, but Kayer was sure the lines of pain had deepened, and his lips were a distressing grey.

The moon was high when Yannis and Arkan arrived. Adil gladly handed over their defence to Arkan, reporting everything Birler had told him. Arkan's face stiffened into a cold mask, and he dispatched riders to help those people escaping from the mountain. Yannis organised her people, and soon, they were encamped.

Time passed, and Kayer managed to get more water into Tiv'erna, but he wouldn't let go of her hand. In the bustle and concern of Atolea's arrival, Kayer leaned over Tiv'erna and whispered in his ear, "I need to find my family. I will come back, I promise, as long as you do what the healer tells you."

He clung to her hand for a moment, but as the Medera arrived, effusive in her concern, Kayer was able to slip away and start the search for her brother and sisters in the mass of caravans and tents being erected.

Adil helped carry Tiv'erna into the healer's tent, and Tiv'erna submitted to the care of the healer, listening for Kin'eril.

"We lead them north. Ber'enger will cut them off," Kin'eril said, his voice confident.

"How many are there chasing you?" Ber'enger asked.

"No more than five," Birler replied. *"Be careful. We don't know if they have any unusual powers."*

"They won't even know we're there until it's too late," Per'ilta said.

"Ride for the border, Kin'eril," Ber'enger said. *"We'll protect you."*

Sir'erle, Arkan's white stallion, stood protectively over Kaf'enir, and they both listened to Ber'enger and Kin'eril's running commentary of a successful ambush. Then Kin'eril passed out of range as they rode north of Mistra, headed towards Berbera and then into Vespiri.

***

Kayer found Lily with the gaggle of kids running chores, fetching things, and helping to furnish the tents. "Lily!" she shouted, and Lily spun, dropped the cushions she was carrying, and bolted towards her.

Kayer dropped to her knees, caught the small body in a hug, and hid her face in Lily's hair. Lily wrapped her arms around Kayer's neck and her legs around her waist and clung tightly. Kayer inhaled Lily's comforting scent and rubbed her sister's back as tears soaked into her shirt.

"I thought we'd lost you," Lily wept, clinging to her.

"Shh. I'm fine. How are Mattie and Daniel?"

"They're here. Auntie is looking after them."

"Why don't you introduce us?" Kayer asked as she smoothed the hair off Lily's face and wiped her tears away. "You can tell me how you met Birler."

Lily's face brightened. "Oh, did he find you? He promised he would." She peered around Kayer, searching for Birler, and then tugged Kayer deeper into the camp. "Is he here? Did he tell you that he showed me how to make a sling? And I can throw a knife now."

"No, he didn't," Kayer replied. "But I'll make sure he explains when we see him next."

"I'll teach you," Lily offered with a grin, and Kayer laughed.

54

BIRLER

GREENS WATCH, VESPIRI

Ten days later, Birler was leading Kin'eril through dense undergrowth. They were off the East Road, south of Deepwater, cutting across country for Greens. They had picked up some new followers who had been closing in on their weary trek through Vespiri, and Birler had decided to hide. They were exhausted. Even Kin'eril's never-ending stamina had a limit. They had quite an in-depth conversation about being honest with each other, and Kin'eril had finally admitted he was pooped.

Birler burst out laughing as he slid out of the saddle and hugged the stallion's sweat-grimed neck. Their dusty robes and elaborate saddle were quite notable. Even covered in road dust, Kin'eril was eye-catching. It wasn't too difficult for their followers to get reports of their passing. He had made a show of them travelling through East Ford, having crossed the wide River Vesp and then left the road, hoping that his followers would be delayed by searching for their trail there.

Kin'eril was nosing the greenery as they passed, amazed at the lush growth. His dust-covered skin shuddered as water droplets landed on him from the surrounding trees. Kin'eril was jittery with the foliage and grey clouds overhead. He hated not being able to see the sky.

Guilt consumed Birler for looking after him so badly. They paused at a shallow stream, and Kin'eril dipped his nose in and out of the running water, a surprised expression on his face.

"There is plenty of water here. Rivers crisscross Vespiri; you don't have to carry canteens. You're more likely to need shelter from the constant rain." Birler watched Kin'eril's reaction with amusement. *"It is also a lot cooler; let me know if you get cold. Tiv'erna would kill me if you caught a chill."*

Birler had purchased a rug and some grain with the last of his coins, not sure how fresh grass and plants would react in a Darian's stomach, so long used to dried hay and grain. The man in the hostelry had eyed him with suspicion, a strange Terolian travelling in Vespiri on his own. Birler felt like a stranger in his own land, surprised that he had adapted to life in Terolia so quickly. He liked both the land and the people.

He shuddered in his thin robes; the chill was slowly stiffening his limbs. Ice rimed the puddles, and the wind had a biting edge that Kin'eril hated. Birler didn't blame him and kept the blanket over his withers most of the time.

They crossed a tributary of the River Vesp high up in Deepwater, where a narrow bridge, a fallen tree trunk cut into rough planks, crossed the deep ravine which housed the river at that point. Birler had to use all his powers of persuasion to get Kin'eril to cross and had eventually resorted to threatening to tell Tiv'erna that his mighty Darian feared a little bridge.

"I am not afraid," Kin'eril snorted.

"I know you're not. You are amazing and wonderful, and see, you're across now. That wasn't scary, was it?"

Kin'eril glanced back at the bridge and then at Birler.

"You won't tell Tiv'erna?"

"Never," Birler promised with a grin, happy to be home in Greens. He stiffened as the hairs on his neck prickled, and he hopped a couple of times before launching himself back up into the saddle. *"We have company. Greens is due west; we just need to keep working our way west."*

"I will find the way," Kin'eril promised, his ears flicking. He lengthened his stride, and the trail passed by in a blur. Birler leaned over his neck, keeping as close to Kin'eril's body as possible, reducing the target he made. He only had Tiv'erna's sword, and that was of no use while they fled.

The vibration in the air was his only warning, and he threw his arm up to deflect the arrow. Kin'eril swerved, changing direction, and Birler clung to him.

"Sorry," Kin'eril said.

"Don't be. Do what you need to. We are exposed; we need some cover."

Kin'eril galloped across an open field and into some trees without stopping, heedless of whatever was before him, and Birler had accused him of being scared. He was strong and fearless, and Birler would tell him so. Later.

They wended their way through the trees until they reached a clearing. Birler recognised the Ancestor tree. "Only five miles from Greens. We are nearly there," he murmured. They flinched as an arrow thunked into his saddle. Birler wrenched Kin'eril around, and they dived back into the trees. *"Are you hurt? Did it hit you?"* Birler twisted around, trying to see as his heart raced.

"No, the saddle stopped it." Kin'eril's voice was breathless, but he kept going. *"We're going the wrong way,"* he said, trying to veer left.

"It's too open. We'll have to work our way around from the north." So near and yet so far. Birler tried to remember the map. Trees ranged all the way from the Guardians' Ridge to the

manor house. Where would Warren's patrols be? He was wondering why he hadn't met any yet when they stumbled straight into one.

"Tianer," Birler gasped as he recognised the fiery ranger who had consistently beaten him in the ring.

Tianer stared at him, taking a moment to recognise him. "Birler? What are you doing up here? And dressed like that."

"We're being chased. We're trying to get to Greens. There are at least four Terolians after us. They have archers, and they keep forcing us north."

Tianer snapped off the arrow protruding from Kin'eril's saddle. "So I see," she said, her face grim. Her expression was questioning, but she snapped out commands, and her men silently fanned out. "Stay here. We'll clear them out. If you go any further north, you hit the ridge, and then you'll be trapped."

Birler slid out of the saddle and leaned against Kin'eril's heaving sides; he had been galloping for miles without complaint. *You are amazing, do you know that? So strong and brave. Tiw'erna is lucky to have you, and I am honoured you allowed me to ride you.*

A soft hum vibrated in his head, and he smiled as Kin'eril nuzzled his shoulder. They stiffened at the sound of approaching horses, and Birler drew the curved sword, only relaxing as Tianer appeared. Tianer eyed him with concern. "Four. You were right. How long have they been chasing you?"

"They picked us up at the border," Birler replied, shoving the sword back in his robe. He eyed the distance back into the saddle; he wasn't sure he could get back up.

It was a sign of his exhaustion that he startled when Tianer murmured in his ear, "Need a leg up?"

"Please."

"Where is Kafinee?" she asked as she lifted Birler into the

saddle. Tianer's face pinched as Birler landed with an inelegant thump, his usual grace absent.

"Long story."

Tianer stared up at him and gripped his leg. "It would be," she agreed. "Come on. Let's get you home."

"Home," Birler repeated, and Tianer grinned at the expression of relief on his face.

Birler clattered into the courtyard behind the Greens manor house, surrounded by Tianer's men. They led four horses with bodies tied over them.

Warren hurried down the steps at the unexpected commotion. "What's wrong?" he asked, and Tianer's men parted to reveal a road-begrimed and tanned Terolian with a wickedly curved sword at his waist, astride a strange black stallion equally covered in dirt.

Warren gasped as he recognised Birler and then strode up to him and pulled him out of the saddle, hugging him tightly. His son was exhausted and strained, but he was alive and home and gripping him back hard. Tears gathered in Warren's eyes at the ferocity of the hug.

Clearing his throat, Warren released Birler. "Who is this?" he asked, offering Kin'eril his hand.

"An amazing Darian lent to me by a very good friend; his name is Rill."

"Rill, welcome to Greens. Thank you for bringing my son home safe." Kin'eril nickered, and Birler smiled, with the dirt creasing his face.

"George," Warren said, his voice raised, "we have a guest."

"So I see." Warren's grizzled stable master pushed his way through the milling horses and smoothed Kin'eril's neck.

"He's far from home, highly strung, and exhausted," Birler said, handing over the reins.

"I know how to look after a Darian."

Birler grinned. "I know you do." Birler smoothed his hand down Kin'eril's neck, and George's eyes widened as his eyes went distant. *"Go with George. He will care for you. Call me if you need me, anytime."*

"I will," Kin'eril replied. *"Do you have any Baliweed?"*

Birler laughed out loud. "You don't have any Baliweed, do you, George?"

"I might have," the stable master said with a grin and then led Kin'eril away.

"What happened here?" Warren asked as he approached one of the bodies and lifted the head up by the hair.

"They were tracking Birler. Fortunately, he stumbled into us, and we were able to stop them," Tianer said.

"Are there any more?"

"Probable. Clary won't give up," Birler said.

Warren glanced up at Tianer. "Hand them over to Sam and then return to your patrol. Pass the word; protocol defence."

Tianer nodded and led her men away. Warren wrapped an arm around Birler's shoulders and escorted him into the house, where Melis pounced on him, determined to reassure herself he was alright. She finally let him go clean up and change out of the exotic robes he was wearing.

She glanced at Warren after he had gone. "He looks like a Terolian."

"I know. It's unnerving, isn't it? You should have seen him on that stallion; I hardly recognised him."

They were seated at the dining table, waiting for him, when he descended the stairs, damp-haired, clean and wearing his ranger's uniform. They breathed a silent sigh of relief to see the boy they knew in the man who walked through the door. "Eat first, Birler. You must be starving," Warren said as he rose.

Birler grinned. "I'm used to travel rations now."

"You have lost weight," Melis agreed, frowning at him.

Birler made quick work of the stew placed before him, drinking deeply of the crystal clear water. He refused the wine, knowing he was too tired to be able to cope with it. He gave them a much-edited report of what he had been up to. Warren raised his eyebrows and, glancing at Melis, let Birler continue.

"It was Clary running the mines. He's been mining crystals, and they are using them to build circular arrays. Whatever skills they've learnt, the crystals enhance it." Birler placed the dull black stone and one of the crystal rods on the table. "I destroyed one of his arrays with the help of a Terolian girl. They almost took out two of Sodera Arkan's patrols in one go. We were lucky we only lost three men.

"I left Kafinee in Terolia because she was exhausted. Arkan's son, Tiv'erna, lent me his Darian. He promised to look after Kafinee. And here we are."

"How come the son of the Sodera of Atolea lends you his horse, and a Darian at that?"

Birler squirmed in his chair. "Did you know Kafinee was a Darian?"

"No, and don't change the subject." Warren glared at him.

Birler grimaced. "I was sent to check the borders. I met Tiv'erna, the Sodera's son, and he recognised Kafinee for what she was. He invited us to guest in his tent because he wanted to make sure Kafinee was well looked after. He could see we had bonded, but I didn't know what that meant.

"Whilst I was a guest of their tent, his cousin tried to kill me. He had been enspelled by this *Mentiserium*. The only reason he didn't kill me was because he fought the compulsion. My proving that meant his life was spared. They were going to banish him for dishonouring the family; it would have torn them apart. So, they owe me a life twice over. They granted me the protection of their Family. They treat me like a son of the Atolea."

"They can't have you," Melis said with a laugh, half serious.

Birler flashed her a gleaming smile, bright in his tanned face. "This is home for as long as you will have me, Ma."

Melis smiled, content.

"I left Kafinee with Tiv'erna, and he lent me Rill; I had to use my sword to splint Tiv'erna's leg, and he gave me his. I will return it when I return Rill. I left Yannis and Arkan clearing up the mess in Melila." Birler held Warren's gaze. "I need to take the crystals to Lady Leyandrii; she needs to know what they are doing."

"We'll escort you. We are due in Vespers for the Year End ball; you can accompany us. Tagerill will be at the palace. He was part of the escort bringing the Ferrantes to Vespers."

Melis scowled. "Though they didn't stop here on the way."

"We'll have him here for a week in the new year," Warren soothed.

Birler smiled through his concern. "What about Greens? What if Clary retaliates?"

"She'll be safe enough. We are on lockdown, and everyone will be alert. Penner knows what to do. I'll send messages to Marian, Versill, and Tagerill. They will be warned."

Birler made the effort to visit Kin'eril, even though Warren said he was well looked after. Kin'eril was gleaming and content, snugged in a warm rug and happily rummaging for Baliweed, which George inexplicably had a stock of.

Returning to the house, Birler collapsed into his own bed and slept long and deep.

55

LEYANDRII

LADY'S PALACE, VESPERS. DECU 31, 1122

The palace was a bustle of preparation for the Lady's ball later that evening. Elegant vases of pink, white, and red roses were appearing all over the building, and their scent permeated the air, and soothed many frantic courtiers. Elliar lengthened her stride to keep up with Leyandrii as she followed her down the corridor.

"What's the rush?" Elliar asked.

Leyandrii glanced at her over her shoulder. "I want to surprise Guerlaire. He keeps badgering me to create my own Guardians, so I'm going to, but I want to see what the uniform looks like. You are going to be my model."

"Me?" Elliar squeaked. She cleared her throat, her eyes brightening. "Are you going to create a gown? I look better in a gown than a uniform; this has never suited me," she said, fingering the deep grey of the rangers uniform.

"*My* uniform will suit you. It will suit all of you."

"Who are you intending to ask to make it?"

"You'll see. Ah good. Birler is before us. Come." Leyandrii swept into the morning room where Birler sat, staring at the swathes of colourful material spread over the chairs and settees. "Birler, I see you have returned full of news, but hold your report. You can tell me when Guerlaire arrives. For now, I have another request of you."

Birler leapt to his feet. "My Lady, it's desperately important that we speak now; it can't wait."

Leyandrii patted his tanned face and smiled as she selected a deep blue cloth. "Yes, it can. It won't change anything. Look, which colour do you prefer? Elliar, what do you think?"

Birler stared at her, perplexed. "Colour?"

"Yes, for your uniform."

Birler looked down at his clothes. "I have a uniform."

Leyandrii laughed, and he relaxed as her invitation filtered into his mind. "Oh," he breathed as he sank to his knees and stared up at her with an expression of awe. *"Always, my Lady. My life and my sword are yours to protect all you command."*

"Ah, my Birlerion, always so quick. And I see you have chosen a colour. Oh, my, it's perfect. Yes." Leyandrii leaned towards him and stared deep into his eyes. He blinked as her green eyes glowed in front of his nose. *"You are mine, and don't you ever forget it."*

"Never, my Lady."

Leyandrii straightened and offered him her hand. "Rise, Birlerion, my Sentinal."

Bemused, he let her pull him up as he watched her in wonder.

"Does this mean I don't get to try on all the different clothes, then?" Elliar asked, folding her arms across her chest.

Leyandrii pursed her lips as she observed Elliar. "Depends," she said, watching her closely.

"On what?"

"Whether you are listening, I suppose."

Elliar stared at Birlerion. "What did you do to him?"

"He accepted my invitation." Leyandrii gestured, and the rolls of material disappeared.

Birlerion swallowed and looked down at his clothes. The silvery-green material shimmered in the light. He patted his pockets and relaxed as he felt the hard edges of crystals. He plucked the material, so soft and fine but durable. It wasn't just the uniform; a soft vibration murmured at the back of his mind as if a precursor for Leyandrii's voice. Soothing, a sense of belonging. He smiled. Leyandrii had claimed him; he was hers. He belonged to yet another family.

Elliar was still looking at him with a strange expression on her face, so Birlerion walked over to the long mirror covering the far wall and stared at his reflection. Silver eyes gleamed back at him. He blinked and raised his hand to his face. His reflection copied him. It was his face. He had liquid silver eyes, startlingly different to his usual deep blue ones.

His uniform was like nothing he had seen before: a high-necked jacket with silver buttons which fitted him perfectly, trim, straight-legged trousers, and calf-length grey leather boots. The material of the shirt beneath the jacket was soft against his skin; it caressed him, and he shivered. The shimmer of the material settled as he watched, leaving a soft sheen.

Leyandrii met his eyes in the mirror.

"Birlerion, you will be my Guardian. You will protect my people when I cannot, help where you see help is needed, and protect when threats are offered. Kill, if necessary, so others won't have to."

"Yes, my Lady."

"Good. You will attend me tonight." An amused expression crossed her face. *"I understand you dance very well. I expect at least one dance out of you."*

Birlerion choked. *"As you command, my Lady."*

Leyandrii laughed out loud. Elliar scowled at them,

narrowing her eyes as she watched Birlerion smooth the material of his new uniform with hesitant fingers.

"What invitation?" Elliar asked, tugging at her dark grey jacket. "What does Birler have that I don't? I'm older than him, and I've been guarding you for months."

"He is called Birlerion, and he is my Sentinal," Leyandrii chided. "Each will find their own way."

"You talk in riddles," Elliar said, huffing out her breath and thinning her lips.

"Then you are not listening well enough." Leyandrii chose a chair. "Guerlaire is on his way. Elliar, if you would be so good as to guard the door. We are not to be disturbed."

"Of course, my Lady."

"Unless another Sentinal turns up. Allow them to enter."

"Yes, my Lady." Elliar turned, her back rigid, and left the room.

"Sit, Birlerion. I'll get a crick in my neck looking up at you. Nice choice, by the way. I like it."

"Was it my choice?" Birlerion asked with a wry grin.

Leyandrii chuckled. "Well, I listened to what you wouldn't like to wear, so it's both our choices: practical and durable but elegant."

"And comfortable. Why does it shimmer?"

"Maybe you could tell me when you figure it out. That was you."

"Me?"

"All you."

"Why didn't you ask Elliar to become a Sentinal?"

"I did, but she wasn't ready to hear me."

Leyandrii looked up as the door opened and Guerlaire strode in. He halted at the sight of Birlerion, who leapt to his feet.

Leyandrii rose. "Well, my Captain?"

"Very well, but you could have warned me. Lord Asher

nearly had heart failure when my clothes changed into these right in front of him." Guerlaire plucked at the shimmering material.

"Oh, dear." Leyandrii chuckled. "I hope he has forgiven me?"

"He said he would speak with you tonight."

Birlerion stared at Guerlaire. His eyes were a brilliant emerald green, just like the Lady's. A soft chime resonated through the gentle hum at the back of his mind. Guerlairion, the Lady's Captain, had arrived. He wore the same silvery green uniform as Birlerion, and his sword was a pulsing bolt of energy at his side.

"Ah, I forgot about that," Leyandrii said. "I'm sorry, Birlerion. Things may be a bit distracting to begin with, but they will settle down as you get used to it. You have some of my perception now; you will perceive those things that are not of this world or are magical in nature. But you'll get used to it."

"Birlerion." Guerlaire crossed the room and grasped his arm. "Well done."

"Thank you, Captain," Birlerion replied, dragging his eyes away from Guerlaire's sword. "Guerlairion?" he asked.

Guerlaire's lips twitched. "I think Guerlaire will be fine. Leyandrii gets a bit carried away at times."

"I do not," Leyandrii said with a mock scowl.

The door opened, and Tagerill stumbled in, his silver eyes wild. Leyandrii chuckled. "Tagerillion, welcome."

"My Lady," he gasped, kneeling at her feet.

"Rise, Tagerillion. I thank you for your sword." She pulled him up, and Tagerillion spun to Birlerion, grinning wildly as he engulfed him in a hug.

Leyandrii watched the door expectantly, and when it duly opened, Serill and Nialler entered, looking just as disoriented as Tagerillion had, closely followed by Marian.

"Serillion, Niallerion, welcome. Marianille, my dear, please come in."

Marianille stared at Tagerillion and Birlerion. "Both of you?" she gasped. "Pa will be climbing his trees, and Ma, as well."

"Good point," Leyandrii said. "Maybe they had better see you all before the ball tonight. I'll arrange a room for you. We wouldn't want my Lord of the Watch caught out, now, would we?" Leyandrii paused, her eyes going distant. "Especially as Versillion has accepted as well."

Tagerillion grinned, regaining his composure. "Marianille, it suits you." He nodded at Serill, his grin widening. "Serillion."

Serillion laughed and grasped his arm. "You'll always be Tagerill." Tagerillion rolled his eyes.

"Or Tage," Birlerion added.

Marianille snorted. "Tagerillion is a bit of a mouthful."

"Blame Ma; she chose it. Anyway, it's no longer than yours or Birlerion's."

Leyandrii held her hands up, and they fell silent. "You are the first to accept. Others accept as we speak. You are my representatives tonight, my Sentinals. You will protect me and my people from whatever threatens us. And when I am unable, you will step in for me. The watches will be responsible for their people, the people will nurture the land, and the land will provide for all. You, my Guardians, will watch over them and speak with my voice. We *will* have peace in Remargaren."

"As you command, my Lady," her Sentinals replied.

"Good. Guerlaire is my Captain, as he is yours. You report to him. He will advise you of your new assignments, but for now, return to your duties. I expect to see all of you tonight." She nodded her dismissal, and they bowed. "Birlerion, stay. Guerlaire needs your report."

Tagerillion tried to catch Birlerion's eye as he left. Birlerion grinned and watched his brother's shoulders drop as he shut the door behind him.

Guerlaire let out a deep sigh as the room emptied. "I should have known you would exceed all expectations. How many have accepted? Asher is going to be upset with you for stealing all his rangers."

"Not all of them, and anyway, they will ease his burden. My Sentinals will be in the watches and the palace. The rangers will be able to become more specialised as he has long planned. And anyway, I have other duties for him."

"What made you change your mind?"

"Birlerion has some worrying news. I believe it is time to take steps."

"He does manage to find trouble, and it seems he doesn't know what the word 'observe' means." Birlerion flushed under Guerlaire's critical gaze.

Leyandrii smiled and patted Birlerion's arm. "At least you are here in time for my ball; you owe me a dance."

She was interrupted by an altercation outside the doors, and they heard Elliar's voice raised in denial. "Guerlaire, would you let Taurillion and Marguerite in, please? Elliar is being over-zealous, I fear."

Guerlaire grinned and went to open the door, where he was met by Elliar's flushed face. "Lady Leyandrii said you were not to be disturbed," she protested.

"Leyandrii didn't mean you to deny her sister," Guerlaire said, keeping his voice calm. "Lady Marguerite, Sentinal Taurillion, please." He stepped back, allowing them to enter.

"You can't have him," Marguerite snapped as soon as the door was shut.

"Then claim him, dear sister."

"I thought I had." Marguerite's voice was sharp as she raised her chin. Her blue eyes flashed with anger.

"I told you, Marguerite, I'm yours, but that doesn't mean I won't serve Remargaren when asked," Taurillion said from behind her.

Marguerite twirled, with sparks flying from her auburn curls. "You're mine," she snarled.

Taurillion smiled and cupped her face. He bent his head. "Always," he murmured against her lips, and as they kissed, his silver eyes darkened to a molten copper.

Marguerite stared up at him and then relaxed into his embrace, hiding her flushed face in his chest. Taurillion wrapped his arms around her and murmured into her ear.

"Well," Leyandrii said, her lips twitching, "now that that is sorted, maybe we can hear Birlerion's report." She perched on the edge of her chair, her skirts swishing as she sat. "Birlerion, please tell us what happened in Terolia."

There was an awed silence as Birlerion finished his report and laid the crystals on the table before Leyandrii.

"Only you," Leyandrii said, picking up the lodestone. "You truly are the embodiment of a Sentinal."

Birlerion flushed, his tan deepening.

"So, that's where that magnificent stallion in our stables came from," Guerlaire said, picking up the clear rod.

"I'm afraid Birlerion has to return him," Leyandrii said, recognising the covetous tone in Guerlaire's voice.

"Pity."

"Maybe if you speak nicely to Sodera Arkan, he'll sort one out for you," Birlerion suggested.

Marguerite snorted. "I suggest that Birlerion asks; he is more likely to be successful now that he is part of the Atolean Family."

Birlerion squirmed in his seat. "What are we going to do

about Clary? I'm afraid I did injure him. He was going to unleash something on those people. I had to stop him."

"It couldn't be helped. At least he won't be at the ball tonight. It will be much nicer without him, but I will consider my response. He attacked one of my rangers, diverted resources from the Terolian people, and threatened people's lives. He has quite an account to settle, I think."

"He said he has more arrays."

Leyandrii frowned at Guerlaire. "That is quite worrying, my Captain. I think that needs to be one of your priorities, dealing with these arrays. They must all be neutralised and destroyed."

Guerlaire nodded. "I think we will pay a lot closer attention to the Clarys' properties."

Birlerion ran a hand through his hair. "When I was working with Dominant Vincent, there was a requisition for an optical array unit that came through his office. I didn't know what it was, nor did he, so I refused the request and asked for more details. By the time the response came, I had moved on, so I don't know what was passed, but if that is the same thing, there may be records in the Administration."

"Taurillion, would you be so good as to investigate for us?" Leyandrii asked.

"Of course, my Lady."

Leyandrii tapped her lip as she observed Birlerion. "After the ball, you must return your gift horse to Terolia. And then you can have a couple of weeks' rest. After that, in the new year, I need you to go to Elothia."

"What is in Elothia?"

"I'll explain nearer the time," Leyandrii replied. "Be warned: it is winter up there, so make sure you take plenty of warm clothes. It will be a shock after Terolia. Oh, and I should tell you. Edrilion is all recovered, as is his Darian. He has agreed to stay in Melila and help that poor village recover."

"I'll call in and see him if the Medera is still encamped there."

"She is," Leyandrii said with a smile.

"How come you couldn't hear us there, my Lady? Edril was distraught."

"The arrays distort the atmosphere. It makes too much noise, and I can't hear you through it."

"So, we should be able to find the arrays by the noise?"

"Possibly, but I won't necessarily know that I am not hearing someone. I can't tell it's blacked out unless you tell me I didn't respond. I only knew there was something wrong in Terolia because I sent you and then I couldn't find you."

Guerlaire frowned in thought. "So, it's not a noise you can identify; it's more a lack if we can't bespeak you, but by then, it could be too late."

Leyandrii nodded. "Which is why you have to destroy the arrays; otherwise, we are vulnerable."

"I will help Taurillion search," Marguerite said. "These arrays would take a lot of resources to develop. It would be difficult to keep it quiet."

"Kayer said they had been mining for years," Birlerion said, suddenly remembering.

"Kayerille," Leyandrii said, emphasising the name with a smile, "will be a good place for you to start, Marguerite."

"Maybe I will travel with Birlerion. I haven't been to Terolia in ages."

"It would be my honour to escort you, my lady," Birlerion said.

Marguerite laughed, and Taurillion glowered at her.

56

BIRLERION

LADY'S PALACE, VESPERS

As soon as Birlerion left Leyandrii's chambers, Tagerillion and Serillion pounced on him.

"I thought you were going to be in there all night!" Tagerillion complained as he dragged Birlerion down the corridor.

"We had a lot to discuss."

"Well, now you can discuss it with us," Serillion said as he peered into a darkened chamber and gestured for them to enter.

Serillion hurried to light the lanterns, and the room was soon revealed to be a small parlour. Tagerillion hauled Birlerion into a hug. "By the Lady, I've missed you. I'm so glad you're back."

"I'm glad to see you, too," Birlerion said, his voice gruff as he hugged his brother back.

Serillion smiled as he watched them, and then when Tagerillion finally released him, he embraced Birlerion as well.

"It seems ages since we were last all together," Serillion murmured.

"I wasn't expecting to see you here," Birlerion said with a tired grin as he released Serillion and collapsed into a chair.

"Nor me. Guerlaire is trying to convince the Lady to recall me to Vespers. I think he thought having me here would strengthen his argument."

"Birtoli does seem to suit you."

Serillion smiled. "It is the most relaxing place I've ever visited."

"Wish I could visit, but I have to return to Terolia; I had to leave Kafinee there."

"Tell us what happened in Terolia," Tagerillion demanded.

Birlerion ran his hands through his hair. "I don't know where to start."

"The beginning is usually a good place. But first, what do you think of all this?" Serillion asked as he waved at their uniforms.

Birlerion wasn't sure how to answer. He hadn't had a moment to himself since he had responded to Leyandrii's invitation. He hadn't thought once, let alone twice, about his decision.

"It seems right," he said.

"But weird, you know?" Serillion said. "I mean, your eyes swirl on occasion, like liquid."

"I'm sure all our eyes are like that."

"But why?"

Birlerion shrugged. "You'd have to ask Lady Leyandrii, but I think it's to do with how we see things. Did you see Captain Guerlaire's sword?"

Tagerillion wrinkled his nose. "What about his sword?"

"It glows a bright blue."

Serillion shook his head. "I didn't see it glowing."

"Lady Leyandrii said it had to do with the way we perceive magic."

"Or the way *you* perceive magic," Tagerillion said, twisting his lips. "You see the energy we throw off sometimes when we don't."

"I'm sure there will be lots of things that have changed," Serillion said in a soothing voice. "I mean, our eyes have changed, along with our names and uniform, so there must be other things as well."

"Let's hope we get time to figure it out before we get thrown into the next mess."

"Talking about messes, how come you ended up in Terolia?" Tagerillion asked as he sat opposite Serillion.

"Any chance there's some water in that jug?" Birlerion asked as he marshalled his thoughts. Serillion rose and brought the tray over to place on the table, and Birlerion helped himself to a glass. Having just given Leyandrii his report, it didn't take long for him to hit his stride.

Serillion's eyes got wider as he talked, and Tagerill's jaw dropped.

"Only you," Serillion said. "Only you would come up with such a story. It's the threat from these crystals that is concerning. We should speak to Parsillion. He's been experimenting on them with Niallerion. The research they were doing showed that crystals can be used to enhance a person's abilities. I know because I was helping them."

Tagerillion grinned. "It's really crazy, but if I think of the person and they are a Sentinal, I have an impression of them in my mind. Like, I know they are alright."

Birlerion frowned as he concentrated, and multiple glows hung in his mind as he pinpointed Marianille, Versillion, Niallerion, and Parsillion. The brightest glow was Captain Guerlaire. He couldn't help smiling, as he knew they were all well. "That is amazing," he said. "How did you figure that out?"

Tagerillion grinned. "I was thinking of Versill … I mean

Versillion. We haven't seen him in ages, and I just had that impression that he was happy."

"I can see him."

"See him?" Serillion asked.

"He's a glow in my mind, and yes, he is well."

"A glow?" Tagerillion asked.

"Yes, isn't that what you said?"

"No. I had a-a feeling. I don't see a glow."

Birlerion hesitated. "Well," he said slowly, "I see a glow, brighter the nearer they are, dimmer the further away, but if I concentrate on them, I know whether they are well or not. Guerlaire is blinding."

Serillion laughed. "Of course he is. Did you see his eyes were an emerald green, the same as the Lady's? He is totally committed to her; it is quite obvious."

Birlerion smirked. "Taurillion's eyes are copper. He committed himself to Lady Marguerite."

Tagerillion stared at him. "Lady Marguerite was claiming guards as well?"

"No, I don't think so. His eyes were silver at first, and then Lady Marguerite said he was hers, and his eyes turned copper, a metallic brown."

"Shouldn't they be blue like hers?" Tagerill asked.

"No idea," Birlerion said and then yawned. "I'm sorry, but I am exhausted."

Serillion laughed. "Not surprising from what you've told us. Go have a nap before the ball this evening. We'll make sure you wake up in time to beautify yourself."

Birlerion laughed. "Make sure you do. Otherwise, I'll miss it." He glanced at Tagerill. "Show me to my room?"

"Of course," Tagerillion said, rising. "You are next to me."

"Thank goodness," Birlerion replied, tucking his hand in Tagerillion's arm. "Lead on."

57

LEYANDRII

LADY'S PALACE, VESPERS

Warren and Melis were ushered into the reception room by the Lady herself, a little bewildered at being diverted from the ballroom.

"Warren," Leyandrii said. "I ought to warn you that your children have accepted my invitation to join my personal guards. They are now Sentinals, bound to me. Protectors of Remargaren in my name."

"I am not surprised, my Lady. You know Greens support all your endeavours," Warren replied.

"Yes, well, I wanted you to know before this evening's festivities." She smiled at Melis. "I have claimed them. They speak with my voice, so they wear my mark."

"Your mark?"

Leyandrii patted her arm. "Don't fret. They wear it proudly. I am very pleased with them. I'll leave them to explain further."

Leyandrii turned expectantly towards the door as it opened. "May I present Marianille, Tagerillion, and Birlerion."

Warren stiffened and his breathing hitched. Melis gasped and covered her mouth with her hands.

Marianille rushed over to her and gave her a hug. "Ma, it's alright; we're still us."

Tagerillion hugged his father as Birlerion hung back, watching. Warren held out his arm, and Birlerion smiled shyly before joining them. "So, what have you all got yourselves into now?" Warren asked as he released them.

Birlerion shrugged, his silver eyes gleaming. "It's no different to the rangers. We still serve the Lady, only now we report directly to her."

"Via Guerlaire, the Lady's Captain," Tagerillion interjected.

"But your eyes," Melis said, her voice wavering. "They look so … so different."

"They don't behave any differently, and I think they are very pretty." Marianille grinned at her mother.

Melis smiled, making an effort. "They are beautiful, almost liquid silver." She stroked the material of Marianille's glimmering uniform. "Such an unusual colour."

"Birlerion chose it," Leyandrii said with a smile, watching them.

"Birlerion," Melis repeated, and a smile spread over her face. "It suits you. Congratulations, Birlerion." She moved to hug him and then Tagerillion. "Tagerillion, that's a bit of a mouthful." She laughed.

Tagerillion grimaced. "Everyone says that, but you chose my name, Ma; the Lady only enhanced it."

"Enhanced it. I like it. Congratulations, my love." She patted his cheek and smiled at her daughter. "Marianille. It is beautiful, just like you. I think the Lady is very fortunate to have you as her Sentinals."

Her children grinned back her, bright-eyed and happy. Warren wrapped an arm around his wife's shoulders. "You still have to come home, no excuses! We expect to see you all at every opportunity."

They all laughed, and Leyandrii breathed a sigh of relief. "I should warn you that Versillion accepted as well. He will visit Greens soon, so you'll be able to speak to him then. I'll leave you to talk. You have about half a chime, and then I expect to see you in the ballroom. Birlerion, you owe me a dance. Don't forget." She smiled at them all and left. They all started talking at once.

"What happened? When did this all change?" Melis asked immediately.

Tagerillion grimaced. "This morning. I was about to leave the barracks when I heard the Lady's voice inside my head. I said yes, and my uniform changed. It was quite startling, and then Serillion came rushing in. I saw he had silver eyes, so I went to look in a mirror, and it was a shock," he admitted with a wry grin. "And then Niallerion stumbled in and we went to find Birlerion. We found him with the Lady."

"I went to report to Leyandrii, as you know," Birlerion said. "There were swathes of material spread out all over the room. When Lady Leyandrii and Elliar arrived, she said to choose a colour. She was more interested in choosing the material for our uniform. And then she asked me to be one of her Sentinals. It wasn't words; it was a feeling deep inside, an understanding." Birlerion struggled to explain. "I embraced it and offered her my sword, and she accepted. And then this happened." He gestured at himself.

Marianille chuckled. "I think we all hear the Lady in our own ways. As long as we hear, that is all that matters."

Birlerion grimaced. "Not everyone heard her. I think she was expecting Elliar to accept, but she just looked at us as if we were mad. Leyandrii said she wasn't listening."

Warren stood up from the settee that he and Melis had collapsed onto when Leyandrii had left. "Well, I think the

Lady is well pleased with you, as are we. We are so proud of you all." He held his hand out to Melis. "But it is time to join her in the ballroom. I am sure you will cause quite a stir." He cast an eye over his children, all tall, competent, and silver-eyed.

His stomach fluttered at the thought that the Lady needed to call her guards, a move she had long resisted. He led Melis out of the room and towards the ballroom, resigned to making an entrance flanked by three Sentinals. Melis gripped his arm, and he relaxed his face into a smile as they entered the brightly lit room.

They reached Leyandrii, who smiled sympathetically. "I didn't mean to make such a statement, but I suppose it is unavoidable."

"They are distinctive; they will be noticed wherever they go," Melis said.

"My Sentinals will represent me when needed. They have my voice. Wherever they go, the people will know I am present."

Warren frowned. "I don't know what's different other than the obvious, but something is."

Smiling, Leyandrii gazed around the room, watching her Sentinals. "They are more assured. They have my trust, and they know it."

Melis tilted her head as she watched Birlerion pause by Lord Asher. "Maybe that is it."

"Please, enjoy the evening. We will speak later." Leyandrii moved to greet her next guest, watching the ripple that spread through the room as her Sentinals dispersed.

Leyandrii smiled in satisfaction.

The same ripple would flow throughout Remargaren, following wherever her guards went. Her Sentinals would speak with her voice, see with her eyes, and keep the peace in her world. They would help protect her people against the

Ascendant threat. Remargaren would flourish under her watch, and if she had to equip her Sentinals with magic to do so, then so be it. They would protect those who could not protect themselves, and they would kill, if necessary, so others would not have to.

To be continued in Sentinals Origins Part Two …

Sign up to my newsletter via www.helengarraway.com to find out when Part Two will release and download free novellas set in the world of Remargaren.

GLOSSARY

<u>Vespers</u>

Lady Leyandrii – Goddess of all Remargaren
Lady Marguerite – Leyandrii's younger sister
Guerlaire – Captain of Lady's Guard
Father Menaret – Temple officiant
Chryll – Lady's Ranger, friend of Guerlaire's
Elliar – Lady Leyandrii's guard
Jarvaine – Leader of Administration
Montserie – Deputy leader
Selby – Minister
Gilbert Clary – Member of Administration
Tilda – Clary's daughter

<u>Rangers Academy Cadets</u>
Birler – Vespers
Serill – Marchwood
Tyrler Clary – Vespers
Parsill Ferantes – Stoneford

Nialler – Vespers
Lorill – Deepwater
Cleo – Stoneford
Adil – Terolian
Edril – Terolian
Samis – Birtolian

Oren Asher – Commander of Lady's Rangers & the Academy
Pallinten – Sparring Master
Demeren – Healer

<u>Lords of Watches</u>
Marchwood – Philip Benoir
Stoneford – Daven Ferantes
Deepwater – Ricard Landeros

<u>Greens</u>
Warren Descelles – Lord of the Watch
Melis – Warren's wife
Penner – eldest son
Versill – son – Ranger
Marian – daughter – Ranger
Tagerill – son – Cadet
Saller – Healer
George – Stable Master

<u>Mayer's Landing</u>
Henry Mayer – Lord of the Watch
Emma Mayer – Wife
Archie – steward
Davis – Captain of guards
Caspar – Lieutenant of guards

Chambers – Clary's steward

<u>Terolia</u>
Frener – Ranger
Ael'vin – Elder
Tiv'erna – Son of Medera Yannis
Janis – Atolea Medera
Arkan – Atolea Sodera
Fer'arne – Tiverna's cousin
Per'ille – Son of Medera Yannis
Ser'ander – Traveller
Kayer – Mistra

<u>Lady's Rangers</u>
Anter
Saer
Taurill – Marguerite's partner
Merill
Eren
Calene
Fonor
Gener
Lorill
Laurel
Samis
Severen
Royor

<u>Elothia</u>
Egryll – Grand Duke
Olaf – Prince, Egryll's son
Aisha – Princess, Olaf's wife
Yaser – Ranger

<u>Birtoli</u>
Emperor Pierien
Empress Olini

ACKNOWLEDGMENTS

The last four years have been an amazing experience, learning the world of self publishing and book promotion. I now have thirteen books published, became a USA TODAY Bestselling author, saw my books up on the Nasdaq board in Times Square, and been the recipient of multiple book awards. I have loved every minute of it, and I hope you have enjoyed accompanying me on this incredible journey.

If it hadn't been for readers like yourself, buying and enjoying my books, I wouldn't still be publishing. Your support and feedback has made all of this possible.

I have to thank my editor, Maddy Glenn of Softwood Books for making me think harder about my stories and writing even more. Jefferson, from First Editing for his guidance on grammar and polishing my book to be the best it can be. To Michael Strick, my alpha reader extraordinaire who has the best ideas! Jeff Brown, for creating my amazing covers. My amazing ARC team which continues to grow. Jan, Daisy, Johnny, Jackie, Bob, Danielle, Barbara, Kris, Chere, Raelene, Vignesh, Cynthia, and Ian, who absorb my books in a flash and make me very happy when they love them! Thank you.

I look forward to sharing new worlds and more stories in the old worlds as more and more ideas bubble.

Make sure you sign up to my newsletter via my website www.helengarraway.com to find out first about my next book release, to let me know who else you want me to write about, all the inside info about my books and free downloads of novellas/short stories set in the world of Remargaren.

Thank you so much for your continued support.

Helen

ABOUT THE AUTHOR

Helen Garraway is the USA Today Bestselling author of the award winning epic fantasy Sentinal series which was first published in 2020, followed by the fantasy romance SoulMist series which is also now complete. Book 1, SoulBreather, was first released in 2022 as part of the Realm of Darkness Anthology.

An avid reader of many different fiction genres, a love she inherited from her mother, Helen writes fantasy novels and also enjoys paper crafting and scrapbooking as an escape from the pressure of the day job.

Having graduated from the University of Southampton with a Degree in Politics and International Relations, she remains an active member of their alumni. You can find out more at www.helengarraway.com.

Patreon

Become a supporter or Join Team Arifel, Team Darian or Team Sentinal and get access to the first chapters of my new books first, free bookish downloads, polls, and early sneak peeks.

instagram.com/helengarrawayauthor

patreon.com/HelenGarraway

bookbub.com/authors/helen-garraway

ONE
THE SENTINAL SERIES

SENTINALS AWAKEN

HELEN GARRAWAY

SENTINALS AWAKEN

Haven't read the original Sentinal series yet? Want to read more? Find out about my award winning epic fantasy series at www.helengarraway.com

Available in the format of your choice.

* Audiobook
* Ebook
* Paperback
* Hardcover

Remargaren is a vibrant, ancient world. With Goddesses, Sentinals, Rangers and Ascendants all trying to protect or attain that which is important to them.

Join me on the journey, as we meet Jerrol Haven, a King's Ranger, who is destined to become Lady Leyandrii's Captain. A role lost in the mists of time after her last Captain spectacularly disappeared with her when she sundered the Bloodstone and banished all magic from the world.

Throw into the mix some magical creatures, magic

seeping back into the world, an insidious disease affecting the Watches of Vespiri and the tall sentinal trees, the only reminder of the Lady's Guards, her faithful Sentinals, and we have the Sentinals Series.

We travel deeper into the world of Remargaren as Jerrol grapples with the expectations of goddesses and kings, and tries to stay alive long enough to figure out how he can wake the ancient guards sleeping in their tall trees. They are his only hope to help him protect their world against the wild magic of the shadowy Ascendants.

Start with book one, Sentinals Awaken:

https://Books2Read.com/SentinalsAwaken

When a long-forgotten threat starts to reemerge, one man stands as the last defense against darkness…

Jerrol Haven serves his king without question. When he finds evidence of corruption and is attacked, the loyal soldier's mind spins after his touch of a sacred tree awakens the dormant spirit of a three-thousand-year-old protector. But he fears he has failed after the crown prince accuses him of treason and orders his execution…

Fleeing the city, Jerrol is stunned when the goddess appears to him, appoints him captain of her warriors, and charges him with a quest to find artifacts that can save the realm. And as he runs into danger and more betrayals, the steadfast hero discovers a rare gift that may be the world's only hope…

Can Jerrol rally the forces of good to stop a rising evil?

Global Book Award Silver Medal, Wishing Shelf Book Award Bronze Medal, Readers' Favorite Finalist.

1
SOULBREATHER
THE SOULMIST SERIES
HELEN GARRAWAY

SOULMIST SERIES

Interested in my Romantic Fantasy SoulMist series? Find out more at www.helengarraway.com

Start the adventure now with book one, SoulBreather. Available in the format of your choice from Amazon and other vendors.

- Audiobook
- Ebook
- Paperback
- Hardcover

If you fall in love with the shadows, does that mean you are fallen too?

A dying angel. A fractured realm. The SoulBreather who might be able to save them both.

Solanji has a secret. One that is becoming increasingly difficult to keep. She can touch souls and see into a person's inner thoughts. Soulbreathing is exhilarating and addictive, until the day Solanji caresses the wrong person's soulmist.

Dragged into a long forgotten angelic mystery, she is forced to venture into Eidolon, the godforsaken last resort for those without souls. In order to save her brother, she must rescue a broken and tortured man. Can she save him from the shadows? Does he even want to be saved? And can she find a way to return to the light before the darkness engulfs them both?

SoulBreather is the first book in the paranormal fantasy SoulMist series. Winner of a BookFest Gold medal, a Global Book Award Silver medal, a Readers' Favorite Finalist medal and a Readers' Favorite Five Star Review.

Order: https://Books2Read.com/SoulBreather

If you love Dystopian Fantasy then check out my standalone novel, Harmony.

Order: https://Books2Read.com/Harmony-dystopian

READER'S NOTES

www.ingramcontent.com/pod-product-compliance
Lightning Source LLC
Chambersburg PA
CBHW060753210726
48292CB00013B/74